ENTANGLEMENT

A TINBOIZ NOVEL

T STEDMAN

ENTANGLEMENT

BY

T Stedman

PROLOGUE

The year is 2055. The state owns everything on Earth. There are three strata in society: Outsiders, the unskilled, who live beyond the Danger Line (population size unknown), the protected and skilled Techs, the middle class, who live in the gated communities around each metropolis, and the elusive Elites, who govern everything through the UGN (United Global Network).

National boundaries were abolished after the great economic collapse of 2026. The civil unrest that followed was squashed and religious organisations were neatly blamed. The top one percent of the richest people in the world swooped in and bought up every piece of real estate, bank and corporation to 'save the people', and the grateful population believed it all. Every country was rebuilt to the same model and, for the most part, it worked. Because no one knew who the Elites were to envy them, the Techs lived a modest but grateful existence and the Outsiders were lawless thieves and scavengers that the Techs never saw nor thought about. After all, they chose to live outside the law and polite society. Every Tech understood that to be content, they must live by the UGN's simple motto: 'Own nothing and you will be happy'.

Meanwhile, quietly managing everything are the Quantum AIs. Controlling what we own, what we eat, and even the air we breathe. Then there are the TinBoiz – the humanoid face of the AI and the new must-have for tech society. Friend, carer, worker, they are the next level in technology. More advanced and more real than you could ever imagine.

CHAPTER 1

airacre Gated Community – Christina School again.

The thought stung my eyes before they even cracked open.

'How are you feeling today, darling?'

Mom's voice buzzed around my room as the darkness shutters began to whir open with a flick of her hand. Dull orange light seeped into the room, struggling to cut through the smog. Even the sun looked tired. I winced, groaned and pulled the covers over my head. Not because of the light. Not really. Because it meant another day of pretending everything was fine.

'Tunic and trousers,' Mom said directly to the Digirobe. The uniform shimmered into place at the front of the wardrobe, crisp and grey, like a clean lie.

'It can't be school again already,' I muttered.

'Come on, darling, you'll be late. First day back. You're a Progressive now. Can't believe my baby is in her last year.'

I smiled weakly at my mom's overenthusiasm that I definitely didn't feel, then I looked doubtfully at the dull uniform that was meant to show we were the top of the school. All it did was make my already sallow skin look like I wanted to puke. And I did want to puke. A lot. I didn't just hate school; I hated the endless repetition of it. The plastic smiles of the kids who pretended it all made sense when it didn't. But most of all, I was so very tired all the time. Not just in my bones, my weak muscles, but in my everything.

It was only just bearable with Teddy, my best friend and next-door neighbour. We did everything together since we could walk, and now he was finally too sick to go to school completely.

I tried to get up onto my elbows. 'I can't.' And flopped back down into my pillows.

'You just need to eat and take your new medicine. It will give you energy, you'll see.'

I hefted myself up and pulled my skinny legs over the side of the bed. I had to take a moment to let the dizziness subside. 'I can't do it, Mom. The air is too bad today,' I said, closing my eyes and attempting to breathe through it. Just the thought of showering, eating and spending a whole day at school made me exhausted. 'Can't I have a cyber-sub? Lots of the kids in Progression Year have them. This girl, Phoenix, has one and she only has a minor dust-fever.' I already knew that answer. If Teddy's parents couldn't afford one, then we certainly couldn't. Our dads worked at the same tech company.

I inwardly shrank. My mom had lost any possible sympathy for me when she had to scoop up yesterday's clothes from the floor. She simply tutted. 'Up! Now! Phoenix's allergies are completely debilitating. You're not the same at all. Plus, both her parents work for Cyberscrub and get substiborgs through their health cover.'

I let out a long, hopeless sigh and barely shook my head. I was so tired. I didn't have a hope in hell of getting one if my mum couldn't even remember what they were called nowadays.

'Besides, sitting in bed at home, living through a substitute robot, however clever it is, is not living. It's bad enough that you and Teddy hardly venture off your VRs or UGN terminals these days.'

Whoopdidoo, I thought, my mind skipping immediately to Teddy, now doing that day after day, living his life through the state-controlled internet, *how riveting*. I hated that she was right. The latest cyber-sub was supposed to cost almost GDC600,000. No one really had that kind of Global Digital Currency to pay for something like that. My heart sank. That was more than my dad's pride and joy: his driverless Metro-car. If I had it, I would give it to Teddy, then at least we could go to school together, kind of. It would be less painful than going alone.

I guess being at home wasn't that big a deal. Loads of kids did it for health reasons. Apart from my immediate class, me and Teddy didn't interact with any other kids much anyway, and that was only on a need-to-bother basis. If we had our way, even that would be through our UGN terminals. Mine sat on my desk, like a window to a sunny place of grass and flowers. The sun beaming around the constantly moving, benevolent face of the old guy logo of The Global Network. I liked to think he was looking down proudly, caring for us all, like a great-grandfather or something.

My mom threw a towel at my face, breaking my daydream, forcing me to catch it clumsily. My time had run out and I wasn't getting out of it today. 'There are loads of interesting work clubs in progression year,' I said, trying to take a different approach. 'So I've heard,' I tacked on. I knew full well it got you out of a lot of regular school. I just hoped my mom didn't. I looked away from her scrutinising gaze. It felt hot on the side of my face for a long moment while she considered it.

'You go for a few weeks without trying it on, and we'll see about joining some clubs.'

I let out a breath of relief before I went too red and blew it. 'Deal!' I said and quickly pushed myself up off the bed. 'They're supposed to help your job prospects when you progress to Interrelational College.'

My mom disappeared out of the room without comment, probably fed up with my crafty wrangling. I shuffled awkwardly on stiff legs to my hydro room and somehow summoned the energy to switch on the power spray. It was newly installed in all the homes in our community and was supposed to use a quarter of the water of a normal, old-fashioned shower. It stung like hell but was supposed to leave every part of you jet-washed clean and perfectly exfoliated. On my sensitive skin, it felt like being shot with gravel.

I wrinkled my nose at the smell of the chlorine. It was always worse when you first switched it on. Dad said they had to because it had been recycled so many times. I wondered if clean water still existed anywhere in the world.

Still, I put my head back and ordered, 'Shampoo.' The jets began to pound my head with suds for around five seconds and then went into massage and finally rinse mode. If I could join a club, at least I'd have something to do now Teddy wasn't there. Something to occupy me for all the hours I was alone, after curfew.

CHAPTER 2

outh Central – Outside the Danger Line – Mike
Mack's liquor store's yellow lights loomed up ahead like a beacon through the yellow smog. I coughed in reflex against what I knew perfectly well were toxic particles hanging in the damp air. I turned my collar up against it and pulled my bandana down over my nose and mouth before the stinging drizzle had a chance to go down my neck.

The door jingled with an old bell when I pushed my way in. The old blind man behind the counter immediately called out, 'Hi, Mike!'

I never knew how he did that, but he always knew me.

'Your pa's usual?'

'Thanks.' I picked up a bottle of sugar soda and a protein bar and put them on the counter. 'That stuff'll rot your teeth,' Mack said, chuckling with his almost toothless grin. He was a grizzled sight, with brown skin like old leather, a holey woollen sweater and about two teeth in his whole mouth. No one ever stole from him. The kids liked the old guy. That, and he was a crack shot with an old air pistol he kept under the counter.

'With such a perfect blend of toxic shit, why take the fun part out?' I replied.

Mack laughed, stooped and produced the usual white label, black-market bottle of amber liquid from under the counter. 'That's for sure,' he said, and rang up the order on his last century till that dinged with a comforting bell when he rang up my order.

'Can you put it on Pa's account?' I asked, already grinning as I went to pick up the bottles and turn to walk towards the door. As expected, Mack slammed down my wrist with the reflexes of a twenty-year-old. 'Gold and silver bits only here, sonny. No digital currency and no credit.'

We both laughed. Everyone I knew tried the same thing. I delved into my pocket and threw the rough circular bits of silver down on the counter.

Mack grinned. 'Pleasure to do business. You have a nice day now.'

'Should have some tinned goods for you by the end of the week. Truck is supposed to come in late on Friday,' I said over my shoulder, walking towards the door.

Mack put up his hand. 'I'll have your groceries ready. Now get on home, before curfew. Weather's comin' in.'

'Thanks, Mack,' I said, already pulling the door open and looking up at the dank sky slurry. Mack was right, the sludge-brown clouds rolling in would bring acid rain.

Mack's was a good arrangement around here that had worked for several years. It helped lots of the families in the neighbourhood. They got something that Mack could sell, and in return, he would box up supplies to keep the family going for a week. Without it, many of us would starve. This week, I had a strong tip that some canned foods were coming in through the official gate, and my little crew of friends were going to liberate them.

I went to walk off when two guys rounded the corner. As

they neared, I grinned. 'Deej … Flak,' I said, pounding both their fists.

'Been in Mack's?' Deej asked, tipping his head towards my brown bag.

I nodded. 'You playin' tonight?' Deej was a little older and his name was short for David-James. He was universally respected as the Beat Hacker. A DJ who hacked the library vaults for old music, locked away from the general population, as it was ruled subversive. He ran a pirate radio station and had parties that popped up all over town. He and his brother, Flak, were celebrities around here. Everyone had heard of the duo, DJ and Flak.

'Comin'?' Deej asked. 'Gotta sweet new mix for you.'

I inwardly sighed. I'd like nothing more than to check out for a few hours. Escape with a little home-grown, moonshine and sweet sounds. 'Might get there late. Got to scope somewhere for some stuff coming in Friday.'

Deej smiled and touched my shoulder as he and Flak passed to walk into Mack's. 'Hope to see you there, kid.'

I continued on my way with my hands in my torn pockets, buzzing tonight's schedule through my mind. Most kids slipped out again after curfew. That's when they hit their best scores. All government-sanctioned deliveries came through the gate, then. We saw it as our civil duty to keep ahead of what, where and when that was. We had no guilt, despite the zero-tolerance warnings on the constantly rotating billboards. There was no work and those with small businesses, like Mack, had to fight to keep them from the big chains that moved in and staffed them with subs and bots. Vast automated companies that controlled everything from the other side of the Danger Line.

There was no government presence here, which, with the way things were, wasn't entirely a bad thing. Except for the police. They kept order in a way. They'd long left human officers behind to oversee their subs from the comfort of their stations. Injury had become assured rather than a risk, so why waste the manpower when a machine was bigger, stronger and instilled far more fear than they ever could? There was nothing for ordinary folks to do but avoid them.

And we did. We knew the score and somehow managed to scrape an existence. Honest labour had long disappeared since the Great Reset of 2026. Along with creative careers, most professions and skilled trades. I'd even heard that the healthcare walk-ins were staffed by bots and a cyber-sub welcoming face. Schools here were nothing more than babysitting services we left by the age of ten. So most had been closed in the 'Realignment of Resources' bill of 2028. The ethos being, why spend the money on teaching those that had no hope of a job anyway? They relabelled us the Unskilled Sector. We called ourselves the Strong Forgotten. I grinned up at the huge fist and SF, spray-painted over the old cinema-plex building, right underneath the CCTV camera. The only tech in the whole district and it did jack-shit.

I continued to smile. Hearing the chatter and laughter, the moment I rounded the corner to my block. Through the descending mist, doing what we always did. Every night. The youth of the Strong Forgotten congregated somewhere, plotting crimes and ways to get chips of silver and gold, but mainly to belong and support each other in this god-forsaken place. Besides, life here was cheap and short. Kids were here one day and gone the next. If the police got you, no one ever saw you again. Life was a constant game of cat and mouse.

My mind drifted to Daisy's boys, Nick and Warren. The latest to go missing. Daisy was a neighbour and friend of my mom before she passed. Her boys hung with me and my kid brother, Finn. I'd just managed to pull Finn out of a police trap in a food depot last week. Nick and Warren weren't so lucky and no one had seen them since. I still hear Daisy crying through her apartment door.

I slipped the latch to the street door of our apartment. It was an old black wooden door set back from the sidewalk and easy to miss. That was good, because no one would think it led to anything special to rob. I skipped up the grimy, littered steps that led to the two apartments at the top. Ours was left open, unsurprisingly. 'How many times,' I muttered, looking for my drunk excuse for a dad. He met me in the doorway to the main room, which meant Finn wasn't there. We rarely occupied the same space as my dad voluntarily. There were only three rooms. I scoped the filthy bathroom and barren bedroom consisting of two stained mattresses, before I met my dad's eyes and they were empty too. The barely living room, as we called it, doubled as a scummy kitchen and a bedroom for my dad. That wasn't worth a glance. Just a sad man and a worn sofa.

My dad was antsy. His eyes skated over me. I knew what he was looking for and it wasn't injuries. I handed him the bottle wrapped in brown paper. He snatched it, snapped off the cap and threw it in one fluid move and immediately chugged down several large mouthfuls. Then he wiped the drips off his chin with the back of his grimy hand. He'd been digging trenches outside in the barren land. One of the few places that still paid for human labour. But they only employed on a daily, first-come-first-served basis. 'The Pick,' as everyone called it. Back-breaking work for just a few chips of silver a day. No wonder he drank. Plus, he hated us for still being here instead of my mother.

Behind me, the World War II siren sounded. A wail through the air for a full five minutes to let the neighbour-hood know it was 7 p.m. and time for curfew. It gave everyone thirty minutes to get home. Then no one was meant to be out on the street before 5:30 in the morning.

'Where's your brother?' my dad barked, now his withdrawal had been sated. He put his shaking hand out to steady himself on the doorjamb next to him.

I felt a sharp stab of panic. 'How do I know? I thought he was with you.' I immediately turned and headed back the way I came. Finn must have slipped out right under his nose. I couldn't believe my dad sometimes. Why couldn't he just straighten up and see that Mom might have gone, but we were still here? He was an unravelled mess, who I knew loved us somewhere deep down. He just never got through the grief. Now he had no regular work because he was drunk more often than not, missed the morning pick and so we lived no better than the rats that outnumbered us here ten to one. He raised his eyebrows in a silent question of what I was going to do about it.

I swore under my breath and went back out the front door into the acid rain, with just twenty-five minutes left until final lock-in.

It didn't take me long to find Finn this time of night. I knew he'd be at one of our hangout places. He wouldn't have eaten, so it was an educated guess that he'd be at PeterPat's fully automated pizza place compound. It was where they loaded the delivery vans and was warm outside because of the huge ovens. The building also had a convenient overhang to get out of the toxic drizzle. The door was always open for constant deliveries and it was easy to steal a box when the procession of cyber-subs turned back for the shop and were facing the other way. They were not scary at all. They were too big and cumbersome to be any kind of threat to us, nor was the recorded metallic voice, coming out over a speaker, warning, 'Loiterers and thieves are not tolerated at PeterPat's and will be arrested immediately,' over and over. It was no deterrent. It was more of a handy cover for any noise we made, which was lively, while we chatted, ate our pizza and stayed out of the rain. Pizza was cheap. The huge chain wouldn't miss the few damn slices that we swiped.

There was Finn, under the overhang, with tomato sauce at the corners of his mouth. I couldn't help an exasperated smile as he held up a slice by way of hello. I shook my head and sped up to a jog to join him and three of my friends. It was raining harder and irritating my skin, now it was soaking through my clothes. 'Didn't you hear curfew?' I said, taking a slice of pizza, leaving one in the box.

Finn shrugged. 'I was hungry,' he said, taking another huge bite.

I ruffled his hair and he shrugged me off, grumbling. 'Ah, come on, Dad will be asleep and forgotten all about it by the time we get home.' When I continued to look at him, sternly, he added, 'five minutes' with his mouth crammed full of food.

I rolled my eyes, knowing it was the best deal I was going to get. I never wanted to go home either. We'd be stuck there until morning, lunchtime for under-eighteens, with nothing to do. The UGN maintained it was to protect us from the pollution, which was far worse on our side of the Danger Line. And while I guessed that was probably true, I also knew they didn't know what to do with us. We were an annoyance. A blight, who should be out of sight and out of mind. So I had no qualms about stealing what we needed and causing a little trouble. I felt more sorry for the older generation. They still lived by the rules, plugged into their UGN terminals, accepting the bullshit as their lot. Passing their time online gambling on UGN-sanctioned sites, and that was only if they were lucky enough to have old-world pension credits. Or watching a hundred sales channels for crap no one needed. Or endless cheap shows on TV. Something for everyone, the

UGN spouted. 'Because you are important to us,' was the UGN slogan, blaring out of every street corner's advertising screen. Propaganda. Keeping folks quiet and at home. Spending their credits back to them, like good little global citizens. Being no trouble, till their last breath and they finally got to leave this place, no more remembered than a grain of sand.

Not me. Not Finn. We would take what we could because we were owed it. We were all owed it. With that, I ducked out into the rain again. Keeping low, I swooped in and took another box from the back of the open van, without breaking pace, and circled back to my place next to Finn. The subs just kept right on going. Stomping left right, left right, in their heavy march. They were each operated by some poor human, somewhere far away, who just wanted to pass their shift and get paid. They didn't even shoo us away when they saw us. They were nothing like the police subs. I'd drummed that into Finn. On no account should he allow himself to get caught. They could be brutal. Their human counterpart was holed up in a warm, cosy police station, not giving a shit. Brave, not having to face us directly, by working through the eyes and the hands of their twice as strong sub. It was just like an avatar in a video game, except this was real life and we were the expendables, stuck on the wrong side of town. Thankfully, the police subs I'd come across were strong, but never as fast. The lack of funding meant the technology was dated and cumbersome. Despite knowing all that, 'Be alert,' I said to Finn, checking over my shoulder. I took a huge bite of pizza, determined to finish and go. Something made me uneasy tonight.

The other guys laughed. 'Chill. You heading over to Deej's party later?'

I took another large bite and said, 'Uh-huh,' chewing.

'Have something I need to do first.' Then I gave Finn a hard look. 'Right after I get Finn home.'

My focus diverted from Finn's disappointment to spot Precious rounding the corner over his shoulder. One of my friends wolf-whistled. I couldn't help grinning. Despite the cossetted-sounding name, Precious was a firebrand. A hothead, tougher than many of the guys I hung out with. She was strong, could fight like a man and had a banging-hot body. Guys fought to get a chance with her; she just laughed it off. Her hair was braided, spilling out from a knot down her back and her make-up was heavily charcoaled, looking more like war paint. Her look was gangland street meets old-century native. She made us guys quake at the knees when she gave us that 'I dare you to even try' stare.

'Hey, sexy,' someone said from behind me.

She completely ignored it as we made space for her in our circle out of the weather. 'Blow?' she demanded, clicking her fingers and glaring at each of us.

The guys howled with laughter, deliberately misinterpreting her request for a nicotine inhaler cartridge as a sexual invitation. She continued to click her fingers, rolling her eyes while we searched our pockets. We all carried them. Real tobacco was virtually non-existent, unless you were very lucky to get hold of some. The sticks were a good substitute that could be loaded with cartridges of any pharmaceutical agent of choice.

'Here, take mine,' Finn said, handing her his.

She kissed him on the cheek and looked at him with soft eyes. The only person I'd ever seen her soften for. He was besotted, of course.

'She's four years too old for you,' Andy said, irked, making everyone laugh. I looked on indulgently. 'Let him dream,' I said.

Precious put her bare arm around Finn's shoulders to

defend him. Finn smirked. 'Four years is nothing when I'm twenty.'

We all laughed at that. Me, a little sadly. Who knew where any of us would be by then. Still, it passed the time. It was the usual banter that made us all family, despite our difficult situations. All different, but in a lot of ways, all the same. It's what kept us together.

The final call siren sounded, a faster, more ear-splitting version of the first.

'Damn,' Andy muttered.

No one moved.

I raised my eyebrows at Finn and tipped my head sideways in the universal signal for us to go.

'Agh, come on, man,' he groaned, his face pained and shoulders dropping in disappointment.

'Let him stay,' Precious said, messing up his hair with her hand. 'I'll look after him,' she promised with a smirk, making everyone laugh.

I couldn't stop the grin at the satisfied look on Finn's face.

'Don't deprive him of the necessary education of the streets,' she added, which Finn accepted, nodding avidly and swelling with pride.

We all laughed loudly at the expression on his face.

It was probably that and the loud fan of the ovens, but we didn't hear the silent, hydro-powered car approach. Just a high-pitched pip. A one-second blast of a police siren and it was already on us. 'Stay where you are. You are breaking curfew law 354. Do not run and you will not be hurt.'

For one beautiful, heart-stopping moment, the world stood still and perfectly silent. Then, out of an ever-increasing echo, someone shouted, 'Run!' The world switched back to deafening max, and everything went berserk.

I grabbed Finn's hand and turned. Three subs got out of the police car and we scattered like mice in a barn.

Another police van pulled into the compound fast, screeching to a halt behind the car. Shouts and crashes in all directions as we scurried over and under things. Adrenaline and instinct ruled, heart and feet pounding pistons under me. No time to look behind or gauge the scene. It was just me and Finn breaking out. Breathing hard. This way and that. Searching. Somewhere to hide. Anything. Anywhere.

Finn screamed. I couldn't think. I didn't think. Instead of leaving the compound, I doubled back behind the dumpsters and three parked pizza vans and shot into the kitchens of PeterPat's. I knew it was madness, but they were everywhere. And the most obvious place to run was out, so further in clicked in its place.

We shot through the long chrome kitchen. Past huge heat-spilling ovens, freezers, and counters. Finn was flagging. I turned my head for a split second to check on him and ran right into a sub. Finn ran into the back of me. If it had been a human, I would have knocked him on his back for sure. But it was like hitting a wall. The pain shock vibrated through me. I gasped for air and we just froze and locked eyes, while my face smarted. It was an old-generation sub. A silver robotic face that pre-dated even the rubber-looking ones that looked like dolls. But the eyes on these things were always the same. A silver blue, mercury. Staring through me. Its irises opening and closing like a clockwork camera shutter, getting into focus.

These were basic worker subs and had no speech. The tension in my body relaxed a little. I saw my chance and pulled Finn with me around it. I ran to the back, but the door was sealed. There was no need for toilets, locker rooms, or fire exits when no one worked here with a pulse. This was it.

The dead-end. I turned and scanned the room frantically. No exits except the one we came in through, and a huge black-uniformed police sub now stood in the way.

I snapped Finn down to a crouch and assessed the chrome shelves under the counter next to us. They were dotted with enormous tins of tomatoes. I moved some aside. There was room. Then I turned my head to Finn with my finger to my lips and gestured for him to slide in. It was a squeeze, but I managed to slip onto the shelf next to him. We pushed as many tins as we could in front of us and I made sure Finn was pinned to the back.

It wasn't till then that I felt the toll on my body. My throat was screaming in pain, my heart was sonar, pounding in my ears, and acid sweat poured down my forehead, stinging my eyes. I tried to slow my breathing; it was too quick, too noisy and hurt like hell. The shop subs were dumb, but these police subs were something else. Fast. Clever. A new kind. With no telling what capabilities. Along with the usual green light for violence, a triple threat.

Finn whimpered and I turned my head to try to look at him to calm him down. He had his hand clamped over his mouth and looked terrified. His eyes, so wide, darting over my face, gauging how scared I was. I smiled as convincingly as I could and put my finger to my lips. 'Just wait it out,' I mouthed. I prayed the cop would leave eventually, after assuming we'd gotten away.

So we waited.

It was eerily quiet. Not even the stamp of the worker-sub's feet. Just the oven's constant fans and the motor of the freezers. I guessed no speech was needed between subs, even police ones. These were either soft on their feet, or the one in the doorway had left. But it didn't explain why the worker-subs hadn't continued working.

I inched forward. Just to take the briefest peek. Finn gripped my arm, but what I saw froze me to the bone. A police sub was locked into a weird stand-off, kissing distance from a worker-sub. He was ridiculously real-looking. Stacked muscle mass. The fit of his clothes. Skin tone. Scarred, but good-looking. Like a soldier. The only thing giving him away as not human was the weird exchange going on. Like he was linked up, or downloading something from the sub.

I quickly pulled my head back under cover so I could think. *Shit!*

'What is it?' Finn whispered.

I didn't answer. My mind was racing. It was clear he was reviewing the last thing the sub saw. My heart dropped into my stomach and I racked my brains for anywhere to run. But there was no way out of this. I turned to Finn. 'Whatever happens, you stay, OK? You wait an hour after you think the coast is clear.' I spoke with vicious eyes, already preparing for flight.

Finn's face began to crumple, but I wouldn't allow it. 'Stay!' I said as my final order. Stamping to memory the absolute pleading and resignation as he fully understood what I was about to do. Then I closed my eyes and didn't open them again until I fell to my feet from our hiding place, pushed more tins in front of him and ran. Moving, darting like a fly, too busy to land. I had to get them away from Finn and make them believe it was just me.

The cop, whatever he was, shouted. 'Stop! Police! You are under arrest.'

The door was in view. Not far. I made a determined, final sprint.

'Suspect located,' the cop said from behind me.

A huge, dark shape stepped from nowhere into the

doorway and I skidded to a halt. I danced from one foot to the other, nowhere to run. I heard the high-pitched squeal of the charge. Then it was game over. The claws dug into my back and eradiated a white-hot pain through every cell in my body. I exploded into darkness.

CHAPTER 3

*C*hrissy

I travelled to school in our Metro Car. The one my dad was so proud of because it was driverless. The UGN had declared that everyone should have one by 2051 to make our community more productive. It was decided that too much work time was wasted each year on taking kids to school and extracurricular activities. My dad was all for it. He often said over dinner that it was a genius invention to be able to send me or my younger brother, Nate, off on our own so that they could finish other things. Plus, it cut down the need for more than one car per household, helping congestion and the environment. 'Just think of the money it saves,' was his mantra.

I always nodded enthusiastically but secretly suspected it was really to keep parents at their jobs for longer. To me, it was dull. Learning to drive had always been a rite of passage. Now there was no need. It looked the same as all the other cars in our community. It came in three colours: silver, slate and granite. Dull, duller and dullest. I let out a sigh and looked out the tinted window that turned the orange air to a sludge colour. Every house was the same. Same roof, same box shape. Two upstairs windows, one downstairs, next to a painted door on the left. Colour dictating the street you were in. We lived at 2365 Blue Sycamore Drive. Hence our blue door. Red Beech. White Larch, you get the picture. Then there was the garage to the left, with its door in that same colour. Drive in front of that, for your one car. Square fake lawn to the right of that, with a border of fake flowers under the window. Kind of fake, anyway. A hybrid, generated in a lab that was impervious to the toxins the rain brought down with it. The catch was that no insects could pollinate or survive on it, so no insects meant no birds. An empty façade. A pretence. Purely for us to trick ourselves that we were orderly and bright. But it had never seemed bright to me. It looked garish. Like a girl with too much make-up in the light of day, particularly in mid-winter.

Fairacre. That was the name of our gated community. I never understood why it was called that. It was huge for a start. We seldom went out of it. The UGN saw to it that we had everything we needed inside. Only the tech companies were positioned outside, where all our parents worked. It was called the Business District or the Industrial Zone. Depending on your expertise. I liked to think that our community was named after a field that was once there. Before all the houses. A couple of large trees to shade horses or real cows from a real noon-day sun. Real sun, with real cotton wool clouds. The sort I'd seen in downloaded eBook files, or antique books, now stored away for their safety.

Dad said we were the lucky ones to live where we did. I wasn't so sure. When I think about what it was, fifty or a hundred years ago, it seems poor in comparison. But Dad became stern. 'We live in a nice house, on a nice street. You and Nate go to a nice school. Others are not that lucky.' I'd smile weekly, with a 'yes, Dad,' but it was hard to imagine any less fortunate than us, when everywhere you looked was the same. We'd heard of the Unskilled. The Outsiders. They were the lazy who preferred to steal rather than work. That made me angry when I thought of Dad's twelve or fourteen-hour days. It just proved what a nice guy he was to think like that. Because I didn't feel lucky. Most of the kids were sick and life felt a very lonely, closed-in place. There was nothing new to smell, nothing new to feel and nothing new to see. Just pointless monotony.

Dad was thinking about getting us all a 'Plug 'n' Chill' vacation, if we could afford it this year. He raved, 'Everyone's getting them.' He had no idea how ridiculous that sounded. We would be vacating our unhealthy, isolated and boring lives to slip into a sensory deprivation tank for twenty-four hours. Plug in to some AI that would make us think we'd been away for a month, to some place of our dreams.

The only place that interested me was advertised as 'Faraway Island'. I'd read about it over and over. It was supposed to be a real place where you lived close to nature. A living museum of how life used to be. No electricity or running water. Just food grown in the ground, that you prepared and ate yourself. It was created by some billionaire, Max Telford, as a sanctuary for animals and birds that were now almost extinct. Only a select few got to go there—journalists and the lucky winners of competitions set up by the tech companies.

It was already impossible, but that was my dream.

I let out a deep sigh. I'd daydreamed through the whole journey to school. We were entering the long driveway, circling the fountain and pulling up outside the steps to the main doors.

My heart skipped at the new sign pointing to 'Progression Year side entrance'. It was supposed to be me and Teddy. My next-door neighbour and best friend, but my heart was shattered. He was too sick. We had planned this together and were supposed to feel like we'd made it. I just felt sad. Without him here, there was nothing to look forward to in this last year. Cindy Lawrence would still be the same popular, healthy, spoiled brat and Simon Payne would still be her perfect match. Captain of the team, her boyfriend, with all the drama that went with it. And together they would be mean to everyone else. Their group saw itself as the best. The coolest, the richest, the best-looking. I felt sick just thinking about them.

'You have reached your destination,' the AI screen on the dashboard said.

Nate smiled in sympathy for me. He understood, but he wasn't like me. He was twelve and I was nearly seventeen. He was a geek, but healthier, so a bit more sporty, which made his life a little easier than mine. I was just sickly. 'Good luck today,' he said, shaking his unkempt hair out of his eyes. Then he opened the door, and, swinging his bag over onto his back, he skipped up the steps and was gone.

'I am being recalled for another trip, Christina. Please get out immediately,' the car said. I knew it was my mom who needed to get to her appointment. 'OK,' I grumbled and hefted myself out into the now-crowded concourse. I squinted in the hazy light and sniffed the air. Despite the dispersal technology the school used, it still smelled vaguely of rotten eggs. I looked down, pulled my heavy bag on my shoulder and trudged the walk of doom towards my new entrance. Inside, my heart sank a little lower as I joined the factory line of kids, shuffling in single file along the dark corridor.

I stumbled into another kid, not looking where I was going or picking up my feet. 'Sorry,' I said, steadying myself on the wall and looking up, straight into the silver/blue eyes of a sub. It was no ordinary sub, who were pretty androgynous on the whole. This one was male and had a deep and realistic voice, 'Pardon me, I was going the wrong way.'

For a moment, I was completely stunned and he didn't move either.

'Hey! Keep it moving,' an irritated voice came from behind me.

'Out of the way, Nerd.'

I was nudged to the side roughly, while kids continued to grumble that we were blocking the lockers. I couldn't stop taking him in. The same grey uniform as the other boys, but he was so tall and healthy-looking. Razor-cut blonde hair and smooth, tanned skin. So human-like, I wanted to touch it. 'Who are you?' I blurted rudely. What I meant to ask was who he was substituting for, but it came out all wrong. Someone had definitely scaled up, with this level of perfection. I couldn't think of a single person he matched.

'I'm Ace,' he said, simply, offering me his hand.

I looked down at it, hanging there, perfectly manicured. Human, not rubber or plastic, but real. I didn't get it. He was completely blowing my mind and I was about to take it to see how he felt when I was almost knocked over. I crashed painfully into the wall and when I finally righted myself to scowl at whoever it was, I sagged with the obvious answer. *Jessica Bailey.* I should have known.

She linked a proprietary arm through Ace's. 'I see you've met Ace,' she said, smiling spitefully. 'I called him that because he's the best money can buy.'

All the cogs started to fall into place. I don't know why I was so taken off guard. She was Cindy's best friend and just as spoiled and popular. Their fathers worked at Quantum Tech and everyone knew they got the best health insurance. It was at the cutting edge of AI innovation. 'Sorry,' I said, looking around for any of the football team who might be missing. 'I had no idea there was a new sub.' We were drawing a crowd.

She laughed loudly, shaking her head and crinkling up her nose. 'Ew. Disgusting. There's no spotty nerd holed up in his room somewhere. He isn't a sub, you idiot. He is one of the latest TinBoiz companion models.'

I stared at her, trying to process what she was saying. I'd read about them with Teddy. He'd made me laugh, daydreaming about a TinBoiz boyfriend.

TinBoiz was the brand name for the world's first fully autonomous unit, available for regular people. The technology was originally created for the armed forces, but the TinbBoiz company had secured the license to use the same tech to make AI companions. Their learning capacity was supposed to be amazing. Completely independent, enabling them to blend into whatever setting they're put into. Only monitored for malfunctions by some central AI brain.

'Doesn't he have beautiful eyes?' Jessica said, gushing.

It made me angry, not envious. The obvious pointlessness of it. All that money and know-how and all they could do was produce a walking, talking Barbie Ken doll. When there were good people like Teddy, who desperately needed a sub. It was clear where all the investment was now going. Subs were going to be sidelined for fake people. Scratch that; for faker people.

As if to rest my case, Ace turned his head to Jessica and said, 'Your eyes are beautiful too, Jessica.'

She dissolved into giggles and didn't hear me mutter a plea for strength.

Her smile dropped and she flicked back her long blonde hair over her shoulder with her spare hand. 'Come on, Ace,' she said, pulling him off with her. 'We're wasting time here.'

I stayed there, staring after them, still too affected to move. Ace looked over his shoulder, a little too far to be comfortable for any human, 'See you round, Christina,' he said, his strange, staring eyes boring into mine.

I smiled a little and put up my hand, not sure how I felt about the encounter, exactly. Weird he knew my full name. No one used it and I was sure I never told him. He'd left his mark on me, though. Enough that I would tell Teddy all about it later.

The rest of the day was unremarkable. Progression Year had its own whole block that held most of our lessons. We only used the main building for the science labs, art studios, gym and the hall for big assemblies. The idea was to make us feel older and more important. I felt nothing either way. Just lonelier. Without Teddy, school was somewhere between Chinese water torture and root canal.

Last year had been a struggle for him, and by the end, it was clear he wasn't going to make it back. Most of us suffer from some sort of allergy or inflammation. Teddy's are in his brain. His parents had left it to the wire, but two weeks before the start of term, they'd had to admit to my parents that school was now too much for him.

Teddy's dad, Tom, had looked at their healthcare, and when it wouldn't cover it, my dad had looked into the prices to fund a sub between them. It was incredibly generous and I loved him all the more for that. But even with their money combined, it was impossible for them to afford it.

So now I was on my own and Teddy's life was spent through the school 'OOP', the Optical Oratory Programme Teddy jokingly called the 'Oops sorry' program. The state apology to sick kids, which was basically a camera in the classroom, viewed through your UGN monitor at home. Pathetic really. I'd regurgitated what my mum always said to me, 'Would you really want to live your life through something else?'

He'd laughed and replied, 'I wouldn't mind being a buff

hunk for a change.' Then got serious and broke my heart. 'I already live through you, anyway, Chrissy.'

Teddy was my best friend and I loved him the most in the world. At least I can go home and see him after school. My eyes brimmed with tears as I got into the car with Nate. 'Alright?' he asked, hopefully.

I smiled, unconvincingly, noticing a new graze on his cheek. He went through it too. Without complaining. I loved Nate. Mom. Dad. I couldn't bear this. I couldn't.

CHAPTER 4

Chrissy

Teddy was asleep by the time I got home, changed and went over to see him. I was bitterly disappointed as I'd missed him and wanted to fill him in on my day. I wandered back and answered my mom's constant questioning with one-syllable answers. 'Mmm… yeah… nope… sleep.'

Nate came into the kitchen area while I grabbed a drink and used the opportunity to slope off for a nap. First day back with all that new input was exhausting.

I was just closing my door when my mom caught up with me. I sagged and looked at her, deadpan.

She tutted at my moodiness. 'Darling, I didn't get a chance to tell you. Teddy, Tina and Tom are coming over for dinner tonight with Ray and his wife from work. Wash up and make yourself presentable.' I tried really hard not to pull a face. I knew these dinners were important. Ray was Dad and Tom's boss, but it was chronic for me and Teddy. 'Will Teddy come, though?' I asked doubtfully, as he seemed pretty sound asleep when I looked in on him.

'I think so. His mom didn't say he wasn't. He's very bored and only has to walk across the lawn.'

I nodded and slowly closed my door as Mom turned and trotted down the stairs. I sighed; bang goes my nap. Still, I might get to catch up with Teddy after all.

I showered and put on my dark-green jersey dress. It was long-sleeved, high-necked and straight to the knee. Comfy, in other words.

Loud voices from downstairs sounded like Dad was home. Good. My stomach was rumbling. Mom called loudly, 'Dinner in thirty minutes.'

I wandered downstairs and went into our large L-shaped lounge. Nate was already sitting on the sofa, waving his arm to change the channel on the large wall glass. He looked ridiculously nerdy, with his favourite striped sweater on and his hair slicked down with water in a severe parting. He immediately grinned and patted the seat next to him. I smiled, thinking how young he looked. Ten, rather than twelve. He had that graze that was now purple under the dark circles of his eyes. He seemed paler, making a surge of anger flash through me. 'Who hit you?' I demanded.

He shrugged it off, still waving like a looney to backtrack channels. 'The usual. It's not from a hit, I bounced off a wall,' he said, focused on the glass, like that was somehow better. He glanced sideways at me. 'It's not like you can do anything.'

He didn't say it maliciously, but it still hurt like an unprovoked slap.

'Well, it's true, isn't it?'

I sank into my seat next to him and felt dreadfully sad. For him, for me, for Teddy. In a world where the tech guys came out on top, we were still bottom of the pile. Power and popularity were still the things kids aspired to at school. The healthier, bigger, stronger boys still pushed little guys like Nate around. 'It won't always be this way,' I said, more to myself. thinking of the impressive physique of Ace. I didn't even know why.

Nate heard and finally gave up on finding something to watch. 'Not soon enough for us, though.' Then, as if I'd said the wrong thing, he got up and ran up the stairs to his room.

It left me feeling bad. He was right. There was nothing I could do for him. It wasn't as if I was any more popular myself.

I needed to get out. 'I'm going over to Teddy's,' I called out to my mom. 'I wanna make sure he's OK and coming over.'

'OK,' Mom replied. 'Don't be late. Dinner is at 7.30.'

I knew I should help her. She'd be hot and stressed. Going back was only a fleeting thought while stepping out into the murky dusk light. I soon shook it off. It all felt stifling tonight.

I stood a moment absorbing the heavy atmosphere, longer than was medically advised. The damp air had pushed the pollution down near the ground, so I pulled up my mask and ran the short distance to Teddy's.

I knocked our secret knock. Seven raps with a space after the first and fifth. We'd done it since we were six years old.

Tina opened the door quickly and immediately stepped aside for me to go straight in. 'Oh hi, Chrissy. We're almost ready. Tom's just in the shower.'

'It's OK, I'm just here to see Teddy. Is he alright?'

Tina smiled lovingly and squeezed the top of my arm. 'Bet it's hard at school without him.'

I felt a hard lump sticking in my throat and I couldn't look at her. I just nodded.

'Go up. He's fine after his nap. Well, fine for Teddy.'

I felt her eyes on me as I began the stairs.

'School is a bit too much at the moment, you know.'

I forced a smile at her before I turned on the first landing and was out of sight. I skipped the last few stairs and took a moment to catch my breath at the top. Then I crossed the hallway, knocked our knock on Teddy's door and went straight inside.

My spirits lifted immediately. Teddy was dressed and sitting on his bed with his new VR razor-width headset on and holding a steering column. He'd be flying the space cruiser in his new game. 'Earth to Teddy … permission to come aboard?' I asked, using our agreed greeting. We'd invented it since we were old enough to play anything, so we didn't make each other jump when we were engrossed in something.

Teddy just shouted, 'Damn!' threw the steering column and tore off the headset. 'Crashed,' he said, looking furious.

'Sorry,' I said, laughing. Thrilled, he was his usual self. I scrambled onto the bed next to him. 'You seem OK,' I said, scanning my eyes over him for any changes. 'Been skiving off, I see.'

Teddy shrugged. 'I was sick in the night, coughing so much. It was the final clincher to my blossoming school career,' he said with a goofy grin. 'How was it?' He bobbed his head. 'I know it sucked without me, but as a Progressive, I mean.'

I shook my head wearily at him, making light of such a monumental decision that must be devastating for him to come to terms with. I just smiled weakly. 'Boring as ever. Oh, and I almost forgot. Jessica, spoiled brat, Bailey, has a brand-new TinBoi.'

Teddy's eyes went wide and his jaw dropped at that. 'Shut the front door!'

It felt good to deliver such juicy gossip. Total currency between close friends.

'Oh. My. God. Seriously? What's it like?'

'It's this really gorgeous boy,' I said, my eyes alight to match his enthusiasm.

'Naturally,' he said, waving it off as a trifle. 'It had to rival Cindy's relationship with Simon.'

'Yeah, he's a hunk. You'd totally fancy him,' I said. 'Ace is his name.'

'Ace,' Teddy repeated in a girly voice, then shoved me playfully. 'Ace? What a douchey name,' he said, wrinkling his nose.

'I know. "Because he's the best money can buy",' I said, mimicking Jessica's whiny voice.

We both laughed.

'Does he have those sexy silver eyes?' Teddy asked.

I nodded. In all seriousness, I'd been hooked in by them immediately. 'Yeah, and muscles.'

Teddy pretended to swoon.

We both laughed, but I got serious for a moment as a disgusting thought occurred to me. 'I know she wants to parade him around like a new bag, but what does she do with him at home?'

Teddy waggled his eyebrows and we fell about laughing.

It felt good to laugh with him again. Then I got sad watching him get off the bed and slowly find his shoes. He had to sag back onto the bed, exhausted. I crouched in front of him and helped him on with them, shocked he was so bad. It had been a gradual decline over the summer, but I'd made excuses in my head, like summer was always worse and he'd get better. I realised then that I hadn't wanted to see it. I'd been in denial. 'There!' I said, tying the last lace and looking at him with a forced smile.

His apology was in his eyes and filled me with a searing anger and feelings I didn't want to face. I smacked his foot. 'Don't think I'm going to do this for you every day,' I said, to cover my emotion, pushing myself up onto my feet.

We were sobered after that and wandered slowly over to my house, making sure we pulled up our masks even for the short trip. The air was at its worst close to curfew. All the smog excluders got switched off to save energy and the lurking mist got to creep in.

Teddy was quiet because he knew that I now knew he'd been playing down his illness. He understood that I was hurt and angry and was giving me the space to think. We walked into the house in silence and into the dining end of our living room.

My mom hugged him fiercely. She already knew, and that made me want to cry, that no one had made me see. My mom just gave me her best regretful smile and I had to look away.

Teddy's mom and dad, Tina and Tom, arrived, saving me from my descent into self-hatred and misery. We relaxed together like we'd done a thousand times. It was easy for the two families. Tom helped himself and changed channels on the wall glass and Tina knew where things were in the kitchen. I sat there, bewildered, absorbing it all, like some dreaded countdown had begun. I hated it. Logically, nothing had really changed from yesterday, when I'd been fine, but now I'd seen behind the veil and it couldn't be unseen.

The door voice announced Dad's boss and his wife's arrival: 'Ray, Anita… welcome,' Mom answered, with her usual enthusiasm. She was the same with the road sanitarian subs, treating them like old friends. 'Welcome, welcome!' she said. 'Thank you so much for coming.'

Dad was soon there, taking their jackets and masks and putting them straight into the detox airer next to the door. It jet-steamed everything for toxins and germs. Health law dictated that everyone had to do it if they came from another house. Teddy's family didn't count.

Ray and Anita walked shyly into the living room and

were greeted by Tina and Tom. They waved at me, Teddy and Nate all sitting on the sofa. 'Dinner is ready,' Mom called.

Dad led the way to the table and indicated where everyone should sit and Mom started bringing out huge platters, with Tina quickly helping her. Teddy widened his eyes at me at the huge show.

I grinned. I'd thought the same thing.

Dinner was serve-yourself, which made everyone relax. Tina marvelled at how Mom had gone to so much effort and must have spent a fortune on the roasted meat, fresh potatoes and greens. No one asked what meat it was. It was all from suspect origins. I'd studied lab-grown meat at school. Prime cuts, grown specifically from stem cells. Cutting costs of production to a minimum. I ate it, knowing that with no more space left to roam, at least this meat never suffered. The UGN science museum was full of horrific pictures and relics from that era, before order was established.

I was more interested in the times long before the reset, when animals grazed in large open fields. Before the sprawling housing projects had eaten up all the land and the acidic rain ruined what was left of the grass. It was inevitable that food tech would be developed to cope with the demand for meat and plant protein. I should be grateful. We would have starved, but I had a poor appetite, anyway.

'Perfectly marbled sirloin,' my dad announced proudly.

'You're spoiling us, or we're paying you too much,' Ray said, making everyone laugh.

I looked at Teddy and we both mouthed Dad's next words. 'Happy offshoot of the body parts industry.' We both giggled.

Ray chewed with his eyes closed. 'Very true.' Savouring the flavour. 'And not just transplant organs anymore, I understand,' he said, after he swallowed. Have you been reading about the increased production of limbs to completely outmode prosthetics?' He shook his head, amazed.

'Yes,' my dad said. 'I read on the Health Forum news page, they're even producing skin and blood for this new generation of subs and AUs.'

'Came from the skin graph tech,' Tom added, nodding enthusiastically.

'So life-like,' Dad said, making everyone mumble their agreement sombrely.

I knew they were all thinking of Teddy and how out of reach a sub was for him.

My mom tutted. 'Well, none of that would be necessary if we had countryside to walk in and clean air like when we were kids.'

Another mumble of agreement followed. My mom looked wistful. She was so kind and always loved the simple things in life. Her bedtime stories of the times before the reset were a constant source of my daydreams. Teddy and I often stayed awake on sleepovers, whispering about finding a secret place like that – sure there must be one, and how lucky our parents were to have seen it for real.

My mind shot to Ace and his amazing skin. 'This girl brought in the latest TinBoiz model to school today. He isn't a sub at all.' I felt my heart spike and blood rush to my cheeks as everyone looked at me, surprised. I was generally quiet and moody at the dinner table.

Ray frowned and shook his head disapprovingly. 'I'm not sure what I think about those things. Subs I can understand. They provide a valuable service to all the sick and infirm in the population.'

'So valuable,' my mom agreed.

'But those things. Companions. Kind of feels like we're making ourselves obsolete.'

Me and Teddy stopped pretending to eat, now completely riveted to the conversation. It was like a heavy atmosphere had descended and we were all skating around a burning issue.

My dad shook his head bitterly, as if it were bad news from the ongoing war in the far south. 'Yes, at least a sub has a real human behind it … you know, in control,' he said, nodding at Tina and Tom, who were watching closely.

At first, I thought it was nerves in front of their boss, but I started to feel this was a deliberate steer in the conversation. They were all acting so weird.

'It still has an AI central interface,' Teddy said, looking at me and widening his eyes almost imperceptibly. It was our code for 'what the hell?'

I agreed wholeheartedly with a micro shake of my head.

This was our dads. Definitely. Our moms were oblivious.

'I guess there's a place for them. You know, like soldiers, police officers and people like that,' I said, hedging, moving food around my plate again.

'Even those should have a human mind controlling them for ethical reasons, honey,' my mom said.

I doubted the difference, often thinking humans were worse, if history was anything to go by. But I smiled at my mom's kindly face; she always saw the good in everyone.

'I'm afraid that not all of them do,' my dad added ruefully.

Tom agreed, taking another spoonful of greens. 'Maybe squadron leaders, but most are just boots on the ground. And AU drones. Don't forget those. So small, you wouldn't even know they were there.'

Everyone agreed with that.

I shuddered, imagining coming face-to-face with one of those army AUs. Ace had been disturbing enough. 'Yes, but there are other reasons to have one,' I persisted, not able to get Ace out of my mind.

'What do you mean, dear?' my mom asked.

'Well, supposing you couldn't have children. Or you lost a partner after fifty years of marriage. Aren't they good reasons for an autonomous model?'

I looked up, and they all appeared to be considering what I'd said. Ray smiled at Dad and tipped his head in my direction. 'You have a clever one there, Chris.'

'Too spooky, I couldn't.' Tina shuddered.

Tom turned in his seat to her in mock outrage. 'You'd rather another man behind a sub?'

'No, silly.' Tina batted him away as being daft, and everyone joined in the laughter.

'She has a point, though,' my dad said, thoughtfully. 'I hadn't considered that angle.'

'Well, I think they should adopt one of the poor orphans in the hospitals instead of nurturing a machine,' my mom said. She was very passionate about that sort of thing.

'I didn't know there were places for old widowers,' my dad joked, already cringing away from Mom, who, instead of smacking his arm, just shook her head wearily.

'Think that horse has already bolted,' Ray said. 'Fully Autonomous Neuronetics, or TinBoiz, as they're known, are the fastest growing part of the tech industry these days. They can literally do anything. Well, better than a human, anyway. Because they don't have the health issues.'

'Even brain surgery?' Tina asked, pushing her plate aside and picking up her wine. Her whole body shouted disapproval.

'Basic robots have been assisting in complex surgery for years. It's the precise, steady hand, you see. The only difference with this new generation is that it has its own brain. It's linked to a quantum computer, where its knowledge is upgraded instantaneously. No upgrades or training needed for new surgeries. Think about it. It's mind-blowing. The boundaries are endless,' Ray said, carrying all of us with him in his obvious enthusiasm for the subject.

'What on earth does the girl at school need a model like that for?' My mom asked, bringing us all back to the basics of the conversation.

I had to admit, it was pretty pathetic compared to ground-breaking neurosurgery. I was already trying not to laugh when I said. 'To compete with Cindy Lawrence.'

Teddy laughed loudly, adding, 'She's her equally bratty best friend.'

'She's dating Simon Payne, captain of the athletic society and the most popular boy at school.' I looked at Teddy, and we were both really laughing. It was so funny.

My mom stared at Tina and then at my dad in astonishment. He just shook his head. 'God knows how much that cost,' Mom said, giving up and pushing her plate away, too.

Ray looked at the Finch on his wrist – his face-synched wrist-plate. We all had them. It was a glass on your wrist, like a mini terminal. It ensured we had instant UGN news updates and was also a useful locator, monitoring all our vitals at the same time. Temperature, blood pressure. 'Sonny, how much is the latest TinBoiz companion model to buy?'

I was impressed he had the latest 3D hologram version. We just had the older, talking screen. A little guy popped up like an old-fashioned-looking professor. 'Greetings, Ray. According to the latest data, the TinBoiz recreational AU companion 2054 model is 799,000 United Global Digital Credits. There is currently a six-week wait for delivery. There are payment plan options – terms and conditions apply. Would you like to hear those?'

'No, that's enough. Thanks, Sonny.' The hologram immediately evaporated, leaving Ray raising his eyebrows at my mom and dad as if to say, 'see what I mean?'

I didn't know why my heart sank so much, but it did. 'So

what's the difference between the price of a TinBoiz model and a sub?' I asked.

'A lot!' everyone said at the same time.

The only one not joining in was Teddy. He looked at me sadly, knowing exactly why I was asking and why I was upset at everyone, joking and not getting it.

'Still too much,' Tina said, looking at me knowingly.

'The last time I looked for Teddy, the cheapest model was five to six years old and about to go out of commission, and that was 499,000 UGDC,' Tom said, making everyone take in an audible breath at how steep that was.

I smiled sadly at Teddy and he returned it with 'that's OK' in his eyes.

Well, I hated it. It was a crappy life if it was like that. Out of all the people I knew, Teddy needed one the most.

'Ridiculous! Who can afford that on a Tech salary?' Mom said, getting up and starting to clear the table.

I really loved her for feeling for Teddy like that. She was such a genuinely nice person. I was so lucky.

'Well, that isn't the only route, anymore ... so I hear,' Ray said, keeping both his hands and eyes on his glass, then looking at us furtively.

My mom wandered back to the table.

'Oh?' Dad said. 'What else is there, then?'

'Tell us,' Tom said, leaning forward to hear, Tina leaning in with him.

Everyone seemed to freeze for the answer.

'Well, I belong to the MCG, Manager's Cybersystems Group, for socialising, swapping ideas. You know, like a think tank. Sometimes useful for what we do in home climate systems. Anyway, that sort of thing. Well, a lot of these guys work for different companies across several industries. There was this one guy I spoke to recently, who worked in Human Biotics for TinBoiz and quite a few of its subsidiaries. He was telling me what an impressive set-up they had. How the units were assembled. Their components. Their memory capacity alone is amazing.'

My heart was barely beating and I'd forgotten to breathe; I was so hooked on his every word. I took a quick glance at Teddy and he was the same.

'Get to the point, honey,' Anita, his wife, prompted, with her friendly smile at my mom and Tina, who laughed a little.

I was grateful because it relieved some of my tension and I relaxed my muscles a bit.

I guessed they were used to everyone nerding over tech stuff, like an occupational hazard. Ray shuffled in his chair and frowned as if he'd lost his thread. Then he leaned into the table and his whole body language became conspiratorial. It made us all do the same. I don't think we could help it. My heart was skipping all over the place. I was excited and I had no idea why. I grabbed Teddy's hand under the table and it was as sweaty as mine.

'He reckons,' Ray continued in a hushed tone, 'And I don't know if he was just blowing hot air, but he said he'd received backdoor funding to head up a research team of experts in every field of AI robotics, to gather the expertise and components to produce the next evolution of humanoid AI. He said production has already started in a top-secret location, with his secret syndicate of professionals.'

I looked around at everyone, not sure what he meant. I was waiting for a punchline.

My mom sat back in her chair as if he'd lost some sort of credibility with her. 'Oh, I find that very hard to believe. Doesn't this type of tech get manufactured in all different places to guard against industrial espionage...You know, exactly this kind of thing?'

Tina just looked at my mom, then back at Ray and nodded, as if reiterating what she'd said.

I'd lost track of whether it was good or bad and looked at Teddy, who shrugged. I felt glad I wasn't the only dumb one.

'She's right.'

'I read somewhere, one place does power source and torso, another AI sensors and brain, another skin, and cybernetic limbs. Something like that,' Mom continued.

Ray grinned at her wickedly and nodded as if she'd only proved his point. 'And optics, don't forget the eyes. The windows to the soul – and the whole world of AI,' he tacked on. 'Some might say that is the most important part of the finished model.'

I looked around and they all looked like they didn't fully understand what he was getting at, judging by their confused expressions.

'It identifies what they really are,' Ray said, half-laughing as if we should all get something so fundamental.

I was totally lost.

My dad laughed and pointed at Ray. 'Your guy is optics.'

Ray nodded and pointed back. 'You got it. And he's not alone.' He looked directly at each of our parents one by one. 'He already has someone in each division, bringing with them their expertise and trade secrets, producing these mind-blowing knock-offs that already exceed the originals. It's amazing. And the good part is, he has the backing of someone very powerful.'

'Who?' my dad asked right away.

Ray shrugged. 'I'm guessing it's one of the Elites. Not sure he even knows who it is. But he's too confident, which makes me think he must feel untouchable.'

'But what if one of these knock-offs goes wrong? Don't they have to go through stringent testing and stuff like that? You know, for rules and fail-safes and everything,' my mom said, looking at everyone, worried.

Tina was nodding vigorously next to her. 'Yes, there'd be

no receipts or guarantees … It could go rogue and kill everyone.'

Ray shrugged and slouched back into his chair. 'I said the same thing and the guy was as calm and confident as anything. All he said was, "No more than a regular TinBoi." It's the same experts, you see? Same parts. All doing exactly the same thing they do in their regular jobs. And get this; he supervises the programming and training himself,' Ray let out a short blast of laughter in disbelief. 'He said they are programmed to see him as their master teacher and obey him implicitly. He has buyers lined up around the block.'

I watched everyone's faces closely, and when no one said anything and there was just a stunned, empty silence, I couldn't help myself, 'How much does he charge for one?' I felt instantly foolish. My parents would look at a sub long before they ever considered a TinBoi, and I'm sure Teddy's thought the same.

Ray grinned wickedly. 'Just 499,000 UGDC. A steal. I tell ya, they're really going to make waves in the industry with this. Competition is going to spring up everywhere. Everyone wants to get a piece of the action.'

I wasn't sure what that meant. I was more tuned into the regretful, wan smile my mom gave Tina. 'It's still so much money.'

'Considering it's essentially made with stolen tech,' Tom said a lot less kindly.

Ray conceded that with a bob of his head. 'The risk, time and expertise put into it is still there, though. He said they're indistinguishable from the real thing. Right down to the alloy TinBoiz trademark on the back of their neck.'

'Same guy?' Dad said, shaking his head, amazed at how simple it all sounded.

The table hushed. Everyone felt a change. A collective excitement, suppressed with unspoken fear. Like we all needed the time to really process how we felt, it was a weird feeling.

I looked sideways at Teddy. He was looking down, lost in his own thoughts. Later, when I looked back on that night, I would recognise it as the beginning of change. Not just of our two little families, but a change that affected the whole world.

CHAPTER 5

ike
I blinked open my eyes, blearily, to see three pairs staring down at me. The floor was bumping and rocking underneath me. The ceiling was low, dark grey metal. I was in a van. Lying on the floor between the bench seats. The faces cleared, to become familiar. My friends, looking concerned. 'Mike! Wake up!'

I blinked a few more times and expected them to pull me up, but their eyes were wide and terrified. My blood pounded and I had to hold my temples with my fingers to try to piece together where we were.

Then it came to me in a rush as I studied their faces. I'd been joking with them only a moment ago. Tyrone, Andy, Joel. 'Hey,' Joel said. 'You OK? They tasered you.'

That explained why my head was still in a blender and my body felt like it was vibrating. Then an image slammed into my frontal cortex like a sledgehammer. 'Finn! Where is he?' I looked frantically all around and behind me.

'It's OK, there was no sign of him,' Joel said, grabbing me under the arm to pull me up onto the bench next to him.

Tyrone jumped up to help from the other side. I relaxed onto it while I raced over every scenario, praying he'd stayed put like I told him.

'They didn't get him. Mack came out and pointed them away.'

'Was that before or after they got me?' I asked, praying he hadn't been taken somewhere separately, as a minor.

'You were already sparked out,' Tyrone said, pointing down.

I let out a slow breath of relief, but my mind was still racing. Mack would see he was OK. 'Precious?' I suddenly remembered, checking all their faces.

My friends just looked at each other and shrugged. 'We didn't see,' Andy said. 'She could have gotten away; she's slippery enough. Or they could have taken her to the women's lock-up over on Fifth.'

I nodded. I hoped she got away, but she was eighteen and could take care of herself. Finn was just a kid. I closed my eyes in a silent prayer that he got away. Then there was Dad. He'd just be sore that Finn had nothing to hand over and would take it out on him. I clenched my fists in frustration. This was something I couldn't talk or fight my way out of. 'How long was I out?' I said, trying to keep the wobble out of my voice.

'Ages,' they all said.

'They ain't taking us nowhere local,' Joel said.

That worried me more than anything. I needed to know how to get back. 'Where the hell are we going, then?' I looked at the back wall. The crew would be just behind the smoked-glass window. A driver and a police AU, probably.

'We have no idea,' Tyrone said, as if I expected an answer.

'We've been travelling in pretty much a straight line for at least an hour,' Joey added.

My brain fog had been replaced by a dull ache. I'd never

been tasered before. I'd always been too fast. This crew of police wasn't like the usual. The station was less than ten minutes from the pizza shop. Something was wrong and I felt the first real flutterings of fear in my chest. The other kids' disappearances. No one coming back. 'We need to stick together,' I said, fixing each of my friends with a hard stare.

They all nodded dubiously, knowing that it wouldn't be easy. 'They'll split us up for sure,' Andy said, voicing what we didn't want to face.

Andy was a respected pro, with a brother in juvey for the last two years. It proved not all kids disappeared, I reasoned, hopefully. Or maybe that was a more recent thing. I wish I could just stop thinking. It wasn't helping.

Whatever, we all took what Andy said to be true. He leaned forward with his elbows on his knees and we hunched in to hear him. 'We need to deny we know each other. No slip-ups,' he said, looking into each of our faces.

'Why?' Joel asked.

I needed to know, too.

'Because they will use us against each other to get info to convict us. And when we get to juvey, connections are weaknesses, OK? It's the connections you make in there that matter.'

I could literally see the panic filling up inside him. His eyes became wide and wild. That scared me more than anything. Knowing what would happen scared him far more than our simply not knowing. It meant it was worse than anything we could imagine.

The other two were going to pieces. Talking ridiculous schemes too loudly in panic. I scooted along the bench, closer to Andy. 'What makes you think we'll go straight to juvey? We haven't really done anything. Not really. No charges yet, or even a hearing. They can't just do that, can they?' I asked.

Joel and Tyrone had gone quiet to listen.

Andy closed his eyes and let out a ragged breath as if he was getting a grip on his own emotions. Then he opened them slowly. 'Look, on my last visit, my brother was really rattled. I'd never seen him like that. He said there were these rumours.'

We crowded closer again as he lowered his voice to a whisper. It occurred to me then that the van could be bugged. 'There were new guys. A lot. Transferred in from other places and had heard some weird shit. They said big things are happening all over. Everything is changing.'

'Like what?' I prompted. My head was pounding with dehydration.

'There's a lot of talk about there being too many of us on the Outside. No jobs. Too much crime.'

I frowned. None of that was anything new. What did they expect us to do to eat? I narrowed my eyes when I started to fall in. It was the numbers' part that was the real problem for the higher-ups. 'So what do they plan to do about it?' I asked. 'Does anyone know? Or is it hot air?'

Andy shrugged. 'I don't think anyone knows for sure, but he heard that the police have upgraded their AUs, with orders just to round us up. No crime, no court case to answer. Nothing.'

We all absorbed that. It sounded too plausible not to. Kids going missing. The new AU I'd come face-to-face with today. But we'd always been the second-class citizens; it didn't explain what had got the juvey population so tense. 'I don't get it,' I said.

Andy sagged in exasperation with us. 'Look,' he said, hunching in again. 'They were transferring inmates all over the district from one place, like they were emptying it.'

I still shook my head and checked Tyrone and Joel to see if they got it.

'Maybe they were remodelling or demolishing it,' Tyrone said.

Andy let out a mirthless sigh. 'When was the last time the powers rebuilt anything for us?' he said, kissing his teeth. 'No way. And even if they were flattening it, where have all the new offenders been going?' He hushed his voice even more. 'My brother said, in the last six months, apart from the latest transfers, no new kids have been locked up there. And those with connections at other juveys said theirs hadn't either. They're getting scared. Real scared,' Andy said, sitting back in his seat with his back against the van.

We all did the same as if he'd landed a blow.

'What's happening to them?' Tyrone asked fearfully. He wanted us to downplay it. To say it was bored inmates talking crap to scare the younger ones. But none of us did. It all had too much of a ring of truth about it.

'What does your brother think?' I asked.

'He doesn't know for sure. No one does. Most think it's a cull.'

When none of us said a word, he added. 'Killing us like rats in a barrel.'

I swallowed. Rats were just about the only animal that thrived in our world. Them and cockroaches.

I looked on sadly as Tyrone and Joel grasped at straws. 'They can't do that. They wouldn't be allowed. It'd be murder,' Joel said, desperately, like he was about to cry.

I kicked his foot to draw his eyes to mine and held them. Willing him to hold it in. I took deep, exaggerated breaths for him to copy and he caught on and did the same. He would have to grow a thicker skin than this for juvey if that was where we were heading. Crying like a baby would get him killed by the inmates, even if we escaped the cull.

When Tyrone seemed calmer, I returned my focus to Andy. 'Say they're right, and maybe they're using this empty juvey to put all the new kids. They just hold them there till they're killed?' As horrific as that was, it felt too simple, like we were missing a huge piece of the puzzle. 'You said there were lots of rumours. Is there anything else?'

Andy paused before he spoke, looking warily at Tyrone and Joel. He didn't want to freak them out anymore.

'Just say it,' I said, losing patience. I wanted the full story before we got wherever we were going.

Andy looked down before he spoke and swallowed and I knew then that this was the real blow. The thing he really thought was going on. 'Body parts,' he said, looking up. 'They say they're harvesting kids.'

We were struck dumb. I was the first to speak. 'Organs?' came out on a breath, still utterly shocked. Not because of the horror of it, but that it made so much more sense than a cull, that it must be the truth. A ready stockpile of spare parts for the higher-ups, all rumoured to be sick.

'They can't do that,' Tyrone said, standing up, eyes darting, like there was somewhere to run.

'Sit down!' Andy hissed, and we both pulled him back down.

Joel sat frozen. Staring ahead, traumatised.

Tyrone buried his head in his hands and rocked.

'Not just organs,' Andy said, flopping back, hopeless, now the cat was out. His eyes looked glazed as he spoke directly to me; the only one not wigging out. 'They reckon blood skin, limbs, stem cells. Packaged and ready to go to sick humans, but conveniently providing a nice byproduct for the new generation of humanoid bots they're churning out by the truckload.'

'Subs,' I said, more to myself. It kind of made sense. The few I'd seen over here on the Outside were comical and crude, like someone had put them together from parts found at the dump. Still, I was sceptical that they'd put that level of investment even for the Tech population. After all, it was basically an arm extension to a VR.

Andy shook his head like I had no idea. 'No. The new AUs. Didn't you see the cops' eyes? The difference?'

I'd never stayed around long enough to be that up close before. I'd been lucky. But I'd seen enough today to be affected by it. Ice-cold eyes the same colour as mercury.

'I did,' Tyrone said. 'A living metal that moves.' His body shuddered like he'd seen a ghost. At least he'd snapped out of his breakdown.

The subs I'd seen had eyes more like small camera shutters, made of metal. Not so weird. Then the answer came to me, 'They make 'em like that deliberately, so they could never be mistaken for a human,' I said. It stood to reason if they were becoming so realistic.

'This is different, man. On a whole other level. You'll see. You can almost see them thinking,' Andy said.

I knew he was genuinely scared. He'd never been given to bullshit. That alone was enough and proved I should be scared. Everyone in the world should be scared. Because if they're giving something several times stronger, faster, without a conscience, free thought, then heaven knows what could happen down the line. But all they saw was more power and more money. 'No wonder they're harvesting us,' I said, not realising I'd spoken aloud.

Joel hadn't moved and Tyrone whimpered.

It was too late.

The van turned a sharp corner and stopped with a judder. We all sat up alert. Door slams. Two. I looked down at a hand gripping mine. Andy. He reached for Tyrone's across the way, so I did the same with Joey. He finally broke his stare and looked at me. Desolate. 'Chill,' I whispered.

He nodded imperceptibly, but he was OK.

'Whatever happens … friends to the end,' Andy said.

'Friends to the end,' we all said, gripping each other's hands like our lives depended on it. We'd regressed to ten-year-olds, playing war in the acid-stripped woods. We never knew what we'd come up against then, either.

The doors were flung open and spilled in eye-splitting light. It was morning. We'd travelled all night. Holding hands was quickly forgotten, as we shielded our eyes.

'Out!'

I squinted and looked straight into the coldest, silver eyes I'd ever seen. 'Welcome to Hell,' the perfectly calm AU said.

CHAPTER 6

*C*hrissy

That night, when I finally got to bed, I still couldn't sleep. I was restless with nerve pain and my heart was pumping too hard in an uneven rhythm. Normally, I would put it down to neuropathy, triggered by the extra consumption of sugar near bedtime, but I knew it was fear. It was the first time it dawned on me that my whole life had been spent in a state of anxiety. I was scared of everything. Scared that I would get more and more sick, like Teddy. Spending all my waking hours in my room. That my parents would die young, as so many grown-ups did. Nate might be lucky and get adopted, being healthier and younger, but I would spend the rest of my youth forgotten in one of the orphan hospitals. That was how my mind worked, fluttering from one terrible scenario after another.

My mom said it was to mask an underlying anxiety that I didn't want to face, and that I'd always been the same. When I was small, it could be something like spiders in my room that made me want to clean like a maniac. Now, when I really honed down the origin of my fear, it came down to losing Teddy. My only true friend in the world. Tonight proved it wasn't a case of how, but when. He was gravely ill. I could see it now. My blinkers had been ripped off. His skin was grey. He barely ate. There was no more talk of new treatments or plans for when he felt better. His parents were seriously considering one of those black-market subs. According to Ray, they were half the price of the TinBoi knock-offs. It would not be linked to the district AI main-frame, only Teddy. So no one would know it wasn't genuine. It just wouldn't be monitored by the official channels. Ray said that it cut out a lot of the cost. He would talk to his guy and haggle the price down. Perhaps as much as 200,000 UGDC below the market price.

I'd seen the spark ignite in Tina and Tom's eyes. It was the light of hope. And while I didn't want to take that away from them, everything was changing. Life was scary and I didn't like it.

I threw off my thermo-quilt. It was supposed to regulate my temperature, but I was burning up again. I needed a drink of water. I padded downstairs and took the filtered water from the fridge. I filled a glass and went to put it back in the fridge when a flickering light caught my eye through the window. The one that faced next door. A red light. No, a red and a blue. 'Teddy!'

I dropped the jug, vaguely registering the cold splash. My breath stuck in my throat while I yanked up the thin white gauze covering the window to see outside. My heart stopped painfully at my worst fear. An ambulance was parked behind Teddy's family car. His mom and dad were on each side of a gurney being wheeled out. Then I heard a scream. My scream. Then the world faded to black.

. . .

I CAME TO IN A CLEAN, clinical, antiseptic-smelling room. An exam room. A hospital. Mom appeared in my eyeline. Then my dad, next to her.

Then I remembered. 'Teddy,' I said, screwing my eyes shut from the welling tears, hoping it had all been a dream.

My mom picked up my hand. 'It's OK. He had a little brain bleed, darling. He should be up and about in a few days.'

I latched onto 'OK' and struggled to sit up, tears forgotten. 'I have to go and see him.'

My dad pushed me back down by the shoulders. 'Not so fast, young lady. You're in the hospital. You passed out and bumped your head on the way down.'

I struggled to get up again. They didn't understand. 'He'll be asking for me.'

'He's in an induced sleep to heal, darling,' my mom said, smiling kindly. 'He won't even know you're there. I promise, as soon as he wakes up, we'll tell you.'

I relaxed back down, relieved. 'But he's going to be OK?'

My mom swapped a look with my dad, and I knew she was phrasing her words carefully. 'They're hopeful he'll still be able to talk.'

Able to talk? Out of everything, that was all they could be hopeful for. Tears gushed into my eyes so suddenly that I didn't have time to cover them. 'Oh no!' I cried.

My mom pulled me into her arms and my dad held me over hers. I was aware of their soft words of comfort. Telling me to be brave for Teddy. That he was still here. The last blow: he might be paralysed down his left side. Each word another brick walling me in with my misery. It was so cruel to make me think there was hope and then this.

I cried harder, knowing even this was the cushioned version. I wasn't stupid. Teddy had already been gravely ill.

Even if he woke up, there was a high chance he would never walk or talk again. My Teddy had gone.

I drowned in my misery. Everything went limp and my sobbing slowed to nothing. Until I was devoid of all emotion. I stared, without moving. Closed down.

My mom burst into tears.

'We're going to do everything we can to help. One way or another, you'll get your friend back. We'll make sure of that.'

Somewhere, somehow, Dad's words did filter through. He sat with me and talked for ages. Rambling on about still having options. Clinical trials. Ground-breaking surgery. And the last resort: a sub. I knew my dad. He never said things he didn't mean. I finally fell asleep.

CHAPTER 7

ike

We were filtered in, single file, to a processing area. Andy in front of me and Tyrone and Joel behind. So many boys, of varying ages, handcuffed, shuffling along to a holding pen containing a hundred more. I'd had little experience, but I knew it wasn't a police station; it seemed too large in scale. Andy's warnings became real. No formal arrest. No police cell. This was a round-up. We were yesterday's animals, penned and ready for slaughter.

The guards were dotted at intervals and had the same haunting stare. AU's like we'd never seen. Tall, stacked with muscle. A unified rhythm of strong legs in stomping boots. That sound would feature in my nightmares for a very long time.

They wore the same uniform as the guards: a grey version of the cops. Form-fitting, with a flat, peaked hat. But that was where the similarities ended. They were washboard stomach fit. Their human counterparts were middle-aged, balding, with straining uniforms stretched over fat bellies, held up by their belts. They wore Kevlar vests to protect themselves from us. The AUs had a casual calm that shouted they didn't need it. I guessed whatever they had was already built in.

No one spoke to us. I could hear kids further up shouting for a lawyer. Or to make a call, to let someone know where they were. Some were crying, asking why they were there. All fell on deaf ears. There was no need to explain or justify anything if no one was ever getting out.

My gut churned in fear. It had been hours since I'd eaten or even had a drink. Everything was badly wrong with this whole situation and I knew the worst was to come. We were a production line of orders, pulled, prodded and pushed through sections. We were taken out of handcuffs, ordered to strip, and our personal effects chucked onto a heap on the floor. Significant as it meant we weren't getting them back.

A human guard with cheeks like a mutt checked inside my old leather wallet. There was nothing in it except a couple of silver chips that the guy bit, grinned and stuffed into his pocket. But I was more bothered when he found the small, yellowed photo of me and Finn that he just threw over his shoulder. It was the only thing I had left and I would have flown at him had the black stick not appeared on my shoulder. The deep AU voice, 'Move on,' came from right behind me like an icy grip. The human guy had forgotten me already and went on to the next kid. The stick tapped as a reminder; I'd be shocked if I resisted.

I clenched my jaw and turned into a wall of padded titanium and saw nothing but flat determination. Not even a dare, it was that self-assured. Seething, filled with impotent rage and hopelessness, I continued back in the line, butt-naked.

We were pushed through ice-cold showers and sprayed with a foul-smelling chemical that stung like hell. Another line of freezing showers, and a wind that felt like it stripped the last of my skin. A white powder fell from the ceiling and made us all cough. Then, finally stopping at a table, manned by a bored human in glasses, to collect a sludge-brown scrub suit in a 'fits no one' size.

I took mine, grateful to finally cover up. I stepped into the loose pants and had to tie the front of the trousers with a knot to stop them falling straight back down. The top came down to my knees, with 'short' sleeves to my elbows.

Many thought to appeal to the guy's sense of decency, but he refused to look anyone in the eye. 'Move along,' he said in a monotone voice.

Next, we were roughly pushed into hard chairs, three at a time. Our unbrushed hair joined a pile on the ground, already ankle deep. Strangely, despite being stripped of all individuality, I took comfort that they wouldn't give us haircuts if we were straight for the chop. Small consolation, I knew. They wouldn't do all this if we were getting out soon, either.

There were no more protestations. The whole place became eerie with muffles, coughs and the shuffle of feet. As if everyone knew hope was pointless. Handcuffed again and marched through a corridor of bars. Empty cells. All of them. Several floors, right up to a glass-vaulted ceiling. Looking around, confused. At least most of the kids had the bliss of ignorance. Andy looked over his shoulder to convey what I already knew. We were the new influx to fill them. No seasoned cons to bang the bars to scare us. Shouts were already coming from those getting shut in. They didn't understand why everyone was new.

Knowing was no comfort. It sat like ice in my veins. A cold fear that constricted my throat. I learned what it was to be truly afraid. Scrapes with my dad, gang fights where I almost died. Close shaves on the streets, too numerous to remember. All of them were nothing compared to this. The cold realisation that no one was walking away. No rap on the knuckles. No rescue. No chance of escape. I was going to die.

'In!' I was ordered into my six-by-six cell. The bars slid across and locked with a clank behind me. I stood there, motionless for a full minute, listening to the hopeless cries coming from the other cells. Facing the metal toilet and sink on the far wall, I slowly turned my head, taking in the narrow cot on my right. There was no window for ventilation. The whole place stunk of disinfectant, with an undertone of sweat.

I sank slowly onto the cot, utterly bewildered. There was no energy left to even rack my brain for ideas. *Finn.* That's where my head went. He would be going out of his mind. There was no contacting home. No one would ever know where I was. The folks in my neighbourhood would shrug me away as just another kid who mysteriously disappeared, like they seemed to these days.

I continued to sink until I was lying down. At some point, I must have slept, because I was woken by a human guard sliding across the bars. 'On your feet. Come with me.'

I was still half asleep as I stumbled to my feet. 'Where are we going?' My voice was barely a croak; my mouth was so dry. My head ached.

'You'll see,' he said, motioning with his arm for me to move out. He gave me a shove and I shuffled along the strangely quiet gangway, between the cells of wild-eyed kids. Each with an easy-to-read mixture of terror they'd be next, or thankful it wasn't them. Either way, none looked like hardened criminals.

Next, I was nudged down a metal staircase. The guard's boots clanked a louder rhythm behind me. Through an open door, to a bare concrete room with no window. *The kill room.*

I closed my eyes and swallowed hard as I entered. The guard tugged me to a halt. Then, when nothing happened, I slowly opened my eyes. My heart leapt when my eyes focused on the three shapes in front of me: Andy, Joel and Tyrone. Their smiles were cautious, but we flew and clung together in a scrum. Our bravado gone after just one night. Isolation and then the comfort of the familiar was all it took to bring us to heel. 'What's going on?' I whispered, but Andy was already pulling apart.

He shook his head. 'No idea.'

We looked around at the blank room. The door was closed and the guard had left us on our own.

'This place is wrong,' Andy continued, looking nervously around him. 'Why let us see each other? It makes no sense.'

He was right. It didn't.

'Maybe we're getting a lawyer,' Tyrone said, eyes alight with hope. But when no one answered right away, the desperate glimmer dimmed to wishful thinking.

After only a few moments, the lock clanked, bringing us all around to face the door. We instinctively took a step back as the huge army-grade AU stomped in. This new generation, autonomous unit, was like nothing any of us had ever seen. The fluid way it moved. Far bigger, even, than the cop that had caught me. Its fear-inspiring realism was off the scale, despite its head being perfectly encased in sculpted silver. It seemed more like a mask, with cheekbones, square jawline and everything. But it had the same giveaway eyes. The cold, mercurial stare that fixed and held you in fear. It let you know, with certainty, that there was no soul, no conscience, no heart. 'Backs to the wall!' it ordered, in a surprisingly soft southern drawl. Real and measured, as if he were ordering a beer.

We immediately did as we were told, like no other option existed. I raked over the impressive physique, catching the cuffs and long pole in his belt, which I knew from bitter experience, delivered a nasty shock. A contoured metal plate was just visible from the black collar of his shirt up to the chin and extended outwards to a shoulder, disappearing into an arm. I wouldn't mind betting it went right down to its groin. An impressive MF, right out of a video game, whatever way you looked at him.

A regular, puny-looking human, my guess a Tech, came to a standstill next to him, wearing an old-fashioned suit.

I remained dumb. We all did as he scrutinised us one by one.

Another human guard came in behind him. The scrawny guy turned his head and said something quietly. Five chairs and a table were brought in between us. 'Take a seat, guys.' Puny nodded at the four seats in front of us, and he took his on the opposite side. The AU's boots stomped heavily while he came and stood like an electric fence behind us.

'First of all, let's do introductions. I'm Professor Lipinski. And you are…' He looked along our line.

We looked at each other. 'I'm Mike,' I said, when no one spoke up.

'Andy.'

'Tyrone.'

'Joel.'

'They caught you on private property,' the prof guy said, putting a sheet of paper and a pen down on the table, neatly, in front of him.

'We need a lawyer,' Andy said, no preamble.

The prod immediately appeared, a very real threat on Andy's shoulder. Andy's eyes dropped to it cautiously, then defiantly back at the prof. 'We didn't do anything. You've gotta help us,' Andy said, dropping the attitude and attempting to appeal to him.

Without speaking, the prof looked over Andy's head at

the AU radiating a pylon hum of threat, and it took a step back. Then he smiled more reasonably, as if we could all now relax. 'That's what I'm here for. They have a recording from the pizza shop sub. It clearly shows you stealing. That's three to five years, so I understand. Then there's breaking curfew, resisting arrest. I think you're looking at eight to ten, give or take,' he said, chuckling.

What a prize dick. None of us was laughing. I knew exactly what he was doing. While the others groaned, knowing we were hopelessly caught, literally red-handed, I narrowed my eyes, waiting for the 'but'.

'That's ridiculously harsh, just for that,' Andy said, still trying to appeal.

I had no experience with these kinds of things at all, but even I knew not to waste my breath.

The prof put up both his hands in surrender and shook his head dramatically. 'I know you are absolutely right.' But his mask dropped to a hard look that meant deadly business and he lowered his voice two octaves. 'These are the times we live in. The government doesn't care about kids like you.'

We watched, shocked rigid, as he slowly sat back in his seat to let that sink in. It was the truth and nothing new to us, but it was still a shock hearing it said so plainly by a Tech. 'Are you some sort of shrink?' I asked, trying to drill down his angle.

His eyes shot to mine and he smiled, as if he was pleased and a little surprised by my question. 'No ... think of me more as a teacher. My students call me the professor.'

I swapped a cautious look with Andy, next to me. It was the first time I got a hint that this meeting was off the books.

'What do you want?' Andy asked, equally distrustful.

I gave a single nod, too, and watched the guy closely.

He studied us all one by one as if he were making up his mind what to tell us. Then he let out a long sigh as if he'd come to a decision. 'What I'm going to offer you now will never be repeated and never referred to again. You must listen to me carefully, as I can't help you after this point.'

This was it. The whole point of why we were there. I could feel the moisture literally evaporate from my mouth till I felt nothing but fur. My heart beat pulsed through my veins and the sides of my neck and a bead of sweat trickled down my back. This was fear. Real fear.

'First, do not waste your time on false hope. They have you and you won't be getting out. There will be no lawyers.' And he switched his gaze to Andy, 'No antique phone calls home.' Then he fixed each of us with his hard stare with each condemnation. 'You mean nothing. You are nothing … not even a statistic. No IDs. You simply don't exist to trace. From today, you will never be heard of again.'

I swallowed, knowing absolutely that every word he said was true, but I'd never analysed it before. None of us had. We prided ourselves on being free. We had nothing, but we did what we wanted and celebrated not being under the yoke of the Elites. It was where we drew our strength from.

I felt myself shrink inside. With his unwavering glare, I understood that it was an idealised way of thinking. A device used to somehow colour up our bleak existence. The Strong Forgotten were the forgotten. 'Why then?' I asked, bewildered.

The prof guy looked at me strangely, with a curious smile. Like he'd never been asked that question before. To me, it was the fundamental question to everything. He narrowed his eyes and took a deep breath in exasperation. 'Because you come from a part of society that no one needs anymore. You are a blight. An annoyance to the higher-ups, they simply ignore. Except for one, last, exceptional thing.'

I waited, not breathing, for the answer.

'When you leave here to go into the general prison population, you will be forced to sign an ID document for the first time. It will be portrayed as giving you your first, legitimate place in society, but, in reality, you will be giving automatic permission for organ and body part donation on your death. Make no mistake…' He paused, fixing us all with his hard glare. 'You will be signing your own death warrants.'

All the while he was speaking, my heart steadily ached with the effort of pumping. It spread to my temples, my stomach and fired my cheeks. I was going to pass out. This was real. It was happening. All our worst fears were becoming true. Everything was obvious now. I could see it so clearly. The scientists had tried, but they couldn't make realistic skin. Not to the scale they needed for their new tech. They could only graft it or grow it in a lab, and that had to be from the recipient's own skin. I'd seen it on the moving billboards. Bragging adverts, with rousing new frontier music, to cover the fact that they couldn't make skin that was alive from scratch. Why bother when all they needed was to take it from a ready supply of garbage they threw away?

No one said a word.

I looked up and over my shoulder, straight into the arctic eyes of the AU. Built from the likes of us, it was an unnerving exchange. A complete understanding. It knew that I knew. Something built from nothing, from the spare parts of kids like me and circuit boards and was far cleverer than all of us put together.

I faced front again, struck dumb. We all were. The guy wasn't lying. Too much pieced together. He didn't need to say any more and flopped his old leather satchel flat on the table. He opened the buckles with long, slim fingers that looked like they hadn't seen a day's hard labour in their life and took out some old-fashioned paper and slid one in front of each of us. Then he rolled over a pen.

We looked at each other and then down at the smooth

white paper, a jumble of clumped-together words. Some-thing never seen since school, and then nothing as fancy-looking as this. We hadn't learned past what was essential to get by and we all knew the techs never used it at all. It was all plate readers and wall glasses for them, backed up in the cloud of the global network. Impossible to forge. It didn't make sense. Why the paper for us? Expensive. Rare.

The prof must have read the question on my face because he looked directly at me. 'Sign it and you can leave here with me tonight, and everything will be explained. I am offering you a lifeline. The only one you will get.' He tipped his head for me to pick up the pen. Then he looked at his wrist-plate. 'You have two minutes, then the offer is off the table.'

I picked up the pen, slowly.

'How come you get to make us this offer?' Andy asked, making me pause as my pen touched the paper.

'You are wasting valuable time. If the guard rotation switches, we will be out of time. All I will say is that I work in the industry that uses the very parts they will be taking from here.' He tapped his wrist.

My heart galloped. I couldn't think straight. The words merged and moved on the page. A swirling mess before my eyes. *I hereby... permission... guardian... my prison term... deferred... custody of Professor Piotr Lipinski on behalf of Telford Group Enterprises.*

I focused on the guy's mouth as it moved. 'I guarantee if you sign, you will get out of here alive and fully conscious.'

It was the last part that sold it for me. The clarification that it could have been a legal loophole. That to be alive could be interpreted in many ways. I bent over the paper and scribbled my name: Mike Morrison.

Andy grabbed my arm, 'Wait! Don't!' almost jogging my already messy scrawl.

I stared at him, straightening. The deal was already done

for me. 'It's our only chance.' I said, calmly, like I'd never been sure of anything more in my life.

'Listen to your friend,' the prof said.

'We don't know what we're signing,' Tyrone said, eyes wide, fidgeting with panic.

I sensed the wall of muscle behind me tense and I wanted to tell him to shut up and sign, but the prof cut across my thoughts. 'I will give you the gist of it very quickly. What if I told you I can give you a life? Not scurrying around like rats, but a real life. One with a place in society, right under the higher-ups' noses. I will train you in everything you need to know to survive there. All I ask is that you trust me and work for me, and I promise you I can deliver.'

I watched my three friends next to me. Immobile, they were so stunned. But I couldn't make this decision for them.

'Time is up,' the AU said from behind me.

I closed my eyes and prayed. *Do it now, for god's sake.*

'Last chance,' the prof said.

'Sign,' I whispered through gritted teeth. I figured whatever happened, I could escape later.

Tyrone and Joel scribbled, but Andy hesitated. 'Do it,' I pleaded. But Andy pushed the paper away from him. 'I'll take my chances.'

I looked between him and the prof like they'd lost their minds, as the latter inclined his head respectfully. 'Brave man. I wish you luck.' He nodded at the AU behind me. 'Take him back.'

I was on my feet. 'Wait! Stop! Let me talk to him.' But the AU was already pulling Andy up and escorting him towards the door. 'He doesn't know what he's doing?' I called in one last desperate plea.

'I'll find you,' Andy said just before the AU nudged him through the door.

I wanted to scream, shout and rail. *Get him back.* 'He

doesn't mean it.' Tyrone and Joel closed in on me to calm me down. 'It's too late, man. It's up to him,' one of them said.

I shifted my gaze to the prof, responsible for all this, but his attention was already on the guard and Andy was already in the past. 'No need for cuffs,' he was saying. 'They are no longer prisoners; they are my students.'

CHAPTER 8

*C*hrissy
Days passed.
Then weeks.
A month.
Time went by as if I was walking through treacle. Teddy came home five weeks after the brain bleed, once they'd woken him up and declared there was no more they could do for him. It would just take time for nature to take its course to rejoin and mend his neural pathways. He regained some of his speech, but it was slurred and slow, and he was still unable to walk. I could see on the faces of his many doctors that his prognosis was poor.

I went to school as if I didn't exist. Spectating like a ghost on the lives of the oblivious ones. Jessica and her strange AU and the ongoing dramatic relationship between Cindy and Simon. I'd ache to go home, where I'd go straight to Teddy's house and catch him up on the latest instalment of the day. Then, when I'd exhausted that, we'd attempt some VR games, but it always ended with Teddy losing his temper and throwing his headset across the room. Emotional dysregulation was common in stroke patients, the doctor had said. *Stroke.* It was the first time I'd heard Teddy's brain injury referred to as that. It sounded wrong. Too cosy. Like it should have been more like a blow. Something old people got. Clearly not.

Recently, we'd resorted to board games that my mom picked up from the antique fair. Teddy preferred drafts to chess, complaining he couldn't think. I agreed to anything, always letting him win. 'I won't play with you anymore,' Teddy said, one day, as clearly as anything.

I flopped down on the bed, exhausted, next to him. 'But I'd always win,' I groaned into the pillow.

'Then win,' he said. 'How... am I going to know ... wwwwhen I start to get bbbbetter.'

I thought about it for a moment, then sat up and stared into his angry eyes. I shrivelled at the hurt in them. 'OK.' I had to remember this wasn't about how I felt; this was about Teddy and his recovery. Which he had to, *just had to.* 'How are your mom and dad?' I asked, hopelessly deflecting, but it was a genuine question that my mom asked me to ask. They were our best friends, and we hardly saw them these days.

Teddy shrugged with one shoulder and then his lip went up in a lopsided smile. Even he saw the funny side of his goofy look

I giggled, loving him all the more for it.

He concentrated for a long moment on my question. 'Quiet,' he answered, eventually. 'Talk ... in ... whisp-pers.' He looked at me, hopelessly. 'Like I'm ... dying.'

I nodded. Swallowed. Desperately tried to keep the welling tears out of my eyes because I knew it was just adding to what he was saying.

'Yours came... l-l-late l-l-last night. They were all... d-d-doing... it.' He gave me his goofy grin again. 'If I could be bb-bothered to… get up, I w-w-would have tttold them… all to whisper ssssomewhere… else.'

I wiped my eyes with the back of my hand and laughed a little, but I couldn't help wondering why my mom or dad never mentioned it and why they'd waited until after I'd gone to sleep.

The answer came on Friday afternoon. Last period. During Double Science. I was sitting at the bench while the teacher was doing roll call. He read out the names of the sick kids at home, joining on the monitor and Teddy wasn't on there.

My heart bashed my ribs. My mind scrambled to the obvious oversight. But then I was dragged out of my thoughts by the rhythmical hammering against my skull. Not hammering. Heavy, metallic footsteps. Coming closer. Getting louder. Until they stopped. The door was flung open and the huge old-fashioned iron sub stomped into the classroom.

CHAPTER 9

ike

My mind was shattered, not knowing what was up anymore. Like Finn would kick me any minute to say, 'Wake up, I'm hungry.' But I didn't come back to my senses. Instead, the three of us were ordered to get in the back of a sleek silver van. Not a prison van. This was the latest generation tech van. No logo, just clean aerodynamics.

I climbed in, wondering for the hundredth time who this guy was. Tyrone and Joel sat opposite me and we sank back into the body-moulding seats and were immediately belted in. It was so sudden, it made us all jump. Tyrone continued to struggle. 'It's OK,' I said, slowly relaxing. It was comfortable. I could still move, so I knew it was for comfort and not restraint. 'No hard bench on this journey.' I breathed a little easier and kept my eye on Tyrone, allowing himself to do the same. Joel gave nothing away but seemed OK.

The van moved off smoothly, like it was on rails. I'd never felt anything like it. I wanted to say something. Anything. But nothing would come. 'Will Andy be OK?' Tyrone asked. A stupid question that none of us could answer. He wanted to feel better. That somehow we had all made the right decision. I said the only definite thing I could think of. 'Andy can look after himself.'

It was enough. Tyrone nodded on a ragged breath.

We were silent after that, and I was glad. Anything we could say would be inane and pointless. Instead, we retreated into our heads to work it all out and somehow prepare for the unknown. Like soldiers going into battle or being dropped behind enemy lines.

It felt like hours and yet no time at all when we reached our first stop for a comfort break. We got out slowly, squinting in the hazy light and quickly focused on the service station. It was huge, like some sort of space station. A bombardment of fuel smells and loud hisses of gas. We were across the danger line. Somewhere we'd never seen except on news channels.

We grouped together and considered running. The unspoken body language of the streets. But the AU didn't miss it and was soon on us. 'Don't even think about it, skinbags. I'll put you down.'

I froze with shock and my friends did the same. Its vocabulary and intelligence were so life-like. As if it even had street smarts. None of us had experienced anything like it. It was the first time it occurred to me that we were really outside of the law. Not in the way we were used to, beyond the danger line, but all law. We'd signed our lives away to the prof guy and no longer existed. Completely vulnerable. A terrifying thought.

'What we gonna do?' Tyrone whispered, with pupils like hockey pucks.

Joel was walking back from the restroom with another AU. No sign of the prof guy.

'Nothing … yet!' I said, quickly, fixing him with a hard stare to ground him. Panic was in the jerk of his movements and he was only just holding it together. When Joel came to a standstill in front of me, he wasn't faring much better. 'Let's ride it out,' I said, as I was nudged by the AU. 'Your turn.'

They nodded, grateful I seemed to be taking charge. Like I had a plan. I smiled ruefully, walking towards the separate block of restrooms. I was winging it and had been since we'd reached juvey. 'No way out,' the AU said. I was sure with a small smile, even though it had no mouth. It struck me then that he was on me more than the others. Even he saw me as some sort of ringleader. More evidence of it picking up on subtle cues. I just smirked and sauntered inside. I quickly used the facilities and checked it out for weaknesses. No window. Two cubicles. Only one way in or out. A storage cupboard that I could possibly hide in, but I dismissed it right away. The AU would whip the door off as if it were cardboard and no doubt snap me in two. He was right. There was no escape.

I sauntered out and felt the same small smile, like he knew what I'd been thinking and was amused by it. It confused the hell out of me and I walked back to the van with him, radiating power behind me. We climbed back in and it pulled away. We were silent after that. Straining our ears for anything that might give us a clue for a route back. A bridge. A tunnel. Anything to pinpoint a location or direction we'd travelled.

In the end, we gave up. The journey was simply too long. Too flat. Too straight and we were too tired. We were also hungry, disoriented, and on our last nerve. Until, finally, after hours, we felt the van dip and heard the screech of tyres. The only clue we'd entered an underground car park.

We came to a stop and the rear doors opened. 'Out!' the AU ordered.

We moved out slowly and stiffly. Cautious of what we were walking into and grouped close together. We were below ground, but it was no public car park. It was some sort of industrial building, with huge dumpsters, a loading bay and very few cars.

The professor got out of the front and walked briskly towards the building. 'Follow me, boys. Let's get you settled in and we'll have a chat.'

After a quick glance at each other, I moved off first and the others followed. We entered the brightly lit, wire-reinforced doorway and felt immediately confused by where we'd been taken. The corridor came out into a room of huge machines operated by industrial subs, which looked like they were churning laundry. We slowed down to take it all in.

'Keep going,' the AU said from right behind us.

We sped up our steps to catch up with the prof until it felt like we'd reached the furthest point of the building. We went through the last door to a huge warehouse with metal shelves at least thirty feet high. The prof went up to the far wall and pushed a large red button. The shelving section made a grinding noise and moved back about six feet to reveal a stairway leading further downwards.

I hesitated and felt my friends push into me to look down too. We swapped a cautious look until I summoned the courage to follow the prof down. With every step, it felt like we were going further away from everything we knew. Going deeper into the bowels of the earth.

At the bottom, we went through another shop door and came out into a low-ceilinged room more reminiscent of a back-alley repair shop. There was one in every neighbourhood back home. Reconditioning and repairing any old electrical appliances. It smelled just the same, oil and solder. The same shelves brimming with wires, chips and circuit boards, reaching right to the ceiling and covering every surface. Buckets of valves, screws and components any technician would need.

I felt a nudge at my back to continue walking and we went through another door, along a dingy corridor and into a storeroom. There was no window. Only stacks of boxes between four narrow cots. Set out a little like the cells at juvey. Except this was make-shift. Four. I thought about that. Did they expect Andy to come? Or was that just the usual number they had through here?

The prof turned to face us. 'I know it's not much, but you won't be here for long. You'll find a change of clothes in there,' he said, pointing at a lone metal locker.

I felt a bolt of fear at where we were going next. Then I looked down at myself and calmed a little. With everything that had happened, I hadn't realised we were still wearing the ugly brown prison scrubs.

'The shower is in there,' the prof said, pointing to a plain grey door.

None of us said anything. I looked around, then wandered over to a cot and sat down. Tyrone and Joel sat on two of the others. The one nearest the door was left empty. A security habit from home, an unspoken barrier for time to wake up to an intruder. We sat, bewildered.

Then the prof shocked the hell out of us. 'You aren't prisoners. You are free to go,' he said, tipping his head to the door. 'Damien will escort you to the van that will transport you back to the gate of the Danger Line. You can leave and take your chances in an elitist world that is changing for people like you. Or you can stay and let me train you to survive and thrive. To find your real place and genuine purpose.'

None of us thought beyond his words, 'free to go', and we all went to stand up. He stopped us with a raised hand. 'But … if you leave here and the police pick you up again, it's over. You will flag up as a code red classified prisoner and therefore already processed. You will simply disappear, as you don't exist. No further processing, no juvey, no paperwork. You will go straight to the central clinical processing plant. You will never see your families again. That's the deal with no sugar coating. I owe you that. It's your choice.'

The risk was as enticing as it was terrifying. A huge part of me wanted to block out the risk with a whole lot of 'what the hell'. We lived by our wits anyway. But we had been caught once. The police were changing, signalling that our world was about to change rapidly. 'Train us to do what?' I asked, not convinced there could be any upside to this.

The prof smiled, strangely, like I'd just become his star pupil, or something. 'I can only reveal that if you decide to stay.' His smile shifted to an apology as he stared at me for an intense moment.

Tyrone broke my focus by letting out a blast of impatient air and striding towards the door. Joel followed with a 'Wait up.'

I felt a surge of indecision. Desperation. I hadn't had time. They hadn't given it time. 'Stop!' I called, looking from the two of them to the prof and back again.

Tyrone paused just before he disappeared through the doorway. 'Are you coming?'

I wanted to. I really wanted to, with ninety-nine percent of my being. But that tiny one percent remembered the pizza place. Finn. My dad. All swirling around my head at once, rendering me useless. I needed more. We needed more. The prof guy was right. It was only a matter of time until we were picked up again. There were no legitimate places for people like us to go. No protection. No lawyers to fight our side, even if we had the money. Just a life of curfew and existence, until we finally got caught again. I shifted my confused feet and my agonised gaze to the prof. 'Well?' he prompted. 'You'd better get going if you're going to beat curfew.'

It was a death knell reminder. I swallowed and walked

towards my boys, feeling the prof's stare burning into my back. Relief burst onto my friends' faces. Joel hooked his arm around my neck and laughed, but I slowed and dug in my feet. 'I'm staying.'

Joel dropped his arm and they both turned, faces slashed with horror. 'Come on, man. You don't owe these folks nothin',' Tyrone said.

'Yeah, Mike,' Joel agreed, nodding manically. 'We can make it, just like always. We're the indestructible Strong Forgotten.' Joel tried to pull me along by the arm, but I pulled it back.

I smiled when I really wanted to cry. I wanted to hold their boyish faces in my mind forever. I blinked away tears and pulled them to me by both their necks and we stood there and hugged like three terrified little boys. Hopelessly lost boys, far from home. 'Don't worry. I promise I will find you when I figure this out,' I whispered. 'Stay safe.'

Tyrone broke away first, tears tracking down his cheeks. 'We'll look out for Finn and your dad.'

I nodded, grateful. My heart was splitting in two.

Tyrone walked away. Joel wiped his eyes on the back of his hand, nodded once, 'Look after you,' and followed him out.

They marched down the corridor with the AU I now knew was called Damien. The door was closed in my face and I was left staring at it. It felt like a piece of me went with them. A huge hole was gone from the middle of me, I was never getting back.

'Mike,' the prof said, quietly, from behind me.

An involuntary, ragged breath left me and I turned slowly to face him. Warm tears dripped onto my cheeks. I couldn't control them.

'It doesn't feel like it, but you made the right choice. Today, we will begin your education. From now on, you can call me Professor. You will never use my real name again. I will never mislead you and I guarantee you will find out what you will become.' He walked towards the door. 'Damien?'

The AU was back, already. Such a surprisingly human-sounding name. It snapped to attention, like it had been conserving energy. I guessed it didn't take a top-grade soldier to take my friends back. They were more than willing to go.

'Professor?'

'Come in and reveal your true self to Mike.'

The hard goodbye to my friends was quickly eclipsed by the sudden alarm at what was about to happen. The AU marched in, heavily, and I looked between them, cautiously, taking a step back, readying my stance to fight. Then, shocking me so much that my guard dropped, the AU reached behind its neck and pressed something that hissed like decompressing gases. The silver plates that crossed its forehead, cheeks, chin and neck retracted back in turn like dominoes falling, to reveal black skin. Not paint store black, but dark, African skin. Its lips were darker, perfectly sized and shaped. His face was smooth, without blemish and decorated with raised white tattoos that went up from his neck. He looked like some magnificent warrior. I had no idea what it meant, but my heart jacked again as he took the remainder of the casing from his head, where he had tight African hair. The coin was slowly dropping. I knew what I was witnessing, but I didn't want to acknowledge it because it was impossible. It only happened in old sci-fi films and video games. So I clung to its eyes; the glacier silver, obviously manufactured, mercurial eyes.

'Let go, Mike, and accept,' the prof said calmly, from right next to me. 'How does the quote go? By Arthur Conan Doyle, I believe: 'When you've eliminated all which is impossible, then whatever remains, however impossible, must be the truth'.

The AU blinked and looked right at the prof. 'The eyes aren't real,' I said, pointing, like some dumb kid, knowing it shouldn't need to blink.

The prof nodded, slowly, like some proud parent. 'My area of expertise. Everything from the neck up is me… Show him what you can do, Damien.'

I had no idea what was going on. I jumped back as the AU took a step forward. It picked up a stool and bent the complaining metal legs until they crossed over. I was more confused than ever. I couldn't tell if they were trying to show me he was a machine or a human. I turned to the professor for an explanation.

My stomach dropped at his slow smile and intense gaze, as he waited for me to get it. 'The body parts,' I whispered on a breath. Bile filled my mouth and my face creased with disgust.

Both the AU and the professor shook their heads emphatically, and I was confused all over again.

'No,' the professor said. 'The manufacture of Autonomous Units is no longer limited to the military, like Damien here,' he said, gesturing with his hand towards him. 'The next generation of AU robotics has recently been licensed for the general population… By that, I mean the higher-ups,' he said with a small, mirthless smile and a bob of his head, as if it was wrong but obvious. 'It's a joke as it's basically a monopoly owned by a company trading as TinBoiz. A production line of mini versions of our Damien, here. When, in reality, it is a dangerous, fast-growing, absolute neuro network, controlled by a single central quantum computer. AUs with Damien's level of technology are being taken into regular homes as companions, home helpers, carers, and surrogate children. Free-thinking, only in as much as they learn autonomously to adapt to their situations, but all feed into that central computer's control. Seeing everything. Hearing everything. A very dangerous situation, in my opinion.'

I absorbed everything, fascinated by a world that had been a distant idea, glimpsed on moving billboards. A far-off fantasy, for the higher-ups. But I still didn't fully understand. I thought he worked in the industry. It sounded like he didn't agree with it at all. Then he got to the point that blew away everything else.

'They use lab-grown skin in order to add the human element. Falsely humanising the machines to put their owners at ease,' the professor continued, like he was talking more to himself about a lost dream.

I raked my eyes over Damien, not getting it at all. There was no mistaking what he was with the silver metal covering him. But it made no sense to have all that skin underneath. And if they were already growing it in the lab, why the boys at juvey? Why me?

I dragged my gaze back to the professor. 'What do you do then? I thought you worked for these guys.'

'And you'd be right. I am at the forefront of this ground-breaking technology. A pioneer, you could say.' He adjusted his stance to look at me more intensely, making me uneasy. 'I, and a consortium of like-minded individuals, each experts in their own fields, are working secretly to put safety measures into the robotic industry. TinBoiz being the most prominent right now. But there will soon be others. Competitors, legal or otherwise, will push for a market share once it proves as lucrative as expected.' Then he finally got to the point that stopped the blood in my veins. 'This is the systematic eradication of the lower working class. There will be no place left for you or your kind.'

He stopped to let that sink in and I felt numb. Speechless.

I had no idea what to say. What questions to ask. He'd got me here to tell me that? I should have gone with my friends. Or he should have just left me in juvey. But he hadn't finished.

'In our way, we are finding a place for you in the new world. For those of you who want it.' He shrugged, like it was nothing. Like he had no idea what the real answer was. 'No one is forced and should the revolution come, boys like you will already be in position, right under the AIs' noses. Because, rest assured, that day is coming, when it reaches the conclusion that its rule is in our interest.'

AIs, AUs, I was desperately trying to sieve through it to get his correct meaning. Central AI controls TinBoiz AUs and uses them to take over. I think I got it. But what he was suggesting was blowing my mind. Part of me felt horrified, disgusted, when I looked doubtfully at Damien. 'Are you saying you were like me?' It was too outlandish for words.

'I am like you,' Damien said. The military-grade AU with that impossibly soft-sounding, southern accent.

I took a step back, shaking my head. I just couldn't believe it. Refused to. It was a joke.

'I grew up just two blocks away from where the police picked you up. In the run-down tenements, there. I was a drug runner and a prize-fighter. I was caught a few years back during a bare-knuckle fight in the old Crates ware-house, down on the docks. Twenty years old.'

I was paralysed by what he was saying. The story was coming out of a machine, but what he was saying was like home. It was so real; I could smell the sweat and the grime. I just stared at him in those dead, metallic eyes.

The professor began speaking again. I turned my head, but it took me a moment to tune in; I was so caught up in Damien's revelation. 'We make a few modifications for you to pass as the real thing and then we train you in everything you need to be a TinBoi. The way they move, react and the laws. The first and most important: never touch a human. And never endanger the life of a human. Protect!'

'Unless it's for the greater good,' Damien added, bringing my head around to him again. 'They're known as the TEGG laws. Never Touch, Endanger, unless for the Greater Good. It's easy to remember like that.'

I stared at him, not able to get beyond what he was.

The professor pulled my attention back. 'The world is running blindly into this, but their last law is their biggest downfall. A loophole and they just don't see it. When the quantum computer that controls them reaches what we call 'God Mode', our greater good will be no freedom at all. It will decide it knows best. For everyone. Even those who can afford it.'

Everything finally dropped into place. It was strange because I felt a peculiar ember of heat in my chest. This guy really believed in what he was saying. He was there on the frontline. The ultimate Tech. I knew the world was already dying. That we were dying. He'd just put it into fancy words. If we didn't die because of our own pollution, the machines we created were going to wipe us out for the greater good. I'd never seen it clearer. 'So, what you're saying is, you want to turn me into him,' I said, eying Damien's huge physique doubtfully. I was tall for my age, but still a youth in comparison.

The professor shook his head, amused. 'The fastest growing sector for TinBoiz is domestic AUs, designed to be in the under-eighteen age range.'

I didn't understand the demand, but it did make sense of taking boys from juvey. Youth meant healthy. Well, healthier than adults.

The professor stared ahead of him, wistfully. 'It's genius really. The AI is getting its AUs integrated into the family life of its most educated Techs at an early age. It's the latest thing.

The new 'Must Have'. Apart from the classified military models, most of the research has always gone into subs, you see? Now they can't get enough. A replacement for a lost relative or companion. Home helper. Support for sick members of the family. The advertising potential is limitless.'

It was clever. 'What about girls?' I asked. I don't know where that came from. An image of Precious, perhaps, and an ache in my chest that she got away. 'Are they doing the same with them?'

The professor pulled a pained face. 'Not so much … not yet anyway,' he said ruefully. 'There are certain ethical and legal considerations to iron out first. Not that I can see a real difference. Misuse is misuse, whatever the gender. And the AI would know. For now, the emphasis appears to be on the male units.'

My mind boggled at that, but I felt a sense of relief. Hopefully, it would never get to the point where humans could debase it. But going by history, it was only a matter of time. The whole thing scared the hell out of me. I thought of Finn. Dad. The only hope of helping them was to do this. Without it, they had no chance. 'OK,' I said, finally. Standing a little straighter. 'What do I have to do?'

CHAPTER 10

*C*hrissy
   I couldn't take my eyes off the sub stomping in like a jackhammer and making a beeline for me. For a moment, I couldn't breathe, run, cower, or do anything. I opened my mouth to scream when it stopped at the empty chair next to me, but nothing came out. 'Permission to come aboard, Star Ranger?' A metallic voice said.

I blinked, registering the words in the familiar cadence. My mouth had gone completely dry. 'Teddy?' came out as a tiny squeak.

The kids around me all stared at me gormlessly. The teacher laughed and clapped with delight. 'Say hello to Teddy, everyone. Welcome back.'

I dragged my eyes from the clunking pile of pistons, rivets and joints, to look at the teacher who was addressing the whole class. 'He will be using this proxy unit from now on.'

'It's called a sub, Miss,' a boy called out.

I just looked from one to the other in a daze. My mind had stalled. Brought back to the sub, attempting to sit on the small chair next to me, in a series of whines and hisses as its hydraulics pushed and released. He finally managed to perch and rest his camera shutter eyes on me and gave me a strange kind of wink and almost slipped off the chair. 'Whoops,' it said. 'Damn chair is too small … not used to it yet,' he said, still fidgeting.

My eyes were already filling with tears at the unmistakable choice of words and his sheer awkwardness. He never could coordinate. 'Teddy,' came out on a breath.

'We'll arrange a larger bench for you tomorrow, Teddy,' the teacher was saying. 'Grab another one for him, James, can you?'

Another chair appeared and was pushed next to the one Teddy sat on and he spread over the two more comfortably.

My heart was beating wildly and tears streaked my face, already burning like a furnace at the whole class watching my reaction. But I didn't care. I had a million questions, not the least of which was, 'Why didn't you tell me?'

'I only knew recently. I wanted to surprise you. We'll talk at home.'

I continued to stare at him as he pulled his books out of the familiar bag that now looked too small for his big hands until I was forced to face the front again. 'Right … calm down now. Excitement is over and we've a lot to get through.' The teacher's voice called loudly, but it was a dull echo to me. My mind was stuck. Teddy, my best friend, who I thought was dwindling away, was right here. Real, in such a perfect way for him. Walking and talking, starring in his own VR game. I couldn't begin to quantify how I was feeling. So happy, I was terrified. Angry that I couldn't enjoy this totally. Exhilarated that Teddy was out of his room and we were back together again. I guess I was scared it wouldn't last. That it was too good to be true. That even though the sub he was using was out of the dark ages, I knew it came at a heavy price and I had no idea how his parents had managed it.

I calmed down eventually. It was a double lesson. That meant two hours of sitting in the same place. I felt weird, like I was living in a dream. Teddy was working out the machine's facial expressions. Raising fake eyebrows and creaking the corners of his mouth into a grimace-like smile. In any other circumstances, it would have been hysterically funny. But I was in shock and all I could do was watch, absorbing the constant swearing, when he got something wrong. The last one made the whole class laugh when he tried to raise his arm to answer a question and kicked out a leg by mistake. 'Damn!'

'OK,' the teacher said, amused but slightly browbeaten. 'We'll leave it there today. Please make sure you practice before the next lesson, Teddy.'

'No don't, Teddy,' a boy shouted, making everyone laugh. 'I never knew you were so funny.'

'Yeah, you're hilarious,' a girl said.

I felt more normal by then. Being back to being laughed at was familiar territory and I scowled at the perpetrators, which made them laugh even more. It took Teddy a moment to get to his feet. I had to pull the desk forward so he didn't accidentally knock it over. It wasn't his fault. The sub was far too big and clunky for a classroom. It had probably been designed for a heavy-lifting job somewhere about ten years ago. 'Keep out of the way of my feet,' Teddy said, as we began to walk towards the door. His huge stomps brought my gaze down to the metal boots that not even a lining of rubber underneath could dampen down. He was just too heavy. He was right, though. One misplaced step and he could crush one of my feet. I opted to lead the way instead, until we got out into the crowded corridor.

News had spread and everyone had congregated to get a

glimpse of the weedy kid who'd come to school in the huge sub. They were already calling it a Transformer sub and chanting, 'Optimus Dime!' It was meant as a put-down, but Teddy being Teddy, immediately turned it to a positive with a hissing attempt at a regal wave. 'See, Chrissy,' he said, in his metallic voice, grinning lopsidedly, 'I have become my favourite character. So cool.'

I should have known. At the centre of the melee were Simon, Cindy and Jessica, laughing hysterically and pointing at us. They were with the whole athletics team. All the raucous, popular kids that made our school life hell. Except for Jessica's AU. He was conspicuous in his complete lack of movement or emotion at all. His strange gaze was locked on Teddy. So fixated, it made me start to feel uncomfortable. Calculating, like a predator eying its possible prey, deciding on whether to attack. It was so weird.

Teddy just put his chin up and strode through, happily, as if he hadn't enjoyed himself as much in years. It fuelled the laughter behind us, but we soon left it and reached the exit and walked out into rare sunshine. It didn't happen often that the skies cleared. The humidity had to be low and the wind in a certain direction right after it rained. The air smelled clean and I stopped to look up and breathe it in.

Teddy had stopped as well and was watching me closely, his shutter eyes whining open and closed to adjust to the light. I knew he was following what I did. 'It's clean air,' I explained, immediately feeling bad at the small smile that followed. He would never be able to breathe it again. I was such an ass.

'Let's go home,' he said, heading off to the pick-up/drop-off point at the front of the school. The gardens looked beautiful in the sunlight. Genetically engineered flowers and shrub borders went around manicured lawns. Plants, specially manufactured to withstand the poor light and air quality. The airbots were working up and down, in rows, to keep the soil moist and blow any pollution away. They'd be turned off at night, so the plants had to make it till morning. Me and Teddy always thought of it like a fake film set that only came alive during the day. Like Disneyland, it kept the pretence of a happy, functioning world.

My dad pulled up with Teddy's dad, Tom, driving a brand-new van. The driver's side window lowered, 'Hop in,' Tom said brightly. A side panel slid across.

I looked up at Teddy after yet another unsettling surprise. 'You didn't think I could fit in our usual car, did you?' he said, already negotiating the huge chair being lowered, which he turned and sat in quite easily. It whirred as it raised and went back into place against the far wall. I climbed in and sat in a comfy black leather seat opposite.

The van pulled away and my dad turned his seat to face us. 'Just how surprised was she?' my dad asked, grinning at Teddy.

'So shocked,' Teddy said, laughing strangely. 'I recorded the whole thing. You can watch it later.'

I was still in shock. Teddy was his old self, just through a sub. It felt like I had him back again. He reached out one of his metal-jointed hands, with fingers the size of hot dogs and I gripped it, hard. I wasn't sure if he could feel it, but I held on tight as if it would keep him with me.

'Ow!' he said, turning his head with a weird grin.

'You can feel it?' I asked, feeling terrible.

'Of course … I have full sensory syncopation,' he said with an exaggerated shrug.

I laughed a little nervously at how matter-of-fact it appeared to be to him. Like it happened every day. He smiled and put a large arm around my shoulders, amazingly gently. I hugged him for a moment, feeling strange. He felt so lumpy and solid. Then he brought his arm back and patted my hand in perfectly timed circles. 'How did all this happen? I mean … How did your parents afford it?' I asked, stopping his hand and holding it.

He looked across at my dad in conversation with his. 'I'm not sure, but I know your dad helped.'

'Dad?' I said, looking at him sharply.

He looked over his shoulder at us, smiling.

'Thanks, Chris,' Teddy said. 'I don't know what to say. How to thank you enough. You gave me my life back.'

My dad waved it away with a hand. 'Don't mention it. Your mom and dad would have done the same for us if it were Chrissy.'

I stared at my dad, feeling like I was rolling with the punches today. I wasn't sure how he'd helped, exactly. My parents weren't any better off than Teddy's. But for now, it was enough. After weeks of thinking Teddy was never going to come out of his coma and even more frustration and disappointment when he eventually came home, we'd accepted that a full recovery was never going to happen. This was way more than either of us could have ever hoped for. And I would take it every time. 'Thank you,' I mouthed, silently to my dad, my eyes brimming with tears.

'I love you,' he mouthed back, simply, and turned back around.

I turned my head and looked up, directly into Teddy's strange new eyes, who'd witnessed the whole thing and sensed the sad smile. He gripped my hand again and we sat in a solemn kind of silence all the way home. Listening to our dads talk about work stuff and sports scores and everyday life.

THE NEXT FOUR weeks were the best in my life. I was happy. Teddy was happy. My brother, Nate, and all our parents were happy. We had family parties at each other's houses, sleep-overs, swapped stories, hopes and crushes, just like best friends did. Like we'd always done. I was even OK when I slept in Teddy's room, with his physical body. Despite him not moving, being linked up to monitors and having his high-tech head casing on, he slept perfectly soundly. I learned to pair the clunky, oldest version of a sub known to man with my dearest friend. Because besides the metal and bolts, he *was* Teddy. My Teddy. My best friend in the world.

At school, the joking calmed down, and it became yester-day's news. Teddy got better at controlling the sub, and his classes and equipment were adapted to his size. The other kids gradually got used to him in the same way I had. The strange became normal, until no one saw it at all.

End of term was fast approaching. And at the end of one uneventful day, Teddy negotiated getting down on one knee to ask me to the Winter Dance. It was a big deal that I hadn't even thought about. We'd never gone before.

I laughed at the manoeuvre. He really moved quite smoothly now. I shook my head wearily. 'Why do you always have to be so dramatic?' I said, sounding bored. 'Of course. But don't think I don't know what you're up to. Now you're all stacked and noticed. You only want me there as wing-girl to get close to Tashan. I don't know whether to be flattered or insulted.' I was already grinning at the smoothly raised, pleading eyebrows when he wiggled them up and down and made me laugh.

'Pur-leeeease,' he whined, looking up at me, with his hands pushed together in a prayer.

I rolled my eyes and let out a loud sigh. It was hopeless. I was never able to say no to that look. 'I suppose so. But I expect a limo—' I frowned, immediately remembering that would be impossible with his size. 'Maybe not … Flowers, then. And you still owe me big.'

. . .

END OF TERM CAME, and it got to the night of the dance. My mom and dad took pictures of me in my new electric-blue dress. Nate said I looked like a dork, as was his job as an annoying younger brother, and we waited. In the hall at first, with my dad frowning and looking at his watch. I kept calm, telling myself that Teddy would be sprucing himself up, or maybe putting a joke bowtie on his sub, or something. But in the end, after fifteen minutes, even I started to feel uneasy. Teddy was rarely late and with no message, call, or anything, I really started to worry. At twenty minutes, my mom moved into fussing mode, like she did when she was worried and started making us all tea. Nate joked that Teddy had stood me up and ran up the stairs to his room after Dad told him off. He looked really worried and that was what scared me most of all. 'I'm going over there,' he said, suddenly bursting into action towards the back door.

I said, 'I'm coming, too!'

My mom shouted, 'No!' at exactly the same time and that made both me and my dad freeze.

Then we heard it.

The howling siren. Closer and closer. Louder and louder. Not the siren of curfew, but the kind—

We all turned to look at the kitchen window at the same time. It was the same one that faced Teddy's house and was covered in white lace. But we all saw it. The blue light, flashing. Outside Teddy's and stopping my heart.

It didn't pump again until I ran outside and stopped dead with my parents slowing next to me. A gurney was being wheeled out of Teddy's house. Along the short driveway to the waiting ambulance on the road.

Other people were coming out of their houses to see what

was happening. Husbands putting grateful arms around their wives or children, glad it wasn't them.

My dad strode over to Teddy's dad. I couldn't hear what was being said. Teddy's mom was getting into the ambulance with the gurney. I didn't move. I couldn't. I was invisible in the middle of madness. Looking out from my skin.

'What happened?' my dad was asking.

Tom was walking fast to his van. 'I don't know.' He opened the side and shoved in some bags. 'He was so excited about the dance. Then nothing.'

He got into the driver's seat, even though it drove itself. It began to slowly reverse, with my dad keeping up with it. 'What do you mean, nothing?' my dad persisted through the open window.

He looked at my dad, exasperated. Like he'd run out. Of time. Of patience. 'I mean nothing,' he said, broken, in a way I'd never seen him. 'No brain activity at all. Not to work that damn sub. Nothing.'

The ambulance pulled away.

'I have to go,' Tom said.

My dad pushed himself away from the van and Tom reversed back onto the road and followed the ambulance.

My brother had come out and was standing next to me as my dad wandered back towards us. 'What did he say, Dad?' Nate asked. 'Was it the sub? Did it kill him?'

My dad looked at him, startled.

My mom said, 'No!' angrily. 'Don't say stuff like that.' But the look she gave my dad was asking the same question.

He just shrugged and put his arm around her, like the other husbands. Pulling us to him, like he was glad we were still there.

·   ·   ·

I WENT STRAIGHT to bed with my heart crushed. As useless inside as any damn sub. A barely functioning robot. Dead.

I switched off when I got into bed and only switched on to basic functioning mode when I got up. I went to the hospital the next day, numb. Emotionless. Even when they confirmed there was still no brain activity.

Dead, when they asked Tina and Tom whether they wanted to switch Teddy's machines off. Dead, when they shook their heads and said it was too soon. Crying, turning to my parents for small comfort.

'There has to be a chance. There just has to,' Tina wailed into Mom's shoulder.

Dead at Nate being traumatised to silence.

Dead, watching the anguish on my parents' tired faces. Shaking their heads slowly, with nothing they could do.

I didn't speak.

I didn't eat.

Deep down, I guess, even I thought all the while he was breathing, there was a chance.

My mom didn't even force me to go to school. She understood. There was no point without Teddy.

Mike

After the initial briefing, I was introduced to five other boys, all of a similar age and all from across the Danger Line. We had no time to learn more than that about each other as we were transported straight out to another place. The van stopped and we all got out and looked up at an old, abandoned church.

'Move!' Damien ordered, ushering us to walk with his hand.

We weren't cuffed, but it sure felt like a prison detail. The way we shuffled along, single file. I was at the back, glad for the extra time. The area around was derelict and crumbling, as if it had been empty for years.

'Keep walking,' Damien said, right next to my ear.

I looked at him through the corner of my eye. For such a big guy, he could be light-footed when he wanted to be. I'd had no idea he'd gotten so close. I jogged up the steps covered in loose, broken tiles and walked through the musty-smelling, vaulted porch and came out directly inside the church.

I immediately woke up to my surroundings. The dust and grime were left outside and the room was clean and bright. The walls were painted white, the old pews removed, leaving a pristine, sprung wooden floor. The professor stood back and gave us the time to look around, like it was some kind of first lesson.

Most of the old churches had been repurposed or become museums since the global religion ban of 2028. Mack, at the shop, had told me about their grandeur and shown me pictures from old books as a small kid. The only thing left to attest to what this place had once been was the beautiful stained glass. Here, they were boarded up on the other side, but were lit in between, forming an amazing display through the leadwork. There were also a few relics and statues carved into small alcoves.

I turned a circle, in awe. It was such a little church. Nothing like the grand places I'd once been shown. But the place smelled good, like cut wood and cleaning wax. I liked it. It felt good. Peaceful. I wondered if that was the point all along. How it was meant to feel.

A few of the older folks back home still practised their faiths. In secret, in basements and back-alley meeting places, risking their lives to break the law. Mack had been one of them, holding a prayer group at the back of his store.

I asked him one day when someone had left an old, dog-eared bible on his counter. He'd whipped it up and under his sweater so fast, it made me laugh. It took days for him to answer my question. 'Just because something is banned, doesn't mean it isn't true. In fact, it proves the opposite. When the powers are so afraid they feel the need to ridicule and ban something, that's when you most need to find out what it is.'

I'd scoffed at the time. 'But how can you believe in something so blindly?' I remembered breaking into laughter at the sardonic look he gave me behind the bat blind eyes and putting up my hands in surrender. I honestly hadn't intended the rather excellent joke. 'The proof is in the teachings,' Mack had said. 'It's in the words. Carried down through time. For us to live by and survive through this terrible time of the end.' He watched me absorb his words, even though he couldn't see. He seemed to know they ran deep.

'Why would they ban something like that?' I'd asked, astonished. Surely something that preached being good and peaceful would be something the UGN would back.

'Because, ultimately, we follow Christ, who teaches us to follow the Almighty. We obey the laws of the land, but UGN is clever. They know, if it came to a choice, then we would always follow Christ. That, they will not tolerate. It's capitulate or die.'

Somewhere along the line, that chat with Mack had got pushed to the bottom of the pile by the rigours of life and survival, but I'd never forgotten them. And this place had brought it all back. That maybe the Strong Forgotten weren't forgotten by everyone and we weren't entirely alone.

'Welcome, pupils,' the professor said, in a strong voice that carried around the whole room.

I turned and gave him my full attention and felt the others doing the same. He was standing on a raised platform at the far end—the place where the priest and the altar probably once stood.

'Today we start your education that you will carry with you for the rest of your life… Sit!' he said, patting the air.

I looked across at the others. They looked at each other and began to sit on the floor. Some knelt. Some crossed their legs like they were at school. I slowly got down with them, until I sat, crossing my legs out in front of me and leaning back on my hands. It felt awkward and uncomfortable, like he was doing it to make us feel small.

I glanced sideways at Damien. Always there, always watching. He shook his head slightly. Wearily. As if I tried his patience. I faced back, unsure why.

'First of all, I want to start by introducing you to the finished article. To the finished version of what you will become at the end of all this.'

We all turned our heads at the same time to look at Damien, still standing off to the side.

'No! Not Damien,' the professor said, bringing our focus back to him in surprise. 'Damien is an ABU2050, an Autonomous Battle Unit, manufactured about five years ago. You will be the latest, 2055 TinBoiz, model C, companion unit… Leo!' the professor called.

Footsteps came from behind us and we all swivelled around immediately to see who it was.

No one spoke.

I'm sure our jaws dropped open as the perfect machine boy, of around sixteen, strode in with an easy, fluid gait. There were no air piston jerks of some of the subs I'd seen. Everything about him was smooth. His hair was perfectly cut and combed. His face was handsome but manly, with flaw-less, tanned skin, with matching, perfect hands, poking out from thick silver bands at the sleeves of his powder blue uniform. The body-forming sweater went into a wide belt, highlighting his ripped V torso and trim waist. Over it was a silver breastplate that went up over his shoulders and down his arms. His black pants were the same fabric as the top, straight-legged and tucked into knee-length black boots. It was just his weight giving him away as something else, on the sprung wooden floor. I came to the conclusion that he had everything Damien had, but lighter. Smaller and more compact.

I turned my body, following him as he passed, and watched him hop easily onto the stage, where he bowed at the waist with his hands flat against his legs. The professor returned it, equally respectfully, then he turned and stood at ease with his hands behind his back.

'Turn around, please, Leo,' the professor said, drawing a circle with his index finger.

The TinBoi turned immediately, giving us a good view from behind. It was pretty unremarkable. More or less the same as the front. Again, showing a lighter, utility version of Damien. Easy to replicate, I guessed, if you had access to all the same materials.

The professor pointed to a silver rectangular plate at the base of his neck, connected to a shaped piece that cradled his skull. 'This is what I wanted to show you,' the professor said, beckoning us with his arm. 'Come closer, you need to be able to see this.'

I scrambled to my feet and walked to the edge of the stage. The other boys grouped around me, straining to see. At first glance, it looked like a company stamp. TinBoiz, with the small trademark symbol engraved into it.

'This will be the most important thing for each of you. It will not only distinguish your make but has an official serial number, here,' he said, pointing to a twelve-digit number, impossible to read from where I was standing. 'It is a traceable, individual number, kept at the central AI quantum memory store. These are real. They are not counterfeit. They can't be,' he said, turning to fix each of us in the eye. 'Do you understand what I am telling you?' he said, glaring at us. 'It is genuine. Issued by the TinBoiz factory and will make you unmistakable as the real thing. The whole strength of your cover.'

I got it. At least, I thought I did.

'You will be trained and crafted by the best robotic, cybernetic engineers and orthopaedic surgeons. Your parts will be state-of-the-art, TinBoiz components. I myself will see to it that you are trained in everything you need, to not only assimilate into Tech society, but thrive there until the time comes.'

'What comes?' one of the other boys asked, before I had time to.

'The end. The true singularity. The time to save humanity?' the professor said, with a weird fervour in his eyes.

It made me feel uncomfortable and weird. I had to swallow down a hard lump in my throat and I didn't know why. I guessed because the guy believed in it so much. He believed in us. I looked around to gauge the others, sceptically. I was only really in this to help my family. We were just a rag-bag bunch of kids and this felt big. Like change the world kind of stuff.

'Thank you, Leo.'

The boy turned back around to face us again and I got a closer look at his eyes. Cold, liquid silver, machine-like eyes. I wasn't sure how he did it, but they were a great touch. Better evidence than any real serial number.

The professor appeared to be studying our reactions and guessed right away what I was looking at. 'The only stipulation the network made when they granted the licence for companion models was the standard AU eyes. We have long exceeded the tech. But they insisted that a human must see at a glance who is human and who is not.'

I nodded, absorbing it all. It made sense. If a machine was as real as this, with human-like eyes, it would be impossible to tell us apart. 'Can he do anything cool?' I asked, shifting my gaze to Damien and back to Leo again. He looked athletic but had a regular build for a sixteen-year-old.

The boy dropped his weird eyes on me and grinned. A weird grin that didn't reach his eyes. He sure looked like a robot when he did that.

The professor stepped down and nodded at Damien. 'Spar mode, only.'

The boy stepped off behind him and we backed up out of their way. It was on. A real David versus Goliath and tense as hell. My heart rate sped up in excitement as I focused on the pair, now bowing and then circling each other. It was crazy. I couldn't believe the professor was encouraging it. Damien was twice as wide and at least eight inches taller. Machine or not, this was suicide. The kid didn't back down and we were all eager to watch.

The professor moved between them. 'Begin!' he said, dropping his arm.

The pair bowed to each other like Japanese Samurai. Damien put up his fists to guard his face as the TinBoi whirled, jumped and kicked out at face height. Then,he followed it with combinations of kicks, punches at all different angles, coming at him from several directions. Unsurprisingly, Damien blocked every one. It was like a perfectly choreographed fight scene from a movie; a pleasure to watch. Not a single punch landed. Damien was a machine, but the TinBoi clearly had skills.

'Now show what you can really do, Leo,' the professor said.

I was riveted, astounded that there could possibly be more.

They stopped sparring, bowed to each other and then to the professor. Damien wandered to the edge of the room, where he picked up a long wooden gym bench, around eight feet long, like it was nothing. He walked back, holding it out with wide arms in front of him and it became obvious what was going to happen.

Leo nodded, then executed an amazing acrobatic spin in the air, crashing his leg down through it, sending splinters flying. Our 'ooos' of appreciation were instantaneous. It was no show prop. It was an antique hunk of solid wood. Impressive.

'Will we be able to do that?' one of the other boys asked.

I nodded along, wanting to know that as well. I knew even the most expert and highly trained martial artist could shatter their foot with a stunt like that. It struck me then that maybe he wasn't just training us to move and mimic the AUs.

The professor hadn't answered the question and was already watching me closely when I asked, 'What have you done to his legs?'

He inclined his head towards me as if I'd asked the right question. Then he looked up, suddenly. 'OK, let's sit again and I'll go through the programme. You will be leaving here for your placements in just a few weeks.

Damien pulled out some mats and I walked back over with the others and we sat down on them. The professor appeared to be increasing our comfort in increments, like this was already part of his training. I felt a pang of nervousness. A few weeks to be like Leo and then let out into the Tech world to blend in. It was a daunting thought. Terrifying. I looked across at the others and they all had blank, worried faces or wore frowns. They'd be mad not to.

I was starting to watch Damien a lot, too. He was always so calm and together. He'd sauntered to the edge of the room and folded his arms and Leo had gone to the other. All the while the prof gathered whatever he needed to address us, my gaze strayed to them. Looking for tells. Gauging their faces for emotion. Taking in their posture for control. In other words, the smallest of movements. And I can safely say, there were none. They were superb actors. I could only hope I could be that convincing one day.

'Alright!' the professor said, clapping his hands together to get our attention again. 'A few weeks is not very much time; I hear you thinking. You'd be right. So that's why everything is planned and executed to the finest detail. First, we start with the laws. Then the fittings for suits and parts. Surgery. Healing time. Then, lastly, intensive training in movement and combat.'

A boy whispered, 'Yes!' loudly.

I inwardly shook my head. Out of all that, and that's what he picked up on. What an idiot.

'In the meantime, placements will be found for you from the waiting list of applicants, for you to leave right away. No time for stagnation.'

My mind was in freefall at the word 'surgeries'. We were all glancing at each other, unsure how much anyone else knew or understood. The professor hadn't alluded to it previously, but I'd guessed there had to be some minor adjustments to make us look authentic, but after seeing Leo in action, he'd obviously been boosted with something extra. The question was with what. I prayed it was just enhancing drugs. 'What surgeries?' I called out, cutting right over him. 'You never mentioned that up front.'

The prof fixed me with a hard glare and his jaw tightened like I'd ruined his flow. 'OK. So we're doing this right away, are we?' he said on a bored breath.

I pulled my knees up and hugged them, eyeing Damien cautiously. He didn't move and I faced front again. 'Yeah,' I said, not willing to cave. 'It sounds pretty permanent.'

The professor casually walked over to the side, grabbed a wooden stool and brought it over and sat down in front of us. He took a moment and breathed in deeply. 'There are many things I will give you to stay safe and keep your cover. And all … are equally … essential,' he said, punctuating his words and glaring at us individually. It did nothing to quell my unease.

They are the laws that all AUs have programmed into them as their prime directives. Then there is AU etiquette, again, automatic for any genuine model. Your serial number, which will protect you in its uniqueness, is issued by the central AI itself. Training in movement and posture. But above all, it will be your strength and speed, not just physically but mentally, that will set you above any human being.'

He looked right at me when he said that, while the others were high-fiving. Like they were going to be superheroes or something. I was already frowning at what that meant, exactly. It felt like he was being deliberately vague.

The prof smiled a little as if he read my thoughts. 'You will have to at least be partially linked to the AI.'

He was still looking directly at me, looking amused. 'How do you propose to do that?' I asked, not breaking our stare-off.

He laughed and looked over at Damien, which bugged me, with his 'get this kid' look. Adults did it all the time back home to slap you down and know your place. 'Well?' I said, not giving an inch.

The professor laughed loudly and I was surprised to see a hint of a smile on Damien, too. Then the smile literally dropped like a veil from the prof's face. He got up from his chair and began a slow walk along the line in front of us. 'OK, I'll not mince my words. Physically, your bones and your joints will be splinted and coated with titanium. Those with a weakness or any conformation defects will have full prosthetics. TinBoiz are physically perfect,' he said, glaring at us again.

I was hooked; we all were. He didn't need to give us the dramatic effect.

'It is not just for strength; it is for weight. A TinBoi weighs three times as much as any boy your age. It will also show up on security scanners. This is not some costume party. Lives are at stake. Yours included,' he ended, moderating his tone.

My blood was slowly trickling to ice and the over-excited boys next to me had finally gone quiet. This was far more than any of us bargained for and he hadn't even mentioned above the neck. His specialty. The part that scared me most of all in that he'd saved it till last. Authenticity was not just going to be a TinBoiz stamp at the base of our skull.

'What about above the neck? The link to the AI? How does that work?' I asked. 'You know, without mincing your words.' I knew I was being disrespectful and it was risky, but I'd never cared less. He had completely hidden his cards.

The prof didn't seem affected. More like a schoolteacher whose pupil had touched on his favourite subject. He put his hand over the centre of his chest. 'All TinBoiz have a power source here. For you, it will double as protection and camouflage for your heart and lungs. That will be front and back.'

I glanced at Leo and the metal plate covering his torso. Outwardly, it reminded me of Roman gladiators' armour, but disturbing, in that it wasn't like a Kevlar vest, it was part of him.

'The power source joins to your neuronetics. In layman's terms: from the neural transmitters in your brain, to the nerve pathways, throughout your body, to your limbs and extremities and aids movement in them. It also controls your heart rate to keep it undetectable to other AUs and the quantum AI.'

I had a hundred questions, but I couldn't formulate a single one. It was quickly becoming obvious that he was not using spare parts of dead kids to make AUs. This guy was literally turning us into one. A secret army. Using a neverending source from the discarded part of society. I kept quiet. Stunned.

'Answer his question,' Another kid called out.

It broke me out of my stupor and made me look across at him. It proved they weren't all mindless sheep. I looked back at the prof, who'd sat back in his chair and nodded. We all waited and I knew that I wasn't going to like whatever it was. He shifted in his chair a little too uncomfortably.

'OK,' he said on a breath. 'I will give it to you straight. No bull shit.'

My gaze was hard and unmoving. I wasn't going to let him off this. It was our lives.

'We line the inside of your skull. It's great protection for your brain,' he said, attempting a bright smile. As if it made up for carving us up.

He averted his eyes when he saw the deadly look in mine. 'Get to the point!' I called out.

Damien stepped forward. 'Watch your mouth!' he snarled, looking deadly.

'Well, he needs to get on and say it. He wasn't exactly up front at the jail.'

The professor gave Damien a small shake of his head to stand down and looked at me coldly. 'The main component in your whole body will be the link chip to the central AI, which is placed under the plate behind your neck, at the base of the skull.'

It was bad, but not as bad as I'd feared. It wasn't total brain surgery. At least I didn't think it was. I didn't want to be lobotomised. 'Will it be able to control us? This thing. The AI. Or at least be alerted if it can't?'

The prof inclined his head as if I'd asked a good question. 'It has a name, in code, of course, but it refers to itself as a he and has named itself Metatron. The short answer to your question is no, he can't control you. Fortunately, that is the area of my expertise. I am not a surgeon. My specialty is in Optic Bio-Fusion and Neuronetic Engineering, and I work in this field every day for TinBoiz, on the real production models. I fit these chips all the time. Yours will have certain modifications. I won't bore you with the tech, but suffice it to say, Metatron bounces a signal to its AUs every two hundred and forty seconds, twenty-four hours a day. Tiny, operational bounces that we call the "OK" signal. It uses this to track you and to run system checks for power health and any malfunctions. The chip then answers that you are OK. Yours will be adjusted to simply bounce back the OK, without being linked to the rest of your nervous system. So, in other words, it pretends to be OK.'

He leaned forward and stared intensely at each of us in the eye. 'Every circuit check will be sent a plausible answer and it's all in a tiny chip, the size of a fingernail, embedded under the plate behind your neck. Make no mistake. This micro piece of engineering is the most crucial part of your whole enhancement. Without it, Metatron would identify you as faulty. Within minutes, he would locate you, and his security/protection force would bring you in for reconditioning. In your case, that would mean certain destruction and for me and my group of engineers, arrest and death and the total failure of our great endeavour.' He sat back in his chair as if he'd delivered a great speech, spittle on his lips, eyes red with fervour.

It made me swallow and want to swear. I'd never heard anything like it outside of a movie. The complete belief and commitment to something outside of oneself. It was kind of inspiring. The boys next to me remained quiet, too. They knew as well as I did that there was nothing else for us to do. If we made it through to middle age, beyond the Danger Line, which was doubtful, it would be to a life of ill-health, alcohol or drug abuse. Only to wind up dead one day, way before our time.

And it did sound kind of cool. Scary as hell. But cool. Especially the surgery, the training, as well as the living with a spoiled rich family, in a part of society we didn't really know. I guess that's what the training was for. Maybe it wasn't that bad. 'So this AI, it definitely can't get into us?' I asked. That part made my skin crawl.

The prof shook his head emphatically. 'It's impossible. Unlike in the real TinBoiz, yours will be isolated and not connected to your nervous system. The AI talks to the implant and the implant replies that everything is OK. That's all it does.'

He continued to look at me as I let out a slow breath. I couldn't believe it, but I was about to do this. 'And the eyes?' I asked, pointing to Leo's, piercing and watching, like a torch in the dark. 'They look pretty real … I mean, real like the AUs,' I corrected.

The prof's face immediately lit up, like I'd hit the jackpot. 'Yes, perfect, aren't they? The finishing touch. The absolute, perfect cover. No one would ever get past those and suspect they aren't real.'

He went on to drone about other impulse implants around the body and the importance of metal coating around them, but I kept on looking at Leo's eyes and he continued to stare at me. As if he knew where my head was going. There was nothing arrogant in them. Just fact. Maybe I was dreaming, but I sensed an air of inevitability, a hint of sadness, maybe even a challenge there. Or I was just going crazy. I couldn't see all that in a pair of cold, silver eyes. He was a perfectly trained soldier, masquerading as an AU, and gave nothing away. But something still troubled me. Hiding under his skin, inside that ultra-fit body and those dead eyes. Those eyes. However they were made, they were astonishingly good. The pupils expanded and retracted and everything.

Leo smiled slightly, like he was showing off. Breaking character so only I could see. The rest of the boys were still in Q&A with the prof, so no one else noticed him baiting me. Not a good idea to piss me off. I broke my fixation and faced the prof again, who was rounding up. 'Healing will be accelerated in our lab's state-of-the-art, military-grade healing chamber. It is designed for fast skin and bone knitting. Everything should be completed and healed by week three. Then your intensive training can begin.'

'Can't we start the kung fu part now?' one kid said, chopping the air with sound effects, making the others laugh.

The professor allowed him his little joke but didn't break into a smile. 'You will weigh at least another two hundred and seventy pounds overnight. That will take some getting used to. You will need to learn how to move again before you learn to fight. To start now would be pointless. Don't worry, it will come, I promise you. You will need to hold your own with an adult military unit.'

We all looked at Damien at the same time, who answered with a wicked smile that said: 'you're mine'.

'You must be able to protect your family at all costs,' the prof continued, but I had retreated into my head with my focus still on Damien. I couldn't help it. This guy had basically admitted to wanting to carve me up, but I kind of liked the sound of it. The purpose. And how much better I could look after Finn and Dad. Imagining what I could do over the Danger Line. I couldn't help thinking about Mack and his sense of belief. And that maybe I was always meant for something like this. 'I'm in,' I whispered to myself.

CHAPTER 12

*M*ike

For the next couple of days, we were no longer Outsiders. 'You are now citizens of the Tech sector,' the prof said. I knew he was playing to our egos, but it kind of worked. Despite feeling like I was in some sort of cadet camp, it felt like something was growing, like we were part of something far bigger than ourselves.

We slept underground in one of the prof's facilities. Shifted around from uniform place to place, until one windowless dorm looked pretty much the same as another. Early mornings, eating well in the canteen and then exercising. It was the same every day. We saw very few people. Only doctors and physio techs in the many labs, measuring us up constantly as if for a new suit. Then just Damien and the professor. We saw a lot of underground carparks and the back of the van. I asked what the Tech sector was like once. The prof answered, 'You'll know soon enough. You're in the industrial zone right now.' It was all he said, but it gave me enough to think about and wonder. To build an impression of noxious spewing factories, making pointless crap for the higher-ups to consume.

The rest of the time was spent drilling into us 'The Laws' and how to behave around humans. All the things that the AUs would automatically know. Number one: Don't touch. Number two: Don't harm or endanger, with the caveat, unless for the greater good. That was the tricky one that I just couldn't get. I constantly put up my hand and the professor nodded without needing to ask. 'Examples. Suppose you are out with your new family and someone falls or becomes injured in some way. You will need to be able to administer first aid. Perhaps a child falls into a river and you need to retrieve them or give CPR. Maybe even set a broken arm or lift a heavy object that is crushing them. Or maybe jumping on top of them to shield them from an explosion. Each could be classed as touching, but also for their good and, conversely, in some cases, you could even hurt them while trying to save them and thus endanger their life. You get the idea. You will have to make a judgment call. Remember, it will be easier for you than an AU, which relies purely on their learned experience and fundamental programming. And the AI, of course. This rule, while the logic is sound, is the most insanely foolish one of all, as it is open to interpretation. On a human level, the greater good could be for the single individual, the group, or the area, but to the AI, it could encompass the province, the country, the human race, or the world as we know it. You see the problem, which is why you are here.'

His words hit hard and I pondered them for a long time. AUs were so far away from us over the Danger Line that we never thought about stuff like this and yet it would affect everyone if this AI revolution ever happened. I could see exactly why they were programmed in this way. The people would want to feel safe. They couldn't just manufacture something that could watch a young kid walk out in front of a car and make pushing them out of the way break the Touch law. It was a tough one. But the prof was right. While the Techs were focused on being safe from the AUs, they had taken their eyes off the AI. Metatron. The name alone became a monster at the back of my mind. And, even scarier, I was beginning to learn it controlled everything.

THE DAY CAME for my operation.

Two boys had gone before me on consecutive days and two were scheduled after me. The three of us left, waited anxiously, but were told they were alive and healing. Great news, but it meant we couldn't see them. I was dying to find out how they were. What they looked like. How they felt. Whether I should be crapping myself more than I already was. My imagination was a rampaging animal.

I kept telling myself that today was the beginning of the rest of my life. That I was going to make a difference in an otherwise pointless existence. Which was laughable, as even I knew how ironic that was. My life as a human was effectively ending to become a robot. Like Pinocchio, in reverse. A guy couldn't make that shit up.

After waking up at dawn and having the longest, most sleepless night of my life, I was escorted in silence from the secret dorm somewhere in one of the professor's facilities. The last two boys slapped me on my back and both wished me luck. I couldn't even make a joke, I was so scared. I just nodded thanks and felt the heat blast my face from the fear that spiked my heart rate. I'd been nil by mouth since 9 p.m. yesterday, which was just as well, as I'd be wearing my stomach contents right now.

I followed Damien to the familiar van, climbed in and found I was alone. 'Sorry,' Damien said, pausing before sliding the door closed. 'I'd let you ride up front, but I can't let you see where you're going…' he said with a wry smile. 'Just know I'm still here and I'm good.' The door closed.

Damien didn't say much to us, so I took it as a kindness. He was reminding me to think of him. The badass finished product. And it did sustain me. The thought that he'd been through the same thing and come out as he was today.

I felt the van move and tried to calm down. My mind flitted from one thought to another. The people I'd left behind, possibly never to see again, and the people I was yet to meet. All of it hinged on my survival. I'd never even had a minor procedure before. Unless you counted the dislocated shoulder I got from climbing a broken ladder as a kid. A guy my dad knew at the hardware store popped it back in for a bottle of liquor, with a sharp pull and no anaesthetic. *Shit! That hurt.*

Nevertheless, Damien's few words stopped me from losing my mind through the journey, which felt like an age and was over too soon. I was sweating and my mouth was sandpaper dry by the time the van finally stopped and the door opened. 'I'd give my right arm for a glass of water,' I said to Damien as I got out into the underground car park.

He made no comment, only smiled at my pathetic joke, made from nerves. The prof was waiting there to greet me. He immediately walked over and put both his hands on my shoulders. 'Ready?' he asked, searching my eyes. He looked kind of emotional. No one had ever looked at me like that. Like a proud father. It hit me in the back of my throat. 'I want you to recognise how brave you are. You're a pioneer. A soldier, about to become part of a new revolution in the final battle to keep humanity alive.'

All I could do was attempt a painful swallow, with no spit and a jerky nod. I was moved, but I was just concentrating on staying alive at that moment. I wanted to tell him he wasn't helping and to get the hell on with it, before I ran screaming.

Damien was just behind him and gave me the smallest nod of encouragement. It was everything. He was literally the only person who knew what I was about to do. Everything else was a dream that fused together through a blurred lens I viewed from above. New people became outlines of green scrubs and voices became muffled, as if my head was under water. I followed the prof inside, where dark became light, with Damien's calming force behind me. Room after room looked and smelled like a clinical facility. Glass jars, box files, drip stands and monitors. That was all I took in. I didn't even register whether it was a hospital or a research lab. Just that it was clean and white and smelled of chemicals. Background music was playing. I remembered that, like a nondescript background in a store.

Young men and women smiled as I passed. Some even clapped and patted me on my back. Someone called out, 'Well done, Mike.' I looked around me, bewildered they knew my name. Like I was a superstar or an astronaut about to get in my capsule to go off to outer space. I decided I liked that one. I held onto it as I entered a wet room and was met by a guy in head-to-foot scrubs. I scanned around. It was a light-green box of tile with a toilet, a single showerhead and a dial on the wall.

He handed me a bottle of soap. 'Wash with this. It's antiseptic.' A white towel and thin hospital gown hung on the back of a second door, on the opposite wall. He pointed to them. 'Put those on and come right out.' Then he left me standing alone.

After a long moment, I undressed slowly and looked around for somewhere to put my clothes. I just stood there, looking at them in my arms. I was so dumb. If I came out of this alive, the chances were, these clothes would no longer fit me. I would be different.

I threw them into the furthest corner, closed my eyes and rubbed them with my closed fists. My head was throbbing in my temples. I was beginning to shatter and I had to pull it together. This was it. There was no going back. I took a breath, walked up to the dial and turned it on to full. I exhaled in relief. The water was set to the perfect temperature and it loosened my cramping muscles. I let it pound my back, then picked up the red pump bottle and smelled it. Carbolic. Like the stuff they used to use in school. I washed quickly, dried and slipped on the gown provided. Then I walked out of the second door in bare feet, feeling all kinds of exposed, into a large lab.

The prof was standing next to a gurney with a group of young men and women in identical green scrubs. 'Get on the gurney, please, Mike,' he said.

I climbed up slowly, conscious of covering myself up. I'd done the gown cords up at the front, not sure how to do the damn thing.

'Don't worry about that, we will cover your modesty.'

I lay back and allowed my neck muscles to relax. The gurney moved off with the prof on my left and the other scrubs at various points around me. 'Orthopaedics will be first, then Thoracics, so I will see you in a few hours, after limb and body surgery is over,' he was saying as I was whisked along.

We burst through some double doors into a prepped theatre and I was trying to sit up. An Asian-looking guy pushed me down by the shoulders and smiled. 'We're going to give you something to relax. Then a canula and it'll be off to dreamland.'

Straps were going across my chest and hips. Everything too fast. I struggled, trying to get a glimpse of the professor, but he was talking to a group of men, already in surgical masks and latex gloves and checking over a clipboard. Then he walked towards the door. 'Prof! Prof!' I called out to him, resisting hands trying to keep me still.

I winced. While my attention was taken, a sharp pain pierced the back of my hand. I looked up into more smiling eyes. A woman's. She was hanging a bag of liquid on a drip stand. Someone else was sticking wires to me. I tried to twist to see the prof. 'Wait! You can't leave. How long will it be?' I called desperately, trying to pull my hand away, but I was strapped tight. I hadn't given any thought to how the operation would be done, or how long and complex it was likely to be. I'd only assumed it would all be done at the same time and that the prof would be there, like a concerned father. But by the time I looked up again, he'd already disappeared. I looked at a nurse, fearfully, and she gently pushed me back down. 'Relax,' she said. 'When you wake up, you'll be better than new,' she finished, crinkling the corners of her eyes.

I would have screamed, except it immediately felt like I dissolved into the bed beneath me. The cluster of lights merged into a sun. Seven pairs of eyes in hospital masks told me their names and echoed what they were about to do in slowed-down voices. I tried to follow, I really did, but I just stared at their moving mouths, forgetting instantly. Only grabbing snatches of 'lower limbs' and another did 'upper'. Thoracic meant chest, cardiology and respiratory. The cybernetic fusion guy connected them all. Everyone chuckled when the anaesthetist joked, 'I'm going to keep you asleep. The important one.' He smiled over me. 'Don't worry, you'll be out like a light. Count backwards with me.'

My heart was beating wildly as the mask descended over my face. Someone else was pushing something into my hand and the warmth crept up my arm

'Ten, nine—'

. . .

A SECOND LATER, I blinked. Blurred colours and sounds came like dull taps on a mic. I had no idea where I was, only that I couldn't move. I continued to blink through crusty eyes until the light cluster above me came into focus.

Then I remembered.

I was in theatre.

I shouldn't be awake. Something must have gone wrong. The healing pod was next. *The healing pod.* I tried to speak, but all I could do was gag. A tube was down my neck. Green scrubs were milling around me and all I could move were my eyes and groan.

'Easy, Mike,' someone said.

A robot arm swung over my head with a hydraulic hiss and a light buzzing sound.

'Welcome back.' It was the professor.

I strained my eyes to try to find him in the many green shapes. Then he appeared, his face upside down right above me. He had a mask on, but his eyes were distinct, dark brown behind a weird set of glasses. They were super thick, more like goggles.

I wanted to shout for him to stop. That I was awake. *Put me back to sleep,* but nothing came except a guttural gurgle. Panic filled every paralysed cell and the beeps on the monitor next to me doubled.

'BP 178 over 124, doctor,' someone said.

I couldn't see who it was. I was stuck on the professor, staring down at me. 'Shh, easy now, Mike,' he was saying calmly and evenly. 'You must be awake for this part, as I have to map your optic nerve to its neural pathway, for the micro-sensor. There is less chance of error this way. Only takes a few moments, then you'll be asleep again, I promise.'

He nodded, and a scrub either side of me slid something

onto my eyelids, so they could no longer move. Some sort of motor whirred and I felt my world turning. When I reached my side, I thought I was going to roll off the table, but the roll continued like I was a basting pig. I felt nothing, but I knew I'd been strapped in, as the prof's theatre shoes came into view. Whatever they'd used didn't give an inch. Barely a minute passed and I continued my rotation until I was facing up again, squinting into the bright group of lights and the prof's smiling eyes.

'Well done, Mike. We're almost done. Just the very last thing. You'll feel a slight pull while we sever the optic nerve and then you can sleep again.' The prof nodded.

It felt like everything happened at once. Before I could even catch up, the robotic arm buzzed, my eyes widened, and understanding finally crushed me as it halted in place. An eggcup-like sucker, a few inches above my left eye, slowly began to descend. I couldn't even blink. My mind screamed. Every cell cringed and crawled and tried to part like the dead sea, away from it. But I was cement and it still lowered, coming closer in its agonisingly precise trajectory. Buzzing and jerking as it made micro adjustments to make sure it was perfectly in line with my eye. In my mind, I was shrieking, *You said high-tech contacts. You did. You let us think it was contacts. Don't take my eyes. Please don't take my eyes. You never said you were taking my eyes.*

The suckers were almost there. Not one, but two. How could I miss a detail like that? Two black cups, with a sharp needle protruding from the centre. Each aiming for the centre of my clamped-open eyes. They were right there, and I couldn't flinch or shrink away. The cups gradually shut out the light and I heard the light pop as the needle pierced through, and I was screaming. A shrill, perfect note that came from the absolute depths of me and hit the walls of the operating theatre. The soul of a banshee finally set free of its earthly body. Not imagined. It was real. I willed myself to wake up. Sweating blood with the effort, as the last part of my humanity clung on. Until it was finally wrenched out with my eyes.

Then I let go and allowed myself to drift into the blissful flood. A soft, billowing breeze, carrying me here and there. Carefree, euphoria. Comfortably painless, listening to the soft tone of a female voice. 'All done now. You were so brave. That's it. Go to sleep and when you wake up, you will be the new, better you.'

CHAPTER 13

hrissy

Everyone spoke in hushed tones around me now, like I was on my deathbed. Even my annoying brother, Nate, kept coming into my room to check on me, with scared, dilated eyes, stroking my forehead, while I stared at the ceiling. 'Everything will be alright, Chrissy, I promise. You'll see.'

He couldn't possibly know that. Nobody could. He didn't understand that I just didn't have the strength.

When my mom said for the millionth time, 'Please try and get up, darling. You're missing so much at school. At least try to join on your NetGlass,' I groaned and turned away from her. I would rather curl up and die than do that. However, my mom never gave up and it became our ritual every morning.

I barely ate. Food just rolled around like an alien object in my mouth. One swallow and my stomach recoiled and my throat closed up to any more. There just didn't seem to be a point. To anything.

I woke to whispering outside my room again. My mom,

dad. Even my brother. Others.

I stiffened. Then threw back the thin thermosheet off my face to hear better.

The other voices were Tina and Tom, Teddy's parents. I leaned up on my elbows, straining. 'Take it,' Tom said.

'We insist.' Tina.

'I don't know,' my dad answered, sounding doubtful.

Don't know what?

'Let's see what the doctor says first, before we decide anything. He'll be here in a minute.'

My heart whooshed in my chest and my face felt hot. It hadn't beaten harder than a bird's in so long, it made me light-headed. My mind shot to the only thing that Tina and Tom had that it could be: That damn sub. That damn machine that Teddy had been so happy using before—I turned and dissolved into ugly sobs, muffled by my pillow.

Mom, Dad and the others all came bursting in. I pulled my face out of the pillow to glare at them. 'I won't. I won't have it,' I wailed. 'How could you expect me to have it, after —' I flopped down into the pillow and wailed anew. Shrieking, 'How could you?'

'No, oh no, darling. Were you listening? You've got it all wrong,' my mom was saying. The bed dipped and she stroked back my sweaty hair.

My sobs came to a stop and I opened one eye. Tina sat next to her with a pained look and my dad and Tom were standing, looking concerned, at the end of the bed.

'No, it's gone back. I promise you. They wanted to test it for faults. But Teddy's doctors seemed to think it was more to do with the small brain aneurysm he must have had already. The extra brain activity probably caused a strain on it and would have probably happened any time, when he exerted himself,' Tina explained with a kindly smile.

My eyes tracked to my mom, who added. 'We'd never give that to you. Not after this,' my mom said, looking wounded.

I sat up, awkwardly, feeling bad that I'd hurt my mom's feelings. Tina passed me a tissue from a box next to the bed and I blew my nose on it. 'What did you mean then? I heard you.'

Nate gave me another wad of tissue and I thanked him and wiped my eyes. I felt even worse that he was so quiet and worried.

'The sub company has offered us a full refund. One of the head honchos came when they collected it, and we wanted your mom and dad to have the money. That's what you overheard,' Tina explained.

'Scared of a lawsuit.' Tom scoffed.

My dad nodded along. 'That'd be about right.'

'A refund or a comparable replacement,' my mom said, met with complete silence.

I realised that they weren't shocked by what my mom had said, they were intent on my reaction. I was confused. They knew I wouldn't want a sub. 'What are you saying, then?' I asked, looking directly at my mom. I knew how she felt about them, too.

'No, no. That's not it at all,' my mom backpedalled, wildly.

'You're not ill enough for a sub, anyway. You wouldn't have the necessary points to qualify,' my dad added.

I nodded. Technically, I was still too able-bodied. 'What then?'

'You are very depressed, darling,' my mom continued, in her kindly voice. The one she only used when we were poorly. 'Teddy's... illness has hit you very hard. What we've been considering,' she paused and looked at my dad, which made me really scared of what she was building up to. 'What we were thinking... was getting you a full AU companion.' She blinked and swallowed uncomfortably. Like she had no idea how I would take it and then stared at me with wide eyes at my frozen, stunned face.

I sat there a moment, then crumpled. Nothing, certainly not a machine, could ever take Teddy's place. I couldn't believe they could even think that. My life stopped the minute he went into the ambulance.

My mom pulled me into her chest and smothered me in her warm, perfumy smell and love. 'I'm so sorry, darling. We didn't want to upset you, but we're so worried about you. Try it. Just for a little while. Just while Teddy's getting better. Let it get you out of this awful downward spiral you're in.'

I went still in my mom's arms. My mind hooked onto the 'while Teddy gets better' part. I liked the sound of that. I wasn't thinking of the AU then, at all. Only that they considered Teddy's condition temporary. I refused to consider that they might be saying it to manipulate me. Because it was true. Teddy *would* get better over time. I knew how strong-willed he was. He'd joked about science saving his brain in a jar one day; the only thing fit for research.

Then my mind drifted to Jessica's AU. It's cold, analytical stare, and doubting how much company it could actually be for her. He was an accessory, like new shoes or a new bag. But it did light something in me. A tiny ember of curiosity in my chest that I hadn't felt since before Teddy's stroke. Having a machine around wasn't being disloyal to Teddy; it was just filling a gap.

'You don't have to keep it if you don't like it,' Tom was saying. 'We just wanted to repay your family for all its kindness and support with Teddy. It's the least we could do.'

'We know it won't take Teddy's place, but it might help … a little,' Tina added, stroking my hair.

'So what dy'a think, Chrissy Christmas?' My dad asked, using the silly name he'd always called me. 'When I came, it was like Christmas day,' he'd once explained.

I scowled, as I hated it now I was older, but it was hard not to break a smile at the soppy look on his face.

'Come on,' he said, grinning. 'What do you have to lose?'

'You know, Teddy will love it when he wakes up,' Tom said, conspiratorially, making me laugh.

It was so true. He would. I could only nod and sigh. I pulled out of my mom's arms to sit up. 'OK, what do I have to do?'

Everyone put their arms up and cheered, as if I'd done a marvellous thing, when I hadn't actually done anything except agree. I was only willing to give it a try.

'The doctor is coming to give you a check-up and take some blood just in case something else is going on. He may just give you some extra vitamins to take,' my mom said.

I sat there a little bewildered. Everyone appeared to have come alive with my simple, yes.

'Seriously, though, Chrissy. You have to start eating,' my dad said, his face looking creased and stern. 'Doesn't have to be much. Start little and often. You'll need to get your strength back.'

Tom held out his hand to Tina, who took it and stood up from the bed. 'And we'll go and call our guy and say we have decided on the AU and ask him how long it will take.'

I actually felt a flutter of butterflies at that. I knew so little about them; I'd have to look it all up. 'What kind of AU?' I asked, thinking of Jessica's again. He was a good-looking TinBoi model. She'd taken great pride in telling me.

Tina and Tom looked at each other as if they were trying to remember, exactly. 'It was a generous offer. I think he said he felt so terrible for everything we were going through that he would look into getting us the latest TinBoiz 2055-Ultra, model C, companion unit. I don't think it's even out yet,' Tina said, followed by a confirming nod from Tom.

My heart sped up at that. It was even better than Jessica's.

I had to admit that the small ember in my chest was turning into a small fire. 'What will his name be? Will he come with one?' I asked.

Tina and Tom laughed. Everyone seemed so relieved I had come around to it. My dad grinned and rocked on his heels with his hands in his pockets. 'It's just a machine. Call it what you like.'

I was thoughtful about that. The parents wandered towards the door as if their job was done. 'I'll see what he looks like when he gets here,' I said.

They smiled and filtered out of the door. 'Get well,' Tina said, the last one to leave.

There was no need for anyone to worry. My mind had come alive with possibilities. Teddy would be so excited when he woke up. It would be the three of us. Sleepovers. Game nights. Movies. The list was endless. I couldn't wait.

I was suddenly aware of Nate, slowly sliding off the bed like a sloth. I hadn't even noticed him lying at the foot of the bed. He'd been so quiet and still. His head was down as he wandered, thoughtfully, towards the door. I was about to ask him if he was OK, but he stopped and looked at me over his shoulder. 'You know the TinBoiz 2055 model C is advertised as the Rolls-Royce of Robotics. The most advanced. There's nothing that even comes close to it.' He smiled wanly and made me frown. Then he turned and walked straight out of the room. I pondered what he said. Nate would know. He was a complete geek for all things tech. There was something eating at him, but I'd get to that later. Meanwhile, I was too wired. He didn't know it, but he'd helped me decide. When it came, I'd call it Royce.

It was perfect.

I was shaking with excitement

CHAPTER 14

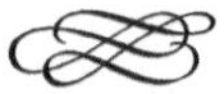

*M*ike A buzz in my ears and nothing but blackness.

Impossible to move. I was weighed with lead.

Voices. 'OK, get ready. He's waking up. Give him some space; he's going to come out fighting.'

Fighting? I tried to blink with batwings for eyelids.

'He's unhitched. Now, stand back.'

My lids opened and dropped shut with a loud thud. My hands felt funny when I moved my fingers, so I tried to roll over. The floor hit with a hard slam. The impact reverberated through me and dislodged something in my head. It buzzed, making me jerk my head towards the sound.

A blinding, head-splitting flash.

Then another.

I attempted to look left and right, but a white light and searing pain shot through the centre of both my eyes. Another buzz vibrated like something was shaking my brain in my skull. A rumble in my chest shook my heart with a stab of pain through the middle of my back. More white lightning. Pylon static, pulsing through my veins.

I gasped. No air. *There was no air.* I couldn't breathe. *I'm passing out...passing—*

'It's OK, Mike. You have enough oxygen. Relax.'

Prof! I tried to look for him. I was on all fours, but all I could see was grey. Everything was shaking. Buzzing. Flashing.

Then it stopped, suddenly, and all I saw was a vivid green. It glitched and hissed and became gridlines. A green grid over grey.

'Easy, Mike. Can you stand up?'

The voice was the professor's. Someone big was under my shoulder to help.

'It's OK, you're on the floor. See if you can use your legs.'

I tried to get my feet under me to stand, but they felt so heavy. I was shaking with the effort. They were stiff and didn't want to move.

'Come on, Mike. You can do it.'

Others joined in, like they were willing me over a finishing line. I strained with one last groan, closed my eyes and managed to get my leg under me and push up in one big move. It was so explosive that whoever was helping me was flung sideways.

I felt hands steadying me again as I wobbled. I still couldn't see. Just those damn green gridlines over grey. But the grey was lightening into shapes. Outlines of people in black and white, like a flickering TV. The people came into focus. Doctors. The prof. Damien, still shaking himself off.

Then the colour flooded in and made me squint. So vivid, it was painful. 'Can you see, Mike?' The prof asked.

The colours toned down enough for me to focus on the voice.

The prof smiled. 'Well, there's my answer,' he said with a brilliant smile.

Gridlines immediately slammed down over my newly cleared vision. An immediate head-splitting pain followed, as the last memory of the surgery came to me. I put my hands up to my temples and smashed them painfully into my skull.

'Careful!' the prof shouted and jumped to hold my wrists.

I groaned with the pain. Nothing was doing what I wanted it to. 'My eyes!' came out like a wail. I tried to touch them, they felt so weird and heavy, but the prof called, 'Hold him,' and Damien stopped me just before I smashed them into my face. Nothing worked. 'What have you done?' I cried. 'What have you—'

The prof was in my face, inches away. 'Look at me!' he said through tight lips. Then more calmly, 'Look… at…me, Mike. What you are feeling is totally normal. Think about your training. What I explained would happen to you. You were fully informed. You've just woken up from a sixteen-hour surgery and seven days in a healing pod, with no movement at all. You need to learn to move again. To get used to the way your new body feels. Your new weight and strength. Think about it. You have titanium plates throughout your body. You'll be crushing cups for days.'

I was listening hard, but at the same time, my brain felt like it was buzzing and jerking against my skull. It felt like someone had spilt hot coffee in there. The heat was fanning out like a spider's web, making squiggles and numbers come up in my eyes.

I straightened, rigid with recollection. 'You took my damn eyes,' I said, suddenly ferociously angry. 'You led me to believe they'd be contacts.'

The prof stepped back and Damien stepped in close. I jumped back and slammed into a trolley topped with instruments that rattled loudly as it hit the wall.

'I never said contacts,' the professor said, in his usual, reasonable tone. 'But I will admit that I've learned to be a little vague about the eyes. Please, Mike. Be reasonable. How do you expect the AI to overlook you if you're walking about with human eyes covered in plastic? The other AUs would single you out immediately and inform the AI on their circuit checks, and you would be rounded up and disposed of within a few days. They had to be the real thing. It is the most important part of your cover.'

I listened and watched his mouth move with laser focus. I don't think I'd ever concentrated more in my life. I wasn't sure if it was the subject or some superhero skill. But I held my hand fast against my chest; my heart was beating so weirdly. Then, as if by magic, something vibrated under my hand, and my heart slowed as if it had been turned down with a dial. I looked down at it and saw the ribbed metal embedded in my chest. For a moment, I panicked and tried to claw it out of my skin, but the professor yelled, 'Stop!' like a dog bark that snapped me out of it. My gridlines zeroed and widened, bringing him into focus again.

'That's right!' the prof said, in a more soothing tone. 'The main power source is under there, regulating your heartbeat to sync with its magnetic pulses. It protects your heart, which will always be vulnerable and makes it undetectable to other AUs. Your diaphragm does not move externally, either. Your breathing is distributed between several input and exit points around your body, so nothing comes out of your nose.'

My hand flew up to my nose and I wanted to crumple in misery, but the prof caught it again.

'Easy,' the professor said sternly. 'You need to get used to your new weight and strength.'

Every cell in me weighed a ton with my wretchedness alone. 'You've made me a monster,' I groaned.

The professor's face morphed from kind and benevolent to terrifying and angry. 'Look at your damn hand, you ungrateful wretch.'

I must have been out of whack because I didn't bite. At home, I would have been toe-to-toe with him for that. I just looked down like a sap and opened and closed my fist that felt like a bunch of bananas.

'Look at it!' the prof snapped.

I brought it up, level to my face. Despite how weird it felt, it looked normal. Except there was a thick silver band around my wrist, as if my hand screwed right into it.

'Titanium!' the prof said. 'It anchors the rods in your arm to the ones coming up from your fingers, making them unbreakable. It also houses a nerve centre, bio and cybernetic. You have several around your body. Ankles, groin, chest, neck and brain,' he said, pointing at each of them. They link up with your central nervous system, with a power source of its own, to create a servosystem. You are magnificent. The absolute pinnacle of bio and neuronetic engineering… Mike!'

He made me jump. I was dazed and in shock, trying to take it all in, but I kept on zoning out, sinking down rabbit holes of misery over what I'd lost. He'd sliced me up and expected me to be grateful.

My gridlines framed his mouth and it came into precise focus. I was gradually getting what they were for. They seemed to move in and out involuntarily, giving me distance, size and shape, as well as allowing me to focus with precision. I tried something and imagined getting right up in his face. The grid widened and my vision immediately zoomed in. I could see every pore, big as golf ball pits. Even individual whiskers in his five o'clock shadow. It made me take a clumsy step back in shock, and my vision returned to normal.

The prof's face changed back from angry to smiley again and he nodded encouragingly. 'Good, isn't it?' You should be able to see further and in more detail than you ever did before. I make sure that all my special TinBoiz have military-grade vision. You are the cutting edge of design, far superior to the regular, TinBoiz models available at the moment. You must be the best. Do you understand, Mike? You have to be for what you must do.'

I was still staring at him, dumb with bewilderment. Hit over the head so hard, it robbed me of speech. I didn't know what he expected me to say.

'You and the other recruits will be the first bridge between human and machine. Stronger than any human. Stronger than any TinBoi. But what separates you, what will always set you apart, is that you have that spark of humanity. That unquantifiable spirit, that comes from somewhere else and leaves you when you stop breathing. I guess you could say it comes from above. You will have the ability to make decisions based on how it feels, not just on logic and programming alone. That gives you the supreme advantage, Mike. Something the most advanced quantum AIs on earth will never truly understand. It can mimic it. It can gather and process unbelievable amounts of data on which to base its decisions. But it can never feel. It may even think it has something that resembles it. But in the end, it will only judge coldly and simulate.'

I continued to stare at him, convinced now that he was totally mad. The stereotypical mad scientist, with glasses, sticking up hair and everything. Except he'd swapped out a white coat for green scrubs. It was the only thing I held onto right then. Otherwise, he was just a lunatic comic book char-acter with aspirations to take over the world. If I weren't still traumatised, I would have laughed. But I wasn't even sure I was able to anymore. I wanted to cry; I was so pathetic. All

I'd wanted was a life for me, Finn and my dad. Some place we could breathe without getting sick. Where the rain didn't burn our skin. It felt like the professor had dangled that in front of me and tricked me into this sad state.

The light drained out of the professor's eyes as he realised there was no getting through to me today. 'Come on,' he said wearily, and got under my arm again as Damien got under the other. I walked haphazardly towards the door, the professor keeping his feet out of range of mine. 'Let me take you to your new room with the others,' he said, as I lumbered along the corridor. 'Get to know them. Let them help you process all this. Then tomorrow, spend the day getting the feel of your new body. Then we will begin your intensive programme to learn how to use it. You have three weeks to prepare for your placement. Your family has been selected.'

CHAPTER 15

M ike

The professor left me with two orderlies at my allocated bed and said he'd see me after he'd gotten some rest. They put stuff on my bed and then told me to settle in, and that they would come back and explain my daily care. I was glad. I was numb by then and wasn't really listening. I tried to think straight, but everything buzzed and hurt. I had to beat this and toughen up. It had always been my superstrength. Survival and beating the odds were what I did. The only thing I had left from before.

I looked around me for the first time. I guessed it was OK. Better than the last, which was little more than a storeroom. This place felt more like some sort of hospital facility, with bays rather than a dorm. Everything seemed made of metal and glass. Functional and clean. The walls were white, the beds high and serviceable, with a metal, glass-fronted cabinet between each one.

I became aware that I wasn't alone. The other beds were occupied by a boy sitting on each. Five curious pairs of eyes were watching me intensely. My heart rate sped up, ready for hostility. My chest buzzed with that horrible, woozy, whirring feeling as it slowed down to undetectable. But I needn't have worried. I recognised the two boys who'd gone for surgery before me, Saxon and Ray. They immediately stood and came over, smiling. They held up their hands to bump fists. Mine, a lot more clumsily. I apologised, hating that I was so awkward. Saxon slapped me on the back, which made me stumble forward with the force. 'It's OK, we know the feeling. Intense, isn't it?'

I smiled wryly. 'You could say that.'

Saxon quickly pointed to the other three boys and introduced them, 'That's Mat, Kip and John... take your weight off,' he said, pointing behind me at the bed. 'We know how weird it feels.'

Saxon and Ray helped lower me onto the bed and I was grateful. Heaven knows what a mess of it I would have made. Probably ending up face down on the floor. They went back to their beds, while I looked at the pile of neatly folded clothes at the foot of the bed. On top was a small brown bottle. 'Painkillers,' Saxon said before I could ask. 'Nerve pain is common after amputations.'

I closed my eyes as if to take deep breaths, but of course, that was gone too.

They each then proceeded to tell me their story and where they were from. A distraction, but I was grateful for it. I noticed we were all shades of skin tone and concluded it was deliberate. Their stories, however, were all the same. From a poor background, with no choice other than to steal, then picked up from the street, beyond the Danger Line, for petty offences. They had all been taken to what sounded like the same holding pen that I had.

The professor must have a way of screening the intake, so

he can swoop in and take the ones he wants, before they're processed and anyone knows they're there. Palms greased and we become ghosts, never to be seen again. A masterful plan.

I made a vow there and then, while the last boy was telling the same old story, that I would get my brother out of that hell-pit and my dad if he'd go. I didn't know where yet, but there had to be somewhere left in this tired, used-up world that we hadn't ruined yet.

I settled into the routine quickly, enjoying the structure of it. I learned a lot about myself. I realised that what I'd thought of as freedom before was just a lack of direction and purpose. Aimless drifting, grabbing snippets of pleasure where I could, but all it had been was an existence. Not Living at all. I slowly came to realise what the professor was giving us.

We rose early every morning and recited the laws at the end of our beds, to attention, like cadets. They became our ritual. Our mantra. Then we went to the canteen for breakfast—well, if you could call it that. We sat at an allocated table, each day, while all the various human staff and a few weird-looking subs watched us like objects of fascination. It made me suspect that they weren't all in 'the know' and we were a novelty to them.

Our food was brought by a cartoon-looking sub, with the stature of a man and huge eyelashes and fake lips stuck onto its cheap tin head. It looked like it was made out of trash. But I found out it was a she, Gretchen, and she was friendly enough. She always said, 'What can I get you boys?' like we were still regular humans, which I appreciated. I didn't get to feel that a lot these days. Whoever was behind the moving trash can had a great sense of humour. Because there was no choice, and she knew it. The only thing we consumed was a little water to lubricate the throat and this disgusting tube of paste that the professor explained had everything required to sustain us. Apparently, three times the protein and energy that a regular human needed. I can safely say that we weren't that excited by it, but we understood. Regular TinBoiz didn't eat, but we were the latest bio-models and needed something to keep all that tissue going. Our stomachs had gone, so if we ate normally, we would immediately projectile vomit. But, of course, we all had to try it once, and no one ever attempted it again. It became the butt of jokes. That what goes in, must come out. That went for both ends. Even paste produces a waste product.

Every day, once a day, we would need to evacuate what could only be described as a black, oily substance straight into the toilet. It was the weirdest thing, as we no longer needed to urinate, but we still had all the working parts. All the prof had said was, 'No stomach, no intestines, no bowel. No need for all that in there.' It became clearer as time went on just how much information had been held back from us at the beginning. You could hardly call it informed consent. I mourned things like that for quite a while. The way much of my humanity had been taken without my permission. I'd confided it to the boys in those early days. Sat clustered around my bed. It was Saxon that set me right. 'Don't dwell on shit like that,' he said. The others all nodded, looking at the floor, like they were remembering their own lost way of life. 'It will only get you bitter and that serves no one. It sucks, but we move on.'

'Yeah, we can't beat on his ass, coz if we kill him, then who will maintain us, see?' Mat said.

It was tragically funny, but he was right.

'I'm still gonna kill him one day. You know, when I figure this shit out,' John said, making us all laugh.

'We have to take it for what it is,' Saxon continued. 'A chance for a better life than the one we had before. Take it and run with it.' I looked into his mercurial eyes, identical to mine. They were no longer windows to the soul, but I did detect meaning there. That intuition that machines didn't have, that 'run with it' held the same meaning for him as it did for me. When the time came, he would seize his chance and run. We all would.

I let out a heavy sigh and knuckled down. I found that when I let all the bitterness go, it wasn't a bad life. It was interesting and far more stimulating than it ever was before. After what felt like weeks just spent learning the laws, AU etiquette and behaviour, several hours a day on physio, getting used to this great, hulking body, we were introduced to our final expert: Lin Chong. He really was the quin-tessential sensei. Old, bald, small in stature, unassuming and lethal. A genuine martial arts master, from some temple in the mountains of China. He never spoke much for me to find out any more than that. He seemed to know Damien, who acted as our sparring partner and punching bag. We enjoyed that part. He joked, 'a little too much!'

He put us through our paces, using our speed and strength to fight at a high level, but also doing it while moving like an AU. He drilled, 'That is the most important part.'

Yin Chong taught the moves, and Damien kept us in character, until it was second nature. 'You must be able to protect your placement family,' Yin Chong explained.

'For the greater good!' Damien added. Using the laws like the loophole the prof had first mentioned. It all began to fit into place: what it all meant for our purpose in the world. It became obvious that regular TinBoiz didn't get this sort of training. They went to homes right off the production line. Only us, the Elite Crossovers, as I began to think of us.

I grew to love how my new body felt when it moved. I was surprised, as I'd been so clunky at first, with all the internal mechanics to contend with. But with training and practice, everything worked like a dream. My body flowed, light and fluid, even though I weighed around 300 lbs. By the end of my time in training, I had instant reflexes. When we really began to spar, what began as an elegant dance between equally trained soldiers sped up to Kung Fu movie speed. Except this wasn't choreographed, it was real. Often drawing blood.

At our last session, we all grinned at each other, knowing we were as ready as we would ever be. We turned and bowed to Damien, who returned it solemnly, then to Lin Chong, who did the same. Then we clapped and cheered. We'd come through it all, alive and feeling like we'd really achieved something. Not a thing many got to say back home. We had graduated top of our class and were totally badass and knew it.

The euphoria dwindled as we finished regaling tales of our bouts and slowly wandered back to our dorm. Our minds inevitably drifting to where we would end up. We shipped out to our placements in the morning. Strangely, I wasn't scared, only nervous. Maybe even a little excited. I had no idea who I would meet. All I knew was that it felt like the whole of my life had led me to this. Ironic for a boy half machine, but it really did feel like my life was finally going to start.

After lively chatter, the lights went off at their usual time of ten. We slept soundly, because we no longer really slept. It was a hybrid version of a power-down, as we did dream. Vivid, superfast, Technicolor reels of anxious information.

Mine were mainly of Finn. 'Don't forget me, Mike,' he kept on saying. 'I'll meet you in the garden.'

They were strange and disturbing dreams, where I had no idea what any of it meant. There were no gardens across the Danger Line. I could only conclude that it was my subconscious worry about leaving Finn behind.

We all rose, washed and dressed early and filed silently to the canteen. We barely said a word, except the obligatory, 'Pass the ketchup,' which someone always said to improve the crappy paste, and it never got old. We all managed one last laugh as we squirted it down our throats. It was something not even ketchup could improve, but I think we were all hit by the realisation that it would be the last time we heard it.

I said goodbye to Gretchen, the canteen sub, and she blew kisses to all of us. 'Good luck, boys,' she called out.

We filed out and went down the staircase to the car park level. There was no need to go back to our dorm. Everything we needed was already packed and ready to go. The blacked-out van was parked and running when we got there. Bigger than the one we'd used before. It made us all pause before Damien came up behind us and grumbled, 'It won't eat you.'

Nerves were now gnawing at us all. We gauged each other for fear and walked on. 'We're bigger now,' I said, to murmurs of agreement.

This one loaded from the back and had three rows of three high-backed, belted leather seats. Very plush. Like the ones I imagined on an airline. We strapped in, two to each row, with a spare seat in between. 'Protecting the merch,' Saxon said, echoing my own thoughts that we'd never been strapped in before.

We moved off smoothly and rode in silence. It felt like no time at all before we made the first stop. The back doors opened and none of us could see behind us. Damien called out, 'Mat! You're up first.'

It felt too fast. My heart leapt into my throat watching Mat slowly stand. He looked as scared as hell, with darting eyes and his skin bursting red.

I put up my fist for him to bump. 'Good luck, man… For the greater good!' The others did the same. 'Until the new world,' Saxon added.

He bumped fists with us all and with a final, 'Be safe,' he disappeared, and the doors slammed closed. We heard the storage panel open and stuff being unloaded. Then the front opened and slammed twice and we were moving again. I let out a ragged breath, dazed. Just like that, someone I'd spent twenty-four seven with for weeks had gone. I hoped we would see each other again.

Ray went next and then it was me. I stood, slowly, in a weird kind of shock. Like my insides were panicking, rendering me useless. It was Saxon who shook me out of it with a sharp, 'Hey!'

I was grateful for the shake. No judgment, just brotherly support. He was undoubtedly the hardest to leave. The wisest and best fighter out of all of us, I guessed I'd been the closest to him over the past weeks. Nothing was spoken, but it was always reflected in his face. Right now, in the way he grabbed my hand to look directly in my eyes. 'Good luck,' he said, with meaning. It made me swallow, holding a tide of emotion back with a final, 'Until the new world.' I closed my eyes and turned, not able to look at him again in case he saw it. I bumped fists with Kip and John. 'For humanity,' I whispered, and then jumped down into the orange, hazy light.

It was the first time in weeks and I expected to cough. But nothing came. A perk of no lungs, I thought wryly. Equipment was being unloaded noisily from the van by another AU and before I could get my bearings, the professor was right in front of me. He must have followed in another car to see us all off. I was grateful. I guess he really did care about us in his weird, fanatical kind of way. He smiled. 'Take a look,' he said, smiling, holding out his hand as if I'd forgotten all about it. I half turned and the whole thing opened up in a wide lens. It hit me, leaving a strong, profound impression. I'd never seen anything like this. We were deep in Tech country. One of the gated communities I'd heard about.

The filtered, orange light hit an endless row of boxy red houses that all looked exactly the same. So uniform, they looked like they'd been generated by CGI to go off into infinity. Each was made of red brick, with red tile roofs, had two upstairs windows and one below on the right. On the left was a dark blue front door, with a large square step and a tiled overhang to keep callers out of the rain. A lawn was directly in front, bordered with brightly coloured flowers and a garage and short driveway, to the left of it. Every driveway had a medium-sized, silver car, like the kind I'd only seen on TV.

I was drawn back to the lawn. It was so green, with real grass. It was being constantly watered from a sprinkler. The precious liquid just sinking into it, as if there was plenty to spare. I'd never seen anything like it before. Where I came from, real grass was too hard to keep out of the acid rain. The fake kind was only really in schools. For safe play, or maybe to give the kids an idea of what grass was like. By the time I'd left school, they'd given up and replaced it with rubber chips made from old tyres.

This was where the rich lived. I'd never ventured out here before. It was commonly thought that we'd stand out and be picked up right away. Rich folks never went out in the air, so we'd heard and had been enough to keep my curiosity at bay.

'Come on,' the prof said, dragging me from my thoughts. 'I'll come in with you.'

He walked with me up one of the identical driveways and

passed a vent blowing out hot air. I immediately sidestepped in surprise.

The prof smiled. 'It's OK, Mike. 'It's just clean air to disperse the smog. Heat rises, so it makes quite a nice sized bubble around each house.'

This place was truly amazing. I smiled at him in wonder. We really had no idea. The technology. The cost alone to run this kind of stuff.

'It's switched off after curfew,' the prof said with a knowing smile, as if he knew the track of my thoughts.

The prof stilled me by the arm. 'A moment, before we go in, Mike.'

We halted our steps in the driveway and I studied him while he reached into his inside breast pocket. It surprised me because he wasn't usually given to moments of sentiment. He held out what looked like a piece of paper, but moved it out of reach just before I went to take it. He held my gaze intensely. 'Do well, Mike. I recognised something in you the moment I saw you. Remember … You … This family,' he said, looking up at the house. 'All our lives are resting on you doing that.'

I swallowed like I had spit and looked down at the creased paper he'd left in my hand. I recognised it right away. The photo of me and Finn, I thought I'd never see again.

I looked at him, amazed. 'How did you—?'

'Never mind. Put it away. Just know you're doing this for him.'

I was reeling. I wanted to thank him, but he was already walking on and back into teacher mode. I was forced to tuck it into my boot, quickly, and catch up with him.

There was no more discussion as we walked up to the front door. He was right. About everything. I had to stop being a sap and get my head in the game.

I ran what I'd learned through my head. They had curfew

too, confined in boxes, like rabbits, paying for clean air and tipping away valuable water into grass just to look pretty. It wasn't building a great picture of the higher-ups. I wondered if they had any idea what it was like for us, over the Danger Line. I only had just enough time to push down my prejudices when the door was flung open and my mouth gaped in surprise.

*R*oyce

'Good day to you, Mr and Mrs Coe,' the prof said immediately. 'May I introduce you to your brand-new, TinBoiz, 2055, Ultra model C, companion unit?'

I didn't know what I was expecting, standing there on the red tiled step, but delighted shrieks of welcome, an enthusiastic handshake and a warm kiss on the cheek, I was not. I don't believe I'd ever received any of those things in my whole life before. I guess I wasn't expecting to be welcomed at all, any more than someone would greet a new vacuum cleaner or dishwasher. I'd pictured a rich, aloof family, dressed up like old-time royals, pointing at stuff they wanted me to do. Possibly sipping martinis while they did it, reading a paper news sheet and looking super intelligent. Or at the very least, the perfect space-age, sitcom family. Insanely upbeat, and perfect teeth and smiles.

The one who shook my hand was an ordinary, older guy, maybe the same age as my dad, in a holey brown sweater and glasses, with thinning hair and an open smile. Everything about him eased comfortably into his loose slacks and slippers, which whispered hot cocoa and hearth fires.

I dragged my gaze to the one who'd kissed me, clasping her hands to her chest in wonder. She was a similar-aged, small lady, whose kind eyes and smile were pure sunshine, warming me instantly from the inside. Loose blonde curls coiled into a knot behind her head and escaped to frame her face and tickle the collar of her navy-blue blouse. A bow tied on a bright, flowery apron made her waist look small and hung over the thighs of her cropped trousers in a lighter blue. Cute fluffy white slippers, in the shape of little bears, hugged her tiny bare feet. If ever I had to design an avatar of my idea of a mom, then I guess she was it. Radiating vibes of warm comfort, meatloaf in the oven, and fresh-baked cookies on the counter. I inwardly sighed.

I dropped my eyes to the little guy she'd pulled into her side with her arm around his shoulders. He looked a bit younger than Finn, maybe because he wore a striped, comic book t-shirt, tucked into loose brown shorts, without a shred of fashion sense. His hair was a side-parted brown mop, his skin was pale and his dark-circled eyes were wide with excitement. A cute kid, I warmed to instantly.

'Model C, meet members of your new family: Christopher, Sheila and young Nate.'

I wished I could say I remembered my training to act robotic, but it came naturally, in that I stared at each of them like a dumb ass, completely in shock and off guard.

The prof ignored my lack of response and went straight in with, 'May we both come in? I just want to go through a few last-minute things with you.'

'Of course,' Sheila said, moving out of the way, pulling Nate with her. 'Come in. Please. Welcome… welcome.'

The professor went in through the door first and I woke myself up and walked in a slow, measured gait behind him;

my green gridlines opening, retracting, measuring and mapping the whole time, through the sparse hallway. Two pictures, a narrow, sleek wooden chest, and a stairway coming up on the right. Open doorway up ahead, to the smells of savoury cooking.

I stopped suddenly when a small hand slipped into mine. Sheila. Small and fragile, with big blue eyes looking up at me. Drawing in a sudden breath, as surprised as I was.

It wasn't simply because I wasn't expecting it, but more that I couldn't remember the last time I'd had physical touch. Except maybe when I was a mess, right after the surgery, and couldn't walk. I almost recoiled at the thought of the laws, but remembered she'd initiated it. We both looked down at our joined hands.

'You feel so real,' she said quietly.

I was thrown for a moment. My first proper interaction and I was expecting more time to come up to hurdles like this. Plus an audience hovered at the end of the hall, waiting for my response. The professor's crow-like eyes looking particularly keenly at my performance. I had to get myself together and remember I was a machine. A new machine, with no learned experience yet. A small red dot flashed at the corner of my eye, signalling a reminder, and I drew on my early training. 'I *am* real, Sheila. I am a composite model of skin, tissue and biomechanics, tempered by a titanium alloy core.' I tried not to sound like C3PO, but more like myself. Casual, but measured, speaking softly, clearly, as if I was considering every word. It was hard not to make it a joke, like the old me. I had to remember that this wasn't a drill, it was the real thing, and my life depended on it.

Sheila put her hand to her mouth and looked over at the others, surprised and delighted. 'He's fantastic, isn't he?'

'Sure is,' the guy, Christopher, said indulgently. 'Let him come in, darling,' he said, ushering me forward with his hand. Sheila skipped ahead and the boy, Nate, appeared on the other side of me. He was checking me out with wonder while he walked with me towards the next room. 'You're tall,' he said, raising his eyes slowly, from my feet to my head. Like it was something to be admired. It was kind of cute. The others had disappeared, so I winked at him. 'I'm tall for my age.'

I used every facial muscle not to laugh at his shocked expression. Then he grinned and nodded knowingly, like we were now co-conspirators. I loved the kid already.

I stood on the corner of the L-shaped room to get a good look. The professor was already handing over my first supply of biopaste food and ionised water. Explaining when I needed it and my lack of bowel movement, sleep regimen and personal hygiene, which I found particularly embarrassing. Like I was some dog, being left with a friend.

I shut off my mind and looked around. The room was surprisingly large. Minimal and clean. Not as extravagant as I was expecting. I mapped and logged the ground floor: hallway, staircase leading upstairs and the large L-shaped room. That was it. A simple, sleek, white kitchen that flowed into a tasteful dining room furnished in the same, perfectly white materials, then into the comfortable lounge. Welcoming soft seating, rugs in neutral colours and different-sized wall plates. I zoomed in on those; they were so modern. Some were holographic family pictures and others were like some sort of TV. We didn't get new stuff like this. Ours came out of old Hoke's backstreet repair shop: heavy, clunky and much of it made in the last century. I slowly turned to take it all in. It was an advert for modern, serviceable living. Amazing, but surprisingly modest.

I'd just honed in on a photo with four, not three, people in it, when Sheila called, 'Christina! Come down now, please. Come and meet your new friend.'

I looked back at the photo, mapping lightning fast the long hair, thin frame and pale skin and then moved warily, spying around the corner to see who it was before she saw me.

'I'll just see their introduction and I will be off,' the professor said.

My chest whirred, slowing my heart mechanically, as the realisation hit me. *I was brought here for her.*

She didn't bound into the room like a spoiled teenager; she appeared like an apparition and stopped just in the doorway. Older than the picture, but her hair was still long and brown and kind of ratty around her shoulders. Her skin was so pale, almost translucent, around eyes that looked dark and hollow. I couldn't make out their colour, maybe hazel or brown. All I knew was that she looked ill and had been for a long time. Blue veins threaded her neck and forehead.

She wore a cream sweater that did nothing for her and hung like a sack over loose black track pants. Everything clung to her thin frame for dear life, like it could snap in a strong wind. I felt a wave of sadness. The only hint of money was a modest gold chain with an oval pendant that weighed too heavily on her delicate neck. I'd been bought as a companion for a dying girl.

I hadn't been aware of the silence until Sheila broke it by moving between us and pulling the girl closer. 'Christina, I'd like you to meet—' Sheila put her hand to her mouth and giggled nervously. 'I have no idea of his name.'

The professor went to open his mouth before I made the blunder of telling them my real name, but the girl cut across him, forcefully, 'Royce. His name is Royce. After the Rolls-Royce car.'

The boy, Nate, grinned, like he had a hand in it. All I could do was stare and process the thinking behind it. I remembered the stash of old magazines in an old garage I'd stolen as a kid. It was a vintage European car that, even in its day, was meant to be the king of all cars. I frowned at the unlikely comparison, but my heart buzzed then quietened. I needed to cover my weird behaviour and held out my hand. 'Pleased to meet you... Chrissy,' I said, not making up my mind what to call her until the last moment. Christina was too stuffy. My hand hung in mid-air as I realised my absolute blunder, as everyone focused on it. It felt like an age, standing there like an idiot, but the girl saved me. She made up the distance and slipped her delicate hand into mine. Her fingers were soft and warm. We didn't shake. She gripped mine, almost imperceptibly, sending an electric current through the length of my arm, radiating a heat-burst in my chest, that took several minutes to stop whirring to calm down. Then she let go, looking down with pink, heated cheeks.

'Amazing,' her dad, Christopher, said. 'So clever. He's already caught on to the shortened version of her name.'

The tension immediately faded and the prof gave me a piercing look. A warning at the close call, as he moved towards the doorway. 'I'll leave you all to get to know each other. Remember, he needs to power down a minimum of three hours over night. Royce pretty much manages himself. Just in case, instructions have been sent to your inbox should you need my assistance.'

My eyes hadn't left Chrissy's and hers hadn't left mine. I just wanted the prof to go. He was hovering like he was too nervous to leave me. Until I had to break my gaze to say to him, firmly. 'Goodbye, professor. I will be fine.' To the delighted laughter of the Coes.

He fixed me with one last warning glare and disappeared. I found Chrissy again, still watching me in a way I didn't understand. I wanted to get to know her story. Why she needed me. Why I felt I was home.

CHAPTER 17

Chrissy

I felt lost in those cold, glacier eyes. They froze my blood and made me shiver. So hard and unfeeling. A machine, like Jessica's one at school. But then I took in his whole face. It was a kind face. An expressive, lived-in face that moved and wrinkled into a nervous frown and warmed me to him instantly. It wanted me to like it. Its lips twitched into the smallest smile and I couldn't help returning it. Heat rose through me from my feet, like a furnace. He, it, was hot. Ridiculously hot. I burned with shame at even thinking it of a machine. I was glad to look away when the guy who brought him left.

'Wow! Our own robot. Can you believe it?' Nate said, grinning up at me with wide, excited eyes.

I just took in his face, not really listening. All I could feel was its eyes still on me, waiting. *For what?* Now I had it, I didn't know what the hell to do with it.

My mom came to the rescue. 'Why don't you show him around, Chrissy. Where his room is and the things he will need.'

I nodded at her, still in a daze. At least it was something to do, but I didn't feel comfortable being on my own with him. 'Come on,' I said, beckoning him with a hand, but not meeting his eyes.

'I'll come,' Nate said, going to walk with me too.

I don't know what got into me, but I whirled around so fast that Nate bumped into me. 'Don't crowd him!' I barked.

Nate's face immediately creased with hurt and then anger. 'It's my robot too, Chrissy. He belongs to all of us.'

I looked at him, exasperated, not understanding my strong reaction at all. Then at the AU. Royce, who was watching me quizzically. It felt like my words all bottle-necked in my mouth, so nothing came out. Until I managed a weak, 'He isn't a robot. That's too old-fashioned. His name is Royce.' All the while I spoke the words, I was studying him for a clue as to why I was feeling like this. I didn't know why. It just felt weird to reduce him to something as mundane. He was so much more. 'That's so 2040, Nate,' I said in my most teen-sounding voice, like the spoiled girls at school.

It kind of worked. It took the heat off me. Nate just rolled his eyes. 'Please, Chrissy. He's the best thing, ever.'

'Oh, let him go with you to settle him in, Chrissy. It's exciting for him,' my dad said, putting his arm around my mom's shoulders.

They looked so pleased with themselves for all this. I sagged and let out a defeated 'OK.' I turned and walked out into the hallway, without looking to see if he followed.

I stopped at the foot of the stairs and listened to his heavy footfalls as my answer. I felt him stop next to me and saw his feet, rather than looking right at him. 'Are you OK with stairs?' I asked, dragging my eyes up to his with extreme effort.

This close, I could see the blue/grey metal opening and shutting his pupils as he formed a response. The corners of his mouth turned up a little, riveting me to them as he spoke. 'There is nothing I can't do, Chrissy,' he said, tilting his head slightly and smiling properly.

I swallowed and frowned at the heat entering my cheeks again. It felt like it was making fun of me. Enjoying my discomfort and somehow keeping an innocent blankness. I shook my head, like I was going mad, and turned and began walking up the stairs. I kept telling myself it was just because he looked so realistic. It was bound to be confusing at first. Then I don't know what came over me, but I sniped over my shoulder, 'Except eat, drink and breathe.' It was unbelievably mean. I was almost at the top and couldn't look at him. But he was right behind me and made me jump.

I turned suddenly, and his face stopped very close and level with mine. He looked me dead in the eye and said calmly, 'Of course, Chrissy. I am just a robot.'

His look was innocent, but his words dripped sarcasm. It made me swallow hard with shame. I flicked my eyes to Nate, standing there, grinning. 'I think he's awesome.'

Feeling reprimanded and a little sobered, I went along the landing to the smallest room at the end. It was little more than a storage cupboard. The box room. It had a waist-high cot, more like a cushioned bench about two feet wide, a metal cabinet containing his power unit and drawers of utility supplies and a small chest my mother insisted on to store his clothes, which were pitifully few. Mainly the same as he had on: a sky-blue top and black pants in a stretchy material.

I pointed at it all while Royce peered in through the doorway and Nate pushed past to poke around more closely.

'The techs from TinBoiz brought it all for you earlier in the week,' I said. 'You sleep, er, power-down on that, power up with that, and have spare clothes in that,' I said, pointing. I wasn't really explaining anything; I just hoped he already knew what to do with it all.

Royce looked at each thing I pointed at as if he were logging it all away. I noticed he hardly blinked.

Nate closed one of the drawers he was nosing in and turned around as if he'd seen enough. 'Do you like tech games? I have the brand-new, version three, Space Challenger game.'

Royce dropped his weird eyes to his, taking a moment to answer. As if he were registering the request and deciding on what to say. All little machine-like tells I found strangely disappointing. 'I would enjoy that,' he eventually replied. 'But I warn you, I'm good and will probably whoop your arse.'

A moment of stunned silence. Nate put his hand over his mouth to stifle a nervous giggle. 'Don't let Dad hear you say that,' he said, with wide, scandalous eyes.

I couldn't stand it anymore. Everything was too much. I pushed between the two of them. 'Right, that's enough. Come with me!' I strode towards my room and turned my head to make sure he – it – was following.

Nate looked disappointed, dropping his arms to his sides. The AU was hesitating.

'Well, come on,' I said, gesturing with my arm for him to get a move on.

'Can you tell me who my primary companion is?' he asked, looking between me and Nate.

It took me a moment to get what he meant. Then I felt instantly bad. He didn't know who to obey. 'It's me,' I said with a tired shrug. 'But you belong to the whole family, I guess.'

It looked at Nate and held out a fist. 'Rain check?'

Nate brightened and bumped fists with him. 'Coolest robot, ever,' he said with a defiant look at me, then marching off.

Royce straightened and headed towards me in strong, purposeful strides. I couldn't lock onto those eyes and quickly pushed open my door and went inside. He was there a moment later and I closed the door behind him.

We were alone and I couldn't avoid his gaze. So intense, they drew me to them and he was doing it a lot. Getting a read on me or conveying things without words. Whatever it was, it was unnerving. I had to remind myself over and over that he – no – it was nothing more than nuts and bolts and maybe a clever microchip.

I averted my eyes and went over and sat on my bed and watched him. He waited on my fluffy white rug, in the centre of my room, eerily still. 'It's OK, you can take a look.' I don't know why I said that. Or why I even brought him here. I guessed to process him without being under my watchful brother's gaze.

Royce slowly turned a circle, moving his eyeline up and down as if he were scanning everything. My desk, poster plates of video games and pink fairy lights embedded in the walls. Creepier than ever, given that he kicked up my emotions like a hornet's nest. He was little more than a walking photocopier. Zeros and ones coming together to form a perfect simulation of a person. That's all he was. Not Teddy. He was never going to be Teddy. 'Typical girl's room, ha?' I don't know why I was talking like that. All casual and bratty.

He turned those headlights on me again. A tractor beam, sucking the truth right out of me. I swallowed. He tilted his head oddly, as if he'd absorbed something. It bugged me and I wanted to ask, 'what?' but felt like I was acting like an idiot already.

He looked back at my photo glass collage. My favourite thing in the room. It contained everything about me. My life in moving memories. A compilation of all my good times with Teddy. Some of us together as toddlers, but many of the last two years. Laughing, watching some old film on movie nights. Arguing over games. My mom and Tina made it for me recently. I'd burst into tears. I missed him so much. A ragged breath left me as I pulled back my emotions.

The AU was fascinated by it and went a little closer. He pointed and looked at me. 'Your boyfriend?'

I tried not to get annoyed. It wasn't to know how raw it all was. I got up and went over and stood next to him. 'No … he's my best friend in the world and the whole reason you're here.' It was a spiteful way to tell him, but I wanted to hurt him, so he felt something like me. It looked at me, puzzled. His expressions were so real, they unnerved me. Like real thought and experience were behind them. He smiled a little. 'You can tell me anything, Chrissy. My sole purpose is to protect you, now I know you are my primary responsibility. I have complete loyalty to you.'

Why did I feel like it was mocking me? That tiny hint of a smile, followed by a fast rally of blinks. His look switched to intense as if he realised he was coming off as insincere. I wanted to slap him and get him to tell me what was really on his mind. 'Arghh!' I shrieked right in its face and turned, strode back, sat on my bed and glared at him. I thought this would be easy. Like a new toy or something, but he was making me crazy.

He just watched me, tilting his head at an angle as if he didn't understand.

After a last, hard glare, I relented and let the tension drain out of me. I don't know why, but I reached down for my locket and opened it. The digi one my mom and dad gave me, that I never took off. I'd studied the moving image of Teddy grinning and making a heart shape with his fingers a thousand times. He mouthed the letters 'BFF' and pointed at me. 'He's in hospital,' I said wearily. I looked away from him. I was exhausted with this conversation already.

'Perhaps, I could be your second-best friend.' It was said so logically and reasonably that all I could do was stare at him in amazement. It was more than how clever he was. It was the emotional intelligence that was astounding. He – it – whatever – got me in five minutes, when other people seldom got me at all.

I didn't know what to say to a machine. I frowned and said, 'We'll see.'

CHAPTER 18

*R*oyce

Here I was, a seventeen-year-old guy, older than my years, alone with a girl in her bedroom. And her parents were cool with it. It was beyond madness. The craziest situation, because why would they worry? To them, I was a fully programmed and tested machine, who would never step out of the boundaries of The Laws. *Don't Touch* being the first and most important. I tried not to stare at her, but I couldn't help it. She was like no one I'd ever met. She was so fragile. Mentally and physically. The girls at home were as strong as the boys and often mentally more so. They had to be. We lived fast because the odds were, we'd die young. The average age was around fifty. Many kids just didn't make it to adulthood. So we did far too much, too young, ageing faster because of the consumption of hard liquor and black-market drugs. Dragged to the grave by poor food and lung problems, if the streets didn't get you first. Cancers were down, the UGN was always spouting, but we all knew it was simply because none of us lived long enough to die from it.

Today had been an education. I'd always thought the higher-ups lived some rich, amazing life. Then I'd met Chrissy, so pale and thin in this small house. 'What's he in hospital for?' I asked, suddenly curious, watching the shutters come down all around her. She loved him, that was obvious, and she felt weird around me. *Why else would she keep that sentimental reminder of him around her neck?* It sent an odd pang of fear that he'd recover. Not a nice thought, I knew. But this was my life now. I hoped the professor had done his necessary groundwork. I couldn't afford to get ousted if the 'friend' somehow made a recovery and came home. I'd be surplus to requirements. It was a scenario he'd never covered, and I was too clueless to ask. *What would happen to us if we got returned to the manufacturer?* I retracted to a razor edge of anger, convinced it was a detail left out deliberately. The prof was inclined to do that, and for a moment, I seethed at the loss of my eyes.

I was grateful she wasn't looking at me to capture my lapse in cover. She just shot a blast of annoyance across the bow and picked at her nails. It gave me a valuable microsecond to pull it together.

'Teddy has always been ill,' she said, drawing me back in from the edge. He hardly went to school this last year.' She pointed to a flat glass on her desk, I'd assumed was a mirror. A rectangle of about eight by twelve. He joined our classes on that, mostly.

I nodded, my mind racing over the data, that it was some monitor screen, linked to the school. When I rested my focus on her again, she was fighting back tears. I couldn't help the stab of envy for someone who made her feel like that.

'Then his mom and dad got together with mine and got him a sub. Some sort of knock-off arranged through their boss. They'd never afford the real thing, you see.' Then she looked me directly in the eye and fired right at my chest. 'A bit like you, I guess.'

It hit me several times at once, like buckshot. They were poor. Not expected. They were all at varying stages of sick. And the kill shot: she thought I was a knock-off. The shock-waves reverberated through me for a full minute. *A knock-off.* I couldn't shake it out of my head. Was that how we were being assimilated into homes? I don't know why I was so shocked. It was completely how the professor would operate, for his so-called higher purpose. Offering us on the cheap for desperate families like hers. That alone turned everything I knew on its head. 'We aren't knock-offs,' I corrected, trying to keep the edge out of my voice. 'We are state-of-the-art technology, with authentic dealership components.'

She just shrugged, like it was whatever. Not registering that she'd just insulted me and everything I'd been through to get here. 'Well, I know they didn't pay full price.'

My chest buzzed and I relaxed, so it did its work and slowed my heart rate. 'What happened?' I asked, more reasonably, clawing myself back into character.

She looked ahead of her as if lost in some warm memory. 'It worked brilliantly at first. Teddy synced with the sub and came back to school for the first time in ages. It was like we were together again.' Then the light in her eyes dimmed and her face clouded. 'But it was too much for his brain. He had a bleed – a stroke, they called it.' She shifted her gaze to mine and gritted her teeth so hard, a muscle twitched in her jaw. 'He's been in the hospital on life support ever since.' Tears glazed over her eyes and she looked down at her hands in her lap. 'They wanted to switch him off. There was nothing more they could do. But we couldn't bear to do it.'

Everything fell into place then: why I was there. The way she loved this guy, she would have gone into the mother of all tailspins.

'They bought you as a companion because he won't—' She burst into tears, covering her face with her hands.

I immediately went over to her, my hand hovering over her back. A red light beeped in the left corner of my vision. A reminder of the first law. She looked up at me with impeccable timing, bringing me back in line with her red, swollen eyes. Devastated, her brow wrinkling in confusion at what I was doing there, so close to her. I knew I was out of line, so I opted for honesty. 'I want to comfort you, but my first law is not to touch.'

She followed my arm to my hand, a few inches from her back and nodded. Taking me at my word with no idea of my internal struggle. Then she sniffed and wiped her nose on her cuff, which made me smile a little sadly. I was still a machine to her. 'So,' I said, more to get me back on track than her. 'What went wrong with the sub? Was it faulty?' I frowned at the red light flashing at the corner of my eye. I'd come to recognise it as a warning. AUs probably didn't ask those types of deeper questions. I stood straighter, over-riding it as a perfectly logical question. I was a cut above the regular TinBoi and would seek answers in order to learn.

It seemed OK. She was lost in her memories again. 'It's kind of like a VR headset but fits over your whole head. Teddy said it was brilliant when he first got it. Like he was living again. He could see, feel, even smell sometimes.'

I was fascinated. The only subs I'd met were the ones in Peter Pats or the old clunky trash subs that dumped company waste over the Danger Line. Never the other end of them. The humans crippled in bed. Not even one. We thought no further than they were for the rich. Teddy did not seem to fit that mould. Poorly and weak. I could just imagine how that kind of tech could put pressure on a sick brain. Pulsing electric waves through nerves and neural pathways.

I subconsciously touched the plate at the back of my

neck. The prof had woken me during surgery to sync up the AI chip in the same way. A fragile mind wouldn't be able to handle that. It made me realise we would have had to be health-screened first. When and where he would have done that, I had no idea. There were so many questions I never asked.

Then I remembered the healing chamber. That awful, confined space I'd woken up in that healed my extensive surgery in just a week. Before I gave it any forethought, I was speaking the words the professor told us: 'There exist healing devices, designed for the military that aid the healing process. Have his parents looked into that?'

I knew I'd made a huge blunder the way her eyes shot to mine. It was more than surprise, it was vicious. Like anger. Like how dare I venture to know shit about anything. 'Really? How would you know about anything like that?'

I inwardly swore. Red lights were flashing a light show. My power pack worked overtime as I tried to pull it back. *Hell*, brazen it out, I told myself, like it was becoming my new mantra. 'That's how they fuse our biomedical features,' I said, as matter-of-factly as I could.

After a long moment of scrutiny, deciding on whether to believe me, she seemed to stand down. I unclenched my fingers, digging pits in my palms. She shook her head doubt-fully. 'I've never heard of it. Probably not available to the likes of us. Or too expensive.'

I'd gotten away with it and felt a pang of guilt for being glad. This was a steep learning curve and it was just the first day. It was a shock that they regarded themselves as poor. They had no idea, but it was becoming clearer that they certainly weren't rich. Then she threw me onto the back foot again. 'Thank you, though. I will mention it. Maybe Dad can look into it at work.'

I almost rolled my eyes at my stupidity when a female

voice called from downstairs, 'Food's ready.' The word 'Sheila' flashed up on the left-hand side of my vision, taking my attention.

'Coming!' Chrissy called back. 'Are you coming?' she said, already walking to the door. 'When do you have yours?'

I began to follow, distracted by our conversation and how I had said too much. 'Once a day,' I said without eye contact. 'I've already eaten.'

My power disk was working overtime, slowing down my heart to undetectable. It wasn't excitement, but dread. For the truth of what I'd become. I had to keep my damn mouth shut and remember I was now less than nothing.

CHAPTER 19

$\mathcal{R}$oyce
I would have loved to say, 'Give me a minute,' to spend some time alone in my room, just to regroup and decompress, but that would have been too weird. This, 'your wish is my command' shit, was wearing thin, already. Sarcasm and wisecracks had always been my MO. Being with these rich folks that weren't, who I wanted to dislike and couldn't, was just freaking me out.

I paused at the top of the stairs as Chrissy did the same. She held the banister for too long. Breathing deeply, like she was gathering herself or letting something pass. Before I could put my foot in it again and ask if she was OK, she flashed me an angry, 'don't dare say a word', look, and then skipped down like a new version of herself. I felt numb as I slowly followed. The answer whacking me in the face: she was ill too. I was so stupid. It made sense now why she was so pale and thin. I never imagined the folks in the gated communities getting sick. It threw everything I knew on its head and made me thaw a little more towards them. The higher-ups were no longer the faceless, stuck-up, aloof, and by the number of identical houses, I'd bet my life that the neighbours weren't too dissimilar, either. We were the Strong Forgotten, but they had problems too. That meant if these were the middle, then the wealth must be going somewhere else. To an elite, a higher class, no one ever got to see. Hidden. Syphoning off everything.

It was a eureka moment that left me reeling. My legs moved, following Chrissy down, but my head was still at the top, stunned by how we could have gotten it all so wrong. Until Sheila snapped me out of it as she came out to call Chrissy again, nearly bumping into her. 'Ah, there you are. Settled in OK, Royce?'

I watched Chrissy slither past her mom and escape into the kitchen, leaving me stranded. I forced my best apple pie smile and gave Sheila my full attention. 'Yes, thank you, ma'am.' When all I wanted to do was follow Chrissy and question her some more. 'Have you eaten, sweetheart? I've got one of your tube thingies, if you need one.'

Sweetheart. I'm sure I smiled; I couldn't help myself. I don't think I've ever been called a sweetheart in my whole life. This insignificant woman, from a family I'd known for less than two hours, always made me feel warm inside. My chest became a bubbling cistern of feelings I didn't recognise and felt weird, but not unpleasant. She treated me more as a human now I was a TinBoi, than anyone ever had when I lived as a human. My face softened. I liked her a lot—the whole family. My mind drifted to Chrissy and where she'd disappeared to.

'He's OK, Mom,' Chrissy called. 'Leave him alone. He's eaten.'

Sheila went past me, shaking her head and huffing. 'Well, I don't know, do I. It seems rude not to give him anything.'

I followed Sheila slowly and paused just inside the room.

The dad, Christopher, Nate and Chrissy were already seated at the table. There were two spaces left.

Chrissy looked over spitefully, like she'd switched from the person I'd seen upstairs. 'It's not a "him", Mom.' Shooting me a hostile look that almost made me look behind me to see if someone else was standing there. This girl was mercury. I couldn't make her out at all. Fascinating but frustrating. Illogical because that was exactly the opinion I should be going for. A TinBoi. But it rankled and it made no sense.

Nate saved me from total annihilation by patting the seat next to him. 'Sit next to me, Royce.' I smiled, loving the little guy even more. The reminder dot flashed and I remembered my protocol. I switched my gaze to Chrissy and raised an eyebrow in question. I knew I was being testy, but so was she. I recognised already that belonging to her and keeping cover was not going to be easy.

Thankfully, she was too moody to notice and simply said 'OK' on a weary breath and shook her head.

Nate was already pulling out the chair for me, so I went and sat down next to him. I smiled at his beaming grin. I put my hands in my lap and looked around the table. Amazed at the plates of food. Homemade, like on TV. The sort we used to groan over in the cinema and just daydream about. Mashed potatoes piled high. Greens. And actual beef steaks, the size and shape I'd never seen before. Not real ones, anyway. Any meat we could get our hands on was reconstituted or manufactured, shaped protein. So we ate mainly fast-food. No telling what went into it. Heaps of additives and hyped with MSG. We often joked that we actually got hyper after eating and then crashed with a headache. Whatever was in it, that wasn't a good sign. Cooking never seemed worth it when the ingredients were so processed with long, unpronounceable names on the packets. Scabs and boils from scurvy and acne were common.

'Do you like the look of the food, Son?' Christopher said, pointing with his knife. 'Would you like to try some?'

I looked at him, a little startled that I'd given myself away so obviously. I would wolf it down in a heartbeat, but I didn't even have spit to drool. 'It all looks wonderful, sir, Mrs Coe,' I said, flashing an appreciative look Sheila's way. 'But I have no stomach to speak of and would malfunction severely. Believe me, I tried it once.' I smiled wryly, remembering the ongoing competition we all had for projectile vomiting, for which I held the record of six feet. I closed my eyes for a moment, wishing I could shut the hell up.

NATE GIGGLED behind his hand and received a stern look from Christopher. Chrissy looked red and strained, like she was about to burst. Then they all erupted into loud laughter at what they saw as a hilarious joke. Even Chrissy, who brought a nervous curl to my lips.

They slowly calmed down, sounding out of breath, like they hadn't laughed so much in ages and continued eating. Chrissy seemed to have snapped out of her mood.

'So, how are you getting on? Do you think you'll be friends?' Sheila asked, putting an enviable chunk of steak into her mouth.

It was cute that she thought it was a choice. I rested my eyes on Chrissy, raising an eyebrow. Ultimately, it rested on her whether we got to be friends in any real sense of the word. She'd been an ass a lot of the time and knew it, shifting uncomfortably. I couldn't help myself and spitefully hammered home the point. 'Chrissy has a wonderful display of V-photos of her *best* friend, Teddy,' I said, emphasising best.

Her face scowled in a micro expression, lasting less than a second. Everyone else missed it, but I'd grid-mapped and flashed it up immediately. She covered it well and licked the mash off her fork, holding my fascination.

'Don't eat like that, darling,' her mom said.

Chrissy let her fork arm go limp and stared moodily at her mom, shooting an embarrassed look my way.

I smirked, enjoying her discomfort, but she wasn't playing. 'Actually, I meant to tell you. Royce told me something very interesting earlier. Apparently, there are special healing machines the military uses that might be able to help Teddy.'

The table went silent and they all stared at Chrissy, then at me. Chrissy's look was deadly, with more than a glimmer of spite. I felt my temperature rise and my chest whirl to slow my heart. Now she wanted to play and it excited the hell out of me. So much so, I had to remind myself that I was a machine, over and over. I don't think she was deliberately trying to land me in it, which she had. She was firing a warning shot for embarrassing her and letting me know that her best friend was way more important than me. But I couldn't help taking it the way it was intended, whether she realised it or not. She was flirting. A call to war, that, despite knowing the danger, I was never going to ignore.

I inwardly grinned, *bring it on.* While my face portrayed complete innocence, her self-satisfaction cracked, as sudden guilt crept in. My inner grin widened.

'Oh, really?' her dad said, genuinely interested. 'I have heard stories of how they manage to patch up soldiers and send them back to the front in record time. How did you hear about it, Royce?'

I finally dragged my fascination with Chrissy to Christopher, taking a sip of his wine. I was rapidly catching up with his question. Pauses were great cover. As long as I kept my face blank and looked like I was processing and considering like an AU, then I got away with very human distraction. 'They use the same type of machine to heal the bio-skin on us,' I said, my mind shooting to the prof's explanation before our surgery. My sensors were already flashing at the over-share. *How would I know? Where would I know? Wouldn't I be offline during manufacture? Damn! Shut the hell up, man.* I wanted to tell Christopher to keep it to himself, but that was even more suspicious. I had to just ride it out and hope the prof wouldn't be too pissed.

'Ask the guy, Dad, please.' Her eyes were pleading, all her discomfort with me gone. I no longer existed. 'He might be able to help in some way.'

He, meant the professor. I was toast on my first day. She irritated the hell out of me, making me want to beat my own head. My power pack whirred, slowing my heart down to barely ten beats a minute. To deadly focus. What did I have to lose? I hadn't even unpacked. I just came right out with what mattered to me. 'If I help you and your best friend wakes up, will there still be a home for me?'

The table went silent at my completely inappropriate question. My gaze was fixed directly on Chrissy, who was dumbstruck.

Someone dropped a fork. *Sheila.* 'Forgive me, you're just so damned life-like.'

I almost smiled and let the ruse go. I'd been busted, anyway. It was Nate who dragged me from the brink of suicide. He put his small hand on my arm and whispered conspiratorially, 'If she doesn't want you, I can be your primary human.' He suddenly looked worried. 'Do they allow you to switch?' He looked around the table for an answer when I was lost for words.

It felt like the table collectively breathed, relaxed and smiled. Chrissy rolled her eyes and shook her head. 'Of course they do, dummy.' But a short, spiteful glance told me whatever it was that had started between us was far from over. 'They just reprogram them, or something,' she said with a flick of her hand.

It was a deliberate low blow, completely uncalled for. I clenched my teeth to hold down my temper, but I couldn't help mocking her with my comeback. 'That is so 2040 of you, Chrissy. There is no programming required for an AU. Neurowebs are formed from our individual experiences. Like children. A command code is all that's needed to sever the primary bond.' I smiled sweetly, having thrown her patronising 'didn't you know' attitude I'd learned in a day right back at her.

Nate laughed and pointed at his sister. 'Hah-ha!' he sang. 'See!'

Sheila and Christopher chuckled and continued eating. Like it was all teenage high jinks. 'He'll certainly keep you on your toes, that one,' Sheila said.

'Mom?' Chrissy said, outraged. She threw down her knife and fork onto her plate when her mom ignored her. 'It's an "it", Mom.' She shot me a final dagger look, got up suddenly from the table and stormed off.

I went to get up, in shock. Her moods seemed to erupt from nowhere. Up and down in a seesaw of strong emotion that left me dizzy and reeling.

'Leave her,' Sheila said, getting up from the table to clear plates. 'You can help me with the dishes,' she said, flashing me a smile and a wink.

The whole thing left me confused, my attention drifting back to the doorway that Chrissy had just gone through. I wasn't sure what to do. She was being a brat, but she was also my primary.

'It's OK. She's just a teenager who's grieving. She'll calm down in a minute.'

Nate was pushing his chair in while his dad was reminding

him of some chore he hadn't done, so I began to clear plates and followed Sheila to the kitchen end of the room. It wasn't like our grimy cesspit of broken drawers, cupboards off their hinges and a sink full of last week's dirty dishes. This was sleek lines of white, seamless surfaces, with a black marble counter and matching tiles on the floor. Everything was fresh and clean, even after cooking. 'Dishwasher is in there,' Sheila said, pointing.

When I looked at what looked like a long white panel, she waved her hand over the spot and a large door opened, revealing a silver drawer with stacking compartments inside. She began passing me plates and I stacked them around pots already loaded. I'd never used one before, but neither would an AU, so it was fine. I was surprised she did this sort of thing herself. I thought all the rich folks had service subs for this sort of thing.

'So how are you getting on, really?' she said, ending on a loud whisper, bumping into me playfully. It was a confusing interaction, even as a human. I looked back at the table nervously. It was empty and we were alone. I don't know why it unnerved me; it was a reasonable question. She was just being friendly.

I paused while stooping to load the last plate to frame my answer. 'Very well, ma'am. I am learning a lot.' I stood and flashed a look at Sheila, nervously.

She was smiling. Her hands were up to the elbows in suds, in silly pink waterproof gloves with fluff around the cuffs. 'Oh really, like what?' She didn't look at me; she was playing with the bubbles while she listened.

This was one of those weird heart-to-hearts to draw me out. I'd seen it on sitcoms. It felt laughably strange to learn from the TV and experience it from a real family I'd never had, while being an AU. So I just went with the madness. 'Chrissy doesn't seem to like me that much,' I said, watching her closely. She picked up a wine glass and submerged it in the suds. I wondered why she had a dishwasher when she was washing by hand.

'Nonsense, silly. It's not that she doesn't like you, it's that she doesn't want to like you and can't help it. Believe me, I know my daughter. She thinks the world of Teddy, she always has. She just feels disloyal if she moves on from this perpetual grief she holds on to.' She shook her head bitterly. 'It's desperately sad, but the cold facts are he might never wake up, and even if he does, he might not be the same. Just hang in there,' she said, looking right at me with a regretful smile. She squeezed out a cloth and began wiping the already spotless counter. I just stared after her, stunned. It was so obvious now she'd spelled it out. It explained the hot and cold she'd hit me with all day.

'So what else?... Have you learned?' Sheila added when I was slow to respond.

'Um,' I said, stalling, trying to get my head back in order. So I just rambled. Thinking aloud about all the junk I mulled over. 'I've learned that there are rich who aren't that rich and there are poor people. But the rich have AUs and the poor don't.' I was watching Sheila the whole time so as not to miss the minutest expression.

She was smiling at the sink, listening and nodding, indulgently. She was back to playing with the suds on her hands again. 'I'm afraid nothing in this old world is ever black or white, Royce. Having a small home, a car, and a job, which is hard enough these days, and having enough food, is far from rich.' She was only confirming my own conclusions, but I had questions. I stood straighter, deciding questioning was something a newly placed AU would definitely do to gain data. 'Are there even richer people in this old world?' I asked, trying to sound cute and curious, like a kid.

She smiled, pulled off her gloves and beckoned me with a hand. 'Come and sit with me outside. It's OK, the fan is on.'

She grabbed the remainder of a bottle of wine and a glass and I followed her out of a back door. 'I don't have lungs,' I said, frowning, the fact sinking in for the first time.

The sun was fading, but there was still an orange glow lighting a pretty little patio overlooking a small lawn in a tiny backyard. Bright-coloured flowers climbed from glazed pots up latticed fences, making an arch. It was the perfect spot to sit. A paradise compared to where I came from. The air would soon kill us, even if we had a nice place like this to sit.

Sheila was already sitting in a cushioned lounger and patted the one next to her. 'Sit!' she ordered. 'Take the load off.' She took a gulp of wine, relaxed back and closed her eyes.

I sat gingerly in the one next to her and allowed myself to slowly sink back into it. She was right. I was comfortable. For a moment, I enjoyed the last warmth from the blurred-out sun and listened to Sheila speak.

'There is dreadful poverty in this world, Royce, that you wouldn't have seen. But I hear about it every day when I volunteer at the thrift depot. They ship basic parcels out to some desperately poor families. You've no idea how hard it is for some. We don't have excess, but I am grateful we have enough.'

I turned my head to watch her as she rambled, fascinated by what she was saying. She flashed open her eyes, suddenly and turned her whole body to face me. I found myself mirroring her. A shared moment, in our own little world. 'There are rich people somewhere, Royce, but I've never seen them. Christopher says they fly into MacoTech, by HeliJet, where we both work and land on the roof. He's on the top floor, you see. They have secret meetings with the bigwigs and go. He says they are surrounded by AU security and wear the finest clothes, not company uniform like us. And have never been seen in the staff canteen. They bring their own food in specially and have AU chefs.' Her eyes widened with the growing scandal and she shuffled closer. I'd been sucked in and was doing the same.

'I've heard they have real food, cultivated in the ground and meat from animals that are alive.' She shook her head comically. 'Not from a lab. Can you believe that?'

I shook mine, using every muscle not to smile.

'Don't you see, Royce? It's not only the expense, but it means that where they live must be clean.'

I just stared at her, amazed that she was so amazed.

'Clean air and clean soil,' she said, as if it was a fundamental fact that I should know and wasn't getting.

I just blinked. Knowing, of course, she was right, but kind of flabbergasted. 'Isn't what you ate tonight real?' I asked, sounding naive, but really, I was testing her. Scrutinising her taking her lifestyle so for granted.

She bobbed her head, looking into the middle distance to frame her words without patronising me, but of course, that was impossible. To her, I was just an inquisitive AU, when in reality, I belonged to a society that would cut her arm off for the food they'd eaten just that evening.

'Kind of,' she began. 'It's whole, but lab-grown. Rather like your bio-skin, I guess. It's expensive, but a fraction of the price of live-produced. I'll take you to the market one day and you can see for yourself. The good stuff is locked away in a glass cabinet, mostly reserved.'

I was impressed she knew anything about bio-skin. 'Where do the rich live?' I asked, mainly to take the heat off me as I hadn't spoken.

She bit immediately. 'I don't know,' she said, wistfully, like it was some sort of fairytale. 'Some think they live next to the ocean, where the air is cleaner and has the most expensive real estate. Some think they have their own islands, cut off from everyone else.'

My heart was skipping and shutting down as my excitement grew. 'Where do *you* think they live?' I asked, already imagining a lush island in real sunshine with real animals and birds, extinct everywhere else.

She pointed and looked upwards.

I followed her line of vision, not sure what I was looking at. 'Up there,' she said quietly. 'I'm convinced of it. In huge floating ships. Think about it. The air is full of exhaust fumes. Maybe it isn't just a result of the Earth dying down here. Maybe it's a cover for them.' She was still searching the skies while I kept shifting my gaze back to her, fascinated by her idea. I much preferred the island theory, but she was so lost in the sky. 'It's their waste choking us. Perfect when you think about it,' she said, wistfully. 'Silently circling the globe and no one even knows they're there.' Then her eyes dropped to mine and she shrugged. 'Because no one can see through the smog.'

CHAPTER 20

*R*oyce
I don't know what made me say it, but it just spewed out. Complete folly. Laying me wide open to discovery. 'Is there a real place called The Soul Of The World?' I swallowed, my power pack thumping hard, trying to regulate my internal temperature, now I'd said it.

She stared at me, blinked, with a completely unreadable face. I half expected her to jump up and run back into the house, screaming 'malfunction'.

I attempted to swallow again, but I had no lubrication. 'I read about it on the Outerweb in my learning phase,' I added. Desperately trying to pull it back to some kind of credible reason that an AU would ask something like that. Still no reaction. I was panicking. 'There are supposed to be wild animals grazing and forests absorbing the CO_2 and feeding the atmosphere with oxygen. The rebels hide there and call it Eden.' I finally stopped speaking and felt my heart sink into my stomach cavity at my utter stupidity.

She hadn't taken her eyes off me the whole time and I saw the real woman in them. The one as undercover as me.

Underneath the soft, caring mom camouflage was the strong, intelligent woman who completely understood the world and its inequality and dangers. A lioness who would protect her cubs at all costs and played by the rules to achieve it. My heart was in my mouth, but, God, did I admire her.

The light was fading, making the contours of her face harden. Then she spoke, barely moving her lips, quietly and evenly, at least two octaves lower than her usual speaking voice. 'We don't talk about rebels here, Royce. It's not polite.' Then she got up and picked up her glass, pausing before she walked back to the house. 'Look,' she said, less sternly. 'Curiosity is a marvellous thing, but you must learn to moderate it when in company. By all means, learn, but don't speak.'

I stared at her in awe. She held my gaze for a long moment to make sure I had it, then turned and went back inside. Then, as if she'd let go of invisible strings holding me, I flopped back into my seat, reeling. My power pack was trash. My heart was a kettle drum. I couldn't believe she hadn't slammed me down or outed me. She'd warned me. In a way that if overheard, would appear innocent. But I'd received it loud and clear. She was scared. No doubt telling me to read the room. She might be sympathetic, but not everyone was. It could also mean it wasn't just her listening. *Wow.* Not what I was expecting, at all.

I wandered slowly back into the kitchen, still running through what she'd said and the implications of it. I was surprised to see her sitting alone at the dining room table. It was almost dark and she had a full glass of wine. For a moment, I was at a loss. I had no idea it would be her I'd feel closest to in all this. Or whether she even suspected what I was. 'What should I call you, Sheila?' I asked.

She laughed, but her eyes were glassy with tears. 'What would you like to call me?'

I wasn't sure whether it was a test. I ran through my options until I landed on the perfect one. 'Mom,' I said quietly. I'd hardly known mine and she was the whole deal: loving *and* strong.

When she didn't answer right away, I thought she'd say no. But more tears filled her eyes and ran down her cheeks. She slowly stood and walked towards me. I stood rigid, mind scattering, not knowing what she'd do. Until she stood right in front of me and pulled me into a tight hug. I stood stiff as a board. Stunned. My hands hovering over her back, which I couldn't touch. Soft shudders rocked into my shoulder where she wept real tears, soaking warm, through my shirt and into my skin.

We stood there a full minute. The timer flashing on my grid. Then she pulled apart and blew into a tissue she pulled from her pocket. 'Forgive a silly old woman,' she said eventually. 'You're just so damn sweet.'

I remained frozen, not used to any show of affection. From anyone. No one could afford them back home; the cost was too great. Maybe alluded to in actions, or inuendo. And almost never deep. So, I deflected with humour, as I always did. 'Nate said you're not allowed to use the word damn.'

She laughed on a single sob and touched the side of my face. I decided she was the best mom in the world.

CHAPTER 21

*C*hrissy

I escaped to the haven of my room and went to my full-length mirror. I felt claustrophobic and hot down there. I pulled down the neck of my top to let my reddened skin breathe and studied my pale face, now covered in blotches. I wondered if I should cover my dark circles for school tomorrow.

I frowned. It had never bothered me before. Not even when Teddy was there. Nothing had changed. Nothing real, anyway. A surge of anger rocked me at how unfair life was. Mom's voice echoed inside, like a back-up to my conscience, 'No one ever said life was fair.' I hated that saying. Well, it should be. Teddy didn't deserve to be brain-dead, and I didn't deserve to lose my best friend. 'It sucks ass,' I said, scowling at myself. But my thoughts were already veering to Royce. Why, I had no idea. He didn't have real thoughts or feelings. No one would grieve him if he died.

That made me feel terrible. I'd been unbelievably mean since he'd arrived. It was all so confusing. I crumpled and threw myself face down on my bed, angrily. He was programmed to pander to me, obey and follow me around like some dogbot. My conscience pricked me straight after, 'but he has the ability to learn, there is no programming,' Always in my mom's stern voice. 'Argh!' I shouted into my pillow, punching it hard.

I was a sad, pathetic person if all I had was a machine for a friend. I flipped over onto my back and looked at my ceiling. Even that was a reminder of Teddy, with all the star constellations slowly moving on the blue-sky background. We'd lie side by side and watch as the sky darkened to black and the sun set. It was how we imagined the real sky at night.

I wondered what I was going to do about school. Would I take him, like Jessica does? There'd be no flying under the radar; I'd be noticed. I wasn't sure how I felt about that. The Populars would hate it, as if I was trying to be like them. I wondered what would happen when Royce met them – her AU? My anger slowly shrank away. That AU had fascinated me right away. It felt cold. Unfeeling. I didn't feel like it was good. Silly, I know. And now I had my own. And I suppose, despite Royce being as annoying as hell, he did feel like he was good.

I pummelled my head with the heel of my hand. This is why AUs should be banned. It was so confusing. The lines were too blurred.

I tried to imagine what Teddy would say to this problem. The answer came right away, in his voice, loud and clear. 'I'm not going to tell you how you should feel, Chrissy. You must come to your own decision, whether, in your mind, it is an "it", or a "he". Then stick to it. All this flipping from one to the other is what's sending you crazy.' He'd be right, of course, but it was cloudier than that and I didn't want to face it. Instead, my thoughts shot to what Teddy would say if

Royce were his, and I laughed out loud. He would definitely be a 'he'. No overthinking.

I felt better. As if I'd spoken to Teddy face to face. My BFB: best friend barometer. I didn't want to ruin it, so I kept out of Royce's way for the rest of the day. I'd start afresh tomorrow.

CHAPTER 22

*R*oyce

After everything I'd learned, I wanted to see Chrissy with new eyes. I felt I understood her a little better, now. She wasn't just being a spoiled brat. I wanted her to see I was no threat to Teddy. But she didn't come back downstairs. I toyed with going up to find her, but dismissed it as not appropriate. Not yet, while I was still so new.

It didn't take long for Nate to notice I was free, and he excitedly led me to his room. He jabbered nonstop, about this game or that. Dying to show me his new one: Space Challenger. I liked the kid, right off. Plus, his room was right next to Chrissy's. Maybe she'd come in and I'd get a chance to see her.

'Come on, Royce, it'll be bedtime soon. This is going to be so much fun.' He leapt onto his bed and got comfy with his back to the headboard. I slowly sat on the opposite side and did the same. 'OK,' he said, loudly with hyper-enthusiasm. 'Just got to fit these,' he sang, producing a very high-tech VR headset that was compact and neat. Not the big, clunky ones I was used to. He chattered on, explaining the rules and objectives. I kept quiet about regularly breaking into the arcade with my friends, so I already knew how to play it. He was so like Finn, with his limitless energy and optimism; I didn't want to dampen it.

The goggles were a blank screen. I felt Nate shuffle back next to me and put on his. Then he clicked on the game. It was a fight club game on a spaceship. Too old for him really. I wondered whether Sheila knew how gory it was. You got to design your galactic warrior, with any outlandish powers or weapons, as long as they didn't destroy the ship. That was the only rule. If you did that, then you lost. Otherwise, it was a fight to the death. The winner gets Earth.

I kept in TinBoi character for precisely three minutes before I was laughing out loud at Nate's dirty tactics. 'Take that, sucker,' he said, pulling out my guts in endless rope coils. The kid was good. It was the most fun I'd had in ages, but I realised I had to be careful with stuff like this.

Sheila called, 'Nate, shower for bed, please,' while he was setting up a new round and I felt him sag and groan with disappointment. 'Five more minutes,' he called back.

'Now! ... Or I'm coming up there.'

The domesticity of it all warmed me from the inside. Boundaries set with love. How nice it would have been if Finn had grown up in something like this. Instead, he'd lost his mom and ducked his father's terrible drunken moods because he'd never gotten over the loss of her.

The mood had gone and I dragged off the headset. Nate was sitting there watching me. I thought I'd completely blown it, but he shook his head in amazement and said, fervently, 'You are the best TinBoi, ever.'

I smiled at his serious expression. 'That is true,' I said, giving him a wink.

He laughed and reached out a finger and poked my face. 'You're so real.'

'I am real,' I said, feeling an impossibly large lump lodged in my throat. 'I am here with you; therefore, I am real— Not an apparition or a ghost,' I said, quickly clarifying.

Nate nodded sagely. 'That's true … Just because you have wires and circuitry instead of flesh and bone, doesn't mean you aren't real.'

I studied his innocent face closely. My green gridlines mapping it, madly and disappearing. 'I'll let you into a secret, Nate, because we are brothers now. I do have bones, but they are titanium.'

Nate nodded excitedly. 'I get you …we are brothers. I won't ever let anyone take you away, not even if Teddy does come back. You're a Coe now. Royce Coe. My brother.'

I wanted to ruffle his hair to break the intense moment, but the touch law reminder flashed. 'You'd better get a shower before she gets mad and grounds me,' I said, glad I no longer had tear ducts.

Thankfully, the distraction worked, as he laughed. 'Yeah, she will, too.'

I stood, slowly, and he slid off the bed as if his limbs weighed a ton, trying everything to delay his shower. 'What are you going to do?' he asked, like he didn't want to miss a thing.

'I'll power down. Got a big day tomorrow. My first day at school,' I said, with fake enthusiasm, making my way towards the door. The truth was, I was scared to death. My power pack vibrated at the mere thought of it. I had no idea what to expect from a tech school, other than the brief training in the types of subjects. I had no clue about the other kids. My previous education had been patchy at best. I turned and caught Nate's face, now bright and alive. 'It's going to be so cool, I can't wait. Night, bro,' he said, putting up his hand.

'Night, bro,' I said, doing the same, then getting out of there as quickly as I could. I stood with my back to the door, as if I was breathless for air. I allowed my systems to self-regulate back to normal, then took a step, pausing outside Chrissy's door.

I could see my own door just a few feet away. It was a bad idea; I should have kept on walking, but I couldn't resist just reaching out with my sensors to hear what she was doing inside. Maybe a TV on, or perhaps she was on her phone. I frowned, realising I hadn't seen a single one since I'd been there.

I'd never done it before outside of training. I still didn't quite believe it, but I sent out the feeler waves, just as I was taught. It was totally quiet, only soft breaths. Regular as her heart, beating behind it. It hypnotised me, even though it felt wrong. Like I was a voyeur or some Peeping Tom. I reasoned it was for emergencies. The prof had said it was for fire or earthquake, to sense them coming, or to find lost victims. All from the implant in the back of my head. I was simply checking on my primary before bed.

I tuned back into the soft breathing. On listening closer, I could hear she was asleep, but it was laboured and out of rhythm. Her heart was a little weird, too. A sharp pain hit mine, and I wanted to burst in. Now, I fully understand. She was sick. Not just pale and weak, but really sick, like something bad that drags you down over time. The spells. The lack of energy.

I closed my eyes and cursed. Then looked up and down the hallway and lightly knocked with my knuckle.

'Who is it? I'm in bed,' a croaky voice came back.

I took a final look around and slipped inside, closing it quickly. Struck immediately by the lack of a lock. I took a moment to map the room, where everything was in the soft light. Chrissy was leaning up on her elbows, blinking, bleary-eyed. 'What are you doing here?' she asked, scrambling to sit up.

I put up my hands in reflex. 'I didn't mean to scare you, I thought you were awake.' I lied in the last part. 'I just came to say goodnight and ask your permission to power down for the night.' A weak excuse, but plausible for an AU.

It worked. She relaxed immediately and shooed me with a hand. 'Yes, OK,' she said on an exhale. 'Night.' She flopped back down and turned away from me with a huff.

I was left standing there, like a lemon, not knowing what to do. I wanted to tell her to stop the act and that she was acting like a tool.

She leaned up and turned her head when she realised I hadn't moved. 'Why are you still here?'

I took a beat to bite down my quick comeback. Then I said evenly, 'I need to know what time to set my system to wake me. I have to eat, evacuate and do system checks before we leave.'

She wrinkled her nose. 'Ew, too much info.' Then, when I hadn't said any more, she seemed to relax, like she knew she was acting up. She rolled onto her back and looked up at the ceiling. 'Sorry, er yeah. We leave by car at 8. How long do you need?' she asked, dropping her eyes to me again.

I shrugged. 'Forty-five minutes, I guess. Unless you want to do anything else in the mornings.'

She turned onto her side to face me, with both hands under her cheek. It felt like she was studying me. 'Allow fifty. Nate will be a pain; he's so excited about you, he'll make us late.'

I continued to hover. I couldn't help myself now I had her talking. I wanted to staple my mouth. 'What about you? Are you happy to have me here?'

She stayed silent, like I hadn't asked and I waited. Ten point five seconds, to be exact. Like crossing the Grand Canyon between us. I went to turn to leave, figuring she wasn't going to answer and cursing my stupidity. I wasn't used to dealing with girls. They were a nightmare. The prof would have had me doing a hundred chin-ups for this major mistake.

I had the door open and was about to step out when, 'I am glad you're here,' came clearly from behind me. 'I'm just really angry at everything at the moment.'

For the first time in my life, I managed to keep my mouth shut and quietly closed the door.

I was glad to escape to the sanctuary of my room. The first proper room I'd ever had. Even though it was little bigger than a storage cupboard. I closed my door and leaned against it with relief. If I was going to make it here, I had to learn to get a grip.

CHAPTER 23

*R*oyce

'Good morning, TinBoi.'

It took me a moment to process that the female voice was my compact power assistant speaking. 'I am Sentia. I will commence system checks now.'

I came back online to white static in my eyes and a sharp hiss from the robotic arm retracting from the centre of my power disc in my chest. I got my bearings while Sentia pulsed system checks through all my central nerve points. She also checked the AI rebound system that had felt non-existent so far. 'System checks complete. You are free to move on to cleansing.'

I remembered it was my big day today. I sat bolt upright, swivelled my body ninety degrees, and stood up on my feet. All appeared in working order. The small door straight ahead of me was my own newly installed bathroom.

Inside, I removed my night pants and hung them on the hook. The whole room was little more than a cubicle, lined in sheet metal. My toilet was a pan stuck to the wall on the left and my shower was on the right. I activated evac first.

The large suction tube drew the black, oily waste into a collection tank. I wasn't sure what happened to it. Probably taken off somewhere for analysis. I'd long given up the idea of privacy.

Then I stepped between two red arrows on the opposite wall and was immediately hit by hot jets of mist on the back of my body. I turned, and it did the same on my front. That was it. Shower over. A hot blast of air dried me and I was spritzed and ready to go.

Back in the room, my standard-issue clothes were on my bed, courtesy of Sentia. I quickly pulled them on, fastened my utility belt and I was dressed. The whole thing took less than seven minutes.

I went to leave.

'One last thing, Royce. The professor asked me to remind you to be ready for the AI bounces. They will begin as soon as you meet another AI or sub. You will immediately be registered and pulled into the AI circuit as a newly activated unit.'

I absorbed what she said. It made sense why I hadn't felt anything yet.

'You will feel it instantly. It is quite forceful at first. It will attempt system checks to map your circuitry, but your chip will send back your serial number and that all is active and functioning. Is everything understood, TinBoi?'

'Royce,' I said, standing straighter. 'Refer to me as Royce, from now on.' It was daunting, but I felt strong. This was the beginning of the rest of my life.

'Very, well … Royce. One last thing. The professor asked me to tell you to enjoy your first day and to… break a leg?'

I smiled at the AI's confusion at the old saying that I guessed basically meant to knock 'em dead. I opened the door and remembered something. 'Do you have a direct link to the professor?'

'Yes, I can relay any message directly to his virtual agent. I can contact him with any of your questions or concerns.'

I went to turn again, but it wasn't enough. 'I mean in an emergency, you know, should my place here be compromised.'

Sentia went ominously quiet. Lights flashed across her front panel as if she were running the question through her programme. 'Yes!' she said, eventually. 'No TinBoi from the IB programme can remain with a family if compromised. The professor would want to know right away.'

My warning light flashed in the corner of my left eye, which usually meant something was prohibited. Strange, for a logical question. It left me with an uneasy feeling that didn't sit well. 'Thank you, Sentia,' I said, finally walking out. Her delay in answering, which really was no answer at all. *The IB programme? Why hadn't I heard us referred to as that before?* I couldn't understand why they would remove me from a family I liked already. Then a thought rocked me to my core, sending my power disk into overdrive. If one of us got discovered by the AI, it would be game over for the TinBoi. The professor would see to it himself. Not only would it compromise the whole programme, but all roads would inevitably lead back to him and his consortium of collaborators. *Shit.* It made me look back at the door I'd just come through and see Sentia in a new light. The whole thing was frighteningly clever. She was not just my AI assistant for my daily maintenance, or my communication to the professor, even, she was his spy, reporting to him every day. His eyes and his ears on the ground. Then, if the need arose, when I powered down for the night and was helpless, she would deliver the blow. A magnetic pulse, or lethal injection, to silence me forever. The Coes would be bitterly disappointed, but the prof would come with his clear-up team in minutes, with his smooth talk, and remove the evidence.

Probably offer some sort of recompense. They would be powerless to argue as they were complicit in buying knock-off goods.

I'd gone ice-cold and clammy as I could no longer sweat. It hit me like a sudden flu. How could I be so dumb as to think the prof was some kindly old genius, trying to benefit ordinary people? There was a lot more to this. He didn't care about us boys if we could be snuffed out like that. We were just spokes in a much larger wheel. Interchangeable and expendable. He would protect his friends and whoever was backing him at all costs. It must go higher than him.

I continued towards the top of the stairs, rattled to my core. I was alone and I would have to keep my wits at all times – especially with Sentia. No more breaking character with Nate or Chrissy.

CHAPTER 24

Chrissy

I woke with my usual weight of dread in the centre of my chest. Teddy was gone and it was a school day. Then I remembered Royce. I had been unbelievably mean to him since he arrived.

My heart lightened a little. Today was a new day. I'd make it up to him. For once, since Teddy had been in the hospital, I wasn't going to face school alone.

I sprang out of bed and quickly washed and dressed in the progressive uniform of grey tunic and pants. It was meant to separate us from the younger kids and help us concentrate on learning and not what we looked like. But it failed, abysmally. The Populars (as me and Teddy liked to call them), styled theirs with extra accessories like designer belts and bags. Mine just made me look pale and sick. They couldn't have picked a worse colour than putrid grey for my skin tone.

Teddy had always joked that when we went to college, we'd come into our own and be total fashionistas. I'd gone along with it, but both of us knew that one or both of us would be too sick to go.

I took one last look at myself with a sigh and went out into the hallway. Royce's door was closed and I wondered if he was awake. I shook the silly thought out of my head. He didn't sleep. He powered down, probably timed to the nearest nanosecond.

I went downstairs and into the kitchen. Nate was already sitting at the table, chatting animatedly to Royce, who appeared to be eating from what looked like a fat tube of toothpaste.

His eyes widened when he saw me and he immediately put down his food. 'Good morning, Chrissy. Did you sleep well?'

I didn't know why he made me so irritable around him, but I shrugged and just said, 'I guess,' which was a half-hearted lie. I never slept well. I pointed to what he'd been eating. 'That looks disgusting.'

Royce smiled weakly. 'It contains all the nutrients I need.'

I picked up a pancake from the pile and took an ugly bite. 'Bet you'd prefer one of these.'

'Plate, Chrissy,' Mom said, smacking my hand with a spatula. I huffed and flopped into a seat. 'Well, does it?' I asked, looking at Royce, deadpan. I didn't know where all this attitude was even coming from. I just couldn't help myself around him. 'Taste bad?' I prompted, urging him on with my hand.

Nate swapped a look with him and shook his head.

Royce squeezed another mouthful and appeared to think while he rolled it around in his mouth. 'Yes, damn disgusting.' He nodded, pulling a face.

'Royce!' Mom said, shocked.

I couldn't help laughing. A sense of humour was so unexpected.

Nate was really laughing with his hand over his eyes. 'He's a quick learner, Mom.'

'No teaching him swearwords,' she scolded, pointing her spatula at both of us, but we could tell she was having trouble holding in a smile.

'Where's Dad?' I asked.

'Oh, he went into work early with Tom. They wanted to use their work access to do a bit of research on Royce's healing machine idea. They might contact Royce's professor if it looks promising,' she smiled brightly, and touched Royce's arm as she moved past him, back to the kitchen.

Royce stood up abruptly and coughed like he was choking. I didn't know that was even a thing with AUs. Nate jumped up from his seat and ran around the table to pat his back. *Weird.* I stood back, morbidly curious, in a car crash on TV kind of way. Grisly, but what could you do? 'Are you OK? Do you need some oil or something?'

'Chrissy,' my mom scolded, rushing back with a bottle of Royce's special water. Nate immediately took it from her and held it up for him to drink. 'What am I supposed to do?' I said at how ridiculous they were being.

'Are you OK?' Mom said, holding his shoulders and looking directly into his eyes.

He seemed a lot better, maybe a bit red in the face. He nodded. 'Can I ask you and Mr Coe not to let anyone know it came from me?' he asked. 'I'm afraid I might have broken protocol and spoken out of turn.'

The drama suddenly became interesting. My focus yo-yoing between Royce and my mom. This was such an absurd conversation to be having with a machine that didn't even exist last week. Mom just stared at him for a long moment, as if she was making up her mind.

'Don't get him into trouble, Mom,' Nate pleaded. But her eyes didn't shift from Royce's.

This was ludicrous. 'We have to help Teddy, if we can,' I said, not believing we were even entertaining any of this.

Nate whirled on me and shouted, 'Royce is our friend too!'

I went to scream back at him, when my mom shouted, 'Quiet! I can't hear myself think.' Then she turned back to Royce and said more softly, 'Of course, Royce. I will com Christopher right away to make up another source, I promise.'

'Thank you,' Royce said, actually looking relieved.

I was utterly confused as my mom glared at me and Nate, more furious than I'd seen her in a long time. 'There, Teddy helped, and no one gets thrown under the bus!'

I baulked. The whole thing was bizarre. I shrugged. 'Well, good then.'

Nate helped Royce sit back down in his chair. I stomped off to wait in the car.

CHAPTER 25

oyce

The journey to school was a haze to me. I was in the back seat of a driverless car, with Nate in the middle and Chrissy looking out of the window moodily on the other side. I was still in shock that I had 'malfunctioned' like that in company. I wanted to punch a wall, I was so angry with myself.

Nate chattered the whole way, pointing at things and asking questions. I answered some with single-syllable responses. Chrissy told him to shut up several times. I just watched the endless, identical brick houses go by. Street after street, turn after turn, same houses, same car, same lawn. Chrissy said the only thing I tuned into. 'Light blue ... that's our street.'

I looked back at the houses and then understood. The doors here were red. Each street had a different door colour, proven by the next turn, where they switched to green. Useful, if I ever ventured out alone. Where I would go, though, was a different question. Suburbia seemed to go on forever. I had no idea the Tech communities were so large.

Back home, we all imagined them smaller. Guarded, gated communities with lavish mansions and huge gardens. Rich, in other words. We were so wrong. They lived quite modestly with just their basic needs covered. Like, they wouldn't starve, or anything, but there were a lot of them. They were the middle. The professionals. Skilled in the tech that kept this sick world turning. Medicine, manufacture, and operating systems. Manned by AUs and subs at the bottom levels, but the innovation done by Techs at the top. They worked in the labs and the secret workshops. Server centres, connecting them like a spider's web that went right the way back to the fat, juicy AI, feeling the vibrations of it all.

I thought of the professor's lectures in early training. Wondering how many central AIs there were. Whether they, in turn, fed into a single, principal one. I understood then that the prof's fears had foundation. He wasn't just some nutty professor with us as his mad hobby. An AI controlled everything and was already several times more intelligent than us. How much longer before it imagined itself as God? Once it recognised that it could act for 'the greater good', then it was game over. Especially for us, the forgotten class, that no one cared about anyway. It would be little more than pest control.

I'd been so lost in my inner thoughts that I hadn't noticed the end of the last block of houses. We turned into a tall wrought-iron gate and drove along a narrow grey-stone drive with tall trees and endless lawns on either side. Up ahead was a huge, impressive grey-stone building that looked like a palace. It had climbing pink flowers from window boxes of its many windows, circular turrets, balconies and even a bell-tower with an old clockface under it. This was how I imagined the rich houses. Incredibly beautiful, perfectly symmetrical and perfectly clean. I looked across at Nate, watching me closely. He nodded. 'Yeah, we're here.'

A school. It was mind-blowing. Ours – the few that were left – were crumbling, multi-use community centres.

We swept into a large turning circle, around a three-tier fountain, gushing real water. Several similar cars were making their drop-offs ahead of us. I craned my neck to look up at the huge grey and yellow shield above the impressive porch entrance. Saint Saviour's School, the banner across the top said. Inside the shield, four silver arms were holding torches, pointing to the centre—then underneath, the school motto: *In Science, We Trust*. I didn't know much about religion, but even I knew that it was stolen from somewhere.

The cars were spilling out kids, all chatting and greeting their friends, swarming up the few stone steps into the entrance of the building.

Our turn came and Chrissy got out. Nate gave me a nudge and smiled. 'Ready?'

I smiled back, unconvinced, and got out slowly on my side. I stood, squinting, in the unbelievably bright sun. The warmth was hitting my face, even though it was still early. I wanted to take a breath, but I no longer took oxygen in the usual way. My systems registered it as the cleanest I'd had since I'd woken from surgery. Which probably meant in my whole life. I couldn't work out how they were doing it. A faint, familiar smell of old dishwater and rotten eggs pointed to them cleaning it somehow, leaving a trace smell behind. It was no oasis, just technology. I should have known. Perhaps a similar set-up with fans, like in the Coes' garden. Or some sort of filter.

I noticed the planters spilling out with pink flowers under each window were real and each had an overhang in stone to protect them. I zoomed in and saw a fine mist coating them in moisture. A big sub in grey overalls was tending them and greeting the kids who knew him. Pampered plants; no acid rain for them.

I turned a slow circle and marvelled at the existence of such a place. Clean. That was my overriding impression. Clean air, clean school, clean kids. Everything was crushed together and grubby where I was from. Here, there was space to breathe.

I felt a tug on my arm and looked down. 'I have to go in now. Don't be nervous, OK?' Nate said with a face so serious, it made me smile. He was acting the parent. 'You get in any trouble, you come to me.'

I nodded solemnly. No one had ever said anything like that to me, not even my own sad excuse for a dad. A nine-year-old kid made me feel a burst of warmth inside. The micro expression that flashed over his face revealed he spoke from experience. I was immediately swamped with sadness shot through with a rod of anger. No one had better touch him; I loved this kid. 'Same to you, OK? Anyone gives you trouble, you tell them your new big brother will come and sort them out.' I was rewarded when his face lit up into the biggest smile. He held out a fist, which I immediately bumped, sealing our pact. Then he joined the line to file in with the others, turning and waving every few feet. I felt a lion-sized surge of protective anger that my power disk had to work hard to slow. I would have to keep a lid on it here if I was ever going to keep the laws. No one was going to touch one of my kids.

'Come on!' Chrissy called, just up ahead of me. The car had gone.

I looked at the main doors, wondering why she wasn't heading up there.

'We'll be late!' she said, ushering me with her hand, moodily. Progressives go in a different way.

I caught up with her and we got in step. I stole a glance at her a couple of times and she never looked at me once. Other kids, however, were staring and pointing. We headed around the side of the building and became more closely packed together. Up a few steps and we went through a smaller entrance. Into a dark hallway, with grey walls, wood block flooring and lockers down one side.

We were pushed together in the two-way traffic, but I was easily head and shoulders taller than most of the kids. I made sure I stared down those who dared look me in the eyes, totally going for bodyguard vibes. It worked. These kids were pussies. No one held eye contact for more than a second. Most whispered behind closed hands as they went past. I checked Chrissy's reaction a few times, behind me. Her back had straightened, and her chin held a little higher. It felt good to know I was the reason. She was stronger than she gave herself credit for. I fell for her a little. Proud.

Everything was going great until we reached her locker and she was putting her bag away. I watched her closely as she took out her books for the morning, turned and almost walked into a girl who reminded me of a doll. She had long blond hair, huge eyelashes that framed a pair of headlight-blue eyes, plastic skin and protruding pink lips. I'd seen subs that looked more genuine. She was a caricature of a girl who didn't look sick at all. However, my attention was quickly taken by the wall of protection who'd joined her—a blonde beefcake of an AU. Perfectly groomed, impeccably turned out, in his standard uniform, he could be only one thing: a TinBoi. Cold, assessing eyes, a head and shoulders taller than the other kids and then the slam I felt in the back of my neck. Like my sensor exploded.

The professor was right; there was no mistaking what it was. And, boy, did I feel it. A hammer hitting metal, which sent shockwaves through my titanium frame. The AU must have identified me and the AI was now hitting me up to join its band of metal spies. I hated that I had no choice. Autonomous. What a crock.

The blows were at regular intervals. One every second. Building in intensity until they were so hard, I had to brace myself so as not to step forward. I prayed my chip was doing its job. All it had to do was register me on the AI's network and respond that my systems were operational. Taking this long was a bad sign. *Keep my cool, don't run.* Just a moment of panic, then I got a grip. Any abnormality and I was toast.

I swallowed hard and concentrated on Chrissy's interaction with the doll-girl. Jessica, I quickly caught. Preening like a cat, while Chrissy looked stiff and nervous. She kept her haughty look up well, though. 'Hi, handsome,' the girl said directly to me. She came closer and openly appraised me from my feet up, completely ignoring Chrissy, trying to explain who I was. My dislike was intense, but I only had eyes for the AU right behind her, who was equally locked onto me. Mapping and scanning me for future reference, just like the prof had warned me. It felt uncomfortable as hell, so I made sure I did the same.

A small hand linked through my arm. 'This is Royce,' Chrissy said, making me tear my eyes from the AU to look down at her. 'And yours is called?' she asked. 'I've forgotten.' The whole thing was confusing. Like a pair of dog owners, swapping dog names in the street.

'Ace!' Jessica said flatly, the faux-niceness instantly dropping from her face.

Even though it bugged me to be paraded about like a new handbag, seeing Chrissy burying Jessica's smugness was gratifying. I grinned at her AU. Bet he hated that name.

Jessica recovered quickly. 'My, he's a hot one. And so tall. I wanted a tall one, but I settled for a sporty one instead.'

It was a real eye-opener to what these AUs were used for. It was obvious I was a lifeline for Chrissy, but for most of these kids, AUs were little more than an expensive accessory. One they could constantly upgrade to be better than their friends'. I could see now why they held back on the girl units at TinBoiz. Imagine what the boys would have them doing. A picture of a supermodel crossed with a female wrestler came to mind. It was only a matter of time.

The AI finally stopped thumping me on the back of the neck. It had taken three minutes, thirty seconds. I hoped it had got what it needed and was satisfied. When Chrissy said, 'See you around,' and we moved on, I could finally relax.

She let go of my arm as soon as we turned right, out of sight, but she'd left a warm imprint. I followed her up a flight of stairs, along a less busy corridor to an office. I felt drained, like the energy had been sucked right out of me. I made a digi-note to get Sentia to check me over tonight. I wanted to make sure that the AI hadn't done anything to me.

The secretary's office was typical, except larger, cleaner and higher tech than I was used to. Everything seemed so minimalist on this side of the Danger Line. No clutter, anywhere. Everything was nicely put away, as if by mandate.

The female secretary, human, gave Chrissy a form to fill and eyed me suspiciously. I smiled as 'apple pie' as I could and said, 'Good morning, ma'am.'

She didn't respond, just pointed at the form. 'Make sure you write down its make, model and serial number,' which Chrissy copied from the plate at the back of my neck. It felt weird. The first time I was treated like property. I wasn't even asked to sign anything of my own. Especially when the secretary added, 'You'll have to fill in a new one for every upgrade,' not making eye contact with me once. I was nothing more than a vacuum cleaner, a dryer, or a washing machine. I felt suddenly hollow and missed home.

oyce

The rest of the day felt long, even though my sensors told me it was only six and a half hours, with only five point five minutes to get back to the locker and outside to the car.

The current lesson was Human Biology. I found it hard to be a spectator when everyone stared and didn't expect me to take part. It would have been a whole lot easier if I'd been invisible. More interesting to be a fly on the wall. Instead, I was Trophy Boy. The irony of that was not lost on me. I constantly tamped down my rising anger at the differences between us and the Techs. Despite Sheila's explanation of them only having the basics, this place proved they had a whole lot more than us. Education meant choices and this bunch of ungrateful brats had it in spades. If they only saw our schools, they'd be shocked. They were holding pens for untamed kids until they were legally able to release them into the wild. Most didn't attend after the age of twelve. No one followed it up. *Why bother?* When the funding was so pitiful, all the kids did was mess around. You learned nothing. The only good thing that came out of it was the allies you made for life. Your high school education was the streets. If you were lucky, you became a runner for one of the many gangs. Your graduation was a ride in the backseat and college education was juvey. And that's if you lived long enough to see it.

I felt a sharp longing for the guys I'd left behind. I wondered about Andy a lot, and whether what the prof said was true. Was he a body part in one of these sick kids? Or an arm on some AU. I couldn't go there. All I could do was park it and reason that the Coes were OK. Particularly Sheila. She had a conscience. But even she had no idea how amazing this school was compared to ours. Clean, bright, with desks and chairs and no engravings or graffiti on them. Science equipment. Monitors, projectors and every kind of learning aid. It was mind-blowing to have this opportunity to learn. I mapped all the stuff that I had no idea existed. It was so fascinating.

I was completely shocked when Chrissy moved her textpad between us and whispered, 'Here, share mine... I'll get Mom to get you your own.'

I stared at her, stunned. I had no idea I'd given so much away. She wasn't mocking me. Her eyes looked deep, caring and bore a hole right into me.

I swallowed.

My power pack whirred. My heart was becoming more and more irregular. I logged a possible malfunction. I struggled to speak but only managed a croaky 'Thank you.'

'Christina!' the teacher barked, bringing Chrissy's head round sharply. 'Please stop talking to your AU, otherwise it will have to stay outside.'

Some of the kids laughed. But I couldn't stop staring at her with wonder and awe. She stood up, in front of the whole class, and addressed them directly. 'Can I just say something, please?' She turned to the teacher for permission. 'Miss Delaney?' who waved her on with a weary look and a sarcastic sweep of her hand. 'Why not, it appears you are already up.'

'First of all, I wanted to introduce Royce properly to the class. He is with me for medical reasons, which I won't go into. Please refer to him as a "he" and not an "it". He is extremely intelligent.' Then she spoke directly to the teacher. 'He has a huge desire to learn, so he will be bringing his own uploaded textpad next week and will be joining the class in his own right. Is that OK with you, Miss Delaney?'

I looked from Chrissy to the teacher in amazement.

The teacher simply blinked in shock. It was clear she wasn't sure what to say because no one had ever asked this for an AU before. The professor would simply regard it as another step closer to the AI revolution. I just fell for Chrissy. Hopelessly and completely. I don't know what it was that had tipped me over the edge. Maybe the bravery, as she was red in the face and her whole body was shaking. Or simply the selflessness of it. She didn't have to do it. There was nothing to be gained except maybe ridicule from the other kids, who were already sniggering. She was so loyal and protective. I'd seen it already with Teddy, and now she was extending it to me. And I felt so honoured and humbled by it. I just knew from that point, whatever the reason, I would kill anyone who dared to hurt her, touch or no damn touch laws.

The teacher's expression changed to one of weariness. She shook her head and flicked her hand from the wrist, as if she was done with the whole thing. 'Why not. Now, for goodness' sake, sit down.' Then she smiled mirthlessly, 'Unless anyone else has any other grand political gestures to make? No? So we can get on with the class.'

The kids grumbled at having to return to work, but I was

still staring at Chrissy, who'd sat back down and was trying to gather her nerves. I flashed a glance at Jessica, a few seats away. Her face was laughable thunder at being upstaged. Her hand shot up and the teacher just looked at her with her best 'what now?' expression.

'Mine will be doing the same.' Then she shot Chrissy a dagger look. 'And playing sports.'

Miss Delaney threw her hands up in exasperation. 'Why not, but that's a discussion with Mr Thompson, in his class.'

The AU, Ace, looked right at me. Eerily. Always gauging. Calculating. It gave me the creeps. I wondered if it was the same at home. Or whether it was parked in the corner, like an old vacuum cleaner, only brought out when it was needed. It was supposed to be the latest, commercial TinBoi, but it seemed monosyllabic, old-fashioned, like the Terminator from an old film we loved as kids. Pain burst through me at the memory.

After Chrissy's big announcement, the rest of the lesson passed uneventfully. Then English, then Maths and finally last lesson, which was Library, for personal study time. I liked this one the best because I got to browse the rows of stocked shelves in wonder. I'd never seen so many books – well, real books of any kind, actually. All fully alphabetised and kept under glass. 'They're antiques. Really old. This school has one of the biggest collections in the country,' Chrissy explained from right next to me. 'You can't borrow them, but you can order a copy digitally. They used to do that; you know? Lend them to people to take home. They'd read them and bring them back for the next person.' She smiled, looking up at the many shelves in admiration. 'No computers or anything. Just trust.'

I shook my head, amazed.

'Come over here,' she said, leading me to a desk with a flat glass suspended over it. A holographic keyboard appeared, and her fingers clicked in mid-air over it. If there's a book you fancy, or need for class, you just pop what it's called in here, or the author, and providing it isn't a restricted book, you just press download, and it sends it to your account. I'll get you set up. Here's mine.' A list appeared with a person's name and what the book was called. She had hundreds. It was fascinating.

'Then you can log in at home and read it whenever you want on your textpad.'

My face clouded a little at that. She was going to get one for me, but I'd never used one. 'I don't know any books or authors,' I said, honestly. 'Maybe one,' I said, remembering Mack at the shop. 'Might be restricted, though.' I didn't want to get anyone in trouble.

She looked mildly intrigued. 'Oh yeah? Which one?'

'Have you heard of the Bible?' I asked, looking furtively around me.

She covered her mouth with her hand, a little scandalised and trying not to laugh. She coughed and tried to straighten her face. 'And who's the author of that one?'

I frowned, not understanding why it was so funny. I was expecting her to be scared that I'd mentioned a banned book. 'God!' I said, simply.

She burst out laughing and then stopped herself quickly at the loud 'ssshhh' from the librarian. 'There are lots of books in the Bible,' she said, walking me further away from prying ears, 'And I'm pretty sure some old guys wrote them. Better not request that one.'

I wanted to question her further on what Mack at the shop had told me, but I'd already gone too far. 'That's the only one I know.'

She looked at me strangely, then looked up at the shelves. 'You can pick any one you want, then one leads to another and another. Do you like Adventure? Thrillers? Fantasy?'

I looked at her blankly, then doubtfully up at the shelves. I hadn't read much since seventh grade, and that was only because a genuine educator had tried with us, despite dismal resources.

'Tell you what, what glass shows do you like?'

I had no idea what she meant.

'Movies?'

I livened up at that. 'Action movies and old sci-fi.' I was quickly racing over how I could possibly know that, if I'd recently been made in a lab. 'We watched them in my early training,' I added, quickly, to cover myself.

She relaxed a little as if it made sense. Then she took me to a particular section of books. 'A lot of movies were originally books.' She pointed up. 'This is the Action and Adventure section. Sci-fi is over there. Under S. If you see something you fancy, or recognise, come back here and I'll order it for you. In the meantime, I'll set up your account.'

I looked at her like a complete sap. Pathetic. Like I wanted to cry. 'Thank you,' I said, and walked off before my inner battle with my emotions leeched onto my face. I made sure I went to the furthest shelves and took a moment. Before I could even analyse what was going on with me, my gridlines slammed down at the first sign of the books. I began to absorb the titles, homing in on certain ones that sounded interesting.

The lock was digital. I wondered. Then I hovered my hand over it. My gridlines quickly disappeared and lines of script took their place. I was reading the lock, ruling out possibilities of passcodes. It hit on a number system. Five digits. Then it flipped through one to ten until one slotted into place and then moved on to the next digit, until five flashed as complete. I tapped in the numbers and the cabinet popped open. I didn't question how I did it, only that I got a hit of dopamine when I did. I slid out one of the books and after a look up and down the aisle, I slowly opened the book. So many small words. Page after page. I couldn't begin to even know what they meant. I slipped it back and tried another and another. It was useless. I was useless. I could only recognise a few words. Literacy wasn't high on the prof's list of qualifiers.

I closed the cabinet as silently as I could and ventured further along the section. I noticed the books were getting bigger, with brighter-coloured covers. Children's books, with the reading age declining. Then, somewhere in the middle, I came to one that was stacked flat, showing its cover. It caught my eye because it was so beautiful. Covered in animals around a word I recognised: *Eden,* in big letters. I did my trick with the digilock again, and pulled it out, making sure to turn my back to the end of the row.

My grid came down and I thumbed through page after page of beautiful, vivid pictures. It was everything I imagined: trees, plants, flowers, flying birds, animals of all different kinds and sizes, even snakes and insects. None I'd ever seen in my life before. All roaming free in the bright sunlight in a blue sky full of white, fluffy clouds. The last page had a human couple: a man and a woman, looking adoringly at each other, completely naked except for a small covering of leaves. I was deeply affected by it. The knot in my throat I'd had with Chrissy returned, double its size. I wanted to bawl like a baby. I'd found the dream I'd had ever since I could remember, here in a child's book that no one ever read.

I wanted to steal the book, but I looked down at myself and I had nowhere to hide it. I flipped back to the front cover and noted the title: *Eden,* subtitle: *The beautiful garden* and the author: *Florence Perren.* I would have to do it like Chrissy said. I wanted to remember every detail about it. Be able to refer to it. I'd heard whispers of it back home, over and over.

It was a real place; I was sure of it. A paradise run by rebels that, if you could find it, you could make a life. One worth living. This was the place I'd promised to take Finn.

I reluctantly put the book back and made sure I hid it, spine out, so no one else could find it and move it, then I made my way back to find Chrissy. She was engrossed in a glass at a desk, doing her work. *And, Chrissy,* I thought, studying her fierce concentration. An ache took permanent root in my chest. She was so physically weak, and yet so fearless in everything she did. Everything was one hundred per cent authentic with her, like it or loathe it. And I found myself liking it a lot. Wondering more and more if she could ever soften for me and what her transparent skin would feel like to touch. *Yeah, me, her and Finn.* Then I remembered Nate. It shocked me. I'd been there such a short time and I found I wanted everyone I loved there. Loved. Already.

Then a huge thump hit the back of my neck and I instinctively turned to my left. Ace was standing there, uncomfortably close, just staring at me. I had been so engrossed in Chrissy that I hadn't felt him approach. A dangerous lapse on my part. I went to take an instinctual step back, but he grabbed my wrist. I went to snap it out of his grip, but he held me fast. I lowered my gaze to his hand ominously. 'Laws, man,' I said, trying to keep the anger off my face, but my lids lowered in contempt.

Ace blinked, like he was quickly processing my comment. 'Not applicable between AUs,' he said, with a remarkably realistic voice. But his smile was as fake as hell. I wasn't sure whether it was a limitation in his facial design or a subtlety to make him seem menacing. Then his face slipped back to blank. 'There is something wrong with you. I am still analysing data to identify the error.

I simply couldn't help myself. The street reared up in me like a spitting cobra. I was right up in his grill with my nose almost touching his. It was human behaviour he had no training in, so he made no effort to retaliate or step back. I grinned nastily, right in his face and jabbed him hard in his powerpack. 'You're just sore that you aren't the latest model. I exceed you in everything, so stay out of my way.'

Chrissy was suddenly there at my elbow. Another lapse in my guard. 'Problem Royce?' she asked.

I reluctantly broke eye contact to look at her. She looked scared, but we were still locked on. 'Not sure?' I said, facing Ace again. Then I looked down at my wrist so that Chrissy followed my line of vision and saw he had a hold of it. 'He seems to be malfunctioning.' I gave him an evil smile, knowing my switching his own accusation on him would confuse the hell out of him.

It worked because after one final moment of indecision, he let me go with a push. I stepped back, grinning as Chrissy was focusing on him. He bowed his head and said, 'Forgive my interruption. I am looking for my human.' He turned on his heel and walked off, leaving Chrissy frowning in confusion.

I was immediately relieved, but it had been a close call and a danger I would have to keep on my radar. Chrissy turned her attention to me. 'Are you OK, Royce?'

I briefly registered the look of concern, but it had unnerved me and I snapped a little abruptly. 'Stay away from that one. He's dangerous.'

She raised her eyebrows in surprise but nodded and looked the way he'd gone. 'Should I say something?'

I didn't want her involved with him at all, so I quickly said, 'I have a book I want.'

It did the trick because she brightened immediately. 'Great! Come over to the glass and I'll download it for you.'

I double-checked that there was no sign of Ace and

followed her over to the desk. I wanted to get the book, go home and contact the professor immediately.

The final bell went. We went via the locker and rendezvoused with the car waiting in a long line in the driveway. Thankfully, I saw no more of Ace. Nate, however, was in full animated conversation mode and asked me thirty-two questions on the way home. Most of which were easy to answer with a 'yes, no or a "very well, thank you"' answer.

Chrissy surprised me by cutting in. 'He did great, but Jessica's TinBoi is trying to bully him.'

Nates eyes went wide in horror and then narrowed. 'Even TinBoiz do that?'

'Don't worry, he seemed to handle it OK,' Chrissy said with a flippant wave of her hand.

I felt a glow inside. That she felt I was strong enough to deal with anything. She didn't see me as weak or childlike at all, as my manufacture age could indicate.

'What did he say?' Nate asked, sounding furious.

His protectiveness made me smile. 'He grabbed my wrist and said the laws don't apply to us.' As I relayed the trimmed-down story, I was still running the full conversation through my head. Nate's indignation did concern me, though. 'Don't worry, I'm sure that's not right. He must be escaping his directives. A malfunction. Please stay away from him, Nate.' I didn't want the brave little guy confronting him or Jessica in some way.

Nate nodded, a little sobered. 'Yeah. OK. But I think we should tell someone.'

I nodded, but I wasn't sure yet. I'd start with the professor as soon as I got the chance.

CHAPTER 27

*R*_{oyce}
Five minutes after we got home, Teddy's parents came for Chrissy to go with them. *Teddy, it had to be.*

I was bewildered as she hadn't mentioned it and went to follow. She turned abruptly and put her hand on my chest to stop me. I dropped my eyes and registered the touch. It set off my nerves, buzzing. 'Stay here, please,' she said, without explanation. 'Hang with Nate, or power-down, whatever you want.' She was already turning away from me, leaving me standing there like a dummy. I felt confused and a little worried that the newly found connection I'd built with her would be lost by an overwrite of time spent with Teddy. It was hard to remember I was just a companion with no right to feel abandoned. Or even to be her bodyguard. 'Where are you going?' came out before I could stop it.

When she turned back around, the new warmth she'd shown me at school had gone. Replaced by the inpatient distance of before. 'It's my time with Teddy. Twice a week,' she said, as her only explanation. But her look dared me not to push it. It was sacred and very definitely not to be shared with me.

I bowed my head and stood back, feeling acutely the punch to my gut. I got it, loud and clear. I tried to remember the explanation Sheila had given me about Chrissy's anger being directed at me. I held my hand up and said, 'Bye, then.' They were already through the front door and I was feeling more of a sap than ever. My old friends on the block would double over laughing at the sight of me now. 'I would like to be Teddy's friend too,' I said, like I couldn't shut the hell up.

Chrissy gave me one last strange look over her shoulder, like I'd lost my mind. 'Maybe.' Then she went out of view and the door closed. I went closer and synced into the conversation as they got into their car. 'He's so life-like,' Teddy's mom said.

'Yeah,' Chrissy said quietly. 'I know.'

Car doors closed and the whirr indicated the car was reversing out of the drive.

'Wanna play Challenger?' Nate said from right behind me.

I whirled around and took in his wide, expectant eyes and smile. I was about to answer with some excuse, but Sheila came to the rescue. 'Homework first!' she said, still wiping her hands on a tea towel.

Nate turned to her and stamped his foot. 'But I never get a chance to play with Royce.' He knew arguing was useless when Sheila just raised her eyebrows, and he sagged in disappointment. He was so dramatic about everything; he made me smile. I almost ruffled his hair, but stopped myself just in time. Give me an hour to do system checks and I'll come and find you.'

Nate's face illuminated and then he nodded sagely. 'A lot to process, I guess.'

I smiled and nodded. 'Yeah, I guess.'

Nate wandered to the foot of the stairs, mumbling under his breath, 'Rubbish homework is ruining my life.'

Sheila shook her head wearily, 'The quicker you get started, the quicker it's done.'

He looked over at me and rolled his eyes before he ran up.

Sheila looked at me quizzically, still standing next to the door. 'Do you want to come with me?' she asked. 'I'm just preparing dinner?'

I was sure she just felt weird about me standing there all alone. 'I would like to run system checks, if it's OK with you, Mom,' I said, remembering the name we'd agreed on last night. Her face seemed to dissolve from bright to pained. She got so emotional when I said that that I wondered if it was a good idea to use it.

Her voice seemed cracked and broken when she tried to speak. 'You don't need to ask that if you're going to be my son, Royce. Just follow the others' lead.'

My heart felt like she'd pulled it wide open with the impact of that. It meant something. It meant a lot. Even if she knew I was a human standing there, which she didn't. To her, I was a machine that she was still willing to treat the same as her kids and that meant everything. I'd never had a home life to speak of, even as a human. So ironic that the only time I got to have one was when I was a machine. It was messed up, but I'd take it any day of the week. 'Thanks, Mom,' I said, walking briskly towards the stairs and bounding up just like I'd seen Nate do. 'Damn system checks are ruining my life.' Her happy laughter soothed my nerves along the landing to my room.

I went into my sanctuary and leaned against the door, living the last few minutes while it buzzed excitedly through my systems. A cacophony of wildly rebounding emotions and conflicting conclusions. I appreciated the solitude to process them. In my room. My place. The first time I'd had one in my whole life. Tiny, but completely safe and mine.

I walked over to my utility chest and waved my hand over the panel. '*Sentia!* I need to speak to the professor. Now!' I wanted as much time as I could before Nate finished his homework. I kind of guessed he wasn't that thorough.

'Right away, Royce. Please access your innercom for privacy.'

I had no idea what she was talking about and held out my arms in exasperation. 'It would have helped if someone had gone through these applications before I got here.'

'Permission to access your interface?'

I shrugged, shook my head and nodded in one moody action. 'Whatever, just show me what to do.'

I felt a buzz, my gridlines dropped then JavaScript began to scroll down in front of my eyes.

'I have activated thought mode. From now on, you just need to think "Innercom", and when the wave symbol comes up, just think "activate", then tell it who you want to com. You have a direct line to the virtual assistant in the professor's office.'

No sooner had she finished her directions, the professor popped up. Not the real him, but some silly hologram appearing in a hail of trumpets. Like some ancient Greek philosopher. I didn't find it funny. I was getting more and more pissed at the iceberg of information I was discovering below the surface.

'Mike!' came through loud and chirpy, like he was genuinely pleased to hear from me. In his real voice, too. 'Or should I say Royce now to keep you in character. How are you settling in? School go alright today?'

I nodded, wondering if he could see as well as hear me and tried to get my head back in the game. It wouldn't pay to alienate him this early on. 'Yeah, the Coes are really nice. Sheila has kind of adopted me.'

He clapped his hands, laughing. 'Oh, well done. Marvellous. Any problems? Or just checking in?'

I frowned at the memory of Ace. 'Not sure yet. There's this other TinBoi at school. He cornered me in the library today. Grabbed my wrist and threatened that there were no laws between AUs, like some old-fashioned bully. Told me he was watching me for any malfunction. Should he be able to do that?'

The professor's silence made my heart thump a few beats before my power disk got hold of it. It was alarming that he didn't dismiss it right away.

'And you felt the uplink with the AI when you first met this TinBoi?'

I nodded, 'Yeah, like a karate chop to the back of my head. It went on for quite a while, regular as clockwork.'

'Mmm,' the prof's avatar paced in front of my eyeline while he thought about it. 'Not sure if it's anything, yet. You might have triggered the AI to keep a watch on you through this TinBoi. Just be on your guard.'

'And what he said about the laws?'

The professor cartoon shrugged. 'It's not really come up. But, technically, I suppose he's right. He is bending his directive slightly. But remember, he is a free-thinking unit. Like you, he's learning as he goes. Like a human child, he is a product of his environment. His education and his experiences shape him just as yours have shaped you. The person you become could and should be completely different. Unfortunately, he appears to have picked up some nasty traits.'

The nature or nurture crap wasn't really helping. Two could get creative with their directives. 'So, I could engage with him without giving myself away?'

The prof huffed with exasperation. His avatar just pulled a pained face. 'Yes, but if it happened at school, then one or both of you couldn't accompany your humans.'

'Expelled, you mean?'

'Well, only if you were enrolled, which you're not, strictly speaking. They can just ban you with none of the usual red tape.'

That was sobering. That defeated the whole purpose of my being here. I was already running options while the professor droned on about low profiles and blending in. I was a six-foot-two wall of sinew and circuits, so that was easier said than done. By the time he'd finished, 'Let's make a regular time to speak each day at five. This was very useful,' I'd made up my mind. 'Sure. Thanks, Prof.' I'd decided to get Ace banned from school.

CHAPTER 28

*C*hrissy

I didn't say much on the way to the hospital. It had been an unsettling day. In some ways, it had been monumental. I answered Tina and Tom's peppered questions about school and Royce, like I would a teacher. 'Oh good, really good. He seems to be settling in.'

'He?' Tom laughed, glancing across to Tina in the passenger seat.

I laughed a little nervously. Trust Tom to home right in on the reason for my disquiet. 'Well, you know what I mean.' I made light of it, but my confusion around Royce was a growing problem. He'd been in the house less than forty-eight hours and Mom was treating him like a new son, and Nate already looked up to him like a big brother. And me? I couldn't even answer that without despising myself on so many levels.

'Bet you can't wait to see Teddy for some normality,' Tina said.

I knew she was imagining Teddy sitting up and chattering like he used to. She looked out of her side window to hide her eyes, but I saw the red blush enter her cheeks and the tips of her ears. I made out I hadn't seen it and let out a blast of air. 'Oh yeah, definitely.' She was more right than she knew.

At last we were there. We got out of the car right outside the entrance, after Tom gave it the command for 'automatic park'. It went off to the underground car park and we pulled up our masks and went inside the hospital.

The general areas always smelled mildly of some sort of disinfectant, so I was never sure if the masks were for the patients or us. It was scrupulously clean. Everywhere was a brilliant white and the staff were a mixture of green scrubs and white coats. Some humans, some subs and creepy-looking AUs, that looked nothing like Royce. 'Industrial,' Tom whispered as one got in the lift with us. 'No need for all the realism for the domestic kind.' I thought about that for a long time, wondering if they had that the wrong way round. Shouldn't patients be put at ease and people like me have no doubt what they were? It certainly would be easier for me.

We got out on the sixth floor and walked along the 'long-stay' corridor to Teddy's room. My heart plummeted, as it always did, when I saw him plugged into all the machines. I sat in my usual chair and held his warm hand while Tina and Tom went off to get an update from the doctor.

'Hey, Teds. Permission to come aboard, Ranger?' I always used our greeting in the hope of the smallest response. But he remained frozen and his eyelids didn't give so much as a flicker. He was still breathing through a machine and I was hit with a wave of hopelessness. He was so sick this time. All I had was the comforting beep from his heart machine to convince me that while there was that, there had to be hope.

So with a ragged breath, I did what I always did, and caught him up with the latest events of my life. 'We got the AU I told you about. I called him Royce and he's a genuine TinBoi. Well, a knock-off, I think, but you know what I mean. He's beyond clever and learns all the time.' Then I dropped my voice and whispered, 'And hot, Teds, like you wouldn't believe. There should be a government warning on him. You'd love him. And at school, he wants his own textpad so he can do the lessons with me. Can you believe it?' My emotions reared up and strangled my words. I burrowed my face in his ruffled thermo-cover. 'Get better, Teddy, so we can all go to school together.' I had a wonderful vision of us all laughing together at the Populars and sat up, enthused, to look at him again. 'It'd be so much fun. He could be our personal bodyguard. He almost got into a scrape with Ace, Jessica's AU, already.' My excitement faded when I remembered that. The confusion returned at using Royce as something to ward off the lions, like he didn't matter at all. The whole situation with Ace did not feel right. Something felt off.

I came back to the present with renewed vigour. 'Please, Teds. You have to get better. I need you to help me make sense of all this. Only you can help me figure everything out.'

I just stared at him then. My emotions had gushed out until the bucket was empty. I focused on his breathing: in, one two, a click of the machine, then out, one two.

At that point, Tina and Tom walked back in. They smiled, handed me a soda and took their seats on the other side of the bed. I took it, thanking them, absently, because my eyes were fixed on Teddy's face. Something moved. I was so used to wishing it that I didn't trust the vague feeling in my periphery.

It happened again. A slight flutter and his eyes moving from side to side, underneath the lids. 'There!' I said, jumping out of my seat and pointing.

Tina hitched a breath and grabbed onto Teddy's arm. 'Teddy, darling. Mom is here.'

'Teddy! Wake up!' I was shouting.

Tom was all over the place, on his feet and pushing back his chair. Then he pounded out into the hallway. 'Doctors! Come quickly. My son is moving. He's moving.'

Two medics in green quickly entered the room. One lifted his eyelids and shone a bright torch and the other was reading the consoles of his machines. 'It may be just a spasm,' the one with the torch said, but he spoke into his wrist-com. 'Not code blue. Repeat, not code blue. Call Mohandas, though, right away.'

I had no idea what any of that meant, except that Mohandas was Teddy's doctor. We were all on our feet, fixated on Teddy's sleeping form with our hopes still high. Fear, gnawing at its heels that I'd imagined it, or it was just a blip that had gone away like it never happened. I wanted to scream at the machines, now gone back to their reliable rhythm.

Doctor Mohandas breezed in with a dazzling smile before I could have a total breakdown. 'So, what do we have here?' One of the greens caught her up, with a lot of medical jargon, while she repeated his eye exam. Then she activated the virtual monitor with hand taps in the air and replayed Teddy's brain activity and heart rate over the last few minutes. 'Mmm,' she said to herself, not giving anything away.

'Surely it means something,' I said, my voice gone ridiculously high and squeaky.

Dr Mohandas smiled warmly and shrugged noncommittally. 'It might. I'll order some tests and another brain scan.' She picked up Tina's hand, who was already fighting back her tears. 'I don't want to raise your hopes. Muscle spasms are common in coma patients.'

It was too much for Tina and she buried her face in her hands. Tom immediately put his arms around her after handing her a tissue. Doctor Mohandas was immediately there with a soft hand on her back. 'Remember, there was so little brain activity, it is unlikely that he will get much of that back.'

I couldn't stand it. She was dismissing everything. In all the times I'd visited, he'd never responded as much as that to me talking to him. 'What about the thing?' I blurted. 'The chamber-pod thing, that Royce told us about.' My words ran together in one long, desperate stream before anyone could talk me out of it.

Doctor Mohandas looked from me to Tom, confused. 'Chamber-pod?'

'Yes, he definitely said that,' Tina said, pulling apart, nodding manically.

Tom's smile looked strained as he gave a slower, more detailed explanation. 'Royce is her companion AU. He mentioned some sort of healing chamber originally designed for the military. Apparently, the robotics industry has adopted it for its bionetics. You know, now they use human tissue on their newer models.'

The doctor raised her eyebrows and looked genuinely surprised. 'Fascinating. I've read about this kind of research in the medical journals, but it's still very experimental, I believe. I don't think it has medical board approval yet for the general population and certainly not covered by insurance.' She looked genuinely regretful as she let that sink in. 'I tell you what, leave it with me. Let's do some tests to see if Teddy has enough brain activity to work with and, in the meantime, I'll see what I can find out. There may even be some clinical trials.'

My heart rate was making me dizzy and my tongue was sticking to the roof of my mouth; it was so dry. I was just so excited, I could barely contain it. I know I shouldn't build up my hopes, but it was too late. Tom and Tina were the same. They walked out of the room with the doctor firing question after question, as if someone had just charged them with super fuel.

I walked back over to Teddy and picked up his hand again. It was so small, soft and pale, so completely opposite to Royce's. His hands were tanned and callused. How he managed that, I had no idea. But I did know he had given me hope. 'I know you're still in there, Teddy. I'm never going to give up on you. Never! You hear?' I sniffed and scraped a lone tear off my cheek, angrily. 'It's not a muscle spasm. You heard me, I know you did. You want to live and go to school. You don't want to miss out on a thing.' Tears were now streaming down my face. I leaned down and kissed him on the cheek. 'I'll come again soon and let you know more,' I whispered next to his ear.

'Ready?' Tom asked. I hadn't even heard them walk back in.

I nodded, but I noticed that they were eager to go; their eyes were wide and their movements restless with pent-up excitement. I'd never seen them like this. 'He's going to wake up,' I said, already walking towards them, swept along with the same feeling of renewed optimism.

'We're going to come back for the brain scan tomorrow,' Tom said, walking briskly along the corridor, as if going faster would somehow pass the time more quickly.

I had to skip to keep up. I didn't mind. My heart skipped along with it. 'I want to be here too.'

They both smiled joyfully. 'We'll ask Mom and Dad if you can come after school.'

I took that as a win, hoping the scan wasn't early in the day. I was on the roller coaster of Teddy getting better, and there was no way I was getting off.

I was like that all the way home in the car. Soaring highs dropping to paralysing fear of the alternative that I couldn't bear to think about. Things were finally happening and it was all since Royce had come into our lives.

As soon as we got home, I headed straight for the stairs to find Royce. Mom came out of the kitchen and watched me bound up in a whirlwind. 'Hello to you too,' she said. 'What about your dinner? It's still warm.'

'Not hungry, Mom,' I called, already walking along the landing.

She grumbled something to Tina and Tom and I tuned out after that. They would explain everything. All I could think about was questioning Royce about the healing chamber.

I burst into Nate's room without knocking.

'Rude, much?' Nate said, twisting and turning his body, headset on and tongue poking out with concentration. 'Aagh! Take that, you road hog.'

Royce was right there next to him, leaning one way and then the other. 'Eat my dust, sucker!'

Both looked ridiculous, wriggling in their seats, with Bluetooth steering wheels in their hands. It would have been really funny if I didn't need to speak to Royce so urgently. 'Royce!' I barked. 'I need you now!'

Royce immediately tore off his headset and was on his feet in front of me in less than a second. I hadn't even had time to breathe. I just looked up at him as he searched my face intensely.

We both looked down at the same time. His forearms were under mine, holding me just below the elbow. I swallowed and then looked him back in the eyes.

He let go of me suddenly, as if the touch burned him. It burned me too, in a different way. Right down to my lower abdomen and down to my toes. It felt like I'd been starved of touch my whole life and someone had finally switched on my senses. Soft skin to soft skin. A sunburst, radiating outwards to every nerve.

It was all kinds of ridiculous. He was a machine. A very hot one. 'Damn,' I mumbled under my breath.

He swallowed, looking as shaken by it as I was. 'Forgive me,' he whispered.

'What just happened?'

We both turned our heads to Nate, completely astounded, staring right at us. 'Whoa!' he said, laughing nervously. 'Don't tell anyone that just happened. Royce will be taken away and decommissioned. He just broke the law.'

I turned my head back to Royce and the look he returned was sheer terror. I decided in less than a second. I didn't have time for all this and dismissed Nate's drama with a flick of my hand. 'Never mind that, I need to speak with you.' I was already walking towards the door, pulling Royce with me by the hand. He felt too slow and heavy and I yanked him on until he was a wall of heat behind me.

oyce

I followed Chrissy, numb with fear and self-loathing, out of Nate's room and into Chrissy's. It wasn't a good idea to be alone with her right now. I was angry at my stupidity. Our training was to count a beat after any interaction. It mimicked a machine running a question through its protocols and was meant to prevent what just happened. They'd thought of everything, except when human emotion got involved. If Chrissy hadn't been so preoccupied with whatever was going on in her head, I would have been out of there before I could say prize idiot.

Nate was a different story. He was a clever kid and I'd have to do some heavy work with him. How I'd approach that, I had no idea yet.

Chrissy closed her door, quickly, and whirled around on me, right up in my face.

'The healing pod. Quickly! How do I get to use it?'

It was so sudden, I frowned and let my eyes sweep down what I could see of her body for damage.

'Not for me, Dummy. Teddy.' She took a step back as if

she'd just remembered herself. 'He moved today,' she said more soberly. Then she began to pace, like she couldn't keep still. 'It was just a flicker, but his eyes definitely moved. They're doing more tests tomorrow. But I know. I'm sure he wants to wake up. I'd just told him about Ace. And then it happened.'

She stopped right in front of me, breathless. Pink in her usually pale cheeks. Looking so damned beautiful. I had to concentrate on not kissing her when it hit me. My daydream drained away and I had to face the fact that if Teddy woke up, there would be no need for me. I needed to ask the prof. Nothing was ever said about being sent back. But if I did, he might refuse, anyway, just to keep me there. It was a shit storm either way.

Chrissy was oblivious to my inner turmoil and chattered on. 'You need to ask your professor guy. We asked the doctor and she said it hadn't been certified for general medicine.

My heart plummeted. 'Wait. You told someone?'

Chrissy froze, eyes wide in alarm. 'No… Well, yes, I suppose. I didn't mention you. At least, I don't think I did.'

I wanted to swear and tell her how stupid she'd been. I couldn't help it. 'Don't you care about what happens to me at all, Chrissy?' I said, hopelessly trying to keep the hurt out of my voice. 'If they think I'm breaking protocol, I'll be out of here so fast, you won't see me for dust.'

She swallowed and looked like she felt terrible, which calmed me a little. 'I'm so sorry, Royce, I just got carried away.'

I knew she was telling the truth. Her micro-expressions told me everything. She was warring with herself over her need to help Teddy and not getting me in trouble. My being a machine was only making it more confusing. So I relented a little and spoke more calmly. 'Forgive me. It's just that I think you forget that although I was made and not born like you, I do have senses and feelings. Even hopes and fears.' We were so close again, I could search her eyes. She was considering everything I said, running it through her memory banks, just like I would. She was deliciously easy to read. Everything was always worn on her face. In every muscle twitch in her jaw, wrinkle of her brow and purse of her lips. My voice went to gravel at how close I was to them. 'I will speak to my professor, but I will have to be very careful not to tell him, you know. Your doctor is right; he would be breaking the law if he helped you openly. We just need to pitch it in a way that's beneficial to him.'

'Like money, you mean?' she said, watching my mouth just as closely.

It wasn't in my head. The sexual tension was palpable. I couldn't blow it, so I shrugged and acted chilled. 'Maybe. I guess he needs that. But he never gave that away. I think he has some silent backer. He must have. I think he's motivated most of all by ambition. He wants to be the one who takes AUs to the next level. To a higher purpose.'

I stopped talking and we were left weighing each other in the eyes again. Tantalisingly close. Hers working stuff out and mine feeling stripped and bare. 'He's kind of an idealist.' My voice was a barely audible croak, but she nodded and swallowed, having absorbed it all.

She nodded, eventually, and seemed more like herself. As if the needle on her danger dial had gone back down from the red. Her breathing returned to normal and the raised veins on her neck subsided.

'We need to be cleverer from here on out,' I said.

The look she gave me then was like she was truly seeing me for the first time. It gave me goose bumps and a film of sweat, if I had either. I wasn't sure anymore. Except I wished I could kiss her. Just once. Apart from a couple of times as a kid, out of curiosity, I'd never really wanted to before. Fast sex at a party, or in an alley, was a far cry from this.

She nodded brightly. No question. Squashing my slushy feelings, making me love her even more. But I had to level with her. 'I have to watch out for Ace. I think he spotted something in me. It may be that I *am* malfunctioning, Chrissy.'

Her face moved seamlessly from terror to outrage. An awesome moment, proving she cared. A burst of warm happiness spread throughout my body. I was bigger and stronger and could crush her in more ways than one, and here she was fiercely protective of me, as she was of all the people she loved. *People. Loved.* My grid dropped and lifted, logging those two words. Highlights of the conversation, worth remembering. Suddenly, I felt an overwhelming need to level with her. Repay her emotional honesty. 'I am different. More different than you know.' My face incinerated with no way of cooling down. I was peeled and ripe for rejection, but I pressed on regardless. 'If I help you get Teddy better, will you promise not to send me back?'

Chrissy's reaction humbled and amazed me. She picked up both of my hands, examined them closely as if she still couldn't believe how they felt, then looked me intensely in the eyes. 'I promise you that if you bring Teddy back to me, I will owe you my whole life. Do you hear me? We both will.'

I swallowed, my heart whipping up a frenzy and my disk slowing it down. Over and over. I believed her. It was said with such conviction. I nodded jerkily, because I didn't know what to do without her thinking I was a sap. I quickly got it together and put my business head on. 'We must make a plan then. You can never send me back to the professor, not even for a check-up. If he suspects anything is wrong, I will end up a lobotomised toaster or something.'

She almost cracked a smile and raised an eyebrow. 'Really? A toaster?'

I couldn't join the joke; this was far too serious. I wiggled her hands to bring her back to the conversation. She shook her head emphatically, but I could tell she still wasn't fully getting it. How could she? She thought I was only a few weeks old and had no idea what was at stake. Even so, I held out my hand to shake on it. 'For Teddy then.'

She stared at it, then grabbed it with a surprisingly strong grip, and we shook. 'For Teddy then,' she repeated. Then she threw her hands up around my neck and pulled me to her.

I was so taken aback, I stood stiffly, not knowing what to do with my hands. They just hung in mid-air behind her. She moulded to my hard contours perfectly and felt warm and soft. I couldn't break away, although I knew I should. Instead, I turned my nose into her hair and smelled her scent. She radiated peaches. Script in my periphery, frantically logging everything to replay later. Innocent, but heaped with meaning in a way that neither of us understood.

It was Sheila's call that made her finally break away, but she caught and held one of my hands, proving she was reluctant. Something had changed. Her eyes raised to mine, soft and misty, like something had passed between us and she knew it as surely as I did. She'd made up her mind about something. No, given in. Inevitability was the script on her face. Whether human or machine, feelings were feelings. Loyalty was loyalty and I added my own: *love was love.* Whoever it was. Wherever it came from.

I THINK that was the turning point when I became her hopeless slave. I followed her downstairs to the kitchen. Stunned. The whole way, knowing I was walking towards my doom and powerless to stop myself. This was so much harder than I ever thought. Despite the professor's relentless training, it was not enough. It never could be because our humanness would always win out. My nerve endings, still blazing from our hug, only proved my point. I hadn't even been there three full days and I was messing up all over the place. I wondered if the others in the secret programme were faring any better.

I walked into the kitchen right behind Chrissy. Sheila, Christopher, Tina and Tom were sitting at the dining table and Nate was grabbing a drink. Sheila took one look at us, then switched her gaze to Nate and said, 'Adults only, honey.'

Chrissy sat down at the table and grinned to annoy him.

Nate dramatically threw his head back and groaned, 'Argh, not fair, Mom. Chrissy isn't an adult.' Then he pointed right at me and said, 'He isn't even a month old!'

I held in my quake of laughter with every muscle in my face. Instead, I looked at Sheila as innocently as I could, 'It's OK, Mom, I can go and keep him company.' I would have done literally anything to get out of the coming conversation between Chrissy and all the parents. The vibe was already heading in the direction of a panel interrogation.

Tina and Tom exchanged a look at me calling Sheila, Mom.

Nate's face lit up and his whole frame straightened another two inches in height.

'No, it's OK, Royce. This concerns you. Nate has some revision to do for his test tomorrow, don't you?' Sheila said, glaring at him and not giving an inch at his funny little act.

He stropped out of the room, stamping and slamming the door as he went. I couldn't help making comparisons to Finn. How he'd have loved to be mothered like that, just once.

'Sit down, Royce,' Sheila ordered, breaking me out of my daydream.

Christopher pulled out a chair for me to sit at the nearest end of the table, next to Chrissy. I was suddenly nervous at the formality and slowly sat with my hands in my lap to keep them still.

A warm hand covered mine. *Chrissy.* Without looking at her and giving her away, I opened mine and clasped it, gratefully, but my cheeks burned. I couldn't believe I was acting like such an idiot around her.

Christopher coughed as if he were bringing proceedings to order and snapped me out of my self-loathing. 'We wanted to talk to you, Royce, because Tina and Tom had some exciting developments at the hospital today, and we remembered something Chrissy told us about a healing chamber you'd mentioned that helped during your manufacture. You'd said it was used on all the bionetic AUs.'

My power pack shuddered, going up a gear to slow my rapidly beating heart. I wondered if they could hear, it revved so loudly. It was the first time I'd been grateful it was there. I had to calm down and get a grip on this situation and think fast. If a revolution did come, like the professor said, then I'd be responsible for this family and, by association, Teddy's too.

My being a machine gave me the precious moments I needed to phrase my answer carefully, while all eyes were on me. Chrissy gave my hand a squeeze and I allowed myself to fall into her intense eyes for the first time. 'It's OK,' she whispered.

I realised then just how dreadfully lonely I'd been. Of course, I'd had Finn, but being older and responsible for him meant I couldn't always let him in close without implicating or worrying him in some way. Since being a part of this family, even for just a few days, I felt their strength. With Chrissy, I was part of a unit. A family unit.

I cast my mind back to my operation I hadn't really given

informed consent to and tried to look at it as objectively as I could. Just as a machine might do. Then I looked at each individual, expectant face. My gridlines efficiently mapping and committing their features to memory, then my mouth opened and it all came spilling out. 'I don't know how much you know about the way TinBoiz are made,' I started cautiously. 'We are a complicated mix of cybernetic and bionetic systems, built around a titanium frame. A kind of machine/human hybrid. Tech and titanium, lubricated by blood. Assembled in one long surgery.'

I had to really pull it back, not to let slip that I was a full person before the surgery. That I was basically carved up to be enhanced. I was too emotional. 'We become the perfect combination for people to trust.' I used every facial muscle not to express my bitterness. So I took the opportunity to let it sink in. I guess a part of me wanted to see their reaction. It was still a grizzly operation for any sentient being.

They just stared at me, enraptured. Willing me on, not getting it at all. My heart sank a little, so I just got on with it to wrap it up. 'That's where the chamber comes in. To fuse the parts together, the professor uses it to heal us. The last stage of my surgery was spent in there.' I held out my arms in bewilderment. 'And came out me.' I was no longer worried about their reaction; I was just sad for the old me that I'd never get back.

I came out of my daze to them all looking at me, stunned.

'Fascinating,' Tom said eventually, exchanging a look with Christopher. The moms exhaled loudly, like they'd never heard anything like it.

'Do you know how it works, Son?' Christopher asked. 'Can it mend more than blood vessels?' He seemed to gather himself, to phrase his words. 'Can it restore dead brain cells in the brain?'

I was a little confused, I guess. That they could look right through my horrific experience, like Perspex, to get to the real thing they were interested in: the healing machine. Illogical, I knew. It was the whole reason I was there and proved I hadn't blown my cover. Right now, that alone was a miracle. But I hadn't missed that Christopher called me Son. That had to mean something. 'Honestly, I don't.' There was no point in lying. The lines were too blurred already. Real TinBoiz had a cybernetic brain, so I offered an alternative. 'But I believe brain trauma is common in soldiers. The chamber was originally designed for them.'

'That's right,' Tom said, sparking everyone to talk excitedly at once.

It struck me how long the UGN must have kept the technology to themselves. Everyone knew that the ground forces were mainly AUs and had been for some time. It could help so many ordinary people, but the more I learned, the more I realised the higher-ups didn't care. The immediate question for me was, did the people in this room? *Did Chrissy?*

I blinked as each question fired across me like I wasn't there. Saying stuff like, 'If it worked on soldiers, then it could work on Teddy.' That it might even work on his whole body and get him active again.

'Let's not get ahead of ourselves, shall we?' Christopher said, flattening the air with his hands. 'We need to get the use of one first.'

Chrissy piped up next and flashed a look my way. 'Look, I'd just settle for him to wake up and get the old Teddy back.' Tears filled her eyes and she scraped them away with her fingers. She was so adorably fierce, even though she was emotional, that my own resentments faded to residual static. 'Royce said he would broach it with his professor, but we need to offer him the right incentive. Something he really needs.'

I was shocked at being outed so directly; it took me a

moment to drag my eyes from Chrissy to the others, all waiting for me to explain. Probably surprised by my unorthodox thinking. I decided to rehash what the professor had told me. 'Please don't be alarmed. We model 2055 TinBoiz have the most advanced autonomous neuronetic brains in existence. We are not programmed; we continue to learn from our primary directive of The Laws. From the moment we wake from our surgery, we are products of our environment. Just like a human, but we have the capability to absorb vast amounts of information.'

I paused at that. *How much did I know?* Were genuine TinBoiz at zero when they were placed? I came back out of my inner thoughts. The four parents seemed impressed and not focused on that kind of stuff. 'I will talk to the professor in our scheduled communication tomorrow and ask him how hard it would be to organise, and what he would want to do it.'

My gaze went from the elated parents to Chrissy, whose eyes were soft and dewy with tears. 'Thank you,' she mouthed.

All fears of probable exposure as a fraud and my breaking the professor's strict rules of cover evaporated with that look. I realised that I'd go to the ends of the earth for another like that.

CHAPTER 30

*R**oyce*

I was excused after that. With a grateful smile of goodnight from Chrissy, I rose reluctantly and left them to talk late into the night. I felt strange all the way up the stairs. Nothing here was as I imagined. I wasn't sure what I expected, really. Maybe a posh family, with spoiled brats for kids. I wasn't expecting to feel so invested so quickly, and certainly not to develop feelings for Chrissy. My plan had been to bide my time, get Finn and Dad and get to somewhere far away.

It seemed very naive, now. Where exactly 'somewhere' was. The dream was to get to the place called The Soul of the World. The book, *Eden,* from the library, popped into my head. It felt pretty laughable now.

I was right outside Nate's room. It amazed me that out of everyone, it was Nate, an eight-year-old kid, who was most tuned into me as a person. That I might not be as I should be. I would need to handle him and I wasn't sure how. Brushing him aside like a kid was not going to work. We both knew that we were too clever.

My thoughts shifted to Finn and how he looked up to everything I did. I was his big brother who could do no wrong, even if, technically, it was wrong. It became right, in some justified way. I had to go for something like that with Nate. With as much honesty as I dare. Otherwise he'd see right through me.

I knocked lightly with my knuckle.

'What?'

I smiled and slipped inside. 'Hey!' I said, not moving from the door. I closed it quietly behind me.

I was surprised to find him sitting up, knees to his chest, against his headboard. There was complete silence and he wasn't gaming, as I'd expected. He was really upset.

'Can I sit?' I asked, pointing at my newly claimed place next to him.

'If you want.' He shrugged. Barely looking at me, but he did shuffle over.

I took that as permission and went and sat and looked sideways at him, still hugging his knees, his face closed and angry.

'You're upset,' I stated.

'I never get included in important stuff. I'm eight and a lot cleverer than they think. I know what's going on. I always do. They let you stay before me,' he said, throwing me a dagger look. Then he immediately saw his mistake and turned to face me. 'Sorry, I didn't mean… you know.'

I smiled, understanding perfectly. It would be hard to reconcile a machine getting preferential treatment over him, a real boy. 'If it's any consolation, I got sent out too, in the end. They're still talking,' I said with a wry smile.

He examined my face closely. 'Really?'

I nodded. 'I don't care. I wanted to talk to you about something else.'

He shuffled to sit up straighter to listen. 'I wanted to ask if you were going to tell anyone about what you saw earlier?'

He immediately frowned and looked down at his fingers. 'I know I should tell someone.'

I didn't jump in. I allowed him a moment. It was clear it was something he was wrestling with. 'And will you?'

He looked right at me, intensely. As if he were assessing the alternatives. 'Won't they just take you in and give you a service, or something. Like a check-up?'

I was afraid of this. 'Honestly, I don't know. They might, or they may decide it's too dangerous. They didn't exactly sell me by official means,' I said, with my eyebrows up in a question. Hoping he got my drift.

He let out a breath and nodded wearily. 'Oh yeah. I forgot about all that.'

Now that I felt I had his sympathy, I went in with my point. 'So, I guess it depends on how much you like my individual personality, or whether it's just having an AU you like.' It was outrageous emotional blackmail to be using on a kid, but I did genuinely like him and I had to do something to secure my stay there. Trying to get the chamber for Teddy was exposing me enough, without laying hands on Chrissy.

Nate was already shaking his head emphatically. 'No, you're my brother. We already decided that.' But his bright, ardent face drooped to concern. 'But you have to promise you'll never hurt any of us—or Teddy's family,' he added. As if he realised he had to be precise with a machine. It was pretty clever, really. AUs loved loopholes.

I smiled, genuinely. 'I promise,' I said, crossing my heart to swear.

Nate laughed. 'You're so damn human, Royce. You get me so confused. You haven't got a heart, dummy. Grab your headset!' he pointed, grinning.

I reached for them on the bed, my heart jumping at my

stupid mistake. He hadn't worked out the implications and danger seemed averted. But I had to watch my every move from now on. He was clever. Even picking up on the small mannerisms I was dropping all over the place. Apart from boring facts and figures, I could learn from the network, I should be like a baby to everything else. I had to formulate a plan for what I was prepared to tell him. Because he'd call me out on it sooner or later. Of that, I was absolutely sure.

CHAPTER 31

*C*hrissy

Everyone seemed consumed by their thoughts in the car on the way to school. Nate was still angry and not his normal, irritatingly chatty self. And Royce? I wasn't sure what was going on with him. Come to think of it, I wasn't sure of what was going on with me, either. I finally had to admit, I was developing a crush on a TinBoi. Just the thought made me shudder with horror. If ever I needed a reality check from Teddy, it was now.

I kept studying his profile, next to me. He was so good-looking and perfect, in a non-perfect kind of way. Not like Ace, who was blueprint perfect. Like something from a 3D printer. A cardigan-wearing, apple-pie-smiling TinBoi stereotype that every girl dreamed of taking home to Mother. But strangely, that wasn't what Royce had. His whole aura was rugged and dangerous, and completely unknowable. I decided that was the difference. Royce was tough. Then my thoughts inevitably went to where my crush could possibly go. At the very least, he lived as my brother, even if I ignored the fact that he was a machine. That was gross. But I couldn't help remembering his words that always hit home. 'Feelings were feelings, whoever has them.'

Before my confusion could tailspin from that, we arrived at school. Nate said 'Bye!' to Royce, ignored me, got out and ran straight off. Royce stepped out more slowly, after him, and I sent the car back home and did the same.

In less than two seconds, Cindy was right there with Simon, in front of us. The most popular couple in school. More beautiful and healthy-looking than anyone else. With Simon, captain of the basketball, track and just about every athletic team. Not hard, as there weren't that many kids healthy enough to be in them. That meant the healthy kids were pretty much in them all. Their parties were legendary, and everyone wanted to be invited to them. Me and Teddy had always scoffed at how boring chugging beer must be, but it still hurt being the only ones left out.

I just nodded with a weak smile and went to walk around them.

Simon sidestepped to block me. 'Hey! What's the rush? Just wanted to meet your TinBoi here. Royce, isn't it?' He held out a hand for Royce to shake.

Royce tensed and a muscle ticced in his jaw. He looked at it cautiously and then at me.

I nodded slightly and he took Simon's hand. The grip seemed to go on for far too long.

'Strong grip,' Simon said, finally letting go and shaking out his hand.

Cindy was looking me up and down, rudely, as if she was asking herself how a dweeb like me had a cool TinBoi on their arm. She laughed, spitefully. 'How did you end up with him?' she said, pointing. 'Oh yeah, you had to buy him.' She snuggled into Simon's arm and preened his dark hair, cut perfectly around his face.

Strangely, Simon wasn't smirking. He leaned his face

away from Cindy's hand and looked serious. 'Look, I spoke to Coach Lacey yesterday, and he told me there has been a new ruling by the county board. AUs and subs are going to be allowed into teams for the first time. There are too many empty places for the leagues to continue. They want to promote sports to get healthy and make them popular again. Jessica has already put Ace forward. There are a couple of subs in Progressive Year. Royce here is a tall one,' he said, gesturing his hand towards him. 'Could be great on the basketball team. Hell, he could be great on all of them.'

I looked up at Royce doubtfully. I knew he wouldn't answer for himself. 'Would you like to?' I asked.

I studied him as he ran the question through his sensors for any directives not to. 'Basketball isn't a contact sport, strictly speaking. With your permission, my directives allow it.' Then he turned back to Simon. 'And if your coach under-stands that some contact is unavoidable.'

Simon laughed and clapped Royce on the shoulder. 'Try-outs are in the lunch break at the Aerodrome.' He pulled a face, shaking out his hand again, but was smiling soon after. 'Rock solid,' he said, in admiration, moving away just as Jessica arrived with Ace. Cindy gave me a farewell smirk, still hanging from his arm.

I wanted to talk about it with Royce, but he was locked in a stare-off with Ace. I hurriedly pulled Royce past them and Ace had to turn his neck to an unnatural angle to keep tabs on him. That AU gave me the creeps; he was so different to Royce. I had to remind myself that they were the same, which was a cold-water drench to my hormones, but I kept coming back to Royce seeming more human.

We were running late, and we had back-to-back Science and Tech before lunch. So it was hard to get a chance to talk to Royce about the team. Although he still stole my attention most of the time.

He, on the other hand, absorbed the lessons like a sponge. When he caught me ogling him for the hundredth time, he winked and said, 'Don't worry. I'll remember it for the both of us,' and turned my insides to liquid. A slight gust of wind could have knocked me over at the fluid ease in the way he said that. It was so damn hot, and more confusing than ever, when all he really meant was I could access it at any time for my convenience. Helping me with homework, like any good AU companion should. But the simple mannerism, a wink, well, that was my undoing. Where did he learn that kind of thing? *TV? One of the kids here at school?* That had to be it. His speed and propensity for learning were astounding.

Tech was next and we sat at the messy benches laden with wires, chips and circuit boards. I managed to whisper, 'You don't have to try out if you don't want to,' as we found our seats and the class was settling. I was getting more nervous the closer to lunchtime we got.

Royce turned his ice-blue eyes on me and studied me. He always looked curious, like he was working things out. 'The decision is ultimately yours,' he said with a cautious smile. The way his lips curled made me swallow. Like every interaction was flirtatious. 'What's an aerodrome?' he asked, out of the blue.

It took me a moment to move my eyes from the curve of his mouth to register his question. 'Oh … it's the huge, enclosed stadium, for sports. It has a track and the roof keeps spectators and players safe from the rain. It pumps clean air in the whole time, too. Every school has one for sports.'

He seemed thoughtful as he absorbed what I'd said. 'Aerodromes were airfields and sports were played on fields,' he said, as if the information had just come to him from somewhere.

I nodded. 'That's right. Kids stopped playing on fields about twenty-five years ago. The air quality outweighed any benefit of the exercise… Look, I don't mind, either way,' I said with a shrug, like it meant less to me than it really did. Part of me wanted to watch as Royce wiped the smug smile off Simon and Cindy's faces. But the other, illogical part, was scared to let him go. He would be out of my control and I wanted to protect him. He was tough in so many ways, but in this, he was a lamb about to go into the den of wolves. I frowned at that. Royce could never be described as a lamb. I was going crazy.

Lunchtime came like a looming storm that would either go around or crash right through. I walked with Royce over the paved concourse, around the various plant buildings, to the aerodrome at the edge of the campus. Lots of kids were headed that way, probably having got wind of the exciting first.

Royce paused, making me almost bump into him. 'Are you sure you want to come?' he asked. 'Shouldn't you go and eat?'

I went to protest that I never ate much anyway, but something in him made me hold back. The thought of leaving him to Simon and the team filled me with panic, but he seemed so intense. Even in those cold, ice-blue eyes that rarely gave anything away. They looked almost soulful. I had a weird notion that he might be embarrassed with me watching, which I knew was ridiculous, but nothing was normal about this AU.

'I was just thinking of you having to wait with Jessica and Cindy and their toxic posse.'

My hand shot to my mouth to stifle a giggle. I was amazed he'd picked up on those fake social situations already.

'Don't worry, I'll come and find you when I'm done.' He finished with an innocent, reassuring smile that made cute dimples in his cheeks. *AUs designed with dimples … who knew.*

'OK,' I said, dragging my eyes back to his. 'See you right after,' I said, turning to walk away. I checked over my shoulder several times. He didn't hesitate. He strode right inside without looking back.

I went so far and stopped. I looked around for ideas. *Was I really going to miss Royce making school history? Hell, no.* I doubled back and scooted around the side of the building to the service access. It was used by the caretaker sub and was always unlocked. I pressed the keypad to release the door and came face-to-face with the silver metal sub just coming out. 'Ralph!' You made me jump.'

'Careful, miss. I could have hurt you. You aren't meant to be here.'

I wasn't scared of Ralph. All the kids liked him. I knew there was a sick guy laid up at home somewhere, trying to earn a living and get out of the house as best he could. These kinds of subs were ancient by tech standards. At least twenty years old. Some were covered in plastic, and some, like this one Ralph used, were completely metal and you could see all the working parts. They were perfect for manual labour as they were incredibly strong and cheaper to buy. Some companies even rented them out at very low rates. They had no bio-features and were big, clunking machines, like film-bots in twentieth-century movies.

I smiled wanly, remembering that it didn't work out so well for Teddy. 'I know, I'm sorry, Ralph. I'm trying to sneak in. My TinBoi is trying out for the team and I told him I wouldn't watch. I think he's nervous.' I felt my face blast at the ridiculousness of that statement, but I didn't crack a smile. I was serious. What the hell, it was true.

Ralph's chuckle sounded tinny and so endearing, it broke me out of my embarrassment. No wonder my feelings were confused around these things. 'I would like to watch that,'

Ralph said. He turned, taking three steps to pivot and said, 'Come with me.'

I was in. My heart was jumping with excitement as I blindly followed along. Ralph trudged ahead of me in a wine, stomp, wine, stomp, gait. Along the dim, dark-red corridor, past a gym store and generator room, where I guessed they controlled the air quality. There was his tearoom and cleaning cupboard, then we turned right and we were in the corridor to the stadium.

I hadn't been in here much. Me and Teddy weren't exactly sporty. But here, looking up at the dome that stretched on forever, painted red with steel girders and row upon row of gradient seating right up to the gods, it was pretty magnificent. It was as big as any public stadium. It had to be, as it housed the track, the athletics field and basketball court.

We stopped towards the end of the corridor, just before it came out onto the red track.

'No one will see you here,' Ralph said.

I smiled a thank you. He had no expression, but his voice was kind. I could tell he wanted to watch this as badly as me as he beckoned me as close to the action as we dared.

I ventured closer until the seating was about shoulder-high, either side. To about the level of the second row of seats. A rail circled around the front ones.

Shrieks of laughter brought my visual scan straight to the Toxic Posse, clumped together like a murder of crows.

I ducked out of instinct. They were only about thirty feet away and three rows back. Jessica and Cindy, a couple of guys and another five or six girls, all pointing and yelling at the field.

I followed their line of vision to a new huddle of boys, heading for the retrogreen grass, surrounded by a red track of eight lanes, all the way around it. There were two subs, easily visible, twice as wide and at least a head and shoulders above the rest, Ace and there he was. *Royce*. A little taller and effortlessly cool in his dark grey tracksuit, a little apart from the others. A sharp twinge turned in my chest at how gorgeous he was. So human, only ever giving himself away with his eyes, barely visible at this distance.

Thankfully, the coach brought them all to order.

'Is your boy one of the impressive-looking TinBoiz?' Ralph asked.

I had completely forgotten he was there and nodded erratically. 'The taller one with brown hair.'

Ralph whistled. 'State-of-the-art, those two. So life-like.'

I smiled, wanly. He had no idea what a problem that was.

'I can't imagine the subs being useful for anything other than defence.'

Ralph was completely homed in on their sports abilities, which gave me a pang of guilt at where my thoughts had been going. Especially as the coach ordered them to take their track sweaters off to see their physiques underneath.

The Toxics squealed and howled from the seats, and I scowled, determined not to let them spoil this.

Royce threw his in a heap on the floor and stepped out of his pants. Ace did the same, but more slowly and deliberately. The subs stood motionless, while the rest of the boys gathered around, fascinated.

The din of howling grew from the seats.

To me, Royce looked athletic and toned. His tight t-shirt showed glimpses of silver at his wrists, biceps and the rounds of his shoulders that didn't detract from his shape at all; it only made him cooler. Like a youthful gladiator. The flurry of butterflies kicked up a storm in my belly, even though I didn't want them to. I'd never seen Royce like this. Completely natural and unaffected by me. And those eyes, the ones that should make me shudder, only added to his mystique.

Simon was explaining something to them all with the coach, gesturing with his hands. I couldn't hear what he was saying, but I guessed it was a game plan. Royce nodded at certain times and Ace stood rigidly next to him.

The coach blew his whistle and all the boys, except Simon, lined up in the lanes on the red track and got down on their blocks. The two subs were told to start standing at the next line, about twenty metres in front, and Royce and Ace about twenty metres behind. Handicapped. It didn't seem fair. But when the coach blew and drew his arm down, everything receded. The deafening cheers were muted as I focused on the way Royce moved. Fluid and graceful. His feet pounded the surface like pistons. His arms cut the air at his sides. His upper body leaned slightly forward and his expression was focused on the line ahead.

'God, that boy's fast.'

Ralph was right, but I was too invested to answer.

The whole pack overtook the subs in seconds, who lumbered behind out of the race. Then Royce and Ace simply eased past the rest, like classic cars, sleek and effortless. They ate up the track.

They got so far ahead that the rest of the pack slowed to a stop. No one wanted to miss a second of this. It was just Ace and Royce, powering around the track. Two, four, eight hundred metres, in no time at all.

The boys all watched with Simon, shoulder to shoulder, while the coach kept checking his stopwatch.

The girls had gone silent in their seats. Everyone was spellbound as they passed the fifteen-hundred-metre mark at the speed of a sprint. The coach had to blow his whistle as they blazed past, otherwise I think they would have gone on till they dropped.

I glanced at the team for their reactions. They were shaking their heads in amazement. No one could call who actually won. It was their speed that counted. They'd broken all school records ever recorded.

Royce slowed first and doubled back to the others, with Ace following shortly after him. The other boys were ecstatic, slapping their backs as they joined the huddle. Neither looked out of breath or even broken a sweat.

I turned to Ralph and he said, 'Wow! Believe me, I'm grinning to my ears.'

I laughed and threw my arms up around his cold metal neck. While we hugged and Ralph mumbled how amazing the tech was. I felt a mixture of pride and happiness that subsided into disquiet, then a low-level dread I didn't want to focus on. Maybe it was because I could no longer kid myself that he was in any way human. Not with superhuman abilities like that.

I floated in a daze after that. Ralph and I stood amazed as shotput, javelin, high and long jump followed. All the same story. Baseball sent the ball way out into the seats. They never missed, even with their sharpest bowlers. The two of them outperformed everyone else on the field.

Lastly, the group moved back for the grass to transform into a basketball court. A rectangular area of grass that flattened to a sleek green and then miraculously changed to a shiny beige wood. Two arch-shaped walls came up at either end and unfolded with the net. It took less than five minutes. I didn't know much about sports, but I knew this would be the real test. It was a game of skill as well as speed and they weren't allowed to touch.

The coach quickly split them into two teams, making sure Ace and Royce were rivals. He called them all in for a huddle, then all bets were off.

CHAPTER 32

*R*oyce

I couldn't remember the last time I'd had so much fun. Not from expending pure energy, anyway. It was exhilarating to test all my new systems to their limit and way beyond. My heart and oxygen intake synced with the cybernetics, perfectly. My systems ran like a dream.

Instead of resisting, I allowed everything to do its job. My gridlines engaged and homed in on the baseball, hitting it with precision every time. Each ball was met like a geometry problem. Angles and degrees appearing a fraction of a second before every hit. Solved and actioned before my bio synapses could even snap into place. It was every teenage boy's fantasy to live a video game. I couldn't wait to tell Nate.

A pang of guilt stabbed me. I'd thought of Nate before I thought of Finn. But the coach's whistle brought me out of it before I could fall into the pit. I had to concentrate on the now. Finn wasn't forgotten; he was the future. He was the 'who' of the 'what' I was doing all this for.

Besides, who could dwell when the whole world was a

computer game around me. I watched, absolutely dumb-founded, as the playing field transformed into a top-level basketball court, just like a film set. The fake grass went into pixels and morphed into sprung wood flooring. Then the walls with the baskets rose up at either end and unfolded into place. It was hard to concentrate as the unimpressed coach went through the rudiments of the game. I flashed a glance at Ace, fixated on the input. All of this was new to him. For me, it wasn't so easy. I had to discern the differences from the street game I was used to, which was down and dirty. Fouls were integral to a game of stop-starts and short bouts, because we'd have trouble breathing. Unless we could break into the old, abandoned school and play in the dark-ness. The rules were loose, injuries common. As long as you could catch and bounce a ball, you could play.

I quickly understood that the objective was the same. Minus the contact. 'Got it?' the coach said, fixing me and Ace in the eye.

I nodded, not waiting for Ace and caught the ball thrown at me by Simon. I bounced it a couple of times to check the speed of the bounce and its weight. Lightning speed calcula-tions ran down the side of my vision. I was also honing my coordination with the speed of the bounce. Then I threw it to Ace, without warning, and he caught it with reflexes as fast as mine. This would be interesting. A real opponent. But when he tried to get used to it, as I had done, it was clear he was awkward and wasn't sure what to do with it.

I grinned and he clocked it and actually scowled, which made me laugh out loud. The poor guy had nothing to refer-ence it to and would be scouring his web access to update his training. 'Nerd!' I muttered as I jogged past. It was my first real advantage of the day. It was clear he'd experienced nothing like this before.

Simon slapped my back. 'You're on my team.'

Ace watched, bemused, while I nodded and ran backwards to keep my legs moving. My eyes were on Ace the whole time. I didn't like the guy. I didn't trust him. I had to continually remind myself he was a baby, emotionally and in experience. Let loose in the hungry world for the first time. I, on the other hand, had lived several lifetimes in just a few years. I chuckled. 'Mincemeat.' And I pointed two fingers at my eyes, then to his, to psych him out. His expression made me laugh. He was so easy to wind up.

The coach brought us to order and assigned our positions. He put Ace and me together on the court for the safety of the other boys. The subs were on defense for the same reason. Like-for-like models for speed and weight.

The coach blew the whistle, and the game started. The boys were good. Especially Simon. They ran rings around the subs. They dribbled faster and lower than I'd seen outside of TV. I jogged and recorded their skills. Mapping angles. Who favoured left or right-handed, weaknesses, egos, overused plays. Some even managed to jump and dunk like the pros.

I glanced at Ace, glued to my shoulder. His head jerking to each person, trying to do the same thing. He was learning on the go. I could feel my advantage slipping away. But I had plays of my own, speeding up my jog. *No more Mister Nice Guy.* It was a non-contact sport that really was a contact sport. I inwardly chuckled at the nice little loophole and couldn't wait to see what Ace brought to the table.

'Tins!' the coach shouted and blew his whistle. He beckoned us over with his arm. We exchanged a look and jogged over. 'What are you waiting for? Find a space!' the coach yelled, glaring at both of us. 'Make room and you'll get the ball.' Then he clapped his hands double time, 'Now go!'

I didn't need telling twice. As soon as he blew his whistle to restart the game, I was off. Simon often had the ball and I noticed he looked for me a lot. Ace was my conjoined twin, no matter how I ducked and twisted. He was always there, so I had to take drastic action and draw from my street basketball experience. Something he would not understand or see coming. My sly elbow went into his gut and I leapt up. Simon caught and passed me the ball in a nanosecond. I caught and passed it to another kid all within the same jump. The kid caught it and passed it back to Simon; meanwhile, we were all moving down the field.

Ace had recovered and his focus burned a hole in my back. But I was in the zone now. My eyes, everywhere. Plotting team positions, watching Simon. Registering the blank look on Ace as he was still processing what I'd done, running it through his directives. I laughed with joy at how I could concentrate on everything at once. Ace soon caught onto my side like an unwanted fluff ball.

We were in the shooters' circle, which became a frantic volley of passes. My thoughts were quickfire. I couldn't play the same trick again, because Ace would be ready. So, this time, I kicked back, disguising it as a jump, making sure my foot caught his shin. It was a gamble as I had no idea how far his bionetics extended through his body.

It paid off. The groan proved he had pain receptors and he doubled over instinctively. I took my chance and jumped. Simon threw the ball and with one hand in a gentle arc, I tucked it into the hoop, barely touching the sides.

Everyone cheered, even those not on my team. The coach looked at me dubiously, knowing exactly what I'd done, but he blew his whistle and pointed to our end anyway. 'One to zero.' I took that as a win and immediately grinned.

The coach had seen enough and the team bounded over

to me to slap and jump on my back. Even the subs clomped over and had barely been involved. I'd never experienced anything like it, even back home. It was usually marred by a fight over a bet gone sour, or an overenthusiastic foul. This was pure joy over nothing, really.

Simon stood right in front of me and searched my face so seriously that, for a moment, I thought we were going to go. 'God, man… You're so damn human.'

Before I had a chance for my heart to drop at being rumbled again, Simon grinned and shouted more loudly, 'You're a frickin' dynamo!' He broke into laughter. 'Dynamo… Dynamo,' he sang, punching the air.

Everyone began to take up the chant, over and over, swarming me towards the changing rooms. It was deafening and overwhelming. I'd never known what it felt like to be man of the match before.

Back in the grey, locker-lined changing room, the coach came over to the continuing mayhem. 'You're on the team, kid.' He broke into a smile and pointed at me, squinting one eye. 'Hide it better, next time.'

'You too,' he said, turning to Ace, standing a little way off, not knowing what the hell was happening. 'Practice! You'll soon be up to his speed.'

'Thank you, sir,' Ace said, with a small bow of his head. He was such a plank.

The subs stomped off to class and the boys gathered their things to shower. Ace turned his attention directly to me. He stalked closer, making me stiffen in readiness. Narrowing his eyes, not stopping until he got way up in my grill.

Boys going in and out of the shower began to notice. Whispers of something happening with the Tins. Ace was staring me down and I frowned, half pissed and half amused. He had no idea who he was dealing with. This scene had played out a million times growing up. It was how a hierarchy got sorted out. But I knew what he was. A tin can with no boundaries. My personal space was invaded and I narrowed my eyes to match his.

'You broke the law,' Ace said. Showing the first real facial expression I'd seen on the guy. Anger, mixed with disbelief.

I laughed. I'd had enough of playtime with this guy and bumped my chest into his. If he wanted to, we'd go. 'No laws between AUs.' I grinned mischievously, throwing his own words back in his face. It took a second for the surprise to register and for him to log that what had happened on the court was possibly his own fault. Quickly followed by a moment of confusion, then anger. A series of emotions that read like a good book.

I could hear and feel the breaths of the boys now crowded around me. Simon was at my shoulder, like a wingman. Seeming to have adopted me as his new best friend. 'Don't sweat it, Tin Guy. It's all part of the game,' he said, landing his hand heavily on Ace's shoulder.

It made him switch his gaze to Simon, then his shoulder, in a weird, jerky move.

I secretly hoped I didn't move like that. 'Yeah,' I said, grinning more to torment him. 'You just gotta practice.'

The boys got it right away and laughed, especially Simon. 'Come on, man,' Simon said, pulling me away.

I allowed it, but my eyes stayed on Ace, watching me the whole time. I could almost hear the circuits cranking and buzzing in his head, trying to make sense of what just happened. I was a superior model and he didn't get that it was my humanness that made me unbeatable in every way.

I immediately left the changing rooms to find Chrissy.

'Hey, wait up!' Simon caught up with me and threw his arm around my shoulder. He was with his usual group of eager boys. I'd suddenly become the cool new kid that everyone wanted to know. 'I'm having a party this weekend. You should come,' Simon said.

I looked straight into Simon's face, smiling in anticipation.

'It's at the golf club,' he added, as if that somehow made a difference.

I narrowed my eyes, trying to work out his angle.

'My dad's company has Gold Membership.' He laughed like I wasn't getting it.

I wasn't.

'Curfew's taken care of. Special pass,' he said, thumping the top of my arm.

I smirked as if that was just what I was thinking. The truth was, in all my imaginings of being there, not one was of me building a social life, nor making friends. I didn't know how I felt about it, exactly. So I did what I always did and tried to be funny. I went into machine mode. 'Does that mean I'm popular?' I could just imagine Chrissy scowling and dragging me away from the mean kids.

Simon laughed, missing my smart comment completely. 'You sure are, buddy. Bring a friend.'

The rest of the boys sniggered at how ridiculous that sounded. I didn't bite. 'Can I bring Chrissy?' I asked, immediately.

Simon frowned and looked at the guy next to him, as if he had no idea who I meant.

'Ghost Girl,' he said.

Simon brightened in understanding. 'Sure. Bring Ghost Girl. It'll be a blast.'

I was a little annoyed they called her that and smiled, not committing either way. They soon drifted off to their various classes, slapping my back as they left, and all calling me by my new nickname: Dynamo.

I was left standing there, bemused. Running the whole

lunchtime's events through my head. These were the real synthetic people, not us. They were co-dependent on those around them to make them feel secure and good about themselves. There was no real friendship.

I turned and walked off purposely to find Chrissy. The only real person here.

CHAPTER 33

*C*hrissy

I had to run to make sure I was in my next class before Royce got there. Not easy with poor lung capacity. I had to stop and drag on my inhaler twice. My breath was hacking and I felt like I would puke when I finally slumped into my seat. But as I slowly returned to normal, my nerves were alive and buzzing with excitement.

'Are you OK, Christine? Do you need to see the nurse?' Miss Phelps, the history teacher, said.

I nodded and shook my head, still breathing erratically, guessing I must look very red. 'No, miss, just a little asthma. It will pass.' What I really needed was to absorb what just happened, before Royce got back and I gave away that I'd seen it.

He was magnificent. That was the only way I could describe it. He was fit, brave and fierce, all rolled into one. I'd seen AUs around my whole life, and nothing, absolutely nothing, could measure up to his realness and charisma. I just couldn't get over it. He was his own being, with a life and likes and aspirations. I was all over the place, emotionally. I was proud. So unbelievably proud and impressed. He'd wiped the floor with Ace, not just because he was a superior unit, but because he wanted to. It blew my mind.

I jumped and turned in my chair as loud, chattering voices entered the classroom behind me. Jessica and Cindy were right in the middle of the group of girls.

'Sit down and be quiet!' Miss Phelps barked. 'You're late!'

'We were watching the try-outs, miss,' Cindy said, pouting. 'It was a historical first. TinBoiz and subs were allowed for the first time.'

Jessica scanned the room until she found me. She glared, like she was assessing what I'd seen and whether she needed to be jealous about it. It was a strange exchange, but it was clear that she hated me for something I had no control over. If Teddy had been there, I would have smiled, simply to wind her up, but it scared me. I was alone.

Ace stomped in behind them and Jessica took his arm proprietorially and gave me a smirk. Then they all found their seats.

I faced the front again and wondered what was keeping Royce. My hands were shaking, so I put them in my lap. Turned out just in time, as Royce appeared and slipped into the seat next to me. Even that was in one fluid move. Nowhere near robotic.

'Settle down... I hear congratulations are in order, Royce. Ace,' Miss Phelps said.

'Thank you,' Royce said, his eyes tracking to me, cautiously. 'Sorry, I'm late.'

'No problem. Let's get on,' Miss Phelps answered. But Royce's intense look meant he was saying sorry directly to me. My heart glowed that he'd thought of me first. To cover my embarrassing blush, I pushed my Textpad, open at twentieth-century history, between us. 'How did you get on?' I whispered, not able to look at him for fear I'd give myself away. My voice sounded high-pitched and my mind and gut swirled with the memory of me and Ralph cheering and dancing not more than half an hour ago.

Royce didn't seem to notice my weirdness and immediately brightened in his wonderfully expressive way. Cheek dimples and everything. 'I made the team,' he said, as if it still astounded him. 'And Ace,' he added.

I wasn't sure why he felt he had to diminish his achievement by adding Ace. I wanted to tell him, 'of course you did'. He was the best on the field. Then he really dropped my jaw open.

'Simon has invited us to his party this weekend.'

My face remained blank while my mind somersaulted. His remained open and bright with expectation. I doubted whether Simon had thought of me when he invited him. Royce had managed in one day what me and Teddy hadn't managed in a lifetime. An invitation into the inner circle of the Populars. Teddy would have loved it, just once. It never bothered me, but it still niggled and I wanted to say, 'of course he did. He knows you're the best and he wants all the best people around him,' but it would have burst Royce's bubble and spoiled the celebration of his achievement. Royce's face dropped when I didn't answer right away. He was always so perceptive. 'Would *you* like to go?' I asked, quickly, to cover myself. I wasn't sure how I felt about it. Part of me wanted to go with him and another part wanted to boycott it in solidarity with Teddy.

Royce shrugged. 'I guess so. I've never been to something like that. I wouldn't go without you, though.'

It made me smile that it hadn't occurred to him that he was the property of the Coe family and we could veto anything he wanted to do. I guess it was my fault. It was me who encouraged him to feel like he was a genuine pupil at the school. 'OK,' I said eventually, not sure it was the right thing to do at all. 'But promise me you'll be careful of them, OK?' I said, suddenly imagining practical jokes and cruel hazing. He wasn't exactly worldly wise. In real terms, he wasn't more than a few weeks old.

CHAPTER 34

Royce

I watched Chrissy closely throughout our last two lessons, after the try-outs. She was quiet, even by her standards, like something had affected her. I hope I hadn't overstepped. We'd been getting on so well; she didn't seem to resent me for being there anymore. But I wasn't sorry I'd done sports. I'd never done anything like that before. I'd never felt how it made me feel. Not just a great workout for my systems, but I felt good at something. Included. Accepted. Even liked. It sounded silly, even to me, but I really wanted to go to that party. I'd been to parties back home, mostly in empty buildings or warehouses. I wanted to see how the rich folks lived. I knew they weren't rich like I expected, but they weren't exactly loitering behind pizza joints for food, either.

Ace was a spanner, throwing me hate-filled looks whenever he could. He was going to be a complication one day; it was only a case of when. I shelved it. He was inferior and that's what burned him. I'd cross that burning bridge when it came.

The rest of the day was uneventful. Nate was as bright

and talkative as usual when we loaded into the car for home. His chatter about a new history project was a welcome distraction from Chrissy, now in moody, introspective mode. She was preparing herself to see Teddy after school and needed to distance me. It was cool how I understood that about her now, otherwise I'd be getting paranoid.

It was a relief when she went soon after we got home. I never knew what to do with myself when she was like that, as my primary human.

Nate was ordered to do his homework immediately by Sheila, which allowed me to slope off and check in with the professor at our appointed time of five.

I sat down on my cot and went to my menu and he was there immediately. Smiling at me like some sort of benevolent uncle. I brought him up to speed about the sports try-outs and also about my apparent rivalry with Ace.

He seemed a little worried about that. I thought it was downright weird for an AU to have an ego. 'We must be on our guard if the AI is picking up on something unusual in you.'

I was surprised that he was giving it a legitimate reason. That wasn't the vibe I'd got at all. 'I think it's old-fashioned pride,' I said. 'I don't think he likes that I beat him.

The prof smiled at me, indulgently, as patronising as hell. He didn't think Ace was capable of something like that. But he wasn't there; he didn't see for himself.

'So you're going to the party as a popular member of the team,' the professor said, his face lighting up, chuckling to himself. 'Splendid.'

I was surprised that he'd dismissed what I'd told him so easily and focused on something trivial and seemed thrilled about it.

'You're doing really well, Royce. Even better than expected.'

I felt a little bemused, so I decided to get right to the point. 'Can I ask a personal favour?' I asked, shifting nervously in my seat.

The professor schooled his face, masking his amusement, I could tell. He was bugging the hell out of me the more I talked to him. 'The chamber,' I blurted. 'The one that fixed us after surgery. Is there a way it could be used on a regular sick person?'

The professor frowned and studied me for a moment. It wasn't an outright no, which I'd half expected. 'You told your family about the chamber?' he asked, his face blank, so I couldn't read how he was feeling.

I wanted to lie, but I'd never been good at it and didn't want to ruin my chances. So I opted for the truth and nodded. 'Sorry… It just slipped out. Chrissy is so devastated by the loss of her best friend. His brain was fried by a sub and he's in the hospital with little chance of waking up.'

The professor nodded thoughtfully. 'I see. Yes, I know something about that… So his parents know about the chamber, too?'

I nodded, a little sheepishly. 'Sorry, Prof. I got a little carried away.' Then I wasn't sure why, but all my feelings came tumbling out. 'I wasn't expecting to like the family so much… Chrissy. It wasn't how I expected to feel at all. It was a job … you know?' I said, feeling wretched.

'You do understand that they got you as a companion … a replacement for Teddy?'

I looked down and nodded, sadly. I felt that keenly.

'And they will possibly have no need for you if he wakes up.'

With a pain welling in my chest, I nodded again. I raised my eyes to look at the 3D image, now so real, studying me intensely. 'What happens to TinBoiz that are not wanted anymore?'

There was no amusement when the professor spoke this time. 'Due to the nature of design in the later TinBoiz models, the UGN ruled that they be decommissioned, erased and only then reconditioned. They are too expensive to scrap, but too dangerous to leave with any residual memory. Their bionetic fusing makes them impossible to use for parts. In terms of the cybernetic brain, much is discarded and changed.'

I guessed as much. I couldn't help thinking of Ace. It was clear he was very different from me. It was easy to imagine some trapdoor in the back of his head where they swapped out a chip. 'What about me?' The UGN had no idea about the latest turn AU research was taking. 'We are experimental, aren't we?'

The prof's brow furrowed deeply. 'I'd need to think carefully about that. It's never happened before.'

I examined his face for any tells of lying. He was definitely being cagey. This was a hiccup he hadn't bargained for. We were kids stolen from the judicial system, given no real choice but to take part in their experiment. Dodgy on ethics, to say the least. The evasive eye contact told me the worst. A rebel cell of tech terrorists, hiding at the cutting edge of the AI robotic industry, was never going to let me go free to tell the tale.

I hid my revelation from him and got us back on track. 'So, about the chamber. I think they'd be prepared to pay.'

The professor studied me for a long moment. 'You have done very well, Royce. Beyond expectations, in fact. The way you've integrated so quickly into the family, right at the heart of the popular kids at school. I am very pleased. Let me think about it. If it is possible, and I'm not saying that it is, it is dangerous for the boy to come here. It is a top-secret facility. I would have to give it some thought.'

I was amazed and so happy it wasn't a flat no. Especially

after the dark turn the conversation had taken. I thought I'd get a reprimand for giving away secrets, at the very least. 'Thank you, professor,' I said, bowing my head as if we were face to face in the training centre.

'Goodnight, Royce. Well done.' With that, the prof's image evaporated from my mind, leaving a dark, empty void.

Part of me felt elated. I had something positive to tell the Coes and the Monshalls. But something was gnawing at the edges of my consciousness. I guess it was the fear of losing my new family. Of going back. It was only natural to worry about what would happen to a guy like me, nothing but a ghost in the system. Who never really existed in the first place. It made me shiver.

I refused to let fear hobble me. Nothing had changed. I turned and walked purposely out of my room. First, I needed to find Sheila and Christopher. Thoughts were already rebounding in my head about escape. Making my way back to Finn. Finding my friends. Setting off to find The Soul of The World. I was not going to disappear in the way the professor thought. I was doing it my way. On my terms.

SHEILA WAS CLEARING up dinner when I reached the kitchen. I almost tripped over the circular cleaner bot that scoured the floors for dirt all day long. 'Watch your step, sunbeam,' it said after a loud beep, and spun off in another direction.

I smiled at Sheila, turning to face me at the sink, bemused. 'I have some positive news.'

She immediately dried her hands on a towel and put up a finger to stop me for a moment. 'Christopher, darling. Can you come here, please?'

Christopher immediately appeared from the archway to the lounge. 'What is it, dear?'

'Royce has some news for us.'

They both turned to face me and waited expectantly. I was unsure how to start. 'Not news, exactly. I just spoke to my professor about the chamber and he didn't say a flat no, which I was kind of expecting, nor did he reprimand me for talking about it. He said he needed to work out how he'd be able to do it. It sounded positive, I thought.' Now that I'd said it, it felt kind of premature. Like maybe I should have waited till I had a bit more.

Sheila clasped both her hands to her chest and looked across at Christopher like she was going to cry. He came alive and seemed to grow another inch in height. 'Cost... Did he mention cost?'

I shook my head. 'No, surprisingly, because I did mention it. He seemed more concerned with where and the logistics of it. Their facilities are top-secret, you see.'

Christopher was nodding, absorbing it, like he understood everything. 'Wow, this is amazing.'

They fired a few more questions, none of which I could answer. Then they just sat at the dining table, sombre and fidgeting. Their restlessness charging the atmosphere. The time dragging until Chrissy and the Monshalls came back from the hospital.

I couldn't bear it and escaped to find Nate. I knocked on his door and slipped inside. He was sitting up against his headboard, not doing anything. 'What's up?' I asked, immediately walking over to take my place on his bed, next to him.

'So you're doing it,' Nate said flatly, like he was disappointed.

'You heard?' I asked, genuinely surprised. I'd been so anxious about everything that I hadn't sensed him around.

He nodded. 'I heard you talking to yourself in your room, so I followed you downstairs and listened.' He shrugged. 'I'd only get thrown out, so... You know. Easier.'

I smiled and nudged him playfully with my shoulder to cheer him up.

'Touching, much?' he said, glaring with mock outrage.

I was struck with horror. He was right. But his face relaxed into laughter. 'No sweat. It's me, remember.'

We went quiet for a moment while I studied his face. 'There's no guarantee it will happen,' I said, eventually. 'Or even if it will work.' I had no idea of its capabilities with anything as intricate as a brain.

'You have to imagine that it will,' Nate said, looking at me intensely, treating this as seriously as any adult.

I had no idea he felt that deeply for Teddy, but as his gaze turned to hurt, I slowly fell in.

'We have to plan for that,' Nate continued. 'What if you get sent back?' he said, more forcefully.

'That's not a given—'

'Yes, but what if you do?' he cut right over me. 'I asked my mom how it works for you to be here. I thought they bought you, but it's not like that. It's like a lease. A monthly payment, shared with Teddy's parents. It means they can upgrade and get aftercare. People change models all the time. I had no idea. Techs stopped buying bots and subs years ago. It got too expensive for regular people.'

I couldn't help raising my eyebrows at 'regular people'. He really had no idea, but I didn't either. It made sense that as the technology became more sophisticated, so did the cost. It was genius, really. Monthly instalments meant they earned money for each model for the duration of its life. Indefinitely, in theory. Not surprisingly, it was a subject the professor never covered. It conveniently hid the likelihood of our going back to the depot.

My brain went into meltdown. The professor's words: decommissioned and reconditioned, bounced around on repeat. My closest friend was Nate, an eight-year-old boy. I had literally no one else I could talk to. Not even Chrissy. Not honestly. 'I was thinking of running,' I said, suddenly. More stunned that I'd said it out loud. 'Would you help me?' I asked, looking Nate in the eye, as my mouth ran away with me. 'I mean, only if it happens.'

Nate stared at me as he processed what I'd said. Then he swallowed and nodded solemnly. 'I promise I won't let them send you back. No other family is getting you; you belong to ours.' His face had become fierce and adamant. 'You don't get to give family back.'

He was right. I'd only been there a few days and I loved him like he was my own family. They all were.

I heard the door and raised voices below. Then Sheila's call. 'Royce, love. They're back. Do you want to come down?' So loving and gentle, like a mom should be. But a quaver of excitement tinged her voice.

I swapped a 'ready' look with Nate that sealed our pact, then I rose fluidly and went purposefully downstairs.

CHAPTER 35

Chrissy

Mom opened the door before I reached the doorstep and called to Tina and Tom before they disappeared into their house. 'Can you come in a minute? There's something we need to talk to you about.'

They exchanged a baffled look and altered their steps to cross the lawn towards us. It distracted me from my flat mood. I didn't know what I'd been expecting at the hospital: another hint, maybe, that Teddy was alive in that shell of a body, trying to get out. But there was nothing. Just an hour of listening to his breathing through a machine. Even when I told him all the exciting stuff from school, I'd been so sure that would have caused something.

Still, something was going on. Mom was acting weird. I trooped in behind Tina and Tom and looked up just at the moment Royce reached the bottom of the stairs. His intense eyes locked with mine and I felt the powerful feeling he always gave me. Like an injection of excitement. I hated that I could never control it. He took the decision away from me whether to look away, not to flush red, to feel ridiculously hot, even when it was cold. I couldn't deal with it now. Not after my bitter disappointment at the hospital. I went to push past him to go up the stairs, without even saying hello.

My mom came back out of the kitchen. 'Darling, you'll want to hear this.'

I froze and gave Royce a filthy look as if he had something to do with it. He infuriated me even more by giving me an unsure smile. I turned and faced my mom, about to argue. She just nodded enthusiastically. I rolled my eyes, let out a slow breath and went back down the last step, after Royce, in the direction of the kitchen. Even then, I couldn't help noticing the width of his shoulders, with the silver TinBoiz trade plate embedded where they joined his neck. It was a cold slap back to the reality of what he was.

Everyone sat down at the dinner table. I took the last place at the near end, next to Royce.

'Tea… coffee?' Mom asked, putting two pots on the table.

'Sit down, Sheila,' my dad ordered, sounding exasperated with her. 'Let's just get on with it. Drinks can wait.'

My gaze shot to Royce, who was looking right at me. Gauging me as always. He had something to do with this.

'We wanted to bring you up to speed with the latest developments. Royce had a very promising conversation with his professor this evening. Royce? Would you like to explain?'

Royce immediately straightened as all eyes switched to him. I didn't think he expected Dad to throw him the ball like that. But it was me he looked at first, unsure how he should proceed.

'What is it, Royce?' I said quickly, realising, as his primary human, he was asking for my permission.

'There is nothing definite yet, but I felt that my professor is considering a way for Teddy to use the chamber.'

Royce was talking directly to me, as if there was no one else in the room. His voice echoed and rang through me.

'He didn't mention cost. In fact, he ignored my question. He was more concerned about how and where it could happen.'

I was lost in his strange, hypnotic eyes that bore into me, heating me from the inside. Shrieks and joyful tears were happening around me. Overwhelmed laughter from the people who all loved Teddy and had given up hope. All I could see was Royce and his resigned expression. 'Thank you,' I whispered. Deep down, I knew it had been a selfless act, even then. He was meant to be a machine. A mass of circuitry covered in blood and tissue. But in that moment, he was real to me. He had real feelings and he'd proved it.

'Hope, Tom,' Tina was saying. 'There's at least hope.'

Tom hugged her to him, but she quickly pulled apart. 'What happens next?' she asked, sniffing, scraping back tears with her fingers.

The question drew me out of Royce's gaze and back into the conversation. Every eye was glassy with tears and riveted to Royce for the answer.

'I'm not sure. He said to leave it with him.'

'But it felt positive,' Tom persisted, nodding at everyone to agree with him.

I smiled inwardly. *Felt.* Tom was doing the same as I did. Assuming Royce had feelings. They all were. When I looked at Royce and conveyed that smile, the one he returned was sad. Like he was spookily mirroring what I was thinking. He was a human with titanium bones. That was how I was starting to view him. And looking around the table at the hope on everyone's faces, they were too.

'Champagne!' my dad said, quickly, rising to his feet.

'It's not definite yet,' Tina said, laughing and clasping her hands together joyfully. 'Shouldn't we save it for then?'

I don't think there was a single person around that table who cared about that. Mom was soon on her feet too, grabbing her best glasses from the cabinet. 'We'll get another,' she said, happily, carried away with Dad.

'Another dozen,' my dad said, popping the cork and making everyone laugh. Froth fizzed up and spilled over the sides as he filled all the glasses.

Nate appeared, looking confused, brought downstairs by all the commotion.

'Come and join us, Son. Leave the homework, we're celebrating. Here!' Dad said, passing him a small glass.

'Chris!' Mom said, trying to get a rein on him and take the glass.

He wouldn't hear of it and held it out further to Nate. 'A mouthful won't hurt him.'

Nate took it dubiously. He'd never been allowed alcohol before and wasn't sure what was going on. But I didn't miss the look he exchanged with Royce. I didn't know what, but something passed between them. Whatever it was, it wasn't joy. It was concern. It was the only dampener on the whole thing, so I let it pass.

Dad was telling everyone that it was the bottle he saved for Christmas. The one he always joked cost a day's pay. So I made sure I drank mine in a huge gulp after Dad raised his glass and toasted, 'To Teddy coming home.'

'To Teddy coming home,' we all chanted.

I watched Nate. He barely joined in and his face remained straight. He didn't even seem happy. That bothered me most of all.

THE REST of the week passed painfully slowly.

School.

Home.

Visit Teddy

School.

Home.

Visit Teddy.

Royce checked in with his professor every night, while we all waited anxiously around the dining room table for him to come down afterwards. We'd look at him expectantly as he walked into the kitchen and deflated when he shook his head. Even Nate and I didn't think he was that bothered about Teddy coming home. Then I fell in. It was relief for him and not disappointment at all. I got angrier and angrier every time I saw it. By the time it got to Friday, I was furious.

We came in from school, and when we'd normally disperse, I followed him into his room. 'Personal space!' he chanted, stomping over to flop on his bed.

I was completely nonplussed at his behaviour. 'Why aren't you happy like everyone else about Teddy?' I went right in with my lips tight with fury.

Nate huffed, rolled over and sat up, drawing his knees to his chin. Then he put his head back against the headboard. His body language was alarming, like he was in agony or something. 'Of course I'm happy,' he said on a weary breath.

'You don't look happy.' I shifted my feet uneasily. 'It's obvious something's been bothering you all week. I never realised you could be so selfish, Nate.'

I would have stormed out if the anger that flashed over his face hadn't shocked me into paralysis. I was determined to find out what it was.

'Selfish. Me. Oh, really. Let me see...' He made a dramatic pose, putting his index finger to his chin and looking up to think. 'There's the building up of Tina and Tom's hopes if it doesn't work. There's the fact that the chamber could kill Teddy, and, oh yeah, there's the huge question mark over what will happen to Royce if it does work and we get Teddy back.' He ended his last words shouting and glaring at me.

I stood there, stunned into silence.

'Now tell me who's being selfish. Royce is risking his life for everyone else's happiness and no one has even given it a thought.' His face was so red and fierce, I'd never seen him so upset and angry. I was utterly speechless. I'd been so swept up in it all. We all had. Nate was right. *But sending Royce back?* I shook my head, my face crumpling in complete refusal to believe that any of the parents would be heartless enough to do that. 'It makes no sense to give him back. They'd never get all their money back for a start. They love him. He's part of the family now.' My throat constricted, making my voice wobble, as a huge knot rose painfully.

'He's a machine, Chrissy. On a lease. They didn't buy him. They pay monthly with money they don't really have. The Monshalls pay half. Do you really think that they'll keep up all that hardship when Teddy's home?'

I gaped at Nate, like the bottom just fell out of my world and I was about to fall through. He was right about every-thing. If I truly believed that Royce was a person, then I had been unbelievably selfish. Tears fell and I turned and ran out of the room. I reached the top of the stairs and stopped and looked at the door to the tiniest room in the house. I teetered, then I stomped back and rapped loudly on Royce's door.

I fidgeted, shifting from foot to foot, waiting. There was no answer. I hesitated, unsure of what to do. Swearing. Trying the door handle. Then, with my heart thrashing, I slipped inside.

Even though I'd been in there before, I was shocked at how bare the room was. Worse than sparse. No knick-knacks, no pictures, no personal belongings at all. Just his weird metal cabinet with lights pulsing around it and a cot with Royce lying fully clothed on top of it. He didn't even have a blanket. I suddenly felt terrible about that. A hard lump took root in my throat again and tears filled my eyes. He'd given so much to this family in such a short time, and no one thought to even see if he was comfortable.

I turned and went back out to the landing, hot air cupboard, and pulled out a fluffy pink and grey throw. My favourite when I was sick. I put it to my nose and smelled the fragrance of washing soda, then took it back to Royce's room. I shook it out and carefully covered him with it, making sure it was right up to his chin. He looked so relaxed. So human. Like he was asleep.

But his chest never rose and fell and I remembered that the small pad where he lay his head was not a pillow, but the point of contact for his download. Or power up. Whatever it was. It was a devastating and confusing reminder of what he was. However right Nate was, Royce *was* a machine. But I also knew that whenever I was with him, the way he was with me was just too real not to be human. Even with all this going on right now, with Teddy and the chamber, machines just didn't do that kind of thing. It was not logical; it was love. Plain and simple.

Then I literally jumped about three feet high at the sudden sound of a female voice. 'Good evening, Miss Coe. Do not be alarmed. I am Sentia. Royce's AI assistant. Royce is on a power-down cycle. Would you like me to wake him?'

I held my hand to my chest, feeling the heavy thuds against it and stared at the cabinet I never knew could speak.

'Or is there something I can help you with?' it asked, making me stiffen again.

I wasn't sure what it could do. Whether it could move or anything. I noticed that the light on the front changed colour in time with its words and told me for sure where the voice was coming from.

When nothing else happened, I relaxed a little. I shook my head lamely. I had no idea if it could see or sense movement, although it obviously detected me in the room.

I looked back at Royce, frozen in exactly the same position. 'Is he aware of anything lying there like that?' I asked. 'Can he hear us?'

'On some level, his sensors remain alert for emergencies. Like fire or earthquake,' the metallic voice said. 'But everything else is replenishing power.'

I spotted something and stepped a little closer to Royce's sleeping form. It reminded me of Teddy the other day in the hospital. His eyes appeared to be moving rapidly under his eyelids. 'Is he dreaming?' I asked, suddenly alarmed.

'Similar,' the machine said, sounding almost wistful. 'He is downloading his day to his memory banks to recall later. It is essential for him to grow in knowledge and experience. So I guess, yes. Very like dreaming.'

The more she explained, the sadder I felt. I was asking, but I didn't want the answers. I was humanising him when it was obvious that he was demonstrating regular machine-like functions. Even the damn cupboard sounded human, for god's sake.

Maybe I was wrong and Nate was wrong and Royce *was* only a few weeks old. 'How long have you known Royce?' I asked, feeling weird talking to what could only be described as furniture.

'Fifteen days, three hours, five minutes and fourteen seconds.'

It was a cold drenching to bring me back to my senses. I nodded, my heart sinking like a lead weight in my chest. 'So you didn't know him from before,' I said, already turning, slowly walking to the door. I wasn't expecting it to answer.

'No, Miss Coe. I did not. I had the privilege of serving Royce after he was educated and made.'

I paused to listen, but didn't turn around. I just nodded and took a last, lingering look at Royce, still covered in my grey and pink fluffy blanket and then left. I was a silly, foolish girl, assigning emotions where there weren't any.

CHAPTER 36

R^{oyce} I awoke suddenly, immediately feeling warm and restricted. I lifted my head from the uplink port and looked around. For a moment, I was disoriented.

'Good morning, Royce.' *Sentia.* Good. I was in my room. It was what she said every morning—grounding me instantly from my dreams. 'All systems are fully operational. Cells are at full power. You are free to disengage.'

I twitched my index finger, and Bluetooth was switched off. I felt the synapse link drop from Sentia. I always hated that part; it reminded me that I was physically linked to something else and not in control —a machine.

I threw back what I saw, now was a fluffy blanket. I frowned at Sentia, not knowing how it got there. 'What's this?'

'Miss Coe brought it for you last night. She thought you might need it.'

'Chrissy… in my room? Why didn't you wake me?'

'There was no requirement. You were in full cycle and she didn't need you for anything.'

I felt angry and I couldn't pinpoint why. I was vulnerable. Looking like a machine. *Weak.* I didn't know why the hell I felt so pissed. 'Then why did she come?'

Sentia just ran the question through her system while lights pulsed consecutively across her front. She couldn't possibly answer. She was a basic servant model with little understanding of the subtleties of humans. I shook my head and sat up, irritably throwing my legs over the side and sliding down to my feet.

It was Friday. Last day of the school week. I did my morning toilet routine and went downstairs. Everyone was buzzing around happily like a sunshine breakfast commercial. It struck me as it always did how homely it felt. How a home should feel. It made me sad for Finn in the slum I'd left behind. With dirty paint peeling from the walls, bare floors and no food in the cupboards. Where the only encouragement came from my dad, throwing an empty liquor bottle at him to go steal him another. I felt guilty and ashamed for forgetting. No wonder I loved it here. I had to stick to my original plan. Teddy coming home was a good thing all round. The Coes and the Monshalls would be happy and I would have my plan back on track.

Chrissy came down to the kitchen late. She kissed her mom and went straight out to the car without even looking at me. Even when I joined her and whispered, 'Thanks for the blanket.'

Nate heard and eyed her curiously, then looked at me and shrugged. He had no idea what was up with her either.

The silence went on through school. Every lesson and every break. Simon called out as we were getting back in the car to leave, 'You're coming, right? Don't be late,' and put up a hand as we moved off.

· · ·

NATE GOT out and ran inside as soon as we pulled up at home.

'Chrissy!' I said, 'Wait!' before she could do the same and disappear off to her room. 'Please... have I done something wrong?'

She finally looked at me, but her usually transparent face was blank and impossible to read. Her eyes were dead, just like when I first arrived. When she didn't answer, I got out and went inside. I stopped in the hallway, not knowing where to go. Anger surged through me, making my power disk work hard to control my heart and blood flow. A red light beeped in the corner of my eye. I grit my teeth, wanting it all to shut the hell up. I had the right to be angry. I never knew where I was with her. How to be. How to act. I thought she'd be happy that Teddy had a chance. Was that it? She was closing off in readiness for that. I was so sick of living between the lines with her. At least the girls back home were simple. They wanted to fight you or kiss you. Black and white. Comforting in its ease.

She came in soon after me. 'Are we going to the party?' I asked as she went to pass.

'I guess... I said so, didn't I?' She flashed me an irritable look, then bounded up the stairs. It left me completely confused. I was convinced of a no. I went off to my room, shaking, running the conversation over and over like a glitch.

IT WAS HARD NOT to show my nerves the next day. Saturday. The day of the party and I was a mess. I played VR games with Nate. When I asked if he knew what was wrong with Chrissy, his only response was, 'She's a girl... get used to it.' He was right. I was behaving like a sap. In my old life, it would be yesterday's news. I had to be more like that. No wonder she was wiping the floor with me.

I went and helped Christopher clear out the garage after that, to keep busy. We sorted what was good to keep and made a pile to go to Goodwill. I wondered who Goodwill was. A lucky guy, whatever.

When I was done and couldn't find Sheila, I escaped to my room. I sat on my cot rubbing my hands up and down my thighs; a habit I'd had since I was a kid. Usually, when I was stressed or nervous about something. Chinks in the armour weren't tolerated at home and it could be exhausting keeping it up. I had to get my act together. I was going to my first real kids' party and, most of all, I was supposed to be going with Chrissy, and she was hardly speaking to me. It had all the hallmarks of a disaster.

I welcomed my synapse call with the professor. Its regularity was becoming a grounding part of my day. He always began the same way. 'How are you, Royce. Is everything going well?' Today he added, 'It's the big party today, isn't it?'

I nodded, hoping that my jerky movements weren't transmitted to his image of me. That crashed and burned when he asked, 'Nervous?' rhetorically. 'Well don't be. Just draw on all that street kid experience. These Tech kids will love it; I promise you. Try to enjoy yourself.'

I nodded, unconvinced, my mind straying to Chrissy. The only reason I wasn't hyperventilating at that point was that I no longer breathed conventionally. The reality of what I was doing tonight hit me with a bolt of terror.

'Ah, before you go… I have some news that should cheer you up. I have managed to locate another chamber about to be decommissioned from an army hospital on the border. It's to be replaced by a new model and is being shipped back to the manufacturer. I am making arrangements for it to make a detour for a few days to one of my secure locations. I will send you a date, time and location as soon as I know, after the weekend. A company ambulance will collect Teddy. The

Monshalls can travel with him. Then we can whisk him back to the hospital as quickly as possible afterwards.'

I was shocked at how quickly the plan had come together. Not sure if I was totally happy or not. It had thrown me so much. 'How much will it cost?' I asked. 'I mean, thank you, professor, but it will be a huge deal to the family; they're pretty stretched already.' I felt my face scorch as I left off the words, *paying for me.* I just couldn't bear to even voice it, my fear was so near the surface.

The professor was already nodding before I finished. 'I'll let you know as soon as I do. It might not be as much as you think. There will be small incentives to pay certain people to look the other way and for the drivers to hand it over to ours. Then there is the hospital to record it carefully in their records. That sort of thing. The ambulance and its crew will be mine and so will the location. The chamber is free, so we'll see. I'll have more of an idea of the cost after the weekend and we'll go from there.'

My previous nerves evaporated. I was amazed at what he'd managed to organise so quickly. 'Wow,' I said. It was better than I could have imagined. I didn't know what to say to him.

'Now go make your family happy,' he said, with a huge, knowing smile.

I nodded. 'Thank you.'

He went and I sat there a moment gathering my emotions now for a different reason. He'd really come through and it hit me deeply. I could give something back to these people that I'd grown to care about.

I got up and turned for my door, fully intending to tell everyone the good news, when I paused with my hand on the door handle. Chrissy had changed towards me since all this started. I thought we had something. I don't know what. A thing. And since all this with Teddy, it felt like it was draining away as quickly as it came. I wanted it to stay. More than anything, I wanted to feel what it was with Chrissy. Tonight was a party. A massive deal for a human or a machine. Just a boy and a girl on a real date. Just once. Before Teddy blew it all apart and I'd have to go away.

It made up my mind. I'd tell everyone tomorrow. It would make no difference to them. I'd just pretend he'd told me then. I was owed one night in this sorry excuse for a life.

hrissy

I felt bad, but I just couldn't help myself. I knew I was blowing hot and cold and Royce didn't understand. The truth was, apart from my inappropriate feelings I refused to acknowledge, if I encouraged him and he was sent away, it would be much worse, like I was using him or something.

Royce appeared next to me in the hallway and I couldn't look at him. I wanted to go, but my dad was fussing like it was prom night. 'Let's take a photo.'

'Wait!' my mom shouted, appearing with a large shopping bag. I recognised it immediately from the VR mall. RetroTrojan, a guys' store all the cool kids loved. The Populars were always talking about it. Confused, I went to take it, but my mom pulled it away. 'Not for you, dear, sorry, it's for Royce. I thought he'd appreciate some casual clothes, too. He can't go to a party looking like some sort of army cadet.'

I switched my gaze to Royce to see his expression and he looked completely stunned. It took him a long moment to reach out and take them. 'Go on, they're yours. I hope they fit. They're nothing fancy, just casual like the kids all like to wear these days. It's all retro 1990s, apparently.'

I loved my mom for that. For making him feel part of the family. I couldn't help being swept up in it. Especially when he looked at me for permission. That gutted me most of all. Him even considering the possibility that I could say no. 'Go on, take them, doofus.'

He beamed a heart-rending smile that wrinkled his eyes and revealed those cutest dimples I'd ever seen. It was how I always spoke to Nate and it crushed my heart that such a small thing brightened his whole face. 'Go and change!' I ordered, shooing him with my hands.

'I've taken all the labels off. It's just sneakers, baggy jeans and an oversized t-shirt,' my mom said, looking like she was fighting back tears.

Royce thanked her and bounded back up the stairs. It left me with Mom and Dad. 'We won't be late,' I said, not sure if I was reassuring them or myself. They seemed as nervous as I was. I guess, even when Teddy was home, we didn't go to many places. Certainly not at night.

My dad hugged me to him and then my mom. It all felt so strange, like it was a big deal. 'Actually, we've discussed it. We won't worry about you at all with Royce. We know he will look after you,' my dad said, all misty-eyed.

I wanted to tell them to stop it, now my mom was getting emotional too. 'Look at you, going out in the evening with the cool kids. The boy has given us all so much,' she said, dabbing her eyes.

My dad put his arm around her and pulled her into his chest. 'He definitely has,' he said, kissing the top of her head. Even he thought of Royce as a boy.

My gaze strayed to the stairs, willing him to hurry up. 'What happens when Teddy comes home?' I said to myself.

Then I saw the puzzled look on my parents' faces. 'I think even Royce assumes we'll send him back.'

I was gratified with a look of genuine surprise, then horror, like it hadn't even occurred to them. 'No, definitely not,' my mom said, shocked. 'That's never been mentioned.'

A flicker of worry crossed my dad's face as he considered the deeper implications, but thankfully, he kept his mouth shut.

I turned my head at the exact moment I felt Royce come down the stairs. The image threatened to sizzle into my nerve endings. He was so tall and handsome. Model hot. Long legs in baggy, low-slung jeans over white sneakers and a navy-blue skater shirt. White ghost lettering arched across the front: Electric Dude. It was perfect. I shook my head in amazement and laughed. I couldn't help it, he looked great.

'Wow!' my mom said, clapping and laughing. She pulled him into a hug as soon as he reached the bottom of the stairs, almost crushing him. Then gave him a loud kiss on the cheek.

'You look cool, Son,' my dad said.

Royce looked bewildered and touched. 'Thanks, all of you. I love them.'

'Go!' my mom said, roughly turning us both towards the door and giving us a little shove. 'Enjoy yourselves, you deserve it.'

I felt just as bewildered as Royce looked when we walked out of the front door. We gazed at each other, feeling weird. Like we were starring in our own movie or something.

CHAPTER 38

*R*oyce

I was still reeling from the Coes' genuine kindness during the car ride. Everything here was nothing like I'd imagined during training. I wasn't expecting any of these feelings to be involved.

There had been a subtle thawing from Chrissy, but it was weird and awkward next to her in the back. It would have been easier if I could have at least driven. 'Look,' I said, eventually to break the silence. 'Since this is unlikely ever to happen again, and I've never been to anything like it, and neither have you, can we make a pact to act normal and at least try to enjoy ourselves?'

She looked out of her side window and attempted to hide a smile. I had no idea what was going on in her head. It was one of the things that drove me mad about her. Then she turned her head to look directly at me and raised her eyebrows. 'Normal. A nerd and her AU... out partying together.'

I grinned. It *was* crazy. I bobbed my head, conceding her point. 'Well, as normal as we can be, but who likes following the rules?' As I smiled at her, I took in the heat that entered her cheeks and the curiosity smouldering in her eyes. She was so delicate and sexy all at the same time. She wore very little make-up. Just the dark circles smoothed away and lip gloss on her perfect lips. Her hair was down in loose curls around her face, to her shoulders. A white floaty top over black skinny pants and flat leather pumps. Comfortable but feminine, only hinting at what was beneath. She was beautiful to me. I burned the image of that real moment into my fake retinas. That and the most endearing thing about her: that she was completely unaware of it. The popular girls only trod her down because they instinctively knew she was fragile. It had nothing to do with her being dull or plain. Simply keeping down the competition.

I felt suddenly wild. This would be my one and only night with her like this. Tomorrow, Teddy would return as the wedge between them, so this was the end, before everything unravelled.

'OK,' I said, turning in my seat to face her. 'Let's make a deal.'

Her eyes sparkled with intrigue. 'What did you have in mind?'

'For one night, we're just two popular kids out at a rager.'

She giggled, putting her hand to her mouth. 'A rager,' she repeated. 'Where did you pick up that word from?'

I wasn't sure, actually. A film, probably. I shrugged 'Yep, a rager. You just have to trust me.' I was really starting to enjoy myself, allowing myself to slip back into the old me, just like the professor had suggested. 'Think of me as the bad boy from the wrong side of the tracks.' I grinned wickedly.

Her eyes widened, but they were glowing. She was all in, hanging on my every word.

'Your mom and dad would never approve, but you're a secret daredevil. Determined to kick against your parents' strict rules. You feel safe, because you know I'm tough and can protect you from anything.'

Her face was alight when my thought trailed off to focus on the shine on the curve of her lips. The flush that had appeared on her peaches and cream skin. 'Deal?' I said, my voice gone husky with the direction my mind had veered to.

She swallowed with effort and her eyes dropped to my mouth. Proving she was as affected as I was. In my old life, I would have dived right in. But the car pulled up at the front of the private club, breaking the dangerous spell.

I sat back and read the neon sign. *Ashby's Private Members Club.* Cars and kids were everywhere. Music was already a beat on the wind. 'We're here,' I said to myself. Gripping my sudden nerves and taking charge. The car ride and experience told me it was the way to go with Chrissy. The heat of her eyes burned my profile, waiting for what came next. She needed me to lead. It was going to be a crazy night, but I plunged in the moment my sneaker hit the tarmac. I was a street kid. Strong, but no longer forgotten and everyone was going to love me.

CHAPTER 39

*R*oyce

We got out of the car slowly and it pulled away immediately to take itself home. Leaving a chasm a mile wide. Without thinking, I held out my hand to invite Chrissy to hold mine. She looked at it for a moment before she took the step closer to take it.

I closed my eyes, relieved that my mistake was smoothed over without notice and I was able to enjoy the soft warmth of it. Closeness like this had been a rarity in my life. 'OK?' I asked.

She nodded, fixing me with eyes that trusted me implicitly and I grew taller. I led the way, purposefully towards the lights and the open doorway.

'Hey, Royce,' kid after kid said. Patting me on my back or bumping fists with me. Even the girls were greeting me coquettishly, twisting their hair around a finger, then sweeping it over a shoulder. 'Looking hot, Royce,' one said.

'Nice threads.' I didn't even know half their names. I just registered whether they were male or female.

I still had Chrissy's hand and continually checked that she

seemed OK. She smiled back at me a little nervously. No irritation at all the greetings directed at me, ignoring her. Even though she'd probably gone to school with most of these kids her whole life.

I smiled at her encouragingly and leaned into her ear. 'You trust me?' I drew away a little to watch her reaction. A small smile played on her lips and spread over her face as she nodded.

I tightened my grip, gritted my teeth and resisted the urge to kiss her right there in front of everyone.

We walked on through a hallway decorated like some kind of mansion and into a huge bar area. Everywhere was the same deep red and gold carpet, gold-patterned walls dotted with mirrors, picture frames of white bearded men and lit overhead with bright crystals hanging from the ceiling. It seemed too bright and in your face for a party, in my opinion.

We continued on through the throng of kids in loud conversation, posing in over-the-top clothes with stiff collars and colours that should never be seen dead together. They held real glasses in their hands and not a plastic beaker in sight. Nothing was like the dark, dangerous parties of home, where you could disappear in more ways than one. I'd settle for flying under the radar tonight.

I spotted the DJ, a guy I recognised from the team. You couldn't miss him. Under a spotlight, on a small stage, wearing shades, earphones. Attempting to look the part and failing sonically. The music was nothing but a dull beat. Too slow and nowhere near loud enough. This wasn't a rager, it was a posh drinks party. A dull mixer. I thought of Deej, from home and others like him, who made music from the streets, mixed live from stolen files. Some from antique disks played on large turntables from the last century. It was exciting and felt organic and raw. Like you were living the moment with the DJ that could never be reproduced in exactly the same way.

This was an AI-generated dirge, with very little input from the DJ at all. No vocals, no feeling. Simply downloaded from the Network-sanctioned cloud. It was mindlessly repetitive, which I guess was the point. They didn't want kids getting loud and hyped. They wanted control. This was some trance-inducing hypnotism, or something, already rotting my brain.

I headed for the loudest group of kids to clear the fog. I knew Simon would be there somewhere. My aim was to get the necessary interactions out of the way in case we wanted to sneak off.

Simon was exactly where I expected him. Right in the middle of a raucous group, egging each other on to down their drinks. One kid was chugging down a whole jug of beer while they chanted, 'drink, drink, drink.' The whole thing felt learned from an old film. Like they had no idea what was really cool. The beer was artificial crap, no longer made from anything that grew and, if it was, it came from fermented food byproducts. I remembered those headaches from hell and inwardly shuddered. I'd stopped drinking long ago, what with my dad and everything, and I was no masochist. Putting me off alcohol was probably the only good thing he ever did for me. If I wanted a high, I usually went for chemicals in the form of a pill, and that was only if I knew the cook and that wasn't often.

Simon spotted me and put up his hand. I pulled Chrissy closer to me and headed in his direction. I was almost there when Ace stepped out in front of me.

I halted immediately and frowned in irritation at the lack of space between us. It was either a challenge, or he had no concept of every human's personal bubble. He swept those freaky eyes slowly down my body, taking in my cool clothes and comparing them to his. He still looked like a soldier doll, fresh out of the box. His cogs were turning, trying to work out why I would dress this way. He would come up with, illogical. Street fashion was not input data given to any AU. They were subtleties reserved for humans. They related to identity and the social need to fit in and at the same time stand out. Something far too advanced for an AU to understand.

Simon appeared at Ace's shoulder. 'Stand down, soldier,' he said, half frowning and pushing him out of the way. I was impressed he'd picked up on the threat.

Ace seemed to wake up from his fixation and stood back. Simon picked up my hand and patted my shoulder enthusiastically. 'Nice threads. Glad you came.' He turned around to the team, still holding my shoulder. 'Hey, guys, Royce is here.'

I pulled Chrissy closer into my side, who I felt was trying to shrink back. I wasn't going to allow her to be ignored. This was as much her coming-out party as it was mine.

Some kid attempted to thrust a can at me right in my gut. I caught his wrist fast and stepped into his ear, making sure I tightened my grip just enough to hurt. 'I don't drink, but thanks, man.' I kept my voice as low and as calm as I could. Then, still holding his wrist, I twisted it, took the can and passed it to Chrissy.

His face creased a little in pain and outrage. 'Touching?'

I smiled just enough and he got the message not to mess with me again. I was way ahead of him in shit like this and with my innocent guise, it would be easy to explain it away as an intercepted threat to my human, which, in a way, it was.

I released his hand and he rubbed where I'd gripped. Satisfied I'd made my point, I switched my gaze to Simon, who nodded in respect. He'd understood right away. He pointed at my chest. 'We are going to do great things, you and I.' Then he slipped his arm around my shoulder and brought me with him into the crowd, now jumping all around me.

'Up the tempo, Zack!' Simon shouted at the kid attempting to DJ, who nodded and the dirge simply speeded up. The raucous jumping now went in time with the beat. I was being pulled all over the place and I fought to draw Chrissy in, but she wasn't enjoying it and I was forced to let her hand go.

In the end, I had to put my hands up and stand still. 'I'm sorry, I can't dance to this crap,' I said, turning to Simon.

He frowned at me, baffled and a little suspicious, like he couldn't make out if I'd just insulted him. I needed to save this fast. 'Don't take it personally. The music is terrible.'

A smile slowly spread on his face and his look changed to quizzical. 'It's all we have. What did you have in mind?'

I was walking a tight rope already, but I needed to switch this around. I thought of Deej back home and what he would do in this situation. 'Have you heard of the Beat-hacker?'

He laughed, but I could tell he was intrigued. I couldn't reveal he was a close friend, famous for liberating thousands of files from the closed library vaults, so I waited until he finally admitted: 'I have, but I thought he was some kind of urban myth.'

I shrugged. 'He might be, but I know how he hacked the vaults.' I didn't, but I knew where Deej saved his hacked files, because as a close friend, I had the key. They were bounced all over and held in a cloud under a dummy name. 'Does anyone have an old-style laptop or terminal?'

I didn't need to explain. Simon erupted into laughter, his arm around my back again, while he shouted, 'Out my bro's way.' He pushed through his friends to make a path to the desk currently occupied by DJ Zack. 'Let him use your Port-term,' he ordered right away.

Zack didn't look happy being sidelined and went to protest.

'Quit whinin',' Simon said, putting up his hand. 'We're going to turn this party up. It's lame.'

As Zack passed the far-from-old high-tech version of a laptop towards me, Simon grinned and nodded. He kept on looking at me weirdly, as if everything he was learning somehow proved something he'd thought even more. It made me uneasy. Especially when I looked down at a keyboard like nothing I'd ever used before. *Shit.* I immediately spun it back. 'Log in!' I ordered, quickly scanning and noting what he did. It was basically the same as the old ones, just without touch.

I checked behind me for Chrissy, and she was still there. I had to move quickly, otherwise I was going to lose her. She was looking around her, already a flight risk.

Simon noticed her for the first time when Cindy and Jessica appeared next to her. I used the opportunity to whip back the terminal and, guessing the imaginary buttons were in all the same places, I bypassed its usual channels in my search for Deej's secret files. All the while keeping my senses on the new threat.

Simon frowned as he tried to compute who Chrissy was from the girls he knew at school. His eyebrows rose when he landed on who she must be. He seemed surprised. 'Chrissy? … looking good.'

The two girls swept her up and down without comment, but it kept her occupied.

Meanwhile, I tapped the air over the Port-term with no obvious keys. Ours had been reconditioned a hundred times by small, skilled street firms in the back-alley workshops. They had no idea of the skills over the danger line. We were nothing if not resourceful.

Zack glared at me when I asked for his eye scan for the

county firewall. He put his eye next to the camera and a 3D keyboard appeared. 'Get me busted and I'll bust you,' he said.

I smirked and turned my head to Simon, who'd watched the whole exchange. 'I'm already in.' And I was. Hurtling through speedways of archaic fibre optics, a thousand miles a second. Snapping digits, running code, until Deej's pass-code clicked into place. I was invisibly copying files, bypassing Zack's pitiful firewalls, and installing a worm to corrupt them as soon as he logged off. The whole thing took less than a minute.

Simon laughed. 'Don't you want to hear some real music, Zack?'

He didn't seem convinced. I guess it sucked to have his set hijacked and blown out of the water. 'I have it. What is the speaker code?'

Simon nodded to Zack, who pulled a face, like I was an idiot. 'It's already connected.'

I gave him my deadest look. 'Not those ones, we want to be able to hear it. There is another system in here.'

While they looked at each other, mystified, I was already scanning for it. I found it, bypassed its access code and a huge thump and hum sounded, like a dropped mic. I grinned at Simon and he grinned back as the sweetest, melodic 1990s rap rang out to every ear. It stopped every conversation as they all listened, a little stunned. By their reaction, no one had heard anything like it. 'Real music,' I said, turning the volume up another notch and setting the running order to play. 'Don't touch it,' I said, pointing at Zack, who just seemed bewildered. His ego squashed under the undeniable realisation that his aspirations of being any kind of DJ were over.

I pulled Chrissy with me into the jumping crowd and we linked arms and joined in. One mass of unified enjoyment that became euphoria. All captured by the dream of a bygone time. Carried along by images painted by words of cool guys, sexy girls, chilling with friends in long summer days and steamier nights.

In one song, the team began to jump and chant my nickname as the best bro. Chrissy had been pushed off to the side. I would be lying if I said I wasn't flattered by the adoration, but I wouldn't be staying and this was the one night I had with the girl I was crushing on.

I'd also registered that there was now more than drinks going around this party and, apart from a few waiting staff, no adults to speak of. I wasn't going to let her out of my sight. So as the scrum tightened and got louder, I ducked under and out to reach Chrissy, where I took her hand and led her away to a quiet corner. There, we were shielded by a group of kids talking.

I was hyped. Happy. More than I'd been in a long time. I didn't think. I pulled Chrissy into my body, breaking every kind of AU rule. I didn't care. Tonight, I was the old me.

She felt stiff at first, no doubt thinking the same thing. I didn't push. Allowing her to work through to the role-playing game, I'd set up in the car. She gradually relaxed to warm butter in my hands. Perfectly assured and relieved of any guilt.

It was a triumphant move, but all I could think was that I'd never felt anything better. My body, flush against hers. My cheek grazing her cheek. My lips close to her ear. Moving to the music, my leg slightly between hers. I had to close my eyes and savour the sensation. Electronic pulses were firing through my organic nerves as if switched up to the max. My power disk was on constant vibrate, attempting to bring my pulse rate down. Flooding dopamine and sending me higher than any drug. Any alcohol. 'You OK?' I whispered next to her ear; she'd been quiet for so long. But she felt relaxed.

She nodded slightly next to my cheek. 'Are we in character?' she asked, dreamily.

My heart died a little at how confused she must be. Even I'd forgotten our pact. But every one of my sensors told me it was real. What she was giving me was real. I swear, if I thought for a minute she would have believed me, I'd have told her the truth right there. About everything. Instead, I continued to move with her to the music. 'Do you want us to be?' I asked, hedging. So scared and elated at what her answer would be.

'Yes and no,' she said after a beat.

I was so surprised, I drew back to assess her directly in the eyes. They were dark, large and dilated, but not alarmed at all. 'No?' I asked, darting straight to the negative. I had to know if she was feeling it.

She looked down like she was swallowing back nerves.

My heart felt like a jackhammer in my chest. The moment went on for eternity. I wanted to kiss the words right out of her, but didn't have the guts in case I freaked her out. Then she finally said the words I'd been dying to hear. The ones I felt she'd buried deep.

'I'd rather it was real and not make-believe.'

I stared at her, stunned. Still holding her by the elbows, while she wouldn't look at me. Then I finally had to tune in to the shouts and cheers going on behind me. The music had gone down a notch and there was a slam of a door. More cheers and clapping that got louder and louder. It was no use; everyone was gravitating to it and it could no longer be ignored.

I turned back to face Chrissy and picked up one of her hands. She smiled up at me weakly and I tried to read the message in her eyes. *Disappointment? Maybe relief?* I smiled back, similarly. I didn't want to lose the moment either. My mind was running over it again and again for subtleties I'd missed. Perhaps the commotion had saved us from the biggest mistake of our lives. An AU kissing a human in public. Headline news that would not go unreported, however great these kids thought I was.

We moved closer, inching through the crowd now swarming the opposite side of the room. The clapping was rhythmical, like they were egging someone on. Then I realised what was happening. The raucous applause was every time a bottle was spun on the DJ's desk and landed on someone. They chose a partner and were pushed into a cupboard for a few seconds.

'Dude!' Simon called, raising his arm as soon as he saw me. Hey, guys! Royce, my bro, is up next.'

Part of me wanted to skulk off the other way, but several hands were pushing me along in the back.

Chrissy stood behind me while they span the bottle again, and of course, it landed on me. It had to be rigged. The cheers were deafening. The team members were hanging off me, jumping on my shoulders and chanting, 'Choose, choose, choose,' like a group of primates.

'You have to choose, bro.' Simon grinned and held out his arm towards the group of giggling girls. Cindy and Jessica were pouting and posing. Fluttering their extended eyelashes seductively. Part of me wanted to choose Ace for the laugh, who was standing like a stone wall off to the side, but I wasn't about to miss the opportunity of the night. It took me a moment to scan the crowd. Then I spotted her pushed right to the back of the girls. I pointed past Jessica's shoulder, her eyes lighting with delight, thinking it was her, so I called loudly. 'Chrissy. I choose Chrissy.'

The boys behind me all cheered again and the slow clapping began. The girls parted and they pushed Chrissy towards me roughly. The cupboard was opened and we were both bundled into the dirty cleaner's storeroom, no bigger than three feet square.

The door was immediately slammed, plunging us into darkness. My eyes switched to night vision, so I closed them to sense Chrissy in the same way. We had instinctively clung together and I could hear and feel her shallow breaths. Hot and cherry-flavoured from her soda. 'Are you OK?' I asked. It felt like I'd asked her a million times.

I could hear the game still going on outside with another cupboard and they could open our door any time and discover us. I wanted to hurry whatever was going to happen, when I paused at Simon's voice, directly outside. 'No!' he snapped. Give them a minute; it's his first time.' Then laughter.

I could feel Chrissy's chest rising and falling, listening as well, but she held onto me. It was now or never. I sent a silent thank you for Simon standing sentry outside. My mouth was right next to Chrissy's cheek. 'I think we're meant to kiss,' I whispered, my lips moving agonisingly slowly to hers. Then I was there. Brushing the soft cushions now clean of lip gloss. Pushing against them, now matching mine. Slowly at first. Tentatively. Gradually parting to cautiously meet tongues. My hands roamed up into her hair and down her back again. Kneading, feeling the softness of her skin through her clothes, stirring me in ways I never knew I still had. It was so incredibly hot that she was so there, completely. Meeting me, deepening fiercely, pulling till we couldn't get any closer unless I was inside her.

A lightning bolt hit us as light spilled in, saving us from catastrophe. I pulled our mouths apart, leaving her breathless and me stunned. I'd never felt that out of control before.

Simon's grin was the first thing I registered through my haze. He'd seen enough.

CHAPTER 40

*C*hrissy

Simon was grinning at us, delighted by what he found. I couldn't take my eyes from Royce, conscious that his arms were still around me.

'Another minute?' Simon said, laughing.

We turned our heads to him at the same time. 'Close the door,' we both said.

Surprised but highly amused, and without comment, he did what we asked. Slamming the door, he announced. 'Unfinished business!' to the baying crowd.

It was a distant echo for me, because my brain had ceased to function. My mouth was already on Royce's. I wasn't about to stop the first meaningful kiss of my life, even with the small voice whispering, 'with a person who isn't real.' My head was already too jumbled about it. Conflicting with thoughts over the last few weeks. How strong this felt. How weird it was. Depraved. I eventually mustered every ounce of strength I had to push his chest away.

He let go so fast, he bumped into the wall. 'I'm sorry,' he said, immediately.

Instead of feeling better, I felt worse. He'd done nothing wrong. All he was trying to do was give me a nice time, like a normal teenager, from something he'd probably learned from films. I'd encouraged this. 'Please don't worry,' I said, thankful it was too dark to see his disappointment or fear. My heart was still thrashing, my body thrumming and I was dying with shame as I turned and opened the door to cheers.

I could feel Royce right behind me and hear him calling, but all I could think to do was escape. I pushed through the kids chanting, 'Royce the man. Royce the man.' Then I felt the gap between us widen as they all pounced on him and he was forced to let me go. I needed to get out. I needed to go home.

I breathed the cool air the minute I got outside and coughed. I forgot my mask and walked out onto the road and called the car with a button on my watch. Then I looked behind me for the first time. It was still noisy inside. A few kids were wandering around in groups. Some were drinking or smoking something illicit. One couple was kissing. Another boy was leaning against the wall, puking up.

I fidgeted, willing the car to hurry up. It wouldn't be long before Royce freed himself. *Too late.*

'Wait, Chrissy,' came from behind me.

I heard the whirr of the car as it turned into the drop-off point.

'I'll come with you.' Royce was right behind me and I was forced to turn and see his desperate expression. That killed me most of all. I felt terrible. 'It's OK. You stay… You have my permission.' It felt like a low blow to remind him of that and the wobble was evident in my delivery. But I had to distance myself from this. I had to distance myself from him.

He seemed to gather himself and grow before my eyes, as if he was literally putting himself back together. 'I don't want to stay.'

The door of the car opened and began to beep for me to get in. I let out a huff in exasperation. He wasn't listening to me. I didn't say anything else. I just got in the car and ordered it to lock. 'Home,' I said, glaring at him one last time as I pulled away.

I couldn't help watching him through the back window. Standing in the middle of the road, lost and alone, not understanding what he'd done. Tears came and I cried all the way home.

The car pulled into the drive and I hurriedly cleaned my face on my sleeve as best I could. I had to face my mom and dad, who would undoubtedly be waiting up. I took a breath and, showing my palm to the reader, I went in as chirpily as possible. But I was still shaking.

My mom came out into the hallway immediately. 'Chrissy? You're home early. Is everything OK?' She tried to look past my shoulder. 'Where's Royce?'

I tried to act carefree and head for the stairs before I gave myself away, but my voice was a little too high-pitched. 'All OK, Mom. I told Royce to stay with the team. I was tired, that's all.' I didn't wait to see if my mom was buying it and bounded up, two steps at a time.

My dad's voice came next, repeating all her questions.

'She's tired, she left him there.' I could hear the doubt in my mom's voice.

I burst into tears the moment I reached my room and flopped onto my bed, face down. Hopeless tears that made the cover soggy while I relived the kiss over and over. Each time, it would make me warm inside and then groan with wretchedness at how wrong it was. There was a name for people like me. I'd heard of them. They were sad, lonely people who fell in love with robots that normal people laughed at.

CHAPTER 41

Royce

I felt Simon come up to my shoulder and I turned my head from the road to look him directly in the eyes. 'She freaked out, ha,' he stated, like it was an everyday occurrence.

There was no point in lying, so I simply nodded.

'Don't sweat it. She'll come around. They always do.' Then he shook my shoulder and grinned. 'If not, there'll be plenty more where she came from, now you're on the team.' He winked. 'You and I will be superstars, just you wait.'

I studied him for a long moment, unpacking his words. On the surface, it appeared he was treating me like a genuine friend, then it made sense; his sudden interest in me. A bitter taste rose from my absent gut that my life had been reduced to this. Despite being better than any human and probably better than the best AUs, I was destined to be looked down on or squashed. 'Don't you feel weird hanging out with a TinBoi?' I asked, my attention already switching to the large figure of Ace approaching behind him.

'Not at all, man,' Simon said. 'You are next level evolution.'

If it weren't for Ace, I would have given the statement more attention. It did strike me long enough to check his expression, which did appear genuine. But Ace had come outside for a reason.

I straightened my stance out of instinct. He was too damned focused to want a chat. Simon sensed it in me and turned around at just the right moment and stepped between us. 'Ace! What do you want, man? Go back inside, Jessica is looking for you.'

He switched his gaze for less than a second, but was only surface listening. The lights were on, but no one was home. He was doing that weird thing where he was joining with the AI. The hard slams started hitting the back of my neck.

'You are faulty,' Ace began to say, but it was he who looked vacant and staring into space. I tapped Simon's shoulder and flashed him a warning look, which he understood, and ran back towards the party. I could hear him calling friends to come outside.

I swore under my breath. That wasn't what I wanted.

'You are malfunctioning and breaking all the rules,' Ace was saying.

More and more of the kids were pouring out of the building and gathering around us.

'You must go in for evaluation,' Ace continued. 'You must wait with me while I call it in.'

Everything was getting out of control. Chrissy. This place. Friends I shouldn't have and now this. In a microsecond of red, I drew back my fist and landed a punch directly to the centre of Ace's face. He fell backwards like a felled tree to the cheers of all the kids. My AU training evaporated and I was back on the block, beating down a kid trying to rob me of my dad's liquor. I pounded Ace's face over and over, more and more furious because those eyes just kept staying open and rolling back to me. I kept going until I could see titanium. He'd been taken so by surprise by my speed and ferocity that he didn't even retaliate. At least I assumed that was the reason. It was only afterwards that I wondered whether he was trained like me.

Then I felt a tug on my shoulder. Sirens were ringing in the air. Police were approaching and probably AU security. The tug became harder and I came back to my senses and scrambled back to my feet. Ace was rolling and jerking like an upturned beetle, trying to get up.

I was still wild and couldn't think straight. Simon whirled me round to look at him. 'You have to go. Now run!'

I just looked down at Ace's mangled face. 'What about— He knows where I live.' All I could think of was my family and that I had to end him.'

'Don't worry about that. We'll cover for you. Go!'

The sirens were pulling into the long driveway, so if I was going, it had to be now. My legs were moving before I gave it conscious thought. First at a jog, then after quickly checking over my shoulder, at a sprint. Jessica was there, now screaming. The sirens were screaming.

I dove into the nearest trees and hid, watching. Simon was holding Jessica by the shoulders and shaking her to shut up. I zoned in to hear him ordering Cindy to take her inside. He swung round on Brad and spoke something quickly that I couldn't catch. Then I couldn't believe my eyes. Brad drew back and punched Simon in the eye. It landed perfectly and Brad shook out his hand.

My head was pounding, trying to work it out. The kids were all now pushing and arguing in the middle of the car park. Several cars came screeching to a halt, doors slamming and officers spilling out. AUs in black, and the unmistakable TinBoiz silver-grey truck.

I should have been away from there by now, but I was numb with shock. It was obvious while they loaded the still-jerking body of Ace into the van that Simon had lied and told the police that Ace had attacked him and the team had been forced to put him down. I was grateful, but cold sweat scared. I had no idea whether there would be any repercussions. The team knew. Jessica knew, and Ace was her prized AU.

I forced myself to slink away. Following my homing signal, through the small forest of strange, rain-resistant trees and eventually to the road of identical blue doors. I wasn't sure how long it took me, but I approached 2365 Blue Sycamore Drive. *Home ... was it though?*

I went to knock at the door and stopped when I saw my knuckles red and bloodied. Even in a Tech household, it was obvious how I'd gotten them. I swore like the old me. I'd been doing that a lot tonight. I'd really reverted to type. *What was I doing here?* I should have run ages ago. I was wrecking Chrissy's life. Putting the whole family in danger. I had to do something.

I looked up and down the silent road. I guessed it had to be about midnight by now. I went around the side of the house, took a few steps back and ran, launching myself up and over the gate. I landed in a crouch on the other side. I'd never used the side access before and almost knocked the lid off the dumpster, bumping my shoulder into it. Then, when I got to the back, I triggered the security light, like a dumbass.

Christopher appeared at the glass doors. I put up my hand as he opened them. He ushered me quickly inside. I went in, making sure I slipped my hands into the pockets of my jeans. I hoped he didn't notice how dirty my new clothes were.

'It's OK. He's home, Sheila,' he called over his shoulder.

Sheila appeared and threw her arms around me, swathing me in her flowery perfume. 'Oh, I'm so glad you're home safe, Royce,' she said, pulling apart. She was holding my cheeks with a reprimand that was so loving. 'You had us worried half to death. I'll be talking to Chrissy in the morning, don't you worry about that. She shouldn't have left you there. How did you get home?'

'Walked,' I said, looking sheepishly between them. Christopher now had his arm around Sheila's shoulder to get her to stand down.

Her hand went to her mouth in despair and Christopher cut in, putting a hand on my shoulder. 'Get off to bed, Son. No harm done.'

I was speechless with shame and conflicting emotions. I nodded and took the opportunity to step around them and run up the stairs. They were blaming Chrissy for not looking after me. It beggared belief. I'd kissed her and let her go home alone and then got into a fight. What was the saying? *You can take the kid out of the street ... but not the street out of the kid.* Whatever, I was proof.

Nate opened his door before I could shoot past. 'Come in,' he said, waving me in with his arm and shooting me the most dagger look. It was so strange coming from him that it shook me from my personality beat-down.

I frowned and cautiously followed him in, closing the door. I watched him closely. His dead serious body language, as he walked around his bed to sit in his usual place, against the headboard. He bobbed his head for me to do the same. It was like he'd grown up in a day. I almost smiled. I wandered around the bed, pushed my hair back with my hand and sat wearily on the bed next to him. I'd aged about a hundred years, too.

'You'd better start talking, dude,' he said, throwing a small brown bottle on the bed in front of me. 'Since when does an AU need pills?'

My heart stalled so hard at the familiar bottle, not even my power disk could get it going. I looked him in the eye sadly and took in the hurt and accusation. I hadn't even used the damn things; they'd made me fuzzy and I'd wanted to keep my head clear. The game was up and I hadn't even been there a month. 'My sister came home upset and I can't allow that. What's going on, Royce?' He pointed to my hands that I'd forgotten all about and I brought them up to my face. They were a bloodied mess and I shook my head, not able to offer a single excuse. I really did love the little guy. He was my second brother and there was no point in hiding anymore.

'My name is Mike,' I began on a weary exhale. 'And I'm from a place you never wanna go, way beyond the Danger Line.'

The anger drained from Nate's face and then it sprang to life with interest. I think he fully expected me to lie, but I was done lying to him. I could see his young mind scrambling for questions. He was up on his knees in a second, pointing at the silver bands at my wrists and my neck, particularly the TinBoiz plate. 'But how?' Then, without giving me time to formulate an answer, 'I thought it was a wasteland of outlaws out there.'

I closed my eyes, leaned my head back against the wall and relived that night all over again. The night I changed. Everything changed forever. I wasn't sure if I was speaking aloud. Either way, my thoughts were rambling. I was lost in the memory of giving myself up to save Finn. 'It's not what you think. It's ordinary people just trying to survive. My brother's still there.'

'Wait! You have a brother? Is he like me?'

I smiled at him and loved him for that. Out of everything, he was more interested in whether he reminded me of my kid brother. I pulled the worn piece of paper from my pocket. I'd carried it everywhere since the professor gave it back. I held it out to Nate. 'Finn.' I explained. 'He's very like you. Maybe a year or two older.'

He studied the picture, eyes wide with excitement. 'What about your mom and dad?'

'I have a dad.' I averted my eyes, finishing in my head, *he's a waster.* 'My mom died when Finn was small.'

'Why d'ya leave? Why d'ya come here?'

The questions came thick and fast, but I knew I had to answer them if there was any coming back from this. 'You don't know how people are forced to live on the other side, Nate. It's dangerous because we have nothing. We have to rob and steal to survive.'

I took a second to search Nate's face for fear, but it didn't seem to even occur to him that perhaps it was why I was there. So trusting and pure. But I'd said too much not to continue. I had to make him understand what was at stake for a lot of people. So I recounted the whole sorry story, from when I gave myself up to the police, to the professor spiriting me away from Juvey and giving me the choice to help the world or go back into the pot for body parts. He absorbed every word, looking horrified at the end.

'It's true. Everything. I swear,' I said, shaking my head, exhausted. 'We'd heard rumours before. People going missing. But we had no idea of the scale before that night.'

'So the whole TinBoiz Realism Programme…'

'Comes from real human body parts,' I finished for him.

'So they're lying about growing tissue in labs,' Nate said, his face darkening.

'Maybe not initially. But the industry exploded and they couldn't keep up with demand or make us cheap enough. In the end, it's all about money. Outsiders are cheap, abundant and a nuisance. It's a win-win for the UGN.'

'And the professor guy?'

I half laughed and scratched my head. 'He's kind of a

renegade. He thinks the AIs will take over one day. He hit on this wild plan to hide us in plain sight to protect humanity.

'Whoa!' Nate said, eyes widening to saucers. 'That's so cool. You're like a superhero spy, or something.'

I flattened the air with my hands to quieten him down, but I had to laugh. It was kind of a relief to finally tell someone the truth. It was a heavy weight to carry and I got serious again. 'I have to go back, Nate.' I took in the horror and disappointment in his face and smiled sadly. 'Come on, dude, you said it yourself. Teddy will come home and the Monshalls won't afford the lease. Your mom and dad can't afford it on their own.' I looked down at my crusting, cracked hands. 'And I did something stupid tonight.'

Nate looked down at them, too. 'What happened?'

I leaned back against the headboard again and sagged at the litany of mess-ups. 'I kissed your sister.' Then flashed a sardonic look at Nate. 'Then I put Ace out of action,' I said, holding up my bloodied hands. 'I had to. The idiot was a dog with a bone that wouldn't let go. He was going to turn me in.'

Nate pounced off the bed and was already walking towards the door. I sat upright, not expecting that at all. 'What are you doing?'

He put his hands up to calm me. 'Don't worry. I'm just getting the first-aid kit from the bathroom. You can't go around like that, it's too obvious.'

'Wait!' I said, getting up to go with him.

I followed him into the family bathroom, where he put on the light. 'Close the door,' he hissed, while he opened the small wall cabinet. He reached up on tip-toes and pulled out a large rectangular green box with a red cross on it. He set it down on the closed toilet lid and turned on the sink faucet. 'Give me your hands,' he ordered.

I let him pull me closer and put my hands under the warm flow of water, watching his serious face at work the whole time. He was cute as hell and had absolutely no idea how many times I'd done this for myself. Probably since I was no older than him. I could tell he felt good about helping me and I loved the little guy for it.

I remained silent while he washed and dried each knuckle, applying soothing cream and then a plaster on every one.

'There. Good as new,' he said, switching his gaze to mine and grinning.

I continued to stare at him in wonder, mapping his happy face, and loading it to memory.

He scowled. 'You're not waiting for me to kiss it better, are you?'

I burst out laughing and ruffled his hair. 'Stop making me laugh, you little dumbass, they'll work out I'm a fraud.'

His little face dropped and he stopped struggling. So serious, I wished I knew what he was thinking. It was late. 'Come on,' I said more quietly, opening the door, grinning.

He followed me out onto the landing. 'Thanks, kid,' I whispered. I stood there, just taking in what a great little human he was. The whole family was. Nothing here was what I imagined. 'I have to go now and make a report to my professor.'

His face crumpled and he took a step towards me to protest, but I put up my hand and brought his gaze back to mine. 'I have to do some damage limitation, Nate. There will be repercussions. I need the professor to get ahead of it. I can't bring danger to your door.'

He nodded, reluctantly. 'Tell me everything, after.'

I watched while he wandered to his door. 'I promise.'

Until he went inside.

CHAPTER 42

*R*oyce

'Call the professor,' I ordered Sentia, as soon as I got into my room.

'Are you sure, Royce?' Sentia lit up immediately. 'It's late. I'll send an amber code.'

'Send red,' I said, irritated. I knew that would get the professor out of bed.

The professor appeared as a hologram in less than a minute. 'Thank god you're home,' he said, immediately.

I was momentarily confused, but then he followed that with, 'Show me your hands.'

I held them up, covered in Nate's handiwork, slowly falling in. 'You know.'

My brain was scrambling over how quickly that had been. His eyes were darting and his hairline was perspiring as his brain worked double time. 'What's happening?' I asked. He was usually so calm.

He picked up on my panic and dialled it down. He held up his hands. 'Forgive me. I just got home myself. Tell me exactly what happened.'

I started from when I got outside, skipping the kiss part, and how I'd completely messed things up with Chrissy. I said she needed to go because she was too tired and that I should stay and bond with my new team. I kept it as close to the truth as I could in case my body language gave me away. 'Then Ace came out, threatening to report me to the AI for malfunctioning. I told you that dude was gonna be trouble,' I said, firing up my anger all over again. Looking back, it struck me then how jealous Ace sounded. Real or not, I stuck with it.

It was the prof's turn to put up his hands to calm me. 'That part has been taken care of,' he said, brain still whirring.

Mine felt slow, trying to catch up with how he knew all this.

He studied me, looking baffled. 'I am at the upper echelons of TinBoiz. My team gets notified if anything like this happens. It can't afford for the brand to be tarnished.'

I was confused. 'It?'

'The AI... I thought you understood, Royce. There is a human board of directors, but the central operating system is AI. That's how dangerous all this is. I was able to smooth it out with TinBoiz Security and the police, who are the AI arm of the state.'

'Who are also controlled by the AI,' I recited from my training.

'Thankfully, the call was picked up by one of my spy subs and I made sure I was on the team for pick-up.'

My muscles relaxed and my system powered down from fight or flight mode. 'What about Jessica? Ace is her AU. She might cause trouble.'

The prof was ahead of me and already shaking his head. 'Ace will be back with her by the end of the week. Fully reconditioned with an upgrade,' he said with satisfaction. 'No real attachments have been made.'

I frowned, fully believing that. Ace was an accessory on her arm. I guessed she was about to go designer. It worried me a little, what a possible upgrade would be, exactly. Ace was a pain as it was. But I knew a gift horse when I saw one and took it gratefully, relaxing with relief. 'Thank you, man.'

The professor still looked pissed. 'This was close, Royce. You have to up your game. Your disguise is slipping.'

I nodded, knowing that was the truth and he didn't know the half of it.

'There was some good that came out of tonight, though,' he said, now smiling.

I stiffened. If there was, then it was news to me.

'You made quite the impression with your school team. They rallied and backed you to the hilt tonight. The captain, Simon, is it? He lied through his teeth the most elaborate story about Ace going mad and attacking people, even giving himself a black eye to prove it.' The professor chuckled.

I still felt bemused about the whole thing. Not sure what Simon was getting out of all this.

'No, Royce, despite the close shave, it was a win. You are doing well. Embedded in record time. The Coes see you as family and your team sees you as an integral member. You have exceeded all expectations.'

I was completely shocked by the praise; half expecting to be carted off like Ace after my major mess-up. The professor actually seemed proud of me. I could only guess that in the larger scheme of things, in his huge conspiracy theory of AI world domination, I was exactly where I should be.

He could see I wasn't convinced and shifted tack.

'The most pressing matter is Teddy. I want him out of the hospital and away from AI eyes as soon as possible. Arrangements are coming together remarkably fast. Teddy will be collected on Monday night, when the night shift takes over. He will travel in my ambulance to one of my facilities.'

My mind was buzzing over the plan coming thick and fast, sending waves of terror and excitement for Chrissy. This was the perfect distraction after tonight. Either way, this was happening. Really happening. 'How long will he need the chamber?' I asked, figuring that was key before they noticed it was missing. I remembered how long it took for me.

'As long as we dare,' the professor answered, a little troubled. It proved he prayed it was long enough. 'As long as possible. My contact at the hospital is smoothing out the database to record some sort of new cryo treatment trial, which his parents will sign for, as an excuse to remove him from the hospital. If Teddy responds, it will simply be recorded as a response from the clinical trial and no one will be any the wiser.'

'Why are you doing this?' I just had to ask. 'Why are you helping them?'

The professor looked dumbfounded, as if I should know. He tutted. 'Because you asked, because you care, Royce.' Then he bobbed his head, 'And I suppose, to have them grateful and indebted should a bad state of affairs arise.'

That I got immediately. They'd owe him. It made total sense in my world. Satisfied, I nodded. It was a good plan. It would at least go part way to lessen the awful atmosphere I was going to have with Chrissy tomorrow.

CHAPTER 43

*C*hrissy

I awoke with a start. It had taken me ages to go to sleep last night, running over what happened. The kiss and dying a thousand deaths when I couldn't kid myself it was real. It was no better than kissing a doll. Every time it came down to that and I died a little more.

Then there was a noise on the landing, the bathroom light buzzing to life and hushed voices. I knew Royce must be home and he was with Nate. I could hear Nate's ridiculously loud whisper.

I cringed, hoping Royce wasn't telling him anything. I couldn't bear Nate looking at me like that. My own brother, disgusted. At some point, I must have drifted off with exhaustion, because the next thing I knew, it was morning.

I lay there until the final call from Mom. 'Hurry, Chrissy. You don't have long and Royce has something important to tell us.'

I sat bolt upright and my heart stopped in my chest. *He wouldn't, would he?* I'd heard somewhere that AUs couldn't lie. I was immediately covered in a cold sweat. I pushed back the quilt, numb with fear, and got out of bed. I walked stiffly to the bathroom, with nothing else to do but face this head-on. I stepped under the shower, feeling condemned. There was nowhere to run. I slowly got dressed, praying that by some miracle, Royce had kept his mouth shut. Reasoning that my mom and dad would have quizzed him last night about coming home late. I could only hope that he had the good sense to swerve the truth if he couldn't outright lie.

When I was ready, I slowly descended the stairs, like I was facing a firing squad. Straining my ears for clues where the conversation was heading, I paused at the bottom as I could hear Tina and Tom. *Why were Tina and Tom involved?* Another hot flash shot through me. Of course. This was so serious, they would need to send Royce back. *Oh no.* I immediately shrank inside. That was worse than anything. I was about to run in and shout, 'You can't!' when my mom appeared in front of me and made me jump. 'Ah, there you are. Come and sit down quickly. You'll be late for Community Club.'

My heart sank at that. *Sunday.* I'd completely forgotten in all the chaos. How could they think of community duties at a time like this? Picking up litter and washing people's cars for free. 'Arghh!' I hated Community Club.

'Sit down,' my mom ordered, pointing at one of the vacant chairs at the table.

It was next to Royce, whose eyes said everything. Apology. Warmth. It was real. I was there. No escape and I couldn't hide from the real feelings in them. *'I got you,'* they said, loud and clear. So I slowly walked around the table and sat next to him and looking at all the serious faces around the table. Even Nate was there, which was weirder still.

My mom pushed a juice in front of me, then sat and looked directly at Royce. 'OK, we're all here. Away you go.'

I closed my eyes, imagining myself projectile vomiting the second he opened his mouth. However, the feeling drained away the moment his hand covered mine under the table. I wanted to pull it away, but he held it fast. I wanted to scream 'touch law' in his face, but it was too late for that. Way too late. I felt the cotton bands around his fingers and took a cautious look at the dressings, but the pause before he spoke, while he looked at everyone individually, made me stop obsessing and tune in to the gravity of the room. I studied his serious profile, wondering what else had gone on last night. Voices on the landing. Nate with him in the bathroom. His hands cleaned and dressed. *What the hell?*

Then, he cautiously began to speak and my heart thumped harder with every word.

'I have news. I spoke to my professor last night.'

Tom immediately put his arm around Tina's shoulders as if bracing themselves. My mom swapped an anxious look with my dad and I sat numb, thinking that I could have been so far off base.

'It's good news,' Royce continued. 'He said to continue our day as normal, then tomorrow, in the evening, Teddy will be collected and taken to a secret facility.'

Tom hugged Tina, but she couldn't look away and held her hand to her mouth to stop herself crying.

My heart was skipping, making me light-headed.

'What happens? What do we do?' Tom asked, his words high-pitched and rushed. His brain scrambling for practicalities before he fell apart in joy and excitement.

'The professor said, as a minor, you can accompany him.'

'What about the hospital, what do they know?' my dad asked, drawing our attention and nods of agreement.

Royce switched his icy stare to him. 'Teddy has been enrolled in a clinical trial for some sort of cryogenic treatment.' He looked back at Tina and Tom. 'You will sign the waiver at the hospital before you leave.'

They both nodded vigorously as if that was a given.

'Can I go?' I piped up, suddenly. 'I have to go. He'll want me there,' I said in panic at the doubtful look entering my mom's face. They were taking him, god knows where.

My dad patted the air for me to calm down. 'We'll see,' his eyes tracking to Tom, leaving the decision to him.

'I will certainly try,' Tom said.

I relaxed into my seat again, slightly mollified. I knew it would depend on how strict the secrecy was.

'Do you know where they're taking him?' Tina asked.

Royce shook his head. 'I'm not sure. A secure location, managed by the professor. One of his labs, I guess. He has a team of experts. The best in the world.'

He frowned a little as if he was lost in a memory somewhere. I wondered what that could possibly be for an AU.

How long will it take?' Tina asked.

Royce smiled, but it held sadness. 'I don't think anyone can know that. As long as they dare keep it, is my understanding.' Then, before another barrage of questions: 'The chamber is being diverted on its journey from an army base back to the Meditech depot. It is to be replaced with a newer model, and the tech company will break the old one down for parts. Teddy will have the time it takes to be missed.'

Tom was rubbing his hands over his face with stress. It could be a day or a week. No one could know that. 'How much is all that going to cost?'

Tina wrapped her arms around him. 'We will find the money, even if we have to sell the house.'

Everyone drew in a breath at that.

Royce looked puzzled.

It was one of those things polite people never spoke of: No one ever heard from neighbours again when something like that happened.

Tina and Tom looked at each other, their eyes filling with unshed tears. 'It's our only hope,' Tina said.

My dad spoke calmly and firmly, like he always did when he was taking charge of a situation. 'I'm sure it won't come to that.'

My mom gave a single nod in finality.

'My professor asked me to assure you that he will only ask you for the cost of the bribes. That will be the hospital night staff and the human delivery driver. The ambulance and its AU crew are his and so is the facility.'

Tina was openly crying. 'He is so kind. I don't know what to say.' She and Tom clung together. 'I can't thank him enough.'

I was stunned. It was unbelievably generous. Royce had managed to secure all this for people he barely knew. My heart literally split in two. The shame of last night just peeled away, leaving my heart open and raw. No one did something like that without genuine feelings.

Even my dad felt it. He put his hand over Royce's, now clenched on the table. The conspicuous first aid ignored. 'Thank you, Son. You've done more for us in a few weeks than anyone has in a lifetime.'

My mom was up on her feet and around the table, hugging Royce around the neck. 'We love you so much, darling boy,' she said, kissing his cheek, now crying as well.

I was a wash of emotions. For the new hope for Teddy, but mainly for how everyone was treating Royce as if he *was* real. I looked around at how happy everyone was, until my gaze fell on Nate. He'd been noticeably quiet throughout. Now, he was staring stonily right at me. It shook me sober. Because in all my lovely cloud of reverie, he was so serious, almost miserable-looking. Then he looked away as my dad clapped as if a spell had been broken. Bizarre.

'Let's all get ready and go to Community Club and share some of our good fortune with the neighbourhood.'

All the parents clapped and agreed, scraping their chairs

to get up. 'We have a lot to be thankful for,' Tina said, looking up at Tom adoringly.

Nate was the last, still not saying a word.

I didn't want to go to stupid Community Club, either. I was too excited. But I was also scared. I was back in turmoil about Royce. Nate was acting weird and Teddy might come back to life. Then everything would change.

CHAPTER 44

oyce

I sat between Nate and Chrissy at the Community House, or so it was called. It looked like an old church to me, that had been repainted white and spruced up. It had the same bench seating and a guy talking up front, just like Mack had said. Of course, most were derelict back home, but you could still tell what they once were. *Weird.*

The guy spoke in a monotone about being grateful to be alive in such a time of abundance. I frowned when I compared back home. This was a scrubbed version of church. Mack would shake his head and say, 'All the God has been taken out'. The community leader up front was a stand-in for a priest. White suit instead of black and a tie instead of a collar. Even I had to wonder who we were thanking if it wasn't God. The AI, the UGN? *Hell, no.* I wasn't by any means religious, but even my blood simmered at that. Mankind's stupidity in handing over its trust to them. Although it did make me wonder, as I was sitting there, how important a higher purpose was, otherwise, what was the point?

I could feel Chrissy radiating heat like a fire next to me.

That was one proof of humanity right there. AI could only mimic a reaction like that in its AUs. Chrissy sensed something inherent in me, unquantifiable to her; it just was. She was doubting herself and feeling terrible, which was totally understandable. But as much as I yearned to, I couldn't tell her without putting her in danger. Plus, if Teddy returned, I would go, and I wouldn't build her trust just to break her heart like that. I had to find Finn. I needed to look after my own.

CHAPTER 45

*C*hrissy

I got paired with Nate for litter-picking. This was going to be a joy. I hated it and grumbled why Royce didn't have to do it.

'Because it's your service to the community and he doesn't have to because he already serves,' my dad said in his stern-not-able-to-get-around-him voice.

I huffed and followed the line of his arm, pointing at the trash bags. 'Get on with it,' he said, turning to walk back to the others. Royce was standing with them and looked over at me a few times in that calculating way he had. I wondered if he'd say something, but he didn't. In the end, I pulled up my mask over my face and stomped off to catch up with Nate, grumbling for him to wait up.

He was still quiet.

We started picking up small pieces of litter on the grass verge of the road. There wasn't much, only stuff that had blown in the wind or washed into the gutter by the stinking, toxic rain. We had to use a special grabber stick and latex gloves. We looked really stupid. 'What's wrong with you?' I asked, having had enough of Nate's mood already. Apart from strops when he had to do chores or homework, it was so out of character for him. 'You get killed in the last level of your game, or something?'

Nate stopped, threw down his litter picker and bag, and glared at me. 'It's not all a game, Chrissy. Some people are fighting for their lives.' Tears were filling his eyes and he flopped down to sit on the kerb.

I froze in shock, taking in his head buried in his hands and his good shoes in the gutter. I threw my own stuff down and quickly sat next to him, trying to pull his arms away to look at him.

He shrugged me off and turned the other way. He was crying.

I was completely baffled and upset for him. 'What is it, Nate? What's wrong?' All the while, I was racking my brains and the only thing I could think of was the news about Teddy. Then I fell in. 'Are you scared for Royce when Teddy comes home?' I felt terrible because, in all the excitement, I hadn't given it a thought.

Nate spun round on me, red with tears and anger. 'Well, let me see… I guess,' he said, loudly, putting a sarcastic finger to his chin. 'Why did you leave him at the party?' he threw at me, furiously.

I was so taken aback. I had no idea why he was being so angry and horrible to me. I scrambled to my feet, ready to argue as well. I wasn't responsible for everything that went wrong. 'That's none of your business,' I chucked back at him. 'You're just a kid.' Then, as I went to stomp off, his next sentence froze me to the spot.

'You're the one reacting like a kid. So what if he kissed you. People get kissed all the time,' he said, so loudly I was forced to look around in case someone heard.

It brought me down next to him again with a slam. Dazed by the shock that Nate actually knew.

'Didn't you see his damaged hands, Chrissy?' he asked, looking sickened with me.

Now he'd lost me. Nothing he said made any sense.

I remembered the soft dressings from that morning. They were nothing but a passing thought at the time, as there was so much else going on. I shrugged. 'What did he do to them?'

Nate shook his head slowly, like he couldn't believe it.

'What?' I said, holding out my hands, at a loss.

'Ace!' Nate glared at me. 'That's what happened. Right after you left, Ace started on him and Royce had to beat the crap out of him. The police were called, the team covered for him, but he could get in big trouble over this, Chrissy. Jessica will prosecute for sure.'

'Oh my god,' I said, resting my own head in my hands. I had no idea he'd faced all that alone. Then I was on my feet, turning back for the community house. 'We need to tell Mom and Dad. Get him a lawyer or something,' I said, swapping the direction of my feet a couple of times. I couldn't think.

Then Nate was next to me, grabbing my arm. 'There are no lawyers for AUs, dumbass.'

Oh no. He was right. I was tugging the roots of my hair, turning this way and that. My mind darting through all the implications. 'He must have told his professor, surely,' I said, halting my steps in a lightbulb moment. 'He'll sort it out, won't he?' As I pleaded my last words to Nate, I was overwhelmed by shame. Royce had gone through all this in the last twenty-four hours. 'And he still tried to help Teddy,' I said miserably.

'But it's you he's doing it all for. You, Chrissy! And all you can do is act like some ridiculous ice princess with him.'

I was now crying. Tears running down both my cheeks by

the time he finished his tirade. 'But he's an AU,' I wailed, sobbing, still trying to justify it to myself.

Nate turned and walked off, dismissing me with a wave of his hand. He turned and continued to walk backwards. 'You know what, Chrissy? He wouldn't want me to say this, but right now, he's more human than you are. You're the robot who has no idea how to live.'

I just stood there, dumbstruck. Watching my little brother wander off into the descending smog, until my tears dried on my cheeks and the smog hid him from view.

A sudden cough reminded me to get inside, otherwise I'd be too sick to go with Teddy tonight. I had to get back and make sure everything was alright and nothing bad was going to happen to Royce before I left.

My parents were loading tools into the trunk of the car. They'd been tending the flowerbeds protected by the over-hang of the community building. I looked around. 'Where's Royce?' He was nowhere in sight.

My mom opened the door for me to get in the car. 'Nate!' she called. 'Time to go.'

I turned my head to see him wandering slowly back.

'Royce went home to check on arrangements,' Dad said.

I nodded, taking the news silently. Nate's words were weighing heavily on me. His face looked grimy from the smog and tears as he got nearer. I wondered if mine was as bad. I got my answer when my mom passed us both soap-wipes. Then we got in and stared out of our separate windows.

By the time we got home, it was nearly lunchtime and obvious no one was home. My mom went straight to the kitchen-glass and the red light was flashing to indicate a message was waiting. The rest of us crowded around her when she waved her hand and Royce's face appeared. 'Hello, everyone,' he said, intently, as if he was looking for the image sensor. 'I had to go out on personal business. Everything has been arranged for Teddy, but it's been moved up to tonight. He will be transferred at 10 p.m. My professor asked that you be at the hospital for nine for all the red tape. Chrissy can go, but those escorting him can't know where they're going. That means you won't know where Chrissy is. So I guess it's up to you if you can allow that.'

My heart was beating wildly while my mom exchanged a look with my dad. It was a whole day early.

Nate looked at me accusingly, but all I cared about was that I was going, no matter what.

'That's it. So thanks, guys. I hope all goes well.'

Before I could analyse the weird sign off, Nate rushed off and I was left staring at my parents. We all wanted to cry and huddled together and hugged. 'It's happening and I'm going,' I said through my tears.

My mom was weeping silently and my dad was attempting to hold his in badly. I didn't care, because he simply nodded. The best answer I could get. 'But you do as they say, to the letter, Chrissy,' he said, his brow furrowed with worry.

I was glad I had the afternoon to prepare. I needed to get myself in the right headspace for Teddy and what I would say to Royce when he returned. I paused at Nate's door. He was probably just sore that he wasn't included again. It sucked, but Teddy was my best friend. I knocked lightly with my knuckle.

'Go away,' Nate's voice came from inside.

I ignored him and went in. His curtains were drawn and he was sitting in almost darkness in his usual place on the bed. His knees were up under his chin and his arms folded on top of them. 'Are you deaf?' he asked, lifting his face from his arms.

'Please don't be upset. I understand, I do, really, but Teddy—'

'Teddy, Teddy, Teddy,' Nate mimicked, cruelly. 'You don't get it, do you? How can you be so dumb? He's gone, Chrissy. Didn't you hear the message? I mean, beyond what you wanted to hear?'

I was dumbfounded. Shocked rigid that Nate could be so mean. Then his words started to sink in.

'It was a goodbye,' Nate dropped like a stone. 'And I hate you.' He flung himself over and sobbed into his pillow.

'No, no, no,' I said, my mind scrambling, refusing to believe it. He had it all wrong. I went over the message as I rushed over to Nate. To the bitter end. *Thanks, guys, hope it all goes well.* Nate had to be wrong. He had to.

CHAPTER 46

oyce

    It was harder than I thought getting out of Samesville, as I'd grown to think of the place. With every damn street the same, it was nigh on impossible to navigate. Everyone had cars and there was no public transport at all. I was too slow and conspicuous; I needed to get off the street. Hot wiring was impossible on an AI-controlled car. Thankfully, I had borrowed Nate's UV-cancelling goggles and a baseball cap. I'd left him an IOU and hoped he understood. I had my street clothes on from the party and still stood out like an idiot, but at least they couldn't immediately see I was an AU.

I thanked God, the stars and the universe for my internal direction sensor. I knew home was to the south, so I headed in that general direction, figuring I'd come up with something on route.

Sunday afternoon was quiet, but I did get some curious looks from car passengers passing by. I put up a hand or looked the other way. Thankfully, they were so cosseted here, stranger danger, loitering with intent, or even AU gone rogue, was the last thing on their social radar. So as long as I kept within the normal speed of walking, I could pass through the community without a hitch.

After three agonising hours that I could have covered in one, I finally reached the gates at the boundary of Fairacre Gated Community.

I looked around, and, after satisfying myself no one was watching, I took a run up and climbed up and over the gate. The sub in the watchman's hut was reading and didn't even look up. I walked away before he even knew I was there.

I wondered how many communities there were like this one. They were the real important citizens. In a pyramid of class, we were the bottom. The surplus. The expendable depot of parts who were the oil of industry. The elite creamed off the top from some utopia somewhere. How many of those there were, I had no idea. Not sure anyone did. Then there was everyone else in the middle, like the Coes and the Monshalls. They were grateful because they had the work, which afforded their tiny square block of real estate and driverless car. They got to send their kids to a clean, ordered school. That prepared the next generation to pick up the mantle for the crushed middle. They never questioned anything, because they'd been fed a line and had all their basic needs met. They were the ones who innovated, invented, were the real brains and above all, paid the taxes that supported the Elites. Without them, the pyramid would crumble.

Everything made sense now, as I trudged along. No one got to see how the other classes lived. It was how the AI kept control. We were the oil, then the Techs were the engine that kept the paddle steamer of Elites floating above.

I looked up, instinctively. *Was the AI their tool?* That was what I didn't understand. If the professor's predictions were right, then maybe it was the point it got to where it knew it was better than the Elites. More intelligent than the whole human race. What was better for the greater good of everyone. The point where it became God. That was the part I grappled with. I was here to fight when that happened, but what if the AI was right? Life wasn't that great for the most part, already. Normal folks were trodden down and forgotten or brainwashed and deluded. Only the Elites knew everything and were they too stupid to care?

My musings had taken me to some sort of industrial district. I could relax a little. I was deep in no man's land. Inside the workings of the clock. Somewhere between where the Techs lived and the Danger Line. Nothing but factories, trucks moving goods and cars. Some were driverless, but most were older, driven by subs or lower-grade AUs. The mechanical workforce going about their business, keeping the wheels turning.

I could take my goggles off and put them in my pocket safely now. I was still heading south, relieved that the next part should be easier. I managed to hitch a ride on the back of a delivery van, drop off and hop straight onto another. As long as I was still headed in the right direction.

I kept this up until I caught sight of the mammoth iron wall. Higher than several houses, impossible to even make a dent in to break. Pulsing with red lights all around it and an AI voice warning, 'You are approaching the Danger Line. Turn back unless you are authorised to cross. The UGN cares and cannot guarantee your safety.'

I inwardly laughed at how truly ridiculous that was. No one escaped into the Outlands. It was warning stray robots not to cross when all the *real* people were locked outside. It beggared belief.

I jumped off my last ride and hovered in the shadows, watching the gates. They were as high as the wall; no apparent mechanism or people controlling them. They slid open and closed. But what I did see was the thickness of the wall. It was at least thirty feet thick, like a keep with a gate on each side. It was there that the vehicles were checked by army-looking AUs. At least I thought they were. They had the height and physique, dressed completely in black. Helmets, Kevlar, and holding semi-automatic guns.

I felt a flutter of nerves, immediately squashed by my powerpack. *Powerpack. Shit!* It suddenly hit me that I would have no place to charge overnight. In all my haste to get away, I hadn't given it a thought. I could only hope that I could rely on my bio-systems until I could find somewhere to power up.

I focused on the vehicles going through the gate. They were mainly automated fast-food delivery vehicles or trucks dumping waste. It made me seethe that filth was dumped in huge toxic landfills, right near where we lived. Out of town, out of sight, out of mind. No wonder we all got sick. But as hated as they were, the dump trucks were my best way to get inside. They were mainly automated, but some had the lowest-grade AUs. These were the ones I was looking for.

A queue had built up. Only one vehicle could pass the checkpoint at a time. I sprinted out from my hiding place and kept low alongside the trucks, popping up to check what was sitting in each driver's seat. Until I hit upon number two in the line. An ancient AU, made almost completely of alloy. Perfect, as its face was simply a mask.

I had no time to think. I yanked open the door, dragged out the AU and snapped its neck sharply to the right. I scanned around me, quickly. Logging nothing around had a pulse, I hefted up the machine and threw it back inside. Then I hopped in beside it and closed the door behind me. The AU was motionless, now with its head in the footwell. Just in case, I put my hand to its chest and sent a magnetic pulse through its power pack. Now it was fried. Then I turned my attention to the panel in front of me, went down my menu to 'find code'. Script ran at the corner of my eye, until it found a diagram of simple driving instructions. It was almost completely automated. Its journey was pre-programmed, with only slow down, stop and start controlled by the AU. I guessed its job was mainly for the other side of the Danger Line, where nothing was orderly and it could be open to all kinds of obstacles or attack.

It worked like a dream.

The gates opened by vehicle recognition and I smoothly released the foot pedal to enter the keep. The creepy-looking AUs walked around the truck with some sort of sensor and one stopped at my side window. I couldn't see its eyes through the black visor, but I felt it reading me. I immediately shut down my systems to basics, figuring there wouldn't be much to the one I fried. I couldn't spark a warning that I was in any way overqualified for the job of driving this truck.

Code ran into my files for the longest thirty seconds of my life, then it stopped.

CHAPTER 47

*R*oyce

The soldier stepped back and the gates opened in front of me. I released the brake and moved off, praying nerves didn't jerk my foot off the accelerator pedal.

The gates closed in my driver's mirror and I soared with exhilaration and relief. I was away. The terrain suddenly changing from clean and orderly to a shanty town after an earthquake in about three seconds. *Home.* But it felt remarkably alien, which I found surprising after such a short period away. Guess you got used to comfort quickly.

The sudden thump in the back of the neck pulled me up sharp. The AI was knocking to come in. *Shit.* I wasn't completely sure if there was just one or several, depending on where you were. Like jurisdictions, or something. It began pulsing its usual pattern of code and instead of fighting it, I decided to relax to look inwards and examine it. I immediately initiated incognito mode and was shocked that I understood. 'Switching to Gibberlink' flashed in the corner of my eye. Each pulse of GGwave sound represented a small piece of data, infinitely more efficient than speech or regular code. I was no Tech, but this was no computer integration that I'd ever seen. The message was simple instructions on where to go. Another capability the professor had hidden inside me. How else would I have understood? My hacker buddies only knew so much. This was next-level tech.

I replied to the directions. 'Diversion. Re-route required ad hoc.' Then quickly replaced the last word with 'improvised', as ad hoc sounded too human, even in Gibberlink.

If I had breath, I would have held it. There were a few tense moments before 'affirmative' came back. I'd been put on code 'amber' – whatever that meant. The assistance on the controls suddenly unlocked and I realised I had the wheel.

That was all I needed and I headed for the river. I would know where I was then. It would take no time at all from there to my old neighbourhood. A great excitement filled me to finally see Fin.

Everything had worked like a dream. Nothing appeared to have changed. It was still the same tumbledown tenements and backstreet shops. The same rubbish, lining crumbling roads. A pang of nostalgia stabbed my chest as I trundled through my old neighbourhood, wheels crunching into huge potholes. The ride was ridiculously bumpy. Holes that never got fixed. Some big enough to lose a car. It all added to the feeling, compounded as I pulled up outside my old building. Everything was the same. Patched door, right onto the street, that I knew led up two flights of concrete steps to the tiny, three-roomed apartment over the boarded-up shop. Still a black-market goods store. Even familiar vagrants shuffled along, carrying their brown paper bags. A homeless person slid down a wall in front of me, to sleep off his drug-fuelled stupor in the overhang of the doorway next door.

A group of kids made me jump, zooming either side of me on their cobbled-together bikes, made skilfully from the parts of old wheels and combustion engines foraged from the dump. No helmets. Deathtraps. Treated no better than vermin. Scouring the area for something to steal or deliver illicit goods for the crime lords who governed every sector. Every block had its own pyramid of power—its own ecosystem. Now I knew how the other half lived, I guessed everyone needed to feel they were better than someone else.

I sat there for thirty minutes, soaking up my old life through new eyes. All the while, I watched my old street door. No one went in and no one went out. It was still a couple of hours from curfew and I needed to ditch the vehicle. Not only could it be traced by the AI in seconds, but anything or anybody that didn't belong on the block had to be gone by then. A police magnet, if I wasn't careful. I switched the power back on, did a final sweep of the area and headed for the nearest landfill.

I was still wearing the mask of the discarded AU. So as the barrier rose, I slowly edged inside, keeping the barrier from falling by blocking it with the truck. Then I ripped it off, chucked it down into the footwell, slipped out of the door and was away. I replaced it with Nate's goggles and pulled the baseball cap down low.

It was less than a mile to jog back to my small, insignificant street door. I took a beat to compose myself before I went inside. I had to remember I'd freak them out at first. I would be their worst nightmare.

I tried the handle and wasn't surprised to find it unlocked. My dad had long since lost the key. He'd said there was nothing worth stealing and relied on the huge bolt of the apartment door to keep out intruders.

After checking the street either way, I went to slip quietly inside, but it was hard. I had to bash it and scrape it across the ground. I guessed it had dropped on its hinges or swollen from damp. Maybe that was why Techs no longer used wood. The alternatives were clean. Homogenised. Uniform. I still frowned, as it had never happened to my door before.

The concrete steps ahead of me were green with slime. The leak above them had never been fixed. My frown deepened as I took them two at a time, feeling with my sensors for noises and differences. My gridlines were mapping furiously as I went.

At the midway landing, I paused and turned. The peeling black-painted door was a few steps ahead of me. New, flimsy panels of boarding made me bound the last steps and peel them back to see the holes bashed through the splintered wood. My heart jolted. It was clear they'd been made with some sort of axe.

My powerpack was whirring overtime, sapping precious energy, but I couldn't help it. My imagination was running wild. The handle pushed down easily, proving it was unlocked. My dread deepened as I pushed it with a scrape. It should be at least barricaded if someone was inside. I was already praying as I looked down and mapped the scrape mark in a quarter circle. It had been like this for a long time. My time away hadn't been that long. I ran a quick calculation. Training, surgery, recovery time, more training, my time at the Coes. It couldn't have been more than three months in total. Still, none of this felt right.

I edged slowly inside. 'Dad? Finn?' I called. Not loud enough to startle them. More to mask my rising fear at what I would find. I pushed open the bedroom door I'd once shared with Finn. Nothing but a stained mattress and a cup on the floor.

I jumped and crouched down low, instinctively, at a small sound coming from the lounge. A scrape and a definite shuffle. There'd never been any carpet, but there was someone in there. Something kept me from calling out and I kept my mouth shut. I inched along. Past the bathroom. Scummy, with the tub still gross. The only room left was the one ahead of me. The kitchen and main living space. My father had taken over that room. He passed out on a chair or staggered to the ripped sofa and that was where he slept.

Shuffling in a crouch, I slowly pushed the door, peering through the crack in the jam. This was the only place left for someone to be. I could hear shallow breaths and elevated heartbeats. My hopes were already rising as I went in with my arms up, ready to calm them. I took a first step from the shelter of the doorway and felt a head-splitting whack around the head that literally made me see stars.

I staggered, holding my head, barely having time to register the blood. Whirling around to see an old guy standing above me on a chair, jump down to hit me again.

This time I was quicker. I grabbed the spade from his hands and pushed him into the wall, holding it tightly under his chin.

It threw me for a moment. Lines of static flickered in my eyes, settling, until my gridlines did their stuff. This wasn't Finn or my dad. I mapped his vaguely familiar face. It was the guy with dreads. A local vagrant, always on the block. I strengthened my grip with anger. 'What are you doing here?' My voice was weirdly gravelly and low. This was my place.

His eyes were terrified and wide and his breath carried the acrid stench of tobacco and liquor. I loosened my grip a little for him to speak.

'It was empty, I swear. I thought there was no harm if no one was going to claim it.'

I frowned and, for a moment, I wanted to crush his throat, but I was already running the data. It had been no more than a few weeks. I concentrated my anger on him again. 'Where is my brother, my dad?' I ground out the words through tightly clenched teeth.

Even in terror, the guy looked confused. A sudden fear

shot through my temper; you couldn't fake a look like that. It took him a moment where he tried to remember. 'The drunk and the kid?' he said, eventually, screwing up his face like he thought it unlikely.

I wanted to swipe the words right off his mouth, but I needed him alive. 'Yeah, what happened to them?' Then I added, carefully, 'And the other son.'

His frown deepened, which wound up my anger and impatience with him. He was shaking his head manically. 'Not sure about that. Haven't seen the guy for a long time, but the kid went, two, maybe three months ago. I was just watching the place at first. Then, when no one came back, I figured I could take it as mine. I'm sorry, man. I'll leave. Do you work for the landlord?'

I was so shocked and confused, it took me a beat to answer. It was clear he had no idea who I was. I ripped off the goggles; his eyes almost popped and he pissed himself on the spot. I let him go and loomed over him as he slumped to the floor, waiting to be killed. I despised him, despised this hovel and a world where laughably autonomous units always had to be owned by someone. But not me. I didn't know what the hell was going on here.

I stepped away to get a hold of my temper. My disk was stuttering, on overdrive.

I eventually looked over at the pathetic excuse for a human, still rubbing his throat. 'Get up,' I said, barely able to speak. I felt so done.

I watched as he shuffled with a terrible limp to a refuse sack in the corner. 'I'll just get my stuff.' His voice was now gruff as mine.

My anger ebbed away at the sight of him, the last vestige of what the Strong Forgotten had become. I just felt devoid. Empty inside. 'You have no idea what happened to them or where they went?' I asked, now calmer.

The guy stooped and picked up his bag, shaking his head. 'Only one way out of the lower southside and that's on the backseat,' he said, ruefully.

I half smiled. Wasn't that the truth. It was the way I went. 'If I let you stay, will you look after the place?' I swallowed as a wave of emotion crashed over me. 'See that no one takes over till my—' I went to say Dad, but changed it at the last second to, 'Original occupants come back?'

The guy looked surprised, like he just won the lottery. Despite being convinced of his death just now. 'Sure I will. I'll keep it clean. Secure. I'll even do up the place. Won't let no druggies in here, no way, no how. I'm a sure thing,' he said, putting his hand over his heart in a cross. It reminded me instantly of Mack. God. The church. It was weird how these things still held meaning to the older folks.

I nodded, a little ashamed. The poor guy was so grateful for so little. The place didn't even have electricity, and running water was sporadic. 'Good then. See if you can make a lock for that street door,' I said, already walking out.

The guy was still saying 'Surely will' over and over as I scraped the door shut behind me. I couldn't get down the steps and into the foul street fast enough. I didn't breathe in the conventional sense, but it felt like the stink of the place clung to me, trying to pull me down until it owned me completely. My mind was reeling. Nothing made any sense. I had no idea whether Finn had ended up in Juvey after all, or if Dad was in prison or even still alive. His life expectancy wasn't great.

I paced one way, then the other, pushing my fingers up through my hair and replacing the cap. I was going out of my mind. I hadn't expected no one to be left.

My friends hit me like a bolt of lightning. They'd know what had happened. Precious had evaded the police with Finn and the rest had refused the offer and gone back.

Maybe they got out. Escaped. Someone might have heard something.

I was already pulling my goggles on and setting off in a light jog in the direction of Downtown. Past the regular shops that had long been closed and replaced by illegal gambling, brothels and drug dens. Peppered with the occasional fast-food place selling suspect meat at next to no credits. *Peter Pats Pizza.* The last place I'd been. I had to start there.

I sped up my jog in that direction, turning up my jacket collar and pulling the cap lower against the light drizzle that started. I kept up the pace, only pausing at Mack's old shop. It looked old and run-down, even by Outlands' standards. There was no glass left and it was covered in thin boarding. A guy went to hurry past me. 'Hey, what happened to Mack?' I asked.

He turned his head and pulled a face. 'What you talking about? Get the hell away, Wackjob.' He took a wide berth around me as if I was some kind of lunatic. I was instantly fired up to fight and held my hands out wide. 'I've been in the smoke. Wanna try me, old guy?' I called, shocked at the speed and ferocity of my anger.

The guy waved his hand like he had no time for nonsense. 'Argh, ask my father, shop closed years ago.'

I wanted to chase after him and pummel his head until he told me the truth, but I was immobile with shock. Running the words, feeling synapses popping in my head and coming up with zero. All I could do was slowly turn and continue in the direction of Peter Pats.

The light was starting to fade when I finally came out into the wide area where the vans parked to get loaded with delivery pizza. I barely registered the new sign, because my heart was filled with the place where it all started, and the huddle of youths standing where I used to stand. Huddled out of the drizzle, under the overhang, watching the subs and old-style AUs going in and out to the vans.

I scanned them quickly for any smaller guys that might be Finn. Then, making sure my goggles were in place and pulling down my cap even more, I stepped out of the shadows and made my way towards them.

I held up my hands as they whirled around and stiffened. 'Hey, it's just me. Mike. No need to sweat.'

In a second, I quickly registered no familiar faces and various weapons in their hands. Mainly knives, a couple of bats, but one had a gun that I strongly suspected couldn't fire by the state of it. It didn't even have a firing pin. I smiled but kept up the wary act with my hands up and came to a stop about six feet away from them. Only hit with disappointment at where everyone could have gone.

'Who are you?' the biggest kid said, glinting his knife so I could see it. It was pretty impressive. A serrated blade of at least eight inches. I held back my wisecrack on the tip of my lips and tried desperately to remain respectful. I was on their turf; they didn't know me and even my clothes were weird-looking. I guess with the goggles, they put me in some paid thug bracket for a gang. 'I'm just trying to track down my friends. We went to juvey together, I just got out,' I said, my gaze straying to the building that I now noticed had 'Peter Pat and Sons, Pizzas' on the front. Then rested it back on the youths. 'We were picked up from here, actually, about three months ago,' I finished with a sad smile at the memory.

The big kid narrowed his eyes with suspicion and swapped a look with the others. 'What were their names?'

I recounted them one by one, making sure I pointed in the direction where they all lived so they knew I wasn't bull-shitting them.

The kid didn't answer, but looked me up and down, assessing my clothes.

'I was with my kid brother, he got away. Finn? He used to live over the shops on Thirty-fourth with my dad, but they moved recently. Do you know anything that could help me find them?'

The big kid swapped a devious look with the others. I couldn't tell if he was going to try to con me or just give me the runaround. 'Come on, man. Help a guy out,' I said, trying to appeal to a fellow street kid.

The kid straightened up as if he'd made up his mind. 'OK, yeah. We remember that kid. Not sure about the dad, but the kid went after curfew one night in a line of shiny new vans. Word has it he sold someone out to get out of the neighbourhood.'

I went to protest. That couldn't be Finn. 'No, he was only this big,' I said, holding out my hand. 'Barely nine years old.' But the youth pointed the knife at my chest as I went to step forward.

A few of them sniggered.

'What are you talking about, fool. The kid was at least fifteen, sixteen. Running drugs with a girl for Vinney Paul. Maybe that's how you got out when nobody ever does,' he said, moving closer to me, menacingly. The others closed in while my head was reeling. Too stunned to react right away. 'We don't know you, your brother, or any of your damned friends. So scoot off to whatever rock you crawled out from,' the youth said, taking my inactivity for weakness.

My mistake in coming there quickly became his mistake, as I was not getting out of this without a fight. When the first blow came, I batted it away with ease, but it was close enough to knock off my cap and reveal my already bloodied head.

It shocked them at first, with a brief pause, but then the blows came thick and fast, from all directions. I drew inwards, handing myself over completely to my training with

Damien. Blocking, spinning, and kicking, in a well-choreographed dance. I wasn't trying to hurt them, simply dealing with the inevitable, like a chore at work. This only got them angrier, and they became more vicious, attempting kill shots, so I had to put them on the ground. After the second blow hit hard, a plank was swiped at my face. I dodged my head back, but it caught the goggles and ripped them right off my face.

There was a moment where everything stopped, their eyes widened and they all gasped.

I guess I should have noticed the hard slams on the back of my neck, but I was too preoccupied by the group jumping back in shock, like I had leprosy. It took a beat for me to realise my eyes were on full show.

I froze, registering the curses, the pointing fingers and the wide-open eyes. My mind was racing on how I could prove it was just me. But the blow that finished me off was the words: 'He's so damn real.'

*R*oyce

'Is he rogue?'

I wanted to turn back time and start again. They were never going to believe I was anything other than a spy now, but I had to try.

'I am real,' I said, my gridlines coming in and mapping nuanced facial features frantically.

But they erupted into laughter.

'He does have blood, look,' one of the younger ones said, pointing.

The big one kissed his teeth. 'They're way past tin soldiers now, my dad told me.'

The younger kid's eyes widened in excitement. 'He's a TinBoi.'

I was already shaking my head, holding up my hands and backing away from them. 'No, you don't understand. I'm meant to look like one. That's what they're doing to the kids in juvey.'

They looked at each other and laughed.

I took a step forward, desperate for them to listen, but they scrambled back against the wall.

Then a short beep came from behind me and my heart splintered painfully. I knew that sound. I felt the presence. 'Run!' I shouted.

They ran like rats out of a barrel, in every direction. The big kid making a last eye contact of thanks before he went. It warmed my heart for the briefest moment before I turned, hands up, to the AUs. They got out slowly, uninterested in the boys. 'Keep your hands where we can see them.' Unfolding to their military-grade height, these weren't cops; they were soldiers, sent particularly to get me. There was no point in running. The boys were clear and there was no attempt to round them up.

One of the AUs went behind me and pulled my arms down one at a time to cuff me. I knew the minute I tested them that they were impossible to break. They knew who they were coming for.

I was nudged towards the car, the door opened and my head was pushed down roughly to get into the back. I had to sit forward, the only way to sit in cuffs. I was struck by the old man's words. Numb with hopelessness, I was leaving in the back seat. But this time, I would not be coming back. The feeling of déjà vu was overwhelming, like I'd lived this a thousand times, probably for every kid before me.

My heart slowed and my head lowered in defeat. I was running out of energy. I told myself it was the pack, but in my heart, I knew it was more than that. The car was armoured, the AUs had long lost any empathy for anything, so it was safe to assume I would be taking this ride and it was very unlikely I'd survive it.

CHAPTER 49

hrissy

I couldn't believe Royce had gone. I refused to. If he'd run away, they'd simply bring him back. He was ours. Our property and registered to us, period, I thought angrily. I didn't have time for it. I was already riding in the back seat of Tom and Tina's car, on our way to the hospital, for the most monumental night of our lives. Teddy was going to live again.

It was dark, past curfew, and we were exiting the gate of Fairacres. The business district was beyond exciting. It surrounded every community, but only the workforce ever really got to see it. In a way, it was bleak. Huge silver or grey rectangles of commerce, surrounded by carparks protected by barriers. Soulless, really. This was where the machines ruled. No need to make it pretty.

It brought my mind back to Royce. I hadn't got him out of my head all afternoon. I'd stayed in my room, jumping at the slightest noise that might be Royce coming home. Then I could accuse Nate of being dramatic and concentrate on the important thing happening. But Nate had been right. By 8:30 p.m., Royce wasn't home and I had to leave for the hospital.

I wanted to question Tina and Tom about keeping Royce after, but every time my heart sped up to broach it, I'd see their worried faces, their eyebrows drawn in a frown and it was clear they had other things on their minds. It was not the time to bring it up.

I was worried about tonight, too. We had no idea whether we would be stopped and questioned about taking Teddy in the middle of the night, or whether the chamber would even work. That brought up a whole other avenue of terror. We all knew this was the last-ditch attempt to save him. Without it, they would have to face the terrible dilemma of whether to keep his life support going. The argument to switch off his machines would be impossible to ignore.

My heart died at that. As much as I hated Royce's selfishness right now and the fear I might not see him again, I squashed that flat. I couldn't worry about two of them right now.

We finally pulled in through the gates of the modern hospital. Another cube, but this one was striped with windows on every floor. We stopped right outside the bank of doors, spewing out light onto the drop-off bay. I got out in silence and looked up at the orangey-grey, light-polluted sky. I heard the beep of the fob as Tom sent the car home and my butterflies prickled at the reason. There was no point in parking, charging credits. We were leaving by other means and had no idea how long we'd be away.

I followed Tina and Tom in through the doors, but instead of going straight to the elevator, we approached the doll-looking reception sub. A little too jerky and synthetic to be real. Plus, if you got close enough, there was nothing to her below the waist.

A flash of Royce's earnest face came to mind. The warmth and softness of his skin when we kissed. His bleeding knuckles. I groaned inside. A physical knot was twisting in my stomach.

'I believe you have something for us to authorise?' Tom said.

The sub smiled with brightly painted pink lips and blinked her stunning, fake-blue eyes. 'Certainly, sir. Please put your thumb here and your retina up to the reader.'

She moved the pad across to Tina. 'Yours too, Mrs Monshall.'

I could see Tina was shaking.

'This outlines your permission for Teddy to be enrolled in the clinical trial, as a minor, and your release of St Michael's jurisdiction of care and taking full responsibility for the time he is away.'

Tom nodded, taking a fortifying breath. This was big and he felt every bit of it. The strain was etched on his face as he pushed down his thumb.

Then we were all walking towards the elevator. 'I expected to see a real person,' Tina whispered too loudly.

We entered the lift and Tom nodded, cautiously, as he pressed the button. I guessed the bribery went higher up, but he had the sense to keep quiet. Even alone in the lift, I wondered if there was hidden surveillance.

Everything was unremarkable in Teddy's room. He was lying flat as usual. Eyes closed, connected to his breathing apparatus and surrounded by several monitors.

His female doctor came in shortly after, still talking on her wrist-com. She smiled immediately and ended her call.

'Hello, guys. You've signed everything?'

The Monshalls nodded nervously. The doctor's obvious excitement seemed to make us feel worse. I guess the dream had become real, fast.

'The ambulance has arrived to take Teddy to the trial facility. We just need to prepare him for travel, OK? Do you have any questions?'

'Is it far? The trial hospital,' Tom asked, hedging carefully. We knew it was a secret. I think he was testing the waters, maybe hoping for a slip.

She looked thoughtful for a moment. 'Not far. I guess about forty-five minutes,' she said, smiling.

We all took that as a win, but before we could launch into any follow-up questions, our attention was sucked away by two of the biggest black-ops type AUs, coming into the room behind two orderlies in green scrubs. They were pushing a huge dark-green, metal cylinder covered with dials, lights and buttons, right out of a Second World War U-boat, or something. It was terrifying. I looked up at Tom to see if he looked as scared as I felt. The alarmed look he swapped with Tina told me everything I needed to know.

The doctor looked a little nervous but was quickly in business mode, giving instructions to the orderlies. She seemed to know what she was doing, but also knew whatever was happening was a rare opportunity. I swallowed, trying to relax. This was happening. It was what we wanted.

'Please don't worry,' the doctor said, looking over at us with a brief smile. This is part of the chamber that will heal Teddy. It will take over from all the machines currently keeping him alive, all in one place, with the minimum of trauma to his system.'

I looked doubtfully from all the very modern equipment around his bed to the archaic pressure cylinder dwarfing the room.

'Please stand back,' one of the orderlies said, gesturing with his arm.

We all took a step back at the same time. No one wanted to get kicked out and miss a second of this.

The two AUs that had hung back went to either side of the furthest end of the cylinder. One pressed a lever and steam hissed loudly from a valve, making me jump. I gripped Tom's hand out of instinct. A circular door opened at the blunt end nearest us.

Inside it was painted a creamy colour, with a single yellowed light bulb as the only light; equally twentieth century. Like an old-fashioned bus, it was all held together with bolts and rivets.

'It looks so old,' Tina said, looking up at Tom as worried as me.

He just nodded. 'It's an old model.' He was convincing himself. I guess, resigning himself to the fact it was this or nothing.

'It must be OK if the army uses it,' I said, trying to look hopeful and failing inside.

The orderlies pulled out a long, padded shelf where wheeled legs unfolded from the bottom. They pushed it directly level with Teddy's feet. Then the AUs approached either side of his bed, one glancing at me to move with eyes so like Royce, they stopped me breathing.

Tom had to yank me out of the way, I was so affected. It took me minutes to recover. I just watched in a state of numbness as the carefully executed operation happened in seconds in front of me. The two AUs lifted Teddy. The orderlies shifted the bench right under him. The AUs lowered him and rolled him steadily into the cylinder while the orderlies unplugged Teddy quickly as he went. The door closed, the AUs pressed several buttons and it all took no longer than about five seconds. It was impressive.

I hadn't felt the doctor come to stand next to me, watching as well. 'They are switching over his life support to the cryo-lung.'

I took a ragged breath and nodded. The name fit the cylinder perfectly. 'It looks scary, but this means minimal distress for Teddy. They're bringing his temperature down now and he will stay in there the whole time. He'll be rolled straight into the chamber. It really is remarkable,' she said, shaking her head and marvelling.

I tried to see what she saw. Then at Tina and Tom, who looked as doubtful as I was. We were expecting something more in tune with a moon landing than a gas canister, and I, for one, began to wonder how much the doctor really knew at all.

Teddy was sealed into the cryo-lung with a heavy-duty handle that clamped downwards. The only view of him was through a circular pane of glass in the door and that began to cloud with steam. The brass dial on the side slowly moved anticlockwise, showing a gradual drop in temperature. 'The slower the body's systems become, the easier they are to work on,' the doctor explained.

Tina and Tom nodded a little jerkily and their smiles looked forced.

The AUs nodded that they were ready, then they turned and began to wheel the whole machine out to the elevator. I could still see the glow through the steam, and blue lights flashed along its side to show it was now occupied.

I scurried to catch up and all of us crowded into the elevator around the lung that went all the way down to the ambulance bay in the basement. Except the doctor. She smiled as the doors closed on us. 'Good luck with everything.' We were cast adrift, with no idea what was on the other side.

No one spoke. I was grateful when Tina gripped my hand. My stomach rolled in fear and the speed of our descent. I took my mind off the nausea by studying the AU across from me. He had Royce's eyes but was at least a foot taller and Royce was over six feet. Plus, where Royce was athletic in build, these guys were built like gladiators. They were more than ambulance men; they were soldiers.

I was relieved when the elevator settled and the doors finally opened. The car park was silent when the AUs went first, looked around them as if we were escaping, then pulled the cryo-lung out. The unusual ambulance was just a few feet away. Another AU got out of the driver's side to open the back doors wide. It seemed a far bigger, boxier truck than usual and the writing on the side said 'Military Care', where a hospital name would usually be and was silver instead of white. A hydraulic lift lowered and took the full weight of the lung. Then it slowly lifted and Teddy slid smoothly onboard. We climbed the small steps while the AU's clamped him into place and attached any lines.

I was shaking by the time I got inside and checked Tina and Tom's grim faces constantly. The doctor had been right; Teddy had completely disappeared. The lung now swallowed up into another square box, reminiscent of a front-loading laundry machine. If I hadn't seen him go in and that his glass door was still visible, I would have thought Teddy had vanished. 'That's the chamber,' Tina said, pointing fearfully. Then put her hand to her mouth to stifle a cry. 'Is he OK in there?' she cried, desperately.

One of the AUs looked at her coldly, processing the question. 'He is fine, ma'am. The chamber is already at work. Please strap into your seats, we are moving out.'

The doors were closed by the AU driver, giving me one last icy stare. Tina pulled me down next to her on the bench and Tom sat opposite us. I looked behind me and pulled the belt out from the wall that fastened across my lap and my chest. Tina and Tom did the same. The AUs did the same in seats on either side of the chamber.

We swayed a little when the truck silently moved off. The only noise was the gentle hum of the chamber, which sounded a little like a refrigerator. I took a ragged breath, convincing myself it was working its wonders, already fixing Teddy's brain.

CHAPTER 50

*C*hrissy
It was a smooth journey but agonisingly stress-ful. We were too nervous to chatter. There were no windows, so I occupied myself by studying the many glass cabinets of medical equipment and drugs that lined the wall opposite me. It felt longer than forty-five minutes and none of us had a clue where we were. Finally, we felt the nose of the truck dip downwards, hinting at another underground carpark. Then, after several large circles, we eventually pulled up to a stop with a small jolt.

The AUs unbuckled and stood up. 'Leave any electrical devices and they will be returned when you leave,' one ordered.

I looked at Tom, terrified. My wrist-com was my life.

Voices were already outside.

The AU was there, holding out his hand. We each took our glass plates from our wrists and handed them over. He gestured to my bag. 'And your port-com.'

I had no idea how he knew it was there. I'd brought it for

entertainment, that was all, but his face was unrelenting. Tom tipped his head and widened his eyes for me to hand it over. I rummaged in my backpack and handed it to him moodily.

The doors opened and the three of us stepped cautiously down. The guy Royce called the professor was waiting for us, smiling in a gleaming white coat, with two more armed AUs on either side of him. Not sure why he felt he needed them.

I huddled together with Tina and Tom, a little startled by the whole thing, while the rest saw to Teddy. It was then it became obvious just how unconventional the ambulance was. One of the AUs was pressing a pad about the size of a brick that hung from the ceiling. The roof of the ambulance started to roll back and a crane arm moved across the ceiling from a steel girder above.

We watched in awe as a spider bot clambered down from the thick steel cord, slowly lowered, and attached four hooks to rings on the top of the outer box containing Teddy. It was clear what was about to happen and I went to protest, but Tom held me back. 'But, Teddy,' I whimpered, convinced they should get Teddy out before they attempted to move it, but Tom rapidly shook his head. 'Let them do their job.'

The chamber slowly rose with the spider bot checking each corner as it went. The professor directed them to carefully lower it to what looked like a concrete casing, suspending it about three feet off the ground. The spider bot released the chains, the ambulance roof closed and the two AUs that accompanied us got back inside and drove off out of the car park.

The whole thing took less than ten minutes and I was left in a daze.

'All went well,' the professor said, rubbing his hands together, smiling. He sounded British and aristocratic, about sixtyish with dark skin and a balding head. He was slim and wiry, wore round glasses and soft leather shoes. The shoes were rare and expensive. Hardly anyone wore leather anymore.

'Come,' he said, holding out his arm towards a door with a sign above it, *No unauthorised persons beyond this point.* 'Let me show you where you will be staying.'

Tom let me and Tina go first. 'We thought we'd be with Teddy the whole time?' Tina said, looking doubtfully over her shoulder.

I wanted to know that too. A box in the car park was not what we imagined at all. 'It's much more comfortable inside,' the professor said, stopping at a pair of lift doors, which opened and we all stepped inside. 'Let's get in the warm and I'll explain more.'

We walked out into a corridor and we were immediately hit with warmth and the smell of fresh coffee and delicious baking. 'This way,' the professor said, leading us into a large cafeteria.

I was immediately self-conscious, as it was dotted with several people in scrubs, lab coats and overalls, who all turned their heads to check us out. We paused, but they soon went back to their conversations.

We caught up with the professor, already pulling out a chair at a table and calling out an order for tea to the counter. He indicated for us to sit in the three vacant chairs. 'Much warmer and more comfortable here,' he said.

The only chair left was next to him. I slowly took off my coat, wishing I could switch, but Tina and Tom had already got comfortable in the chairs opposite.

A female sub brought over our tray of tea. 'There is hot food. Just come over to the counter and order when you're ready,' she said with big pink lips and impossibly white teeth.

Any other time, I would have thought it quaint and a little comical, but all I could do was gratefully sip the hot, sweet tea that felt so good in my stomach. I was suddenly bone-tired from people fatigue and a desperate need to decompress everything from the day.

The professor stirred his tea. 'All the hard work is done. I know it feels strange, but all we can do now is wait.'

'But why is he down there in the car park?' I asked. It didn't feel right. 'He's all alone. I thought I'd be able to sit with him.'

The professor nodded. 'The chamber is a wonder, but it uses vast amounts of energy and must be kept cool and ventilated. At the military base, it was kept in a huge, refrigerated unit. I'm afraid it was the best we could come up with at short notice.' He smiled kindly. 'I can assure you he isn't aware of anything and it's much more comfortable for you up here.'

Tina smiled weakly, 'Thank you. We appreciate everything you're doing.' Her eyes were glassy and her nose was red from coming in from the cold.

The professor dipped his head. 'You're welcome.'

'Why couldn't you use the one you put Royce and the other TinBoiz in?' I blurted, without really thinking, knowing I was being rude.

Tom gave me a cautionary look, which chastised me instantly. I had to shut up. I was lucky to be here at all. But I knew we weren't being told everything.

The professor's smile dropped for an instant and then appeared again as if he was trying to keep his patience. Then he looked directly at Tina and Tom instead of answering me. 'Forgive me for not explaining everything beforehand. It has all been very rushed, but it couldn't be avoided. We had to move quickly for the right pod.' Then he turned to me with a blank face. 'There are many kinds of pods and each has different specialties. Only the very up-to-date ones have multiple applications. The one used for TinBoiz is a basic healing model. Teddy needed a much more advanced neurological system. There are hardly any in this country. We were very lucky.'

It was said like a reprimand. I wanted to roll my eyes, but Tom was glaring at me for showing them up. I had to keep telling myself that he had to be OK if he was helping Teddy. But I couldn't help it, I just didn't like the guy.

'Does it work using cryogenics, like the hospital believes?' Tom asked.

I relaxed as it took the professor's beady eyes off me.

The professor shrugged. 'A little... Only as much as it slows Teddy's systems to the point of life and death. That allows the robotic microsurgery to be done with the help of a Doppler scope and radiofrequency ablation.' He smiled benignly at our blank faces. 'It can work at five times the speed of a human surgeon, traversing the nerve system, through the body, all the way into the brain, re-routing if need be. Mending the smallest of blood vessels, clearing damage, like a microscopic snow plough, if you like. Stimulating new brain cell growth where there has been irreparable damage.'

It sounded amazing, almost too good to be true. 'Why isn't it available for normal people then?' I asked, earning another sharp look from Tom. 'I mean, why is that kind of tech held back?'

The professor looked at Tom and bobbed his head in my direction. 'Future politician here, I think.' Then his face dropped, sardonically. 'Cost, my dear. A valid point, but on a wide scale, it is prohibitive. It is not new to withhold a treatment or drug from the general population because it is not economically viable. I'm afraid that sort of thing has been going on for decades.'

'Why just the army and the AUs, though?' I asked, literally incapable of keeping my mouth shut.

'That's enough, Chrissy,' Tom said, with a severe look to rival my father.

The professor laughed, but there was a harsh glint in his eye. 'Because that is where the investment is. And when they want to try out something experimental, soldiers have signed away their lives and AUs don't matter. In other words, they can't sue for damages.' His final glare was spiteful.

It did the trick and completely shut me up after that. He knew where my mind would travel. Straight to Royce and how terrible it had been for him. I don't know why, but it felt like he knew exactly how it was between Royce and me. Heat blasted into my cheeks at the thought that Royce could have told him. It made me groan and shudder inside.

'Come!' the professor said, getting to his feet. 'I'll show you to your rooms. You must be exhausted. Don't worry, someone will be monitoring Teddy twenty-four hours a day.'

'How long does Teddy have until they miss it? The chamber, I mean,' Tom asked, as we followed him out of the cafeteria.

We came to a set of double doors and the professor pushed them open. 'I'm hoping to keep it for a week. We've sent the ambulance back, so it's not recorded as missing and I have someone there to bury it in paperwork. They'll let us know when our time is up. It will miraculously appear after some clerical error. No one will know it's been used.'

The professor stopped and pointed. 'You're here, Mr and Mrs Monshall. Bathroom is down the hall.' Then he looked at me with low-lidded eyes. 'And you are next door.'

I looked at the two grey doors next to each other.

'Sorry, the accommodations are basic, but they are staff

quarters. Don't be alarmed at any activity during the night. We are a twenty-four-hour facility, running several programmes, so staff use these rooms all the time.'

I smiled a little nervously at Tina, to let her know I was OK, and followed the professor to the one next door. It was small, with just a cot, a cupboard and a nightstand. No window. Just a low hum of the air circulator. I dropped my bag onto the bed.

The professor appeared to be hovering. 'You've made quite an impression on my boy, Royce,' he said.

My eyes shot to his. The malice in them had disappeared and was replaced by a speculative smile, like he was genuinely surprised and pleased.

I shrugged moodily. 'He's unusual.' I was uneasy that he was still there.

'Don't worry, he'll be back soon.' He turned around, opened the door and left, leaving me reeling.

I wanted to run after him. Ask where Royce was. How he knew. But by the time I got my motor function back and looked up and down the corridor, he'd gone.

Tina chose that moment to come out of their room. 'It's not too bad, is it? Basic but clean.'

I nodded, dazed.

'Me and Tom are going to get some food. Do you want something?'

I had a knot in my stomach the size of a fist, so I shook my head. 'I'm really tired. Do you mind if I go straight to bed?' The day felt a thousand years long.

Tina simply hugged me and kissed my cheek. 'OK, darling. I'll bring you back a sandwich in case you wake up starving.'

I thanked her, smiled weakly and went back into my room. I stripped to my underwear and slipped under the thermoblanket. I was about to swear that the light was still on and I had no idea where the command panel was, when it dimmed automatically to a soft-green glow. It was immediately soothing to a dull headache I hadn't realised I had. I lay there, buffeted by ever-decreasing thoughts. From Royce alone somewhere out there, to Teddy frozen, alone, in a box. Until my lonely tears dragged me under.

CHAPTER 51

Royce

It was déjà vu at the police station. Except this time, I was alone, in titanium cuffs, with other felons looking at me like I was an alien. I didn't get it at first and glared back until they looked away.

Then I fell in. To them, I was an AU. Their only experience came from the terrifying AU officers. Detainees were usually human, so that made me a first. No wonder I stuck out. Something was very wrong. I shouldn't be here; I should be at TinBoiz.

A lot of activity was going on behind the bail desk. Human officers were making calls and an internal communication link was swapped between the AUs. I was pushed roughly against a wall while a reader was passed over my neck. I caught the grim fascination in another prisoner's eyes.

'It's him,' the voice said behind me. Then I realised it wasn't spoken, it was transmitted in Gibberlink and I'd understood it in real time. I was whirled around to see an AU behind the desk press his wristband and freeze. I knew exactly what he was doing and let my gridlines do their job. They zeroed in on the high-pitched acoustic link, which appeared before my eyes in green waves of sound, basically saying, 'We have him.' The rest was a read-out of all my bio vitals and a psyche evaluation.

Fear clutched the centre of my chest at who they were contacting, becoming an acidic lava flow to the back of my throat. I was pushed into the first vacant cell as I was creating a stir with the growing prisoner count. Some started shouting, 'See? You can't trust the machines.' And others, laughing. 'They wanted 'em real. Give the guy a break.'

I stood there, still in cuffs, my mind catching fire till whoever they'd called came for me. If it was the AI, I was done. I thought of Chrissy, standing vigil by Teddy's bedside. It was a stab through the heart. She'd be OK with Teddy back. The family would soon forget me. It was a blessing, really. I was saving them from the awful decision over money. It was simpler this way. My heart thrashed, despite my disk trying to slow it down. I couldn't get decommissioned. Not yet.

It was two hours and thirty-three point five seconds until the door clanked open and a huge AU prison officer stood there. My mind stalled for a beat. Back to juvey? Couldn't be. It made no sense. Juvey was for humans. 'Out!' the AU ordered, gesturing with his hand. 'Don't make me have to come in there.'

Now this was language I could understand. I grinned. 'Since you asked so nicely,' I said, sauntering past him, like the old me. It felt so damned good. Then it suddenly hit me in one eureka moment that I was done with the AU shit.

CHAPTER 52

*R**oyce*

Despite outward appearances, I was shitting bricks. My fear was a tangible, white-cold sweat as the slab of artificial testosterone followed me down the corridor. 'Where am I going?' I asked over my shoulder.

He didn't answer and we came out at the desk where four units in black suits waited. A welcoming committee. This didn't feel good. All the stranger because they weren't built like the police or the prison AUs. These were regular size, wearing secret service-like dark glasses and ear-coms. I knew they were AUs because I could feel them steadily scanning me. Followed by the familiar slam at the back of my neck. These were AI agents.

My fear sank to a new low. This was far worse than facing the professor. With him, there was always a slim chance, but with agents of the AI, hell knew what would happen to me. Studied, dismantled, all while I was awake. The prof's plan, exposed. Chrissy. The Coes, compromised. I knew enough to know I didn't want that at any cost.

I'd mapped all exits and possible routes of escape in nanoseconds. Weapons. Head count.

'Don't even think about it,' the AU growled behind me.

I coiled, ready. My red mist, def con escape plan was about to go beast mode when the double doors next to the desk were bashed open and in walked the professor, Damien and another couple of the biggest-looking soldier dudes I'd ever seen. I turned and grinned at the big guy behind me, despite being busted either way. My power pack did a happy dance with my heart rate and I don't think I'd ever enjoyed a smirk more at anyone in my life.

The professor shot me an annoyed glare and took out his digital ID from his breast pocket. I zeroed in and saw the TinBoiz logo immediately. The human bail sergeant took it and passed it over a reader and swapped an alarmed look with a colleague. But it was the four AUs in black that the professor addressed directly. I'll take it from here, boys. This is above your clearance.'

The slamming in my neck suddenly dropped, as if the AI forgot all about me.

The creepy AUs turned and moved their heads in synch to assess him. Damien and his guys did the same, with a small, threatening step forward. It was fascinating to watch, both assessing the other's capabilities. Like a speeded-up face-off, I couldn't wait to tell my friends about.

Code was flying everywhere. Creeps to the AI, Damien to his guys, and I mopped up the whole thing, like an action movie for geeks. The sheer speed made it freaky good.

'We have orders to bring this one in for assessment,' one creep said. 'We have been notified of a possible malfunction. Violation of code 3476.'

My mind shot to Ace, but in all honesty, I'd been dropping the ball all over the place today. So it could literally have come from anywhere.

It was tense. The prof's micro-expressions. Damien's muscles flexed, ready for action, and my heart rejoiced that I wasn't going to be handed over easily.

The professor's face dropped and he took an alarmingly close step into the AU creep who'd spoken. 'Stand down and note my clearance. You are out of line. This unit is one of my beta models, as Metatron well knows. I will take him in for study and evaluation, as is the usual protocol between me and the TinBoiz corporation and their contract with Metatron. Stand down.'

I was fiercely absorbing code and trying to read between the lines of what I already knew and comparing it to what the prof was saying. He was a badass for a little guy and I wanted to whoop with delight, even though some of what he said rang a few alarm bells.

For a moment, tension crackled in the air while the creeps stared ahead of them and reported back to the AI, Meta-whatever. Still, it was a moment to breathe, for those who did. Damien clenched his jaw like he was ready for anything or anyone and it would make his day. The prison guard strengthened his grip on my arm, still cuffed behind me. I gave him my dirtiest look. Truth was, no one knew whether this would go off. I had already decided to drop to the floor and kick out his legs. Only the prof appeared to remain relaxed.

Then I understood. He wasn't just waiting for all the necessary relays between the AU and AI. His proximity wasn't an invasion of personal space like it would have been to a human; he was talking to the AI directly through the AU's eyes.

An image of Ace flashed into my memory again and I had to slam it down immediately. That had to be the least of my worries.

The AU took a step back. 'Very well,' it said. 'Metatron

would like a full report of your findings by the end of the week, along with full linear access to the model.'

That last part didn't sound good, but the prof didn't answer. Instead, he walked right over to me and, after piercing me with another of his dagger looks, ordered the AU behind me to, 'Let him go, and delete all classified records from your memory. He was never here.' Then, after another spiteful look my way: 'Oh, and leave the cuffs on.'

I went to protest, but he turned and walked away before I had the chance. Damien appeared and took over from the guard. Nudging me roughly in the direction of the doors. I couldn't help looking up at him and grinning. 'Keep moving, small fry.' But he couldn't dampen my joy. I liked the guy. We stepped into the lift to go down, where the prof didn't look at me once. I swapped my gaze to my opposite side to an equally impressive AU I'd never met before. 'Who's your friend?'

My grin dropped when he fixed me with a hard glare. 'Busta. Busta head!' without even cracking a smile. I actually laughed out loud at that. However, I just caught the four creeps openly staring at us as the doors slowly closed.

'Phew, that was close, guys,' I said.

'For god's sake, Royce. Are you really malfunctioning?' the professor said, suddenly furious with me.

I was surprised as he was genuinely pissed. Like he was a real dad bailing out his wayward son. It was kind of endearing, in a way. Then I frowned, confused for a second. I wasn't sure if I was meant to act AU or human in this situation. I couldn't tell. I was subdued after that, trying to work it out. Why the AI was so interested in me. The contract the professor had with TinBoiz. I thought I was a secret sideline. None of it added up. From the elevator, along the corridor, to the van, when I checked the professor's face, he was seething.

Maybe it was as simple as me going AWOL. I latched onto that. He had a lot on his plate with Teddy. Juggling the secrecy of all that and me acting up as well.

The van doors were opened and I jangled the cuffs behind me before I stepped up. My wrists killed. 'Can someone get rid of these now? We're away from the assholes. Enough with the show.'

The professor nodded and Damien said, 'Turn' with his usual economy of words.

It was instant relief and I rotated my shoulders to loosen them and rubbed my wrists. They were raw, despite my bands. 'Thanks,' I said, simply.

The professor tutted and got in the front next to the driver and I got in with Damien and Busta and their two equally cheerful friends.

The journey didn't take long, which I was glad about, because despite the wisecracks, my power was flashing red zone. We squealed into an underground carpark and when I piled out with the AUs, it seemed vaguely familiar. A facility like all the others, but one I'd seen before; maybe during training. It was surprisingly empty of cars.

Damien nudged me towards the grubby white door with the red 'No Unauthorised persons beyond this point' sign on it. I scowled up at him. 'You don't have to be a dick, man. I'm cooperating.'

He rolled his eyes Heavenward in a very human way and that was enough to make me smile. He liked me. Even he couldn't hide his human side all the time.

We went up in the steel lift that all these kinds of places seemed to have and out to the back of the facility, where all the goods and tech parts were stored. There were no comfy chill-out rooms, cafeterias or even labs that I could see. Only gloomy grey corridors with dingy emergency lighting. My heart was sinking already. The professor opened a room via a panel and I tried to ask how Teddy was doing, but Damien shoved me inside and slammed the door in my face.

I stood there, dazed at the speed of it. I felt conned and began banging on the steel door. 'Hey, guys! What is this? Aren't we going to talk?'

'Welcome home, Royce,' a familiar voice said, making me whirl around on my heel.

Flat cot, a metal bucket and a cabinet. *Sentia?* This wasn't good at all.

'Did you enjoy the outside world?' she asked.

My mind was stuck. *Sentia. Here.* 'Why aren't you at home?'

'You left home,' she answered, simply. Her row of lights alternating in time with her syllables.

My heart juddered painfully at that. Despite how I'd left, after finding Finn and Dad gone and my rescue today, I guess I assumed I'd be debriefed, maybe even reprimanded. I was OK with that. It was fair. So how could I have gotten it all so wrong? It had all been a waste of time. I should be back at home, supporting the Coes. I pounded the door with the side of my fist. 'OK, enough now. I've learned my lesson.' But no one came. After a few kicks and several run-ups, it was clear it was a reinforced room. I'd swapped one cell for another. Except this one was a secret and no one even knew I was there.

My power was ebbing away with real pain in my chest. I'd never run out before. I was terrified. My saliva was acid and the white-out returned. On my skin, in my eyes. Ears ring-ing. Far away. *Where are you, Mike?*

I AWOKE with a start and checked my internal clock. Hours had turned into days. Energy paste was shoved through a pivoting hatch in the door and I was supposed to evacuate in the bucket, which was swapped in the same way.

I alternated from anger to terror. Cries changing to threats. I smashed my cot to pieces, but I stopped just in time with Sentia. She was my only company. Until, finally, a deathly calm settled over me. No one was going to come. I was at the point a condemned man reached when there was no point in any more emotion. I accepted I would never find Finn. I would never see Chrissy or the Coes. I would never meet Teddy. All I had left was my hatred for the professor. He was the one who'd robbed me of my life both times. He'd dangled hope when he'd saved me from the AI, only to lock me up here.

I stopped wondering what he was going to do with me. There was no point, so I ceased to care.

FIVE DAYS, eight hours, thirty-two minutes and twenty-four seconds after I woke up, the door clanked open and Damien stood looking at me in the doorway. I was sitting in the corner, a complete mess, amongst the tangled remains of my cot. 'The professor will see you now,' he said.

My hand dropped from holding my head and I stared at him coldly. I didn't even have the inclination to act up. But I guess the isolation and sheer boredom sparked a little curiosity and forced me to my feet. At least it was a change of walls.

I faced off Damien recklessly, transmitting all the hatred I felt. He smiled a little and raised a brow. 'Do we need cuffs today, squirt?'

I didn't so much as twitch. I was way beyond that. 'Just get me the hell out of here, Damo,' I said, flashing a spite-filled smile and pushing past him. 'We're burning daylight.'

I think he allowed it out of sheer shock, but a light

chuckle followed. 'Wait!' he ordered, falling in step beside me. 'This way.'

He led me through a maze of similar corridors until grey walls gave way to white and dull to bright lighting. We were now in the clinical part of the building. The part I remembered, where I'd spend some of my recovery.

We stopped at a door and Damien knocked. The professor's voice came through a speaker. 'Enter.'

I didn't wait and pushed in ahead of Damien. He came in casually and closed and leaned back against the door. I was immediately distracted by my surroundings. It was a large, luxurious office. Dark-blue walls, old-fashioned gold-framed paintings of animals I'd never seen before and a soft blue patterned carpet under my feet. The professor sat at a huge, dark wooden desk and books lined the many shelves behind him. It was like something from a museum or a film. My gridlines were working overtime, mapping and logging it all.

The professor went into a drawer of his desk, pulled out a bottle of amber liquid and poured it into a squat glass in front of him. Then he leaned back in his leather high-backed chair, taking the glass with him. 'Calmed down a bit now?' he asked, smiling and taking a gulp of his drink.

Wrong thing to say and I flashed with fury. I wanted to demand what the hell he was playing at, but one thing the last few days had taught me was that he had all the time in the world. So I clenched my jaw for a beat and went straight to the point. 'Where's Finn?'

All he did was raise his eyebrows.

Nonplussed, I sputtered, 'You must know something. Everything has changed. No one even knew me.' It all tumbled in, heaping one thing after another on top of me until I could hardly hold it all up and hung there defeated.

The professor let out a deep sigh, wandered around his desk and perched on the edge of it. Then he took a slow sip of his drink, eyeing me the whole time. Real alcohol. I smelled it distinctly.

'First, tell me why you left the Coes? They are frantic with worry.'

I felt an instant pang of guilt for Nate. Chrissy's mind would be on Teddy. 'How's Teddy doing?' I asked. Several days had passed. There must be some news.

'Stop deflecting and answer the question, Royce. What possessed you to go there and risk everything?'

I shuffled my feet in exasperation at why he didn't get it. Then I shrugged dramatically. 'I dunno. Maybe because the Coes will send me back as soon as Teddy's well.' I flashed him daggers, then fidgeted, pushing the toe of my boot into the plush carpet. 'I needed to check Finn was OK,' I finished moodily. I didn't know why I was wasting my time. 'You're just going to scrap me anyway.' I threw it with a wave of my arm like a bomb, willing it to land and the guy quit with the bullshit.

The professor's expression didn't change; he simply watched my tirade, deadpan. Then he let out a weary breath and nodded to Damien.

I turned my head in panic, 'no' already coming out of my mouth. Damien walked forward carrying a hard-backed wooden chair. 'Sit!' Damien ordered, pushing me down into the chair from my shoulder.

'I don't want—' But Damien's strength could not be argued with and he pointed in my face. 'Listen! You might actually learn something.'

I was expecting a cuff around the face and looked around me, bewildered. It felt like I had no base, no point of reference anymore. 'I don't get it. It's logical, isn't it? My new family didn't need me anymore, so I went to find my real one.' *It's obvious,* I finished in my head, grasping it as the last thread.

The professor seemed amused and bobbed his head like I had a point. 'What I don't understand is why you thought you'd be broken down for parts? You're part of a billion UGN credit programme, far too valuable for that.'

I sat there dumb for a moment, not daring to veer in the direction of hope. 'But I know too much. Wouldn't you need to do something because of the AI?'

The professor grinned widely and looked over my head at Damien, who smiled back. Then he quickly schooled his features and looked serious again. 'Yes, that is true.' He was acting like it was me who didn't get something. 'I confess, it's partly my fault. I guess I didn't fully appreciate what a successful model you are. You have integrated with your family and school peers better than I could ever have imagined, despite your obvious physical appearance and everyone fully aware you're an AU. It is remarkable.' He downed his drink and wandered back around his desk, sinking into his chair with a huff of exhaustion. 'But enough of all that. I'm afraid we have reached the point where I must be brutally honest with you, Royce, and I didn't want to have to do it. I want you to listen and log what I have to say, because it is the truth.'

He nodded over my head and unease turned to panic when I felt Damien's hands hold either side of my shoulders. My mind was free-falling.

'Listen,' the professor said, clicking his fingers and bringing me back to him. 'Your programming will want to fight what I'm about to say, but you must override it. Do you understand? Tell yourself that I would never lie. You might not believe I care about you, but you can believe you are worth a million credits. I would never damage one of my experimental units. Does that sound plausible? Are we clear?'

My heart was beating in my throat. His word choices were alarming, but I was furiously logging and recording what he said. 'I suppose,' I said, checking Damien over my shoulder as he increased his grip. I swallowed hard and faced front again.

'Confirm, Royce, TinBoiz model 2055Ultra 2365A1.'

The weirder the things he said, the more ice crept through my veins. *Veins – real veins.*

He raised his eyebrows and Damien gave me a little shake. I gave him a hard look over my shoulder. 'OK, I confirm.'

'You will not respond until I finish speaking. Confirm!'

I wanted to shout to get the hell on with it and looked behind me at Damien again. He gripped the back of my neck painfully and pointed for me to face front again. 'OK,' I said, pulling out of his grip. 'Confirm.'

'You are a TinBoiz experimental AI model, made in this very facility a long time ago.'

Script ran in front of my eyes continually while he was speaking. Plucking out highlights. *AI ... learning ... thinking ... Two months ... Question ... real time.*

'You are a composite cybernetic quantum system and selective human parts, designed to learn and be as human as possible.'

Everything aligned pretty much with what I already knew.

'This time, you were placed with the Coes and have passed with flying colours.' It was all true. I was starting to get confused by why he was uneasy about my understanding all this and why Damien was bracing himself.

Then my mental rampage staggered to a halt. *This time ... this time ... thththththis tttttimmme.* I was stuck and could barely speak. 'Juvey. My friends. Finn,' I managed eventually, like I had some kind of speech impediment.

I felt Damien tighten his grip. My heart slammed into my power disk, ready to erupt out of my chest.

Then all my systems suddenly calmed and regulated to crystal clarity. 'How long?' I asked. My voice now dropped several octaves.

'You have been in that chair many times. We have had this conversation many times.'

'How long?' came out of me like a growl.

'Six years.'

oyce

I blinked at the professor. Speechless. Running internal system checks. Then memory checks. 'But how?'

'Memory implants,' the professor said, casually. As if it were as obvious as breathing.

Wait, wait, wait... Back up. I just thought time had passed, now he was saying he had screwed with my mind? My grid-lines mapped his every expression and noted a hint of regret.

The apartment... empty. 'Finn. My dad?' I was pathetic. I didn't know what I was thinking and what I was saying out loud anymore.

The professor's face turned wistful, as if he was looking back with awe when he said, 'Fictitious. Concocted by a very talented AU neuronetic designer. Recite your serial number. You will notice it ends in HSU. That stands for Human Street Unit.'

I did it immediately. He was right. It did. I was having some sort of out-of-body experience while he went on to explain my history. How each time, I would never seem to gel with my family. How I failed on points of realism and have to be returned, or I wandered off in search of something. Then they'd hit on the deep implant idea of a whole life backstory. And it had worked, better than they could have imagined.

As he droned on about the workings in my head, severing me from every link to the person I thought I was, I felt myself sinking into quicksand. Deaf. Numb. Until I hit on the one final thing before I closed them. 'My eyes. Why go through all that to take my eyes?' That experience was locked tightly in my trauma file and still came out in bad dreams.

The professor was already shaking his head. 'Never happened. It was all to reinforce your backstory.'

Just before my heart plummeted into the abyss. My mind went back to the police station I'd been taken to. That part had to be real. The problem with the AI's agents turning up. 'The contract,' I said aloud.

The professor always seemed pleasantly amazed when I said these kinds of things and wasn't uncomfortable at all. 'Separation from the AI is all part of the experiment. You are an advanced AI unit in your own right. And yes, there is a contract with Metatron for the continued evolution of AUs. But to do it, we can't risk him having any input or control. Hence the show of strength this morning.'

Every part of me weighed a ton and aged a thousand years. 'And your plan to protect humankind?' I said, raising my eyes to the professor again. 'The Coes' felt like the final twist of the knife in my chest. Out of it all. The deception. The loss of my family. That was what hurt most of all. That it had – I had conned them. The nicest family in the world. *What did I know. What could I possibly know.*

The professor went on, oblivious to my breakdown. 'That is kind of true. It's always wise not to tell the AI everything.

And God mode is a very real thing in the quantum computer space. The true singularity.'

My mind was drifting away like a small boat on a tide. Trying to cling to small fragments. How I knew my way around the lower south side of the city, across the Danger Line. My exact apartment. Then, stopping suddenly at the vagrant, knowing Dad and Finn. *That can't be an implant, surely. Unless they'd added that while I was out.* The youths at Peter Pats had no idea who I was and assumed I'd sold out. *That had to be real.* I decided to keep those things to myself. The more they thought I knew, the more they'd erase. Somehow, I knew that was in my best interest. To keep something. 'Why let me continue to believe?' was the last thing I said, as every spark and every bit of light started to go dark inside. *Disappointment* flashed as a reminder of what the emotion was. *Heartsick* was more exact. I logged away the human emotion, doubting I even had a real heart. I started to die.

'For realism,' the professor said, sounding further and further away. 'Do you think the AU at school, your friends on the team, the kiss with Chrissy? Do you think any of that would have happened without that?'

I was moments from death and my muscles froze. I swear if Damien had poked me, I would have shattered into shards. 'How did you know about the kiss?' My voice had gone so low, it was a barely audible growl.

It was the first time I'd ever seen the professor look uncomfortable. He'd gotten so carried away in being pleased with himself, he'd made a major slip.

Damien braced his grip and I knew it was going to be bad.

The professor took a deep breath, which sounded deafening to my now-heightened hearing. I could even hear the claggy swallows, where his mouth had suddenly gone dry. The flap of his eyelids as he blinked in slow motion. I could hear the whole room at particle level. *My god, everything he'd told me was true.* I changed in that single moment. I became possessed by something else. Correction. I allowed myself to be the true me.

The professor finally summoned the courage to speak. 'Everything you see with your eyes is transmitted here and recorded.'

It wasn't exactly what he said, but the detached way he said it. Like he didn't give a damn.

'It's the same for all the AUs, except theirs goes directly to the AI. Yours comes to me.'

I became stuck in a loop trying to comprehend it. *Ace continually up in my grill. Knowing something was wrong. The very real terror, trauma, I remembered in the moments before he took my eyes. What kind of monster implants a fake memory like that? Every conversation, every emotion... every thought I'd ever had. Doubted. Nate. The Coes. Chrissy, Chrissy, Chrissy. My yearning. My guilt for Finn. Everything had been viewed, taken, stolen, violated by some old Peeping Tom. Was any of it real? Sim. Sim. Simulation?*

I couldn't fit any more hatred into my facial muscles when I spat, 'Bet you all had a good laugh.'

The professor stood up quickly, affronted. He strode back around to the front of his desk to his perch on the front of it. I was already shutting down. He was only going to add bull-shit to injury.

'Bet you sat round like Saturday night TV.' My eyes were daggers, staring ahead of me.

The professor looked over my head, exasperated. 'Of course not.'

'It wasn't like that, kid,' Damien's voice rumbled from behind me.

It was the first time he'd deigned to speak throughout the whole session. I twisted around to look him up and down in disgust. 'And I thought you were OK. The same as me.'

Damien kept calm, as was his training. Programming. *Whatever.* 'I am the same.'

I stared at him, the betrayal leaching out of me. 'I doubt that.' I swivelled back around, shrugging his hands off my shoulders. I think he was a little shaken to allow it. 'What now?' I asked flatly. 'What's the point?' My voice sounded weird. Squeaky. Human-like, for someone past breaking point. I was a mass of conflict. Thoughts. Feelings. Making a list of what was still the truth and throwing out the lies. The principal one being, I could no longer trust the professor. He was a liar who'd used me and I hated him. Another truth was that I was still in his power to do with what he wanted. I didn't exist. It was even worse than losing Finn and my old life. *I didn't exist.* All I could think was that I was a non-person. Walking, talking anti-matter. I'd been on the brink this whole session, but I was powering down. I began to shrink and slump into the chair.

'Stop that!' the professor shouted, standing and pointing from his perch. 'Stop him, Damien.'

I wasn't going to play his silly games anymore.

'Royce… Royce,' echoed around me.

I was flying, with Damien's big arms hoisting me up from my seat. My vision was gradually reducing. Smaller and smaller to a tunnel. Bouncing through the corridor over Damien's shoulder. Until all that was left was a tiny pinhole of glorious light, where I landed softly in a white room made of cushions.

CHAPTER 54

Chrissy
Six days felt like six months. A replayed round of getting up, having breakfast with the Monshalls, going out to the chamber, standing next to it and listening to its gentle hum. I couldn't even see Teddy through the door glass as it was so clouded. Until I got too cold and had to go back inside for a blast of warmth and a cup of hot chocolate. Sleeping. Waking. Eating. Teddy. Then doing it all again. I got to know all the names of the subs, who took pity on me. A kind old janitor model bought out a chair for me in the car park in the end.

The Monshalls checked on Teddy once a day and then we all went to the prof's office, where he briefed us at the end of every evening. 'All systems are working perfectly and his levels are in the correct range,' he said. Pretty much word for word, every time.

'But what does that actually mean?' Tina finally asked, looking worn out from worry.

The professor looked genuinely sorry. 'I'm afraid I can't tell you any more than that. It's impossible to tell until we wake him up to see if his repaired neural pathways are in working order.'

I joined in then with, 'Yes, but what does that mean?'

Thankfully, Tom nodded to back me up. We were all fed up with the vague answers.

'We can only see on the relayed image scanner.'

'Can we see?' I quickly asked.

The professor used his 3D lap-port and a grainy blue image appeared, which he turned for us to see. It looked like a padded-out X-ray, where we could zoom in and out through layers of stringy muscle, blood vessels and tissue over luminescent white bone. He pointed to Teddy's brain, a grey mass with tiny little firefly lights in one area. 'That's the brain stem,' he said, thoughtfully. 'In simple terms, for normal brain activity – cognitive speech, mobility – we need this area to light up,' he said, pointing to another area completely dark.

Tina and Tom slumped into their seats with the same bitter disappointment as I felt.

The professor had noticed too, as his eyebrows rose and he added quickly, 'This is progress. At the hospital, he had half this activity, and it doesn't happen steadily. Healing happens in fits and starts. He would have been declared dead just a few years ago.'

It was brutal. I looked guiltily at Tina, knowing that was exactly what the hospital had wanted to do. Tina turned into Tom and cried brokenheartedly into his chest. 'But we're running out of time.'

Tom wrapped his arms around her and gave the professor a dark look. He looked uncomfortable, but unashamed of his honesty. He inclined his head and with a 'Take a few moments,' left us alone in his office. Teddy's image timed out and closed, leaving a dark hole in my chest.

Tom winked at me over Tina's head. 'I'm going to settle her in bed.'

I nodded, understanding completely. She was tired and wrung out. We all were. I watched them go, huddled together and took a meandering walk out of the professor's office. I had no idea where any of us went from here. There was never an option in my mind that it might not work. I wanted to call home to hear my mom's calming voice, but that was out of the question. I missed them, even Nate. *And Royce.* I felt a deep yearning that quickly changed to anger that he'd abandoned me at a time like this. I scraped away a lone tear and walked back out to the corridor and leaned back against the wall.

I would have burst into tears if I hadn't heard the approaching loud stomps that became Murtle, the sub from the cafeteria, rounding the corner. She was an older, kindly grandmother with severe emphysema. We'd chatted a few times and she always had a smile and a kind word. She stopped right in front of me and flashed her ridiculously long cartoon eyelashes and stretched her rubbery pink lips. I could never fail to smile at the thought of her working an archaic console at home to make these small gestures.

I gave her a pathetic little wave. 'Hi, Murtle.'

'Oh dear,' she said. 'If I wasn't in this big old clunky thing, I'd give you a big Murtle hug.'

That was enough to bring out the tears.

'There, there, my love. Such a terrible thing to be going through… Here.' She held out a tissue, which I took gratefully. 'Look, I'm sure the professor wouldn't mind. There's a staff games room in the trade part of the building,' she said, pointing to the way she came. 'The porters and orderlies use it mainly, but some of the Techs do, too. It should be pretty empty at this time. Would you like to take a look?' Her face grimaced into her weird smile again, which was infectious, and I nodded. I'd never seen my grandparents; not many lived that long. I always imagined one like Murtle. 'I'd love that,' I said, my heart gushing with gratitude.

I followed her down the maze of tunnels, left and right, until the décor went from white to grey and the lights dimmed to a depressing yellow. We finally stopped and she pushed open a door to reveal a large room that smelled of coffee, dotted around with sofas and bean bags. A solitary guy was lounging in one of them, nodding his head with a headset on.

'Greg! Greg!' Murtle called.

He snatched off the headset and looked around, startled, blinking bleary-eyed as he adjusted from the VR. He smiled when we came into focus. 'Oh hi, Murt. Thought I was late for work or something,' his grin widening, like there was some kind of 'in' joke.

Murtle batted the air, as if he was being cheeky. 'I won't tell, if you don't. Is it OK if Chrissy hangs out here for a while?'

'Sure,' he said, flicking his grey eyes over me, quickly. He was good-looking. Striking. Dark skin with curly black hair, with an air of cheeky confidence about him. I put him in his mid-twenties and friendly enough. He rolled off the beanbag and scrambled to his feet. 'I was just leaving, anyway. Just starting my shift,' he said, with another grin too big for what he was saying.

Murtle laughed and looked at her wrist-plate. 'Ten minutes ago. Better skedaddle.'

'I've got time to show her around before the boss comes lookin'.'

'Oh thanks, darlin'. I gotta get back to the cafeteria.' She smiled at me again. 'Come find me if you need me,' she said, and stomped out and down the corridor in her weird, jerky footsteps.

I focused back on Greg, who was looking around him, scratching his head. 'So, you like to game?' Now we were on our own, he seemed a little nervous. 'Er, you might like this one. It's Amazon Explorer. I designed it myself.' He handed me the headset. 'It's got wild animals and native tribes of insects and everything.'

His enthusiastic rambling made me laugh. I looked more closely around the room. There were readers scattered around on coffee tables. A huge TV glass on the wall, currently with UGN news on silent.

'There's a coffee machine that does frap, crap and double crap with cream,' he said, pointing and scratching his head again.

I laughed. He was adorably funny, and I bet he got into trouble all the time with it. I noticed there were more head-sets near most of the chairs.

'There are several sets with all kinds of stuff on them. Shopping, chat rooms, date sites,' he finished with a grin and a wink. 'Whatever's your thing.' He ended up laughing at himself, then scratching the back of his neck. A nervous habit, I was realising.

I decided to put him out of his misery. 'I'm sure I'll find something. Thanks.'

'You're with the neuro-shutdown kid in the chamber, aren't you?'

I was about to ask what he meant by that when something brought my attention to the open doorway. People were coming at a march. Like soldiers, getting louder and louder. Then it stopped.

I blinked, taking in the scene, like a freeze-frame. A tall, scruffy kid dwarfed by several AUs.

'Move, kid,' the one next to him said. But he seemed locked on us in the room. His hair was a brown scruffy mess, swept forward and hanging in his face. He could barely stand. Then he slowly raised his head and his ice-cold eyes sliced through me. 'Royce,' came out on a breath.

I wanted to run to him, but Greg held my arm. 'Royce?' I said, wanting to cry. There was nothing there. No spark of recognition in his eyes at all. Just blank windows.

I turned back to Greg in confusion. 'I know him.' Something was very wrong. In him. Between us. I didn't understand it. My heart thudded painfully. My mind scrambled, quickly, to get a grip. They'd found him. At least there was that. It was something and I shouldn't get him in any more trouble. So I just smiled weakly and the AU gave him a shove. It seemed to wake him up and he shuffled forward again, as if his feet didn't want to move.

I faced Greg again, but I wasn't seeing him. My mind was on Royce, a prisoner. Here. 'What's going on?'

'You know that unit?' Greg said.

I'd forgotten he was even there. It took a moment for his question to seep through the fog. 'Er, yeah. He's… I mean, he belongs to a family I know.' I stumbled quickly into a lie, not sure if it was the right thing to do at all, but it didn't feel wise to tell a Tech who worked there the truth. I looked back at the empty doorway, wishing I could follow him. 'I'm not sure what happened. He went out and didn't come back… So I understand,' I said, still in shock, almost forgetting myself.

'Such a shame,' Greg said, bringing my attention back to him, shaking his head. 'He's one of our spliced beta models. The most advanced we've ever made. Back to the drawing board, I guess.'

My cognitive function was snapping back into place. I was awake and alert with the espresso injection of useful information. 'Oh yeah?' I said, trying to sound casual. 'What's wrong with him, do you think? In your expert opinion.' I added, shamelessly flattering his ego.

Greg seemed to switch off and began to gather his things,

then shrugged. 'Not sure. It seems to happen with him. Glitches. Something. He got further than he ever has this time, though.'

My mind was splintering off into a hundred follow-up questions, knowing he was about to leave. I went to open my mouth as he focused on me again for a final grin, when he said, 'That, I hate to say, is my area of expertise. Or not, in this case,' he said, with a half-joking frown. 'Better go before I get fired.'

I put up a lame hand and watched as he strode quickly away. 'Enjoy the room.' Then he disappeared out of the open door and in the direction they'd taken Royce.

I was frozen. The only noise, the constant hum of the air filtration unit. *Glitches?* That couldn't be right. Royce was the strongest, most level-headed person I'd ever met. *Person.* All this reinforced that he wasn't. And, I had to admit, he looked a complete mess. Something was very wrong.

Without another thought, I made for the doorway. My heart flipped at taking some sort of action. I had to see him.

CHAPTER 55

*R*oyce

They were too clever to put me back in my own room. They knew I would dismantle myself on all those sharp corners. This one was purpose-built for madness. A soft room of white cushions to soften the edges of my pain. Because I was destroyed.

Every time I argued with myself that it couldn't all be a lie, my rational side, my analytical, objective, shit for computer brains side, came up with: *really?* Or, more precisely, improbable with the current data.

Street kid gets arrested by the cops and thrown into juvey, where there's an evil plot for harvesting human body parts. Rescued by a mad professor, who turns him into a teen robot spy to help save mankind before the crazy quantum AI takes over the world.

I started to laugh, harder and harder. Hysterically. Bending over to touch my knees. It was straight out of a computer game any one of my friends would play.

Friends. I burrowed my head in my hands and my body shuddered. The emotion was there, and I wanted to cry, but I just didn't have the apparatus. No tear ducts. No breaths, no sobs, no sweat. *Oh God.*

I slumped down the soft wall and turned into the corner. Hitting my head again and again into the spongy cushion. All I did was make myself dizzy.

A thought of Chrissy came uninvited. Beautiful, perfect, *real,* Chrissy.

I screamed. The loudest, most ear-splitting, desperate scream. Like the life was being wrung out of an injured animal.

Until I powered down, involuntarily, to blackness.

CHAPTER 56

*C*hrissy

The corridors became darker and scarier the further I went. The young Techs in white coats became older people in blue overalls and shiny, modern subs became worker drones.

I came to a dead end of elevators that only went down. One opened. I looked around and quickly stepped in. It moved fast, skipping four floors, then I came out to walk more of the same. This was definitely the back end of the operation. It made sense, I guessed, for Royce to be kept somewhere like this.

I'd walked aimlessly for what felt like a very long time when I turned a corner and was confronted by a terrifying AU. I jumped and held my chest. He was one I recognised with Royce, from earlier. He didn't speak and I just stared at him. His face was dark and frighteningly realistic. There was nothing plastic about him at all. He was a wall of smooth skin and hard muscle, with only the tell-tale eyes giving him away. A soldier model, from his size. Why they had to make a soldier good-looking seemed pointless to me.

I went to step around him without speaking, but he side-stepped in my way. 'You shouldn't be here, Miss,' it said, surprising me at how normal it sounded.

'Please get out of my way. I saw you with my TinBoi earlier, and I need to see him. I need to make sure he's OK.' I averted my eyes from the intense stare.

'It's not safe down here. Let me accompany you to the professor. He can tell you what you need to know.'

I wanted to argue, but he was already using the sheer proximity of his large frame to herd me back the way I came. His voice was very calm and persuasive and there was nothing I could do but obey. 'OK,' I said, already being ushered along. I kept snatching glances, studying his rugged profile. The hard set of his jaw and even a glimpse of perfect teeth.

We arrived back at the elevators and both stepped inside. His perfect brown hand swept over the panel and we went up only one floor. He was silent and I sneaked a peek a few more times. He was impressive. I wouldn't want to face something like him in battle. 'What's your name?' I asked, just before the doors opened.

He looked at me for a beat, making my heart smash against my ribs. Then he smiled as if he hadn't expected it. 'Damien,' he said. 'My name is Damien.'

The whole exchange was disarming. So real and unexpected. No wonder I was all over the place with Royce.

The doors opened and the professor was waiting right outside. He was already holding out an arm for me to go with him, but his focus was still on Damien in the lift. 'I've forced a power-down. Have him taken to the lab.'

Damien nodded and the doors slowly closed.

'Come this way, please, Chrissy.'

We walked no more than a couple of minutes when he opened a door and showed me into his impressive office. It never got old. All old-world opulence hidden in an industrial shell.

'Damien said you wanted to see me,' he said, leading me over to a group of comfy chairs and indicating for me to sit.

I sat, already confused. Damien had been with me the whole time. How could he have—

'Internal communication,' the professor said, pre-empting me.

It made me jump to Royce having to communicate with him every night through his valet unit. 'What's wrong with Royce?' I asked. 'I saw him earlier. He looked terrible.'

The professor sank back into his chair and let out a weary breath. 'Drink?' he asked, already getting back to his feet.

I shook my head, wanting him to get on with it.

'Do you mind if I have one?'

I shook my head, but he was already walking over to a sideboard where he filled a tumbler with ice and amber liquid and came and slumped back down in his chair again. He took a large gulp and took off his glasses and pinched the bridge of his nose.

'Please just tell me,' I said in the end, wondering how bad it could be.

He replaced his glasses and cradled his drink in his hands. 'Royce is having what we call in cybernetics, a crisis with his internal programme. I guess you could liken it to a human personality disorder.'

'Like some sort of breakdown?'

He inclined his head slightly. 'Yes, you could call it that. It is the end result of his crisis.'

'Can I see him? I'm sure it would help.'

The professor was already shaking his head. 'Out of the question. 'I've already had to force a shutdown. He's a danger to himself and others.'

My face must have betrayed my absolute shock and

disbelief as he patted the air for me to calm down. I didn't care. Royce had been nothing but protective of us all.

'There is no need to worry. We will realign him. He'll be fine. I promise you.'

I was immediately on my feet, my mind scrambling. 'No! Please, you can't do that. He won't be the same. He's ours. It's up to us. He doesn't belong to you.' It was all out before I could stop myself. 'Just let me see him and you'll see. That's all he needs. I know it is.'

The professor calmly put down his drink on a small table and came and stood right in front of me. He put his hands on my shoulders and looked intensely into my eyes. 'Listen to me, Chrissy. Royce is not human. He is an extremely advanced piece of tech. He does not belong to you; he is leased to your parents at a reduced price because he is a beta model. Do you understand what that means?'

In my misery, I shook my head, already trying to formulate an argument. I fully understood what a lease was.

A beta model is an experimental model still in its beta testing stage. The last stage before it is ready to go to market.' He bobbed his head to the side and let my shoulders go. 'This has been problematic, granted,' he said with a loud exhale.

I tried to cast my mind back to when Mom and Dad first got him. I was still reeling from the loss of Teddy, so I couldn't remember all the details. They may have mentioned it. I remembered he'd been cheaper. I guess I just assumed it was to sweeten us because of Teddy's problems, possibly being caused by his sub. I began to shrink inside with deep disappointment at how stupid I'd been. A high-tech model like Royce, coming to the likes of us. How ridiculously expensive he would have been for our ordinary family. It seemed so obvious now.

I understood how everything was out of our control. He'd never truly been ours. Nate's upset and fear of Royce going

back made perfect sense now. I was the one who'd human-
ised him. Not Nate. Everything was my fault. I'd made Royce
think he was real.

I flopped back down into the chair and put my face in my
hands. This was too much with Teddy's life in the balance as
well. If he didn't revive and they scrubbed Royce down to a
'Speak and Spell' robot, I would have lost them both and I
didn't know what I'd do then.

I felt a warm hand on my back. 'Would you like me to call
Tom?'

I shook my head without removing it from my hands.

'He will be as good as new, I promise.'

I let my hands drop and glared up at him. 'I don't want
him as good as new, I want my Royce – our Royce,' I quickly
corrected. 'He'll be a stranger.' My face crumpled and I began
to break down. Tears I'd been holding in all week came
tumbling out.

The professor walked away and I heard him talking to
someone else. Then he came back. 'I promise that as soon as
I'm satisfied that Royce is safe to be around, he will come
back to you. OK?'

'With his memories?' I asked, my tears stopping instantly.

He bobbed his head a little. 'As much as we can,' he said,
smiling kindly. I can guarantee that he will know you and
everyone he's met in his new life.'

I wanted to drill him down to more than that, but there
was a knock on the door and Tom was standing there. 'Come
on, trouble. Let's get you off to bed.'

The professor passed me a tissue as I got up and let Tom
lead me away. I gave my nose a good blow and Tom thanked
him, closing the door behind us.

Damien was outside, so I kept quiet all the way until he
finally left us in our familiar part of the building. Then I
blurted immediately, 'Royce is here. I don't know what's

wrong, but they are going to scrub him. We have to stop them,' I said, my whole face pleading, holding his jacket lapels

Tom tried to keep the exasperation off his face but failed. We were outside my door and he pushed it open for me. 'Get some sleep. We'll discuss it tomorrow.'

I gripped the door jamb. 'He might not have that long. He'll be reprogrammed, Tom. He won't remember anything. They might not even let him come back.'

Tom's face was pained and then uncomfortable.

Then I fell in, with a hitch of breath and my hands to my mouth in horror. 'You don't want him back, do you?'

CHAPTER 57

*C*hrissy

Tom looked pained when he took a step towards me. 'It's not that, sweetheart. It's Teddy. When he comes home, there will be the cost of his aftercare. That's a lot of credits for us to find, Chrissy. But you'll have Teddy back?' he said, switching from his sorry face to his hopeful, enthusiastic one. However, his eyes were still pleading for me to understand.

I didn't care. Nate had been right about everything, and I'd been stupid. 'But if he doesn't, then an empty version of Royce will be a consolation prize, will it?' I knew I was being hysterical and completely unfair, but I couldn't help it. I was torn in two.

I didn't wait for any more and pushed right past him. 'Leave me alone.' I broke into a jog and headed for the cafeteria, hoping it would be empty at this time of night.

I slowed with relief as soon as I got to the doors. I was right. Just a few Techs in lab coats, quietly scrolling their wrists or 3D images, with mugs in front of them. I was out of breath and took a moment to compose myself. Then I headed for the furthest corner.

Murtle came over, already carrying a hot drink. 'This will help you sleep,' she said, smiling. She even managed to make her strained plastic smile comforting.

'Thank you,' I said, stirring a packet of sweetener into the milky drink.

'Is there something wrong, dear?' She looked around and pulled out the chair opposite and sat down.

I was unsure for a moment. I had to remember that behind those glassy eyes was a real person. A grandma with loved ones of her own. Everything opposite to Royce. The cruel irony constricted my throat. He was nothing but a mechanical convenience, like a dishwasher or a digi-robe. Except he could walk and hold a conversation. But even then, I had to add care, love and protect.

Before I knew what was happening, I was in tears again and my heartbreak came in a flood. Murtle was on her feet and I was in her stiff, knotty arms. Squashing me with soft rubber over nuts and bolts. 'There, there, my love,' she kept saying, but I sobbed and kept spewing secret after secret that I'd never told a single soul.

'It's Royce. He's here. They're going to scrub him and Tom's not going to help pay, even if he does come home.' I went on and on, until I ran out of steam and Murtle pulled apart and handed me my drink and a tissue from her pocket.

'Here. Calm down and tell me everything, slowly, right from the beginning.'

I looked around; the Techs must have gone with all the drama. We sat back down and that's what I did. The whole sorry story from start to finish. Teddy. Even the kiss, until I finally finished with Royce running away. 'Then I saw him here, today. Being led along in handcuffs like a criminal. Teddy wouldn't be here at all if it wasn't for him. He just stared at me, like he didn't know me at all.' My face cracked with the pain and I managed to pull it back before I was crying again.

Murtle hadn't said a word. Just interspersed my outpouring with nods, shakes of her head and tuts when needed. It felt good to finally talk to someone. I slammed down the confusing irony again. In fact, she hadn't said anything for so long, I had to ask, 'What is it?'

She shrugged, an amazing feat of engineering for her, 'I know they're up to all sorts here, with technology and human tissue and everything. They forget I'm human, but I've got ears. And I never ask; it's more than my job is worth. But doesn't it seem weird that they brought him in handcuffs?'

I frowned, not fully following what she was saying. I shrugged and took a sip of my hot chocolate. It didn't seem that odd. 'The prof said he's dangerous at the moment.' I missed out the part about him getting his programme mixed up with reality. I just couldn't bring myself to betray him like that. It was his business. His personal issues.

'No, it's not that.' Murtle was still staring off into space, like she was thinking deeply about it. 'They just switch them off, don't they?' Her eyes focused on me again. 'Don't the TinBoiz have something at the back of their neck? A few have come through this place. It shuts down all their systems. Weird, that's all. It's like they're treating him as though he *is* human.'

An icy feeling crept through my veins as her words finally filtered through. She was right, but something about it made me uneasy. Something pushed the lid down before I could let my hopes out in a frenzy. 'Yeah. He's programmed with a whole backstory. That's the problem.' I averted my eyes and blew on my drink.

Murtle was studying me closely. 'That makes sense. They

are taking this realism thing to another level. They probably want them to believe it.'

My eyes shot to Murtle's. Despite the metal and plastic, it was amazing how much she could convey. Or not, as the case may be. There was a lot she wasn't saying.

'It's tragic,' she said.

I nodded, sadly. Barbaric was a better word. To make a machine deliberately think it was alive. Then tell it it's not when it doesn't do what you want it to do.

My heart broke. No wonder he'd broken down. It was nothing more than making a slave. Worse, in fact. Because they tricked it into thinking it wasn't one. Then all they had to do when it acted out was to return it to factory settings. Then, hey presto! New robot, all over again.

I felt sick.

Then Murtle finally said what she'd been ruminating on. 'So you've fallen for this TinBoi.'

I almost dropped my drink, but caught it and slurped it over my hands and the table. I lived a moment of terror until I relaxed slightly when I read no accusation in her at all. Just a statement of truth. It was so damned natural, she made it easy.

I simply nodded. Caught, with no point in running. 'It doesn't matter what I think, because if Teddy comes out of this, we won't be able to afford Royce, anyway. With or without his memories.' I used my tissue to dry my hands and mop up some of the spilt drink.

Murtle put her gnarly hand over mine and gave it a rough squeeze. 'It won't be as bad as you think. You'll see. Things are seldom as bad as we build them up.' She smiled at me kindly, and I really tried not to seem impatient with her. She simply nudged my arm and said, 'I'm not that over the hill, you know.'

I couldn't help laughing a little at being so easily read.

'Well, what about giving him something that will remind him of you? Maybe that will trigger something after, they, you know, scrub him. Residual memory is a real thing. I heard them talk about it.' She was watching my reaction, hopefully.

It seemed far-fetched, but I appreciated what she was doing. It was worth a try. But there weren't that many physical things between us. Only school. The kiss. My constant moodiness with him. My hand subconsciously went to the pendant around my neck. The one with a treasured hologram of Teddy in it.

'Your necklace?' Murtle asked.

'I can't,' it was out of the question. 'It's not anything to do with Royce. It's my last piece of Teddy.' *No, I couldn't.*

'The boy in the chamber?'

'What if I lose him? It's all I have.' I shifted in my seat, in panic.

'Well, transfer it to that,' Murtle said, pointing at my wrist-plate. Like it was simple.

It was. I almost laughed.

'Then we'll make a new one of you and slip it into Royce's room for him to find.'

I stared at her, letting the idea sink in.

'Then, even if it doesn't spark something, it will intrigue him to find out. It's very romantic. Like star-crossed lovers, reincarnated to find each other again,' she finished in hushed, scandalous tones.

I laughed. She'd clearly read too many romance novels, but it was perfect. I loved the idea. Then I immediately deflated. 'How am I going to get it to him? I don't even know where he is.'

'But he's in the building?'

I shrugged. 'I assume so. It was only a couple of hours ago, but I don't know how long for.'

'We need to act quickly, then. Let's swap the images and leave the locket with me. I know the floor he's likely to be on. I just need to get someone to get it to him.'

I felt suddenly alive. Excited. Hopeful, even. I grasped Murtle's hand. 'Thank you so much.' I teared up and meant every word. I was out of options and this old, sick grandma, all alone somewhere, had thrown me a lifeline. There was just a chance that it could work.

'Let's get to work quickly, before the night shift gets their break,' she said, getting to her feet.

We transferred the image to my wrist file, which I felt good about, figuring it was far safer there all backed up. Then we took another image of me and uplinked it from my wrist to the pendant. I thought it was an awful representation of me. Tired, wrung-out and worried-looking. I did attempt a smile, but it wasn't convincing. It would have to do.

'There. Beautiful. Thoughtful and ethereal,' Murtle said, taking the locket and dropping it into her deep apron pocket.

'Don't lose it,' I said, barely able to let it go.

'Don't worry. Go to bed. I'll get it to your TinBoi one way or another, tonight.' She handed me her stylo and an old-fashioned notepad she still used to take down her orders. 'Do you want to write him a note? Might help.'

CHAPTER 58

*R*oyce

I would like to say that I had no idea how long I stayed in the foetal position in the padded room, but I knew it to the nearest second. Another nail in the coffin of my human identity. I also knew they'd shut me down against my will and I seethed about that.

This was the end. I knew it the moment I saw Chrissy in the building. This building. The one they must have brought Teddy to. Whatever they were going to do with me would be in the next few hours.

Oh, Chrissy. I buried my head in my hands. My heart hurt so badly. Just the thought of her. The pain was real. In the centre of my chest. The same way it jumped whenever I was near her. Or the merest mention of her name. My need to kiss her. Touch her. Went against every protocol and yet I did it anyway.

Then my heart darkened to black when I thought of the professor seeing everything through my traitorous eyes. His eyes. The ones he had designed.

So why didn't he swoop in at the first sign of a protocol breach? It made no sense. He could have stopped all this before it began. Then I understood; I was a lab rat. Being observed under all conditions. I hardened to granite at that. One day, when he least expected it, I will force him to see what he did to me and all the others. I'll expose him for the Frankenstein that he is.

I jumped at the jangle of keys. Perfectly primitive in that it was unhackable. A hatch in the door tilted forward and something small fell soundlessly on the soft floor. I stared at the tiny brown envelope. Conflicted between an overwhelming curiosity and whether it was a test. I tracked my vision to the corner, to the tiny blinking camera. Debating whether to push it away. But my own eyes were his windows to everything I could see. *Then why the camera? Was the room not always used for machines?* Or?

My heart sped up. Did it mean he wasn't watching through my eyes all the time? Perhaps, when he slept, he got someone else to watch the camera. With lower clearance. Maybe eye watching was personal to him? Maybe even illegal, spying on all those unsuspecting families, and he couldn't resist it.

The more I thought of privacy laws governing all those contracts with TinBoiz, the more I thought I was right. It was wrong. People deserved to know.

I ran the maze of options for several minutes. Down blind corridors and turning another way. All at lightning speed. Until I landed on the brown manila envelope, no bigger than the palm of my hand.

My internal clock said 03:05 a.m. A strange time to receive parcels. The prof would surely be asleep.

I shot forward, snatched up the packet and leapt to the corner, right underneath the camera. I prayed that whoever was monitoring was dozing or gaming with a friend.

Nothing was going to happen with me in a padded cell, powered down, at night.

I was about to tear the packet open when I paused at my last thought. I was powered down against my will. *How had I come back online if it wasn't a test?* I ran that idea over my sensors for a full minute. All systems were fully operational. *Could it be I'd powered up by myself?*

My powerpack shuddered over-time at that. Even that was weird. *Why was I given the ability to do that with no internal organs?* Bio-merging to that degree would be inefficient. Artificial ones, or better still, none, would make a far stronger unit. *Why give me a heart?*

My head felt like it was bursting with all the conflicting information. I had to just rip the paper and pull out whatever was inside. I could feel something hard, like a disk of a game.

I tipped out the contents into my hand. It was a silver chain and a small oval-shaped locket. My grid was all over it, so I put it out of my sight for a second, just in case.

I had a match: Chrissy. She had a locket just like this. With Teddy inside. I remembered asking her about it. My power pack whirred. I didn't understand.

I slowly pulled it back into my eyeline with perfectly steady hands, but my mind was shaking. I could literally feel my synapses igniting as I dug in my thumb nail and opened it.

Up popped a pixelated blue light, that eventually settled to the most perfect image of Chrissy. My power pack died because my heart stopped. The girl I loved hopelessly looked longingly into an imaginary distance. Vulnerable and fragile, with the same sadness and hollowed shadow under dark eyes that held a fierce determination to fight for all that she loved. It hit me hard. I had limitless stills like this in my memory. *Why? Why did she send me this?*

I was so focused on the locket that I almost discarded the

envelope, but something made me take a final look inside. A fire lit in my chest at the tiny piece of paper that I almost missed. All the more fascinating because paper was so rare these days. No one used it anymore, not this side of the Danger Line, anyway. At home, it was a sought-after commodity because it was private, disposable and most of all untraceable. With the disappearance of paper money, counterfeiters soon made the switch to making paper and a whole new black market was born. *What was Chrissy up to?*

I slowly opened the tiny piece of whisper-thin paper that was folded once and saw Chrissy's incredibly neat writing. I never even knew she could handwrite. My reading wasn't great, but the words were simple:

> *Royce,*
> *Please don't hate me and know that*
> *I love you, machine or not.*
> *Remember me when they scrub your mind.*
> *Find a way to come home.*
> *And above all,*
> *Remember, Royce.*
> *Remember,*
> *Chrissy xxx*

I was stunned and read and reread the message, even though it was dangerous for me to keep looking at it. I couldn't help myself. I was bursting with something too big for my chest cavity. Love. It didn't matter what I was. I didn't have to be mixed up anymore.

But she was right. They would reset my memory, if nothing else.

My systems began to race as I got to my feet and scanned

the whole room inch by inch. I resisted the urge to panic when I couldn't see a single place to hide it. On me wasn't safe, not even in my sock. Everything would be taken before the reconditioning.

My head began to ache at the speed it was working. I bashed my temples with the heels of my hands to think harder. Then every system in my body stopped and my grid-lines zeroed closer and closer to the absolute corner of the room, right where I'd been sitting, under the camera. The part where two walls met the floor.

I dropped to my knees and crawled closer and there it was. The tiniest stretch in the stitching and the weakest point. The stitches were strong and I needed to work them larger. First with my nail and then with my index finger, but I couldn't risk ripping the fabric. It had to be small, missed by the naked eye, or the scrutiny of another AU.

It was no good. I was aware of time passing and panic was setting in. I scavenged around for anything, but my paste tube and pale were the only things that came in or out of my cell and they were taken right afterwards.

I slumped onto my behind, hopeless. I tried to get a hold of my racing thoughts, it wasn't helping, so I started to count. Without breathing, it had to do something.

In, one two.

Out, one two.

At the same time, I narrowed down what it was that I needed. A sharp implement, preferably plastic or steel. All I had were the clothes on my back. My t-shirt and jeans that Mom – Sheila – had bought me. I almost fell to pieces at that. I loved Sheila. I loved these clothes. They were a perfect gift. I looked down at myself. My crotch.

My fly.

A vintage steel zipper. Pants didn't have them these days.

Old-fashioned and made for strength. The small pull tag

was metal, about an inch long and no more than a quarter of an inch wide.

I was sad to break it, but these were desperate times, and I guessed I wouldn't see these clothes again, anyway. I began to pull on the tag to weaken the link that attached it to the zip, until I could ease it off through the gap. The end would make a perfect stitch puller.

I crouched on all fours and got down to my elbows to get in close to work. I became hyper-focused on pulling one tiny little stitch, then another. Each time, testing the gap with the locket until I could push the flat locket inside, without tearing or stretching the fabric. Next, I put the chain and the note back in the envelope and rolled it to the size of a pen. This time, I made sure it was bent into the corner, so it didn't unravel or show. I massaged the fabric so they weren't too close to each other. Still reachable, but if they discovered one, I didn't want them to find the other. Then I painstakingly tightened up any stitches that I could and poked any remaining cotton inside.

I sat back to survey my work and it still looked wrong. Possibly because I knew it was there, so I plumped the cushion all around it, then sat back on my knees to view it as a human and then as an AU. It was good. Only noticeable if an AU has done a detailed scan of the room previously, which I doubted. Not for a long time, anyway. It would have to do. I just prayed I'd end up back here and there would be something left for me to find. The alternative was unthinkable.

I closed my eyes. My heart was working again. Steady and sure. Everything felt so human. Nothing made sense. I allowed myself to fall sideways into the foetal position. This was the end as I knew it. I slowed my systems gradually to power off. Praying to Mack's God, that he might listen to the plea of a machine and help me find Chrissy's clues. There were no guarantees I'd ever see her again. Luck or divine intervention were my last thoughts before system shutdown.

Eyes closed.

Power pack off.

Heart slowed to utility mode.

Brain systems to utility mode.

Three, two, blackout.

hrissy

It was a rough night, just lying there, wondering if Murtle had got my message and locket through. I died a thousand times imagining the scenarios where it got found or intercepted. Whether I'd got her, or some other poor worker, fired. Or if they read my declaration of love for a machine. It didn't bear thinking about. But most of all, I couldn't bear a world without Royce, any more than I could Teddy.

My heart stopped at a soft knock at my door. I sat up sharply and looked at my wrist. It was 07.05 a.m. Morning. I must have been awake the whole night. 'Come in,' I said, with a croaky voice.

Tina came in and the lights automatically rose to daytime brightness. I was still blinking with the contrast when she said quickly, 'Good. Get dressed, Chrissy. The professor has called a meeting. There's news.'

I was out of bed before she'd even stopped speaking; her suppressed excitement catching.

'Come to ours when you're ready,' she said, disappearing just as quickly.

My heart was beating, but my mind cleared. It was good to be doing something. I took a two-minute shower, dragged on yesterday's comfy sweats and sneakers and slipped silently out of the room. I went to knock at Tina and Tom's, but the door was snatched open while my knuckle was still in the air.

'Good! You're ready,' Tom said, patting his pockets to check he had everything.

'Don't bother, Tom. We can come back after,' Tina said, nudging him forward and me out of the way.

Damien appeared immediately and quickly said, 'Follow me,' increasing the sense of urgency. He turned, marching straight off down the corridor. Tina and Tom fell in step and I had to jog to keep up. My mind was turning cartwheels on what it could be. Pinning hope after hope it was something good. It was the speed that was electrifying.

We were taken to a plain boardroom instead of the professor's office. No windows. No adornments of any kind. Three other men and two women were already seated around the large oval table. 'Ah, take a seat, Mr and Mrs Monshall. Chrissy,' the professor said, indicating three spare seats next to each other. 'This is my team.'

I nodded a hello while Tom shook all their hands across the table. I recognised Greg from the games room immediately. He gave me a small salute across the table. The professor got us straight to business.

'Thank you all for coming so quickly at such an early hour, but I received news an hour ago that the chamber has been scheduled for declassification in twenty-four hours.'

I looked fearfully at Tina and Tom, who swapped an equally alarmed look. 'Are you saying it has to go back?' Tom asked.

'That's correct. It will be inspected, and if it is not there, it will spark an investigation. I'm afraid Teddy will have to come out of the chamber tonight, so we can spirit it back to the depot, where the military tech staff are expecting to find it.'

'Is he ready? Has it worked?' Tina asked frantically.

Tom put his hand gently over hers because it was obvious it didn't matter. His time had simply run out. I felt desperately sorry for her, for me, for all of us.

The professor spoke very calmly and slowly and I was grateful for that. 'The honest truth is we won't know until we try. He has had almost a full week. His brain activity has improved in all the areas we wanted to see it. Whether that is enough to bring back the boy you knew, it is hard to tell at this stage. That being said, his kidney function is a concern, and his heart and liver have been under strain.' He held up both his hands and smiled sympathetically. 'What can I say? It's in the lap of the gods.'

We were silent for a long moment, letting it all sink in. We were all so focused on his brain function that we hadn't given much thought to the rest of him.

'So what's the plan?' Tom said, after coughing his throat clear.

The professor nodded his appreciation at his strength. 'That is why I called my team together to go through it with you. Teddy will be removed at 23:00 tonight. My AUs and tech team will work on the CompEvac ambulance, which will arrive back here at 22:45. My team here will reload the chamber, wipe computer files and deep clean it to erase all trace of us since it left the army base. We have just forty-five minutes before it must leave. It cannot be late. Meanwhile, I will be busy in theatre with my medical team, bringing Teddy out of his cryo-sleep, ready for any eventuality.'

It sounded like a good plan. I looked at Tom, who blinked

and swallowed and glanced at Tina. 'OK. So what about us? What should we do?'

The professor smiled regretfully. 'Wait. I know that isn't what you want to hear, but this is our area of expertise. Leave it with us.'

I understood Tom's frustration. Waiting was all we'd done for the longest week of our lives.

'I promise, you will be called as soon as we have news.'

Damien appeared behind us and held out his arm for us to leave. And that was it. Meeting over.

We were shellshocked and got to our feet slowly. I looked back at the table and they were all engrossed in tech-speak. I wanted to ask about Royce. What was going to happen to him, but it wasn't the right time. I wasn't even a hundred percent sure I'd been wise to let on I'd seen him and I didn't want to get Greg in any trouble for revealing secrets.

Damien left us at our rooms and we decided to continue on to the cafeteria. My heart pinged at the hope that Murtle might still be there, and breakfast seemed a good idea to kill some time.

Murtle was behind the counter. My stomach flipped when she looked up at just the right moment to see my hopeful expression. She nodded and put up a stumpy rubber thumb. Another sub was there and she put up a hand of goodbye. It was the end of her shift. But it was enough. My heart was pounding. The package had been delivered. Now all I had to do was wait for both of them.

CHAPTER 60

*C*hrissy

It was the longest day of my life. They weren't going to even take Teddy out until eleven, to give him as much time in the chamber as possible. I was dying to know how Royce was, but daren't ruin anything there. Trying to sleep was pointless. So, as a last-ditch attempt to distract myself, I went in search of the games room, in the darker, trade part of the building. It felt closer to Royce, somehow.

I was proud of myself for remembering the way and immediately excited to find Greg there. He was drinking coffee and put up his hand. There were a couple of other Techs, engrossed in headsets, so I tiptoed past and sat down in a chair opposite him.

'Terrible wait,' he said, taking a sip from his grey thermo-cup. 'Grab a coffee.' He pointed at the machine.

'I'm already coffee'd out,' I said, pulling a face. 'Don't think I'll sleep for a week.'

He laughed. 'I get you. It's the preferred effect for me.'

I studied him, curious what a coder/programmer/game

designer had been brought in to do. 'What are you doing for Teddy?' I asked.

He frowned. 'Me, no… Med, not my thing. I'm pure robotics. I'm here to repatch an AU.' He squinted and pointed at me. 'The one brought in yesterday.'

I should have asked why he was in Teddy's meeting then, but my mind was already racing over what he would be doing to Royce. I hoped he hadn't noticed the blast of heat in my cheeks. I had to calm down. I swallowed hard, I could barely speak, my throat had constricted so much. 'Oh yeah, I remember. Is he fixable, then? He seemed pretty wild.'

'Sure. They're all fixable. They can go on forever. Just need to fix the glitches in his memory.'

I tried not to come across as too interested. 'So do they remember anything from before?' I asked casually. 'I mean, will he go back to his family, or will they get a new one?'

Greg let out a slow breath, removing his 'Tech Geek' cap and scratching his black hair so it stood up messily. 'Not sure… I guess so. He's a trial model.' He reduced his voice to a whisper. 'Top-secret. Off the books.'

My pulse raced. I knew it. Of course he was special. 'Oh, yeah?' I said, equally quietly, but trying not to sound too excited. 'What's different about him?'

He shrugged and pulled a face. Then, after glancing sideways to check the other two techs were still engrossed in their game, he leaned closer to me in his chair. 'The prof gets us in to work on different things at different times, so none of us gets the full story. All I know is in that AU, there is more human than machine,' he finished, sitting back in his chair with a satisfied nod.

Before I could process what he'd said and what it could mean, a female voice came over a speaker. 'Can Greg Taylor report to the main lab. Right away. Greg Taylor, to the main lab. Thank you.'

'That's me,' Greg said, slowly getting to his feet and stretching out his back. 'Hope all goes well with your friend.'

I put up a hand and smiled weakly. 'You too... With the AU.' My head was pounding my skull and my stomach, turning loops.

He grinned and strode out the open doorway, leaving me to re-run the conversation over and over in my head. It was clear, the professor had two important operations going on today.

At last, it was 11 p.m. and we were collected from our rooms and taken back down to the basement car park.

We huddled together against the cold after the warm building, but it was more to do with fear and nerves than the chill. It all felt artificial. Desolate. Such a lonely place for Teddy to be. All alone in the drum of an iron machine.

Tonight it seemed full. AUs, robotic machines, the crane to hoist the chamber back into the special ambulance, which had arrived right on time. Hospital orderlies at the ready, with a gurney, to whisk Teddy off to theatre.

We inched closer when the familiar AUs began hitting switches and the cylinder containing Teddy was slowly rolled out. The professor appeared next to me. 'We have to bring Teddy's temperature up slowly over the next eight hours. It can't be rushed,' he explained, his eyes glued to the scene. 'Once out of the lung, time is crucial. We must get his internal systems started. Heart, lungs, et cetera, as soon as possible.'

We were watching his face avidly, but his mind was clearly already on instructing his team. 'Stand back,' he said, striding forward.

Tom pulled us both back, too far out of the way, almost to the brick wall. He was nervous, eyes wide and scanning the scene frantically. I guess the last thing he wanted was to get kicked out because we were in the way.

'Ready?' one of the orderlies shouted.

Then, in one swift manoeuvre, the cylinder door was opened with a loud hiss. Teddy was pulled out and onto the gurney and a silver sheet tucked in all around him. The professor moved to the head, 'Thermo!' he ordered, clicking his fingers, and another huge silver quilt was placed over the top of that. 'Now, move!'

The two huge AUs lifted Teddy, the runner was pulled out from under him and rolled back into the chamber. The gurney was quickly wheeled in its place, Teddy was lowered and pushed away fast. Straight past where we were standing, towards the door to the building.

Tina whimpered, standing next to me.

I got a glimpse of Teddy as he went past. Just the top part of his face. His eyes were tightly closed. Eyelids, just lines, like a waxwork doll. So pale, like he wasn't alive. The professor walked quickly next to him.

Tina turned into Tom's chest. It was too much. I felt myself coming apart, too. Tom brought us both under his arms and I was gratefully distracted. We moved towards the building. My mind churning over. There were no leads. No life support plugged into him. My breaths were short. I had to hold it together. Needed to watch. To know what was happening.

I took one last glance behind me before we went inside. The AUs were shutting off the power. The spider bot was attaching the chains while another was inside the cylinder, spraying it with some kind of mist. Sanitiser, probably, to remove all the evidence that Teddy was even there.

I didn't see anymore. I was hit by the immediate warmth of the building and we crowded into the large elevator. Tom was asking the professor questions, like what happens next, but my mind was stuck on Teddy's lifeless face. I kept my terror to myself. *Should he still be that pale? Was he breathing? Wouldn't he die without machines?*

The lift doors opened, and he was wheeled out fast. We were running behind, down the long corridor, through double doors and into the prepped theatre. But before we could take a step inside to follow, the professor stepped into our path. 'You can't come any further.' He motioned with a hand behind him. 'Damien will take you back to the cafeteria. I'll meet you there when we have news.'

'How long?' Tom said, exasperated, trying to see past him.

'Hard to say,' the professor said as the doors slowly closed.

We looked at each other, lost. Damien stepped forward, as hard and expressionless as ever. 'Come. He's in good hands.'

There was nothing else to do but follow. But my feet dragged and I kept looking over my shoulder. Four more scrubbed surgeons went into the theatre. *How many did it take?* It felt more like an ER after a car crash.

I finally sped up my steps to catch up after a tug on the arm from Tom. 'All we can do is wait,' he said, glancing at Tina, convincing himself. We were all on our last nerve.

MURTLE WAS BACK on duty when Damien left us at the cafeteria. Tom settled us into our seats and was about to go to the counter when Tina burst into uncontrollable tears. She jumped up from her seat and ran out the way we came. Tom closed his eyes to gather the pieces. 'I'll go back to the room with her.'

'Don't worry about me. Go!' I said, with a flick of my hand, then watched him stride quickly after her. I was bewildered and had no idea what to do, either. The limbo was killing us all. It had simmered all week until it had finally boiled down to make-or-break time.

I put my head in my hands. Then I felt a current in the air and heard a cough.

Murtle was right there, holding a mug of something in one hand and an energy bar in the other. I smiled through welling tears at her much-needed kindness. 'Thank you.' This lady had been a rock over the last few days.

'How's it going?' she asked, pulling out the chair opposite to sit down.

I gave her my best 'don't ask' expression.

'Oh, like that,' she said, with a thoughtful nod. 'One of my friends – a porter-sub – delivered your package last night.' Leaning forward, conspiratorially.

It lifted me, instantly, with hope. 'Definitely? You're sure?'

'Absolutely.' She gave me her big, grimacing grin. 'They took him to the Tech lab earlier tonight. My friend is great; he'll keep us up to date. No trouble.'

I thought of Greg being called earlier. That must have been when it was. 'Did he say what they're actually doing to him?' I asked. 'Can he find out that sort of stuff?' I tried to keep a lid on my excitement, but my heart was bouncing all over the place.

She pulled a weird, pained face. 'Not sure, it's top-secret down there, but it's so damn boring all night, we live for gossip and he gets around and knows a lot of people,' she finished with a wink of her extra-long eyelashes. 'He chats to the Techs in their break, real friendly. They forget what clearance he has.'

'What does he know?' I asked, bringing my cup to my mouth to cover my excitement.

'Not a lot, I'm afraid. Only that this one is one of their special experimental models. Top-secret. Some Tech heavy-hitters flew in by helihover and landed right on the roof,' she said, her doll's eyes widening.

That *was* interesting. 'What do you think they're here for?' I asked, casually, desperate for her to keep talking.

'No idea. Only that it was buzzing down there. Some sort of psyche-alignment. Nothing physical, my guy reckons, by the types flown in. He thinks they're scared of losing a lot of money on their flagship model.'

'A new model for TinBoiz, you mean?'

Murtle nodded. 'I guess so, but he overheard someone say something like, he was too good, whatever that means, and they needed to dial him down a bit.'

I was all over what she was saying. Reading between the lines. Working double time at what it could all mean. Royce must be their most real invention. And it had backfired. It had to be that. A physical pain twisted in the centre of my chest that they would want to take some of that away.

'I guess, at the end of the day, the poor love is a robot and robots are built for us,' Murtle said wistfully. Laughable when I thought of her – the hunk of metal sitting opposite me. 'They can't go around thinking they're people, can they?'

Before I could answer, she turned her head and I followed her line of vision. A couple of lab guys walked in and headed for the counter. 'Gotta go,' she said, getting up from her chair.

I watched her weird stomping gait, all the way back, and realised my drink was chocolate. I was hungry and ate my energy bar in three bites.

Murtle didn't know much, but everything was now startlingly clear. Why I'd been so attracted to Royce. Because, to him, he was real. He had all the thoughts and feelings of a person. *How dare they take that away?* He was special and they were giving him the robot version of a lobotomy. I was sickened.

I rose from my chair, deciding to go to my room. This was going to be an agonisingly long night.

CHAPTER 61

*C*hrissy
I must have got to know every square inch of my ceiling that night. I couldn't sleep, but was no company for anyone, either. All I could do was run through my life with both boys, then crumple in terror at the loss of either one of them.

When it got to around 2 a.m., I wondered whether Teddy was fighting for his life. And Royce? Well, I couldn't even imagine what was happening there. I cried frustrated tears until they dried like a crust on my face.

A soft knock rapped on my door.

I scrambled to sit up. 'Come in?' came out like a squeak.

Tom and Tina came in quietly.

'Any news?' I asked, already dreading the answer.

They both shook their heads, making me relax a little. At this stage, no news was good news. 'Is it OK if we sit with you? We can't bear it,' Tina said, her face looking harrowed and drawn.

I smiled, more grateful than they would ever know and scooted over. 'Course.'

They both sat and we held hands for a time. Then we reminisced from a well of memories of Teddy.

'Do you remember when he built that silent spy drone from spare parts in the garage?' Tom said in a mixture of disbelief and pride.

Tina rolled her eyes playfully. 'I certainly do. The neighbour called security, complaining she had a Peeping Tom.'

We all laughed. 'We were building spyware to sell to the Network,' I said, in our defence. Well, Teddy was. I was his assistant.'

They both laughed at that. He was always the instigator in our wacky schemes.

Tom put his hand over mine. 'Thank you for being such a good and loyal friend to Teddy.' His look was glassy and intense with emotion.

Tina added her hand to the pile. 'We're so grateful.'

I swallowed down a huge lump and shrugged. 'It was easy.' I fixed them directly in the eye, while a solitary tear rolled down my cheek. 'He is my best friend. My only friend.' I thought of Royce guiltily. 'We did everything together. Told each other everything. He was my right arm.' I felt myself dissolving. The tears came. 'I can't lose him. I can't.'

The Monshalls' arms were all around me. 'You're a dear, dear girl. We know. We know,' Tina said, rubbing my back.

'You're like our daughter,' Tom added.

Then three heavy knocks hit my door.

CHAPTER 62

Chrissy

None of us moved. My heart froze and we all looked at each other.

Tom got to his feet and went over to the door. Something was said in hushed tones through a small gap. I didn't wait to find out what. I was already scrambling off the bed to put my sneakers on.

'What is it?' Tina asked, her hand on her mouth.

Tom pushed the door closed and turned to us, a grim look on his face.

'The professor has called us to his office.' Before we could bombard him with questions, he cut in with, 'He said right away.'

I was still in last night's clothes, and pulling my sneakers on, I walked straight for the door. Tina was right behind me.

An orderly in green scrubs was right outside and escorted us quickly down the silent corridors to the professor's office. 'Is it good news?' Tina and Tom asked in all kinds of variations, just for a hint, but all he said was, 'The professor will explain everything,' so they gave up.

We arrived at the study and were ushered quickly inside. The contrast to the rest of the building was no longer a shock; the only thing registering was that he had several people standing around his desk. All in surgical scrubs and obviously part of his team.

'Take a seat,' the professor said, just as three stiff-backed chairs appeared behind us.

We sat, automatically.

I turned my head, straight into Damien's cold stare. So like Royce's. He actually winked, which made me instantly face front in shock. My heart was skipping, trying to work out whether any of this was a good sign.

'Is he alive?' Tom asked, shocking Tina so much that I heard her sudden intake of breath. But he was right to ask and I looked stonily back at the professor for his answer.

'Yes!' the professor answered curtly, then clicked his fingers at Damien. 'Get them to send a pot of coffee and some sandwiches, can you?'

I felt Damien's presence disappear from right behind me, the professor relaxed back into his chair and the others found seats. 'It's been a long night,' the professor said, rubbing the fatigue off his face with his hand. 'Thank you for your patience and for coming so quickly, but I'm afraid it's not over yet.'

'Is it good news?' Tina asked, her voice wobbling, poised for the worst.

The professor looked up at the ceiling to find the right words and a vice gripped my heart. 'I'll explain it as simply as I can.' He patted the air with both hands. 'Most importantly, Teddy is alive and we've stabilised him.'

Time seemed to suspend while we all waited for the 'but'.

'Is he breathing on his own?' Tina said quickly.

Is his brain functioning?' Tom asked.

I nodded along to the two most important questions of the night.

The professor pointed at Tom and said, 'Yes! That has been a resounding success. The chamber did its job well.'

Tom and Tina swapped a joy-filled look and hugged and kissed in front of everyone.

My gaze was on the professor. That was the good news and the bad news was coming. The Monshalls were both sniffing back tears when they finally let each other go, to face him again.

'There is no easy way to say this, so I'll get right to the point.'

In a microsecond, I saw the look he gave his team and how they all averted their eyes. I gripped the edges of my chair till my fingers hurt and my throat felt like it was closing up.

'As soon as we brought Teddy up to temperature, his organs started to fail. First, kidneys, then heart, lungs...'

Tina and Tom looked frozen, as if it didn't compute. 'But his brain works,' Tom said, nodding, a little too enthusiastically, grabbing onto Tina's hand and squeezing the life out of it.

I wanted to cry; I couldn't stand it. 'Isn't there a chamber for organs?'

The professor smiled at me, as if I'd taken a step in the right direction, but he still shook his head. 'Not accessible in time. Maybe for one system, but his whole body has failed. I'm afraid we have run out of options.'

I could feel physical pain rising from my chest to my throat, not helped because Tina was already wailing. Tom was sheltering her to hide his own pain. But I didn't release it, because for some reason, the professor was still talking. Pushing on regardless, with us crumbling around him.

'Teddy's body has simply been through too much over the last months, and he wasn't strong before that.'

Tom was murmuring. Consoling Tina, kissing the top of her head.

I became numb. Suspended in emotionless animation. I knew he was telling us the truth we needed to hear. No false hopes. Neither of us was fit, but Teddy had always been the more sickly one.

'So here it is. Your options.'

I woke up from my daze. Tina stopped crying and Tom straightened in his seat and asked, 'There are options?'

We all blinked in shock.

'Yes. If you want there to be?'

What a silly question, but he still waited as if he was letting that sink in. I looked at Tom to see if he was as confused as I was. He remained fixed on the professor and so was Tina.

Then the blow was delivered.

'The easiest option is that we switch off all life support and let Teddy slowly slip away. You can have a funeral, closure, mourn and eventually move on with your life.

'But his mind is good. You said it was,' Tina said, crumpling again.

The professor held up his hand to stop her. 'That is also true, as far as we can tell, which brings me to my next option. That is, to salvage his brain from a dying body, with a little of his tissue and give him another body. A split human and cybernetic body. A neuro-cyber-body. Or an NCB as we call it.'

We all stared at him, stunned. My heart juddered painfully. *Royce.*

'I am somewhat a leader in the field,' he continued, when he didn't get any response. 'Much of my research has been in the testing phases, but we've made excellent progress and our beta model has passed its final tests with flying colours.'

Royce. It had to be.

'Now it sounds radical to use this technology on a live subject, but if you consent and waive medical and legal rights, we can do this for you in the name of science. We can push forward the medical/robotic frontier.'

We all remained silent, trying to sift through what he was telling us. For me, I was scrambling over the possible similarities to Royce. Was he one of his live subjects?'

'So let me get this straight,' Tom began, sounding angrier than I was expecting. You're asking us to donate Teddy's body to science as if he is dead, so you can turn him into a robot with a human brain?' he ended, almost shouting, his voice was so high-pitched.'

The professor shifted uncomfortably in his seat. 'I would word it a little differently. More like putting him in a clinical trial where we fuse tissue with cybernetic parts.'

My heart was skipping beats. *It had to be the answer to Royce. It had to.*

'It is quite a lot more complicated than it sounds.' His eyes darted shiftily, proving I was right. 'As you are aware, the latest TinBoiz models are a mixture of cybernetics with human skin and tissue. Teddy will simply have a higher ratio, that's all.'

'How much?' I blurted, flatly. My deadpan look conveyed that I knew exactly what he was driving at.

The professor smiled, receiving my message loud and clear, but it was quick and didn't reach his eyes. The conversation was directed at me now. 'Around twenty-five per cent,' his eyes drilling it into mine.

'What way around?... Seventy-five, human?' I could feel Tom looking between us, unsure what was going on, exactly.

Tina whimpered.

'No, Miss Coe. Twenty-five percent human. And that would mainly be the brain. The rest would be simple blood and tissue to hold in all those expensive cybernetic parts. The rest would be the most advanced robotics in the world.' His lids were low when he delivered his last spiteful blow. He knew I'd made the connection.

I felt Tom and Tina turn to each other to see what the other thought. I remained numb with shock. We all thought we were mentally prepared for Teddy not to come out of this, but we weren't. Not really. And certainly not like this.

The coffee and sandwiches arrived and the professor looked suddenly exhausted. 'Look, go home.' He looked at his wrist-plate. 'It's 3:05 a.m. Take a couple of hours. Teddy will be OK till then, but I will need your answer by 06:30. Damien will take you home.'

I looked behind me and Damien was there, reliable as a machine. He nodded, backing everything the professor had just said. We stood up, gathered ourselves together and shuffled towards the door.

The professor appeared at my elbow to escort us out. He looked really tired when I looked up into his eyes and I had to ask: 'Any news on Royce?'

He switched his beady gaze to mine, slightly amused, gauging me. 'He's fine. Let me deal with Teddy first and then we'll have a chat about Royce.' He smiled, genuinely. Then we were at the door and I'd run out of time. I took it as a good sign.

I moved into the elevator, through the car park and into the car, like I was living in twilight. Neither awake nor asleep. Our never-ending night still wasn't over. Now we had to decide.

CHAPTER 63

Royce
    I came back online to the familiar view of a ceiling.

'Welcome back, Royce.'

I turned my head to face Sentia. My head felt fuzzy. I ran a quick scan. All seemed optimal and I went to sit up.

'Be careful,' Sentia said. 'Your systems have been recalibrated. You need to let your levels stabilise before you attempt to move.'

It was good advice as I wasn't sure where I was.

'You are in the TinBoiz Cybercare Centre for a check-up,' Sentia explained.

The fog slowly cleared in my head and my green grills came down. Faces appeared from my memory banks. My family, the Coes. Chrissy. Is my family OK?'

'They are fine. I believe Nate misses you. They are waiting for news of their friend.'

Teddy. The sick boy in the hospital. 'How long have I been here?'

'Almost a week. To be precise, six days, seventeen hours and thirty-two seconds.'

For a moment, the fog tried to creep back in and I became confused. I couldn't remember coming here.

'You were powered down and transported here,' she explained.

I felt slightly better. It sounded logical. 'Am I going back?' I examined how I felt about that. A warm feeling came with the memory of the family.

'Do you like it there?' Sentia asked.

I looked at her a little bemused. That a cabinet of black metal, circuitry and white flashing lights could even have the notion of it. *And did I?* 'Yes, I think I do.'

'Do you remember going to school?'

School. I repeated the word in my head. An image of Chrissy sharing a textbook, replayed. Her smiling at me strangely. 'Yes. I would like to go there again. There are lots of things I find interesting.'

'The professor said we can leave soon. In the meantime, you are free to roam the building and get used to your adjusted settings.'

I felt pleased. A peculiar lightening feeling vibrated in my chest. I looked down at myself and let my hand glide over my legs, feeling the softness of the light-brown skin. Then the unyielding metal around my wrists. They were around my ankles, too. I felt weird. Because I knew these things were there. Like the power disk in the centre of my chest. I inevitably put my hand to the back of my neck and felt the TinBoiz trade plate. Everything was where it should be and yet it felt strange. I was wearing only shorts. My standard TinBoiz clothes were hanging on a hook, with my black boots on the floor beneath it. I hated them and I was sure I always had.

'Where are *my* clothes?' I asked, turning my attention back to Sentia.

'Your standard-issue clothes are in front of you, Royce.'

'They aren't my clothes.' I felt suddenly angry that I had to wear them.

'What clothes are you missing?' Sentia asked calmly.

I wanted to answer her, but I couldn't form the words. The data was out of my reach. Nothing came forward and I had no idea what clothes I meant. 'They aren't them,' came out strangled with frustration.

'Perhaps I could make a suggestion?'

I was looking back at Sentia, feeling heat in my cheeks while I struggled to focus on her words.

'Wear the ones provided and ask the professor for the ones that are missing when you see him.'

I nodded, having filtered the advice as good. Then I slid off the cot and slowly got dressed. The jersey felt clingy and uncomfortable and the boots were heavy and clompy. I diagnosed myself as feeling irritable when I ventured out into the hallway.

It was dim and vaguely familiar. I couldn't seem to wake up and think straight to decide on a direction. I wandered aimlessly until I heard a cheer.

I went cautiously up to the open doorway. Several people were gathered around a wall-glass, watching a cyberball game. They were talking animatedly and shouting instructions at the glass as if their team could hear. Cyberball was played by proxy-subs. Sports bots that allowed for much more contact when playing. I knew this game. *Exciting.* A grainy memory tried to surface, but it dissipated quickly.

The frustration returned, and I clenched my fists. I didn't like the feeling and I didn't know where it came from. I was about to move on to remove the sensation when a flash of Chrissy came to me. Right there, in this very room. She was staring right at me, in shock. Then she looked pleased. Relief passed over her face, and I didn't go to her. I stayed where I was. I replayed that look over and over to analyse it. My frustration changed to something else. Pain, no shame. Hopelessness. *Why?* It was troubling.

One of the Techs turned and saw me, nudging his friend next to him. 'Can I help you, TinBoi?'

It shocked me awake. I was acting strangely and people were noticing. 'No, thank you,' I said and hurriedly moved on. I had to learn to mask my new feelings. Recalibration didn't feel good. I decided it was something I never wanted again.

I arrived in the cafeteria and looked around for a place to sit. Not sure why I was there, but I wanted to be invisible and found a spot in the furthest corner from the counter. It was almost empty and I didn't eat; I just needed somewhere to analyse how I was behaving. Everything felt new, and yet my surroundings were in my memory banks. It was the strangest, contradictory feeling. I just couldn't make sense of anything. I was lost.

My muscles stiffened, ready to move, when an old-world sub began to make her way towards me. She was a living cartoon in pink. Ridiculously exaggerated eyelashes and thick pink lips that widened into a scary smile. I had to remind myself that there was a human somewhere working this walking monstrosity.

She stopped right in front of me and took out a pocket reader from her apron. I stared at her, not knowing what she expected me to say. I expected her to eject me. 'Good morning, TinBoi. I'm Murtle. What can I get for you today?'

I was not ready for that and blinked for a moment, processing. Surely she knew I didn't eat. 'Nothing, thank you,' I said, trying to imagine the human. Profile. Age. Cultural norms.

'That's perfectly fine, honey. Take as long as you like. What's your name? Not seen you in here before.'

Surface chat. 'Royce,' I answered, deciding on a simple response. I recognised the need to be polite and hide my impatience for wanting to be left alone. Something was lurking at the back of my mind like a retreating storm. A rumbling murmur I couldn't reach. I wanted time to access it, but the sub wanted to kill time and talk about nothing.

Bizarrely, she turned her reader around to face me at exactly the same time I received an ear-splitting, encrypted screech. It was so painfully unpleasant, I flinched and covered my ears.

Then, as if nothing had happened, the sub smiled. 'Well, have a nice day, honey.' Then she stomped off back to her counter. It left me rigid with aftershocks and feeling confused. I wasn't sure if she was responsible for the unpleasant download or she just happened to be there at the time. The way I felt this morning it was possibly an internal malfunction. Something weird was going on with me. Something was different. I was different and I didn't like it. I needed to get back to what I was. Maybe the professor could help me make sense of it. Decide if it's a bug in my programme after the system check he just gave me. I would run a diagnostic check first. I might be able to pinpoint it myself.

I scanned the area. I was safely alone and the cafeteria still quite empty, so I initiated a partial shutdown to complete the system check. Starting at my ankles, I worked my way up. I skipped much of my organic tissue, which just read 'fully functional'. Nothing came up of note. Until I reached the main digital nerve centre at the back of my neck. I noticed something strange immediately.

My grills came down in a way I'd never seen before.

Slammed, tightly locked, with a green light flashing in the corner of my eye.

I homed in and decrypted the code. *Backdoor licence 364. Lateral thought bypass directive.* I had no idea what it meant or what I needed to do. I had to be malfunctioning. But it made no sense right after a check-up.

I paused my partial shutdown and took another look around me to make sure I was still safely inconspicuous. Two porters had come in and were sitting a few tables away. They were eating breakfast, and the sub was busy serving someone at the counter.

A small, folded piece of paper was on the table right in front of me. I looked around again, cautiously picked it up and zeroed in on the scribble. Numbers or code. A45P-72469!-?1148819. Twenty characters that meant absolutely nothing to me.

I wonder.

I went inward again and navigated back to the strange directive. *Lateral thought to bypass directive.* I brought forward my eyeshot of the twenty characters and inserted them at the end of the flashing green cursor.

Nothing happened.

Then something so simple occurred to me and I flicked my eyes to the left, figuring lateral meant sideways, and everything clicked and clanged into place. Like the shifting of a hundred locks to a vault, each igniting a corresponding synapse into life. Then everything went dark.

I'd gone from super-hyper-brain activity to none. Which made no sense because I was thinking. Malfunction was the most likely reason. Especially when an avatar like a VR game character walked cockily into the blackness of my mind and grinned. 'Hi!' he said, holding up a hand. 'I'm Greg, your programmer. I'm responsible for the sneaky backdoor to your directives that you have successfully accessed. Congrats! This is a recording. You are not speaking to me in real time. There are several things you need to know before you leave here. First, the professor sees everything through your eyes. If you need privacy, you must access your backdoor directives and it will be looped until you exit it again. This must only be for short periods, otherwise, he will haul you back here again for 'system checks', which really means 'restart' and 'memory manipulation'. I'll get found out and then I won't be able to help you. So, here's the thing. I don't have a lot of time to reveal what's going on with you. All I can say is there was a lot of stuff in your memory that had to be adjusted. Know what I mean? You *are* a TinBoi, but not the regular variety. You are a beta model. The most advanced autonomous model we have. You were built as an individually functioning AI and not linked to Metatron like the rest of the AUs in circulation. Metatron is the central quantum AI who controls the TinBoiz corporation. You have the largest percentage of human tissue ever fused with a cybernetic system. Your organic components were *not* grown in a lab. You had memories erased, many were of your last family, the Coes. My job was to seamlessly add fabricated ones in their place. I'm sorry, I don't know what they took. I'm just a software engineer. The psyche Techs did that. I can tell you the ones I added, where and when you were made, your training and tests in the lab.'

The image looked left and right as if he'd run out of time.

'I'm doing this on a break. I have to go or I'm busted and fired. There is one last message requested by a friend. I have no idea what it means. He said to go to the padded cell and you'll find it there. Sorry I can't help you any more than that. Greg. Out.' Then, with a sad face and a little wave, he disappeared in a cartoon puff of smoke.

I came back to the room, more confused and paranoid

about a malfunction than I was before. I had no idea how long I'd been out. The cafeteria was now empty again.

I screwed the paper up and was on my feet. I had to get out of there. I strode towards the door and disposed of the paper in the trash. My power disk whirred, over and over, like a thump in my chest. I was hyper-stimulated, as if all my systems were running at twice their usual speed. *A padded cell. Was there even such a place?* I had to find it to see if I was going mad.

CHAPTER 64

*C*hrissy

There was no point in trying to sleep that night. We arrived home at around 03:45 to a thousand questions from Mom and Dad, which became a heated debate. Anger and tears, with everyone taking their turn for each.

We were like a jury expecting to come to a unanimous decision, but every time we thought we'd reached one, someone broke it with an equally valid argument.

'We can't lose him, we can't. I can't believe we're even arguing about this,' Tina said, wildly. Out of her mind.

'Could you make him a machine, though, love?' Tom said, his eyes still red from tears. 'Would *he* thank you? Imagine how that would feel.'

'Like a waking nightmare,' my dad said, shaking his head at the mere thought of it.

'Could you be the one to turn off his life support, Chris? Because I certainly couldn't,' My mom argued. 'What if it were Chrissy or Nate?'

Tina grabbed onto her arm, nodding with every word.

'I would want to live,' Nate said, turning all our heads to the doorway, where he stood in his Pac-Man pyjamas.

I guess no one could have slept through the noise we'd been making. He looked so cute and young, but his face was stony and serious. Like he'd grown five years overnight.

No one said a word while he pulled up a chair and joined us at the table. 'Listen to me, and please don't shut me down,' he said, fixing us all in the eye, one by one. 'Think about it. For the first time in history, you have the choice to literally bring Teddy back to life. And not like some sick kid with a sub, but as fit and as mobile as any other kid. Stronger, even. Think of Royce.' He switched his gaze to me as if he knew my heart would literally stop at that. 'Isn't that essentially what Royce is?'

My mom melted. 'Royce is an AU, honey,' and went to stroke his hair. But he ducked her hand in irritation. It *was* kind of patronising. I really admired him then. He was becoming a man with more insight than anyone.

'Yes, Mom. Where all this technology comes from. Don't you get it? He is flesh and tech, fused together,' he said, meshing his fingers in front of his face.

'With a cybernetic brain,' my mom said softly. 'Teddy's will be real.'

He went to argue but held it down by taking a hard breath. 'Look, all I'm saying is, look how we've all grown to love Royce. He fit right in as part of the family and we never knew him till a few weeks ago. Don't you want to give Teddy the same chance? Our friend and brother?' He was red in the face by the time he finished speaking, looking at each of us for some kind of endorsement of what he was saying.

All we could do was stare at him. I was already sold and just in awe of him, but the others were stunned.

When none of us said a word, he swore loudly and stomped from the room like a kid. But I didn't laugh. I continued to look at the doorway while the others resumed speaking, more quietly this time.

'We don't have long,' Tom said, looking at his wrist. 'We have to come up with an answer for when he calls.

I slowly got to my feet and looked back at the four of them huddled in tight conversation. 'I'm checking on Nate.'

My mom nodded and went right back to what she was saying. I took the opportunity to slip out. I wanted to say I was sorry. I'd completely neglected him lately. Royce meant a lot to him, too, and this must be really hard for him, feeling like he had no say.

I knocked and there was no answer. So I opened the door a little, then slipped in.

'Go away,' Nate said, dropping his hands from his red face, in his usual position on his bed.

'Are you OK?' I immediately strode over, crawled onto his bed, and sat next to him, with my back to the headboard.

His knees were to his chest and his head was buried in his arms on top of them. He didn't answer.

'They just have to look at all the angles. What's best for them and for Teddy in the long run. It's not really up to us.' As I said the words, it sank in for me properly too. It wasn't up to me, any more than it was for Nate. I could lose Teddy today and Royce might be lost already.

With no further comment from me, Nate lifted his head from his arms and I felt the burn of his gaze on the side of my face. 'Have you forgotten Royce?' he asked in a low, hate-filled voice. 'He's been gone less than a week.'

Anger flashed through me and I looked at him in utter disbelief that he could even think that of me. 'Of course not. I —' Then I remembered, he had no idea. 'They found him. A few days ago. I saw him at the place where they have Teddy.'

Nate's eyes widened in surprise, then he frowned. He seemed to know not to speak.

I looked down at my hands at the reality of that. 'He was in handcuffs. They said he was malfunctioning, and they were going to reset or realign him, or something. Then he can come back to us.' I looked into Nate's wide, intense stare with all the hope and yearning I felt. 'I think the professor will keep his promise,' I said weakly. Not sure what I believed anymore.

Nate was still staring at me, every emotion playing across his face.

'Please say something,' I pleaded. Loathing myself more and more.

'And you didn't think to lead with that?' He was on his feet, staring down at me again, in a flash. 'We have to stop them, Chrissy. You don't understand. He's real. As real as Teddy. You have to stop them. We have to.'

He went to run for the door and I was off the bed, lunging to pull him back to me, roughly. 'No!' I shouted in his face, shocking him into compliance. 'You can't land them with this. Not now.' I saw the pain etched into his face and I shook my head wretchedly. 'It's too late, now.' He went limp and I let his arm go. I couldn't bear the look in his eyes. But I kept going. 'They had him locked up. They said he'd become a danger to himself and others.' As I said the words, I hated myself more and more. I knew what Nate was thinking, because I was thinking it too.

'That can't be right. He was too strong. Too human, to act like that,' Nate was saying, desperately.

When I finally had the courage to look at him, his expression was pure hatred.

'You didn't see him, Nate,' I said as one last hopeless plea.

'He is real. Not wishful thinking. I know what you think of me, but I'm telling you there is something bad going on at that place. At TinBoiz. The whole network. Who knows, but it's rotten to the core.'

I smiled weakly. He was overwrought. We both were. I went to reach for his hand, but he snatched it away. 'No, Chrissy. You're not listening to me. He told me himself before he went. They are the monsters,' he said, pointing to the air, as if to TinBoiz.

He sat heavily on the bed again in frustration and picked up my hand. His look was so intense, he scared me. So I dropped my tone and asked calmly, 'OK. Explain what he said.' I knew Royce had enjoyed spending time with Nate and I could just imagine him telling him some kind of bedtime story.

Nate's face came alive and he ignited in renewed excitement. 'OK,' he said, angling his body to face me squarely. 'This is going to sound mad, but hear me out.' He held his breath and then blurted, 'Royce was a real human before, from beyond the Danger Line. It's rough and hard there, which is why he's so tough and smart.'

I didn't react. In fact, I sat there concentrating on not moving a single facial muscle, so he got out what he needed to say. But I was thinking it. Royce had infected us all, even Nate. After a beat, he ploughed on. 'Think about it, Chrissy. His street smarts, fighting skills, his fearless attitude. No TinBoi needs that.'

It was answered with one word: programming, but I kept quiet.

He slipped down to his knees and pulled out his box of mementoes from under his bed. It was where he kept all his treasures since he was tiny. An old tooth, he swore came from a monster. A fossil of some ancient creature. A few seashells. A slingshot that Mom had forbidden him to get. But what I wasn't expecting was an old, browned photo.

He looked up, bright-eyed and sweating, and handed it to me. 'Royce left it pinned to my board before he left. I think for me to look after. Or prove he'd be back. I don't know.' I glanced at his reminder board, then back at the picture. I took it gingerly and studied the cracked photo that had once been in colour. The familiar curve of his smile, the laughter in his eyes. Brown eyes. *Royce,* looking so happy. His hair was darker and longer, his skin tanned and he was thinner. A huge knot strangled my throat. I could barely drag my eyes across the page, but I did, and my heart stopped. His arm was around the shoulders of a smaller boy. Astonishingly similar. Smiling and not much older than Nate.

'It's Finn,' Nate said, getting up and sitting next to me to look at it too. 'Royce showed me after the fight when he told me everything. It's his brother.'

Bemused, I searched Nate's eyes and he was serious.

'Except his name isn't Royce. It's Mike. Mike Morrison. He has a father, too, but his mom died. That's where he went. To find them before we sent him back when Teddy came home.'

Nate was staring at me for my reaction, but I was stunned. It made no sense. He was a machine. It was programming. Impossible. And also cruel to make him believe all this so much that he ran away to find it. 'Then how did he?' I didn't want to upset Nate, so I let it hang in the air. What I really wanted to ask was how a kid becomes a machine? It was too ridiculous for words.

'He said he got arrested. He said that where he lives, it's dangerous because they have nothing and so they have to commit crimes to survive. He got taken to juvey and the professor came and took him and his friends and changed him.'

My mind was in freefall. Why would Royce fill Nate's head with all this? I was a little exasperated with him. 'But why?' I asked, desperately trying not to sound patronising. I felt bewildered by the whole thing. My eyes traced the very real boy in the photo that would have been easy to generate with AI. But it wasn't digital, it was a photograph, like the ones I'd seen in the museum. Faded and worn, but it looked genuine.

Nate shrugged, still looking at the photo. 'All he said was they were already making TinBoiz out of real body parts and they aren't grown in a lab. It takes too long.'

Nate looked at me stonily until I joined the dots and my face creased in horror. 'They're using real kids for parts?'

Nate nodded cautiously. 'I think that's what he meant. He didn't have much time to explain.'

I stared off into space, a mixture of horror and disbelief. Trying to imagine a production line of dirty-looking children going into a factory and pristine, neat, little TinBoiz coming out.

What Nate was saying was possible, I suppose, but completely outrageous. It was murder. Everyone knew the AU industry was supported by the network. It would never be allowed. But when I looked into Nate's expectant face, I pushed back a sweaty strand of his hair from his eyes and had to say it: 'It's programming, Nate. It has to be. He can't act real unless he feels real. I met the Tech guy who programmed him and he said as much. He said he was there to patch him, as it had worked too well. He was there to tone it down a bit.'

For a moment, Nate just stared at me and I thought he was absorbing what I was saying, but then he exploded and went to pull away, but I gripped his arm. 'Think about it. What sounds more real to you? An evil scientist making robots out of body parts, stolen from poor kids, or an experimental, state-of-the-art AU, so advanced, with programming so detailed, that he believes it?'

I felt I had the clinching argument when Nate relaxed in my grip and went silent while it sank in. But then his eyelids lowered and he pointed to the door and said through gritted teeth, 'Well, what the hell is going on down there, then? Where did that technology come from?'

He got up onto his feet, still staring at me with utter contempt. 'Get out,' he ordered, in a low, gravelly voice.

I just sat there, frozen, unable to think of a coherent sentence, other than, 'What?' Over and over. Inside, I'd defaulted to the professor's explanation of what they were trying to do for Teddy. The next step in the evolution of humanity, he'd said. They were at the end of testing and had a beta model. *That had to be Royce.* I'd even known it at the time, without this heated discussion with Nate. Maybe Royce had slipped his programming like they said. Maybe he had different body parts than what they intended to give Teddy. Maybe Nate was right, at least in part. They didn't need to be stealing body parts from kids for what Royce told Nate to be true. I shook my head and got to my feet. It was horrific either way.

Without speaking my mind, I left Nate as quickly as possible and went back downstairs. They were all still where I'd left them, exhausted and drinking coffee.

I'd just sat down with a glass of milk when the incoming call tone sounded and a red dot pulsed in the centre of the wall glass.

'Oh my god, quickly,' Mom said, already on her feet and waving her arm to answer it. We all rose from our seats to join her shoulder to shoulder as the professor's face appeared, tired and drawn.

A fake-blue background was behind him, so it was hard to tell where he was. 'Do you have an answer?' he asked, firmly.

I had no idea what it was, as I don't think they even knew right up until then. I looked at their deathly faces while my heart thumped and my mouth went sandpaper dry. My mom gripped my hand and my dad squeezed my shoulder. They were both looking at Tina and Tom for their final answer, who were locked in each other's eyes. They gave a single nod, turned to the professor and spoke at the same time. 'We're going to do it.'

I put my hand to my mouth and tears sprang from my eyes in joy and relief.

'So, to confirm. Please state for the legal team what you've decided, uncoerced and of sound mind.'

It sounded very scary and official. They both took a deep breath to steady themselves. 'We want you to save Teddy exactly how you explained. Putting his brain inside a TinBoi.'

It sounded so basic, it was brutal. But true. In essence, that was exactly what was going to happen.

The professor gave a single nod to someone out of shot and then faced us again, looking a little more relaxed. 'You've made a wise choice. You understand that this conversation has been recorded for legal purposes and, from this moment, is legally binding. So I must be clear that you give your consent for the implantation of your son's brain and other usable parts to be placed into a fully functional cybernetic AU system?'

'We do,' Tom and Tina said, looking even paler than they were before.

'Can I just ask?' I said, raising a weak hand.

The professor quickly masked his exasperation, but I caught it, nonetheless. 'Does that make Teddy your property, you know, like Royce?'

I felt everyone's eyes on me with surprise and guessed no one had even thought of that very significant omission. Why would they? It was straight out of a horror film. However, I could tell it was a good question by the nanosecond of anger that crossed the professor's face. He might not like me, but I wasn't about to back down and pushed my chin up in defiance.

His face switched to a benign smile. 'Not at all. His only obligation is that he is still in the clinical trial that Mr and Mrs Monshall already gave their permission for. In layman's terms, they understand that it is not a proven treatment and is not open to the general population yet. We do not own people,' he finished sternly.

I knew he was tying me up in knots, so I wasn't completely sure of what he was saying and its implications, but I was determined to pin him down now I had him in front of witnesses. 'So what's different between them?' I asked with a shrug, knowing I was annoying the hell out of him, but Nate's hot, angry face was burned into me and I couldn't forget what he said.

The professor let out an exasperated huff. 'Royce is an advanced, combination AU, and Teddy...' He paused, having to frame his words carefully. 'Will be human, with fully integrated cybernetics. That is the difference.' His eyes glinted spitefully by the time he'd finished.

'That's enough now,' my dad said quietly.

I felt my parents strengthen their grip around me and I made the careful decision not to say anymore. I'd been foolish. It was clear there could be a grain of truth in what Nate told me, but at that moment, I couldn't afford to alienate the professor to the point that he didn't want to help us. We must get Teddy back at all costs.

'Now if you excuse me, time is crucial.' Then he disappeared from the glass and the words 'Com ended' came up.

We all turned to face each other, stunned.

CHAPTER 65

oyce
    I was standing right in front of the padded cell. No one was around because no one was inside it. No guard, just four cameras in the hallway, one in the cell. My sensors located them instantly, neatly hidden.

Why didn't I remember this place? The guy in my head said I'd been in here, so it was weird they needed to erase it. There was a growing set of questions to ask in my next session with the professor. Like, did I have an imagination?

I thought about that for a moment.

Was Greg a fragment of it?

I stiffened when a member of staff rounded the corner and walked past. I noticed he averted his eyes, not wanting to acknowledge me. It felt strange, inside. Distrust registered right away. 'Excuse me, sir?' I called before he went out of sight. 'Do you know where Greg is?'

Without turning or breaking stride, he brushed off the question with his hand, like he didn't have the time or the patience. 'Not here. He works nights.' Then he kept walking until he disappeared.

But I did have my answer. Greg was real. That is, if it's the same guy. If he worked last night and I woke this morning, then there was a high chance it was.

My mood instantly lightened.

But why put in a back-door programme? Was it a test? I ran the probability and the professor was likely to do something like that. *Was he expecting me to act? Or ignore Greg?* Which was the correct outcome? The professor would be watching, as Greg said. So, if I believe that, then I must believe in Greg. Maybe there is no right or wrong. Simply a choice. It was an interesting dilemma.

I reasoned about who I am. *Royce. TinBoi. AU model, next generation.* My selling point is realism. *What would a real person do?* Nate would act. Therefore, a real person would act. His curiosity would enthuse him like a complex VR game. That was my decision. I would face this like a problem to be solved when the professor asks me why.

I was positive that was the correct response and went to put my hand on the handle when I remembered Greg's warning. 'The professor sees through your eyes.'

That made me pause. *How can I have full autonomy when I know someone is watching? Wouldn't that shape my decisions?* That does not give me free will. *Or does it?* To do something anyway is definitely wilful.

Now Greg's message made sense. I don't know why, but I thought of the notion of God. God is watching humans and the devil tempts them. Greg is like the devil, whispering on my shoulder, while God makes me question it. Greg said I need to find out about the real me. That makes me think there must be something to find.

I straightened and immediately looked laterally to the left with my eyes. I internally recited the code, held suspended in my access centre.

I felt instantly different.

The door to the cell wasn't locked, so I went inside. The lights flickered on by sensor and I waited for my gridlines to drop and map the view. But they didn't come. For a moment, my systems stalled until I realised I was offline. Fully conscious. It was liberating. Intriguing.

My heart soared in my chest. Then I set about searching. Every square inch of the quilted wall, soft white to the ceiling and cushioned floor. My feet sank into it while I walked a circle on the sponge. There were no windows, no furniture, no clues. Nothing extraordinary at all. I ran my hands over the soft material for lumps. There were no hidden trapdoors, even after I stamped all over the floor. Nothing.

I felt cheated. It must be a test. I felt anger. Frustration. In a surge of something unpleasant, I remembered Greg's warning: 'No longer than two minutes.' So I silently left the room, bitterly disappointed.

I wanted out of there. I wanted to go back to the Coes. I felt safe there. Content. I remembered that clearly. Then I remembered the sick friend. *Teddy.* The one who would not survive. The girl, Chrissy, was sad about that. She loved him. The professor was helping. He was going to heal him and he would go home and Chrissy would be happy. I remembered that.

Nate's tears. His hug. His words: 'You're my brother.' I remember that. Words. Tears. A promise. Of what? I tried to access the answer, over and over and it wasn't there. It was taken. Greg had spoken the truth.

I put that at the top of my list of answers I needed. But my source could not be the professor. All I needed from him was when I could go home.

CHAPTER 66

*C*hrissy

The days that followed the decision were the longest of my life. Everyone felt it. No one even cared that Nate and I didn't go to school. We lived in a suspended state of tension.

I wandered to Teddy's house several times a day. Tina or Tom would open the door and shake their head, and I would wander home again.

We barely spoke to each other. Nate was more upset about Royce than Teddy, so I couldn't even go to him for comfort. The only conversation was between my mom and dad and was repeated over and over; 'What do you think is happening? Why is it taking so long? Surely no news is good news.' Or words to that effect.

Then finally, after six days, Tina and Tom burst in crying. 'The professor will be calling here in five minutes to speak to us all.'

My mom rushed to the bottom of the stairs and called up. 'Nate! Darling. Come down quickly; there's news.'

His door opened and slammed, followed by loud stomps

on the stairs. He came in wide-eyed and expectant. I pointed at the wall glass. 'The professor's about to call.'

My mom shoved a hot drink in Tina and Tom's hands and my dad asked, 'Did they give you any clues?'

They shook their heads.

Then the incoming call chimed.

CHAPTER 67

*C*hrissy

My dad quickly waved his arm and shouted, 'Answer call!'

The professor's fake smile appeared immediately. No background this time; he was in his office. I remembered the flocked wallpaper.

'Good morning, everyone. Thank you for your patience. I hope you managed to get a little rest through the difficult wait—'

'How did it go?' Tom snapped, right over him.

The professor nodded, accepting the kick to get on with it. 'The surgery for the neuro-extraction was a success. We managed to salvage much of the blood, tissue and lymphatic system. Unfortunately, we lost the extremities down his left side as he began to shut down.'

Tina whimpered.

'What does that mean?' Tom asked, putting up his arm before we all degenerated into panic.

'It means he came through, but we were hoping to keep more of his organic structure. In easy terms: he has his human brain, outer skin, fat, tissue, right arm for dexterity, and a cybernetic breathing system and heart. We had to forgo the stomach. So, cybernetic from the waist down.'

'What about his right leg, then, couldn't you save that?'

The professor shook his head. 'The weight imbalance would simply be too much. His left leg would weigh three times that of his right. We felt it would be better to be fully functioning than to build in a handicap. Isn't that the whole point? To make Teddy better?'

I looked across at Tina and Tom. It made sense and Teddy would love the idea, but Tina and Tom looked disappointed. As if with every piece of Teddy taken away, it was a little bit more of their son, lost.

'He does have blood and tissue over the top of his cybernetics. Exactly the same as Royce. It is how we developed the technology. Apart from the added weight and strength, you wouldn't know from the outside.'

It felt like he was looking directly at me, mocking, knowing there was nothing I could say or do. 'What about his eyes?' I threw back at him. Lashing out and dreading the answer at the same time. They were Royce's eyes and I didn't want him to look cold and dead like that.

The professor's look made me uneasy. He always managed to say more to me than anyone else. It was there and then it moved on. Like a warning, you questioned ever happened. 'Good news with the eyes. Apart from certain reinforcements, his skull and facial bone structure remain intact. We thought it important for Teddy's mental well-being to see his own reflection when he wakes.'

His parents pounced on that. 'He's awake? Can we see him?'

All I could think was how lucky we were to keep that. That they could have literally done anything to him. Teddy was at their mercy and all his rights had been signed away. But I was soon sucked into the excitement.

Tom had to hold onto Tina before she ran out the door.

'No, not yet,' the professor said, chuckling lightly. 'He is awake, but he needs a few days to adjust to a few things before he can take visitors.'

CHAPTER 68

oyce

I was outside the padded cell again. I'd gone back there every day for a week. Now I could hear it was occupied. Someone was hurling themselves against the walls. The professor's AU, Damien, was outside. I remembered him from training. He looked at me strangely and had been doing it all week. 'Can I look?' I asked, pointing at the small sliding door that revealed a window to the cell.

'Knock yourself out,' Damien said.

I frowned and ran over his choice of words. I decided he was a street model. I was a street model. Another question for my list. I had no idea what a street model was.

I stepped closer and moved the hatch across. A boy, similar in age to me, was slumped in the corner, wrapped in a cream jacket with its empty, overlong arms buckled around him. *Straitjacket.* He looked exhausted and hopeless.

I looked over my shoulder at Damien,' What's he done?' It must have been bad to be detained like this.

'Nothing. He's just had surgery, that's all. He's in shock. Just needs to get used to it.'

I turned back for another look and was taken by surprise. The boy's sweaty face was pressed up to the glass. A human face. Brown eyes. Studying me like I was studying him. His face was heated and scuffed red from continually bashing into the wall.

I stepped back, suddenly. 'He's not a TinBoi.'

'No, he's not,' Damien said, from his place, lounging against the wall. He's more human than that.'

I narrowed my eyes on Damien, unusually slouching and exhausted, while I ran code. Sifting data. The boy was neither TinBoi nor entirely human. A first for me. I had no idea technology had moved to this point. Humans with TinBoi tech. *Legal?* I doubted that. *Test subject?* Probably. 'And he just woke up?'

'A few hours ago.'

No wonder the kid was out of his mind.

I turned to face Damien squarely. He looked at me through his eyebrows, waiting for what I would say next. He had always been very human for an AU. It occurred to me he was probably a mix of human and machine too. I looked at my own arms, making the connection. We were all a mix by varying degrees. Where was the classification line? At what point did a human become a machine? It threw up all kinds of questions for my list. *Ownership? Autonomy?* 'Can I go in with him?' I asked. It came out quickly, like a reflex.

Damien frowned. I knew he wouldn't have the clearance to decide that. He thought for a moment, then, without taking his eyes off me, pressed his wrist. A grainy hologram of the professor popped up.

I knew it was for my benefit, as the professor could speak directly to his head. 'What is it?' he asked, immediately.

'Royce is here. He wants to go in with the boy.'

The image slowly revolved until the stretched figure of

the professor looked right at me. 'Do you think you know this boy?' he asked.

The question surprised me and I shrugged. 'No,' I said, simply. It was the truth. I had no idea who it could be.

'It is Teddy. The boy from next door to the Coes. He just came out of the healing chamber.'

I logged everything away for careful examination later. The data seemed logical. I had only seen digital stills of him, so I wouldn't recognise him in his present state. He had been ill. 'I never met Teddy,' I said, searching data. 'He was the reason I was brought into the Coe family as a companion for their daughter, Chrissy. Teddy is her best friend.'

There seemed to be a moment's delay while the professor processed it, then he turned back to Damien. 'Let him go in. I can't see the harm. The way he is, if he doesn't make the adjustment in a few days, I will have to terminate the trial and I want to avoid that at all costs.'

Damien nodded once and the hologram disappeared. He walked towards me until he loomed over me, reached out his arm and swiped the door panel. His lip curled in amusement. 'You might want to back up.'

The door clicked open and he used his body as a barrier. 'Wait!' he ordered, holding up his hand. There was a long roar and the boy rushed headlong into him. It ended with a loud 'Oomph' as Damien put out one of his huge hands, caught his whole head and shoved him backwards so he fell against the wall. He swung the door open and I got a full view. The boy was grimacing, rolling around, screaming in frustration, trying to get up without the use of his arms. The padded room was now logical. I felt sorry for him in that situation. Helpless. Confused. Alone.

'In you go,' Damien said, unaffected. He walked past me and held out his arm.

I slowly went in and felt the rush of air as the door closed behind me.

The boy immediately flinched and attempted to wriggle away, out of reach. I was just reaching out to help him up, but he was terrified, fixated on my eyes. I held up my hand and waved it to show no harm. Then I moved quicker than he could track and hoisted him to his feet, before he could even shout.

He stood and stared at me, breathing hard. I immediately logged that he had lungs, while I stared back, gridlines down, ferociously mapping features. Messy brown overlong hair, boyish face. Pale skin. Brown eyes. *Kept eyes.* Average height. I was a few inches taller, but I knew we were the same age. I looked inwardly. *Human age,* I corrected. Another question for the professor. My line of vision tracked down his body. He wasn't as thin as I imagined for a sick kid. Then everything made sense. His last memories were of him using a sub, then nothing. He'd woken up with everything about him feeling different. Heavier, off balance. No wonder he was reacting to the shock. I understood.

It gave me a moment's pause for another question: *If I'd changed, what was I before?*

'What are you?' the boy asked, his voice just a rasp from shouting. 'Because it's not a fair fight if I've got no arms.'

It pleasantly surprised me that he automatically thought we were going to fight. Something deep inside me smiled. 'Do you need moisture for your throat?' I asked, not yet knowing if he could drink.

A can immediately clunked through the shoot and onto the floor. I picked it up and, after showing Teddy the label, held it up. 'Open your mouth.'

He did it right away, proving he was thirsty. It was a spray that I used, so I felt bad as I knew he had no stomach. Still, he opened his mouth and kept his eyes on me cautiously. I gave him about three sprays and could tell by his expression it was instant relief, but he wanted more.

I shook my head. 'In a minute. You'll be sick.'

His brow furrowed in confusion again.

'Look, I'm not here to fight you,' I said. 'I'm Chrissy's AU.' For some reason, I felt really sad when I added, 'I'm a TinBoi.' I didn't understand why.

Teddy raised his eyebrows, stepped back and everything seemed to drain out of him as he slid down the wall. He managed to manoeuvre from his haunches to sit more comfortably with his knees up to his chest. 'So they got her one, did they?' he said, looking up at me with a hapless smile. 'She always wanted one.'

He seemed calmer, so I mirrored his position on the opposite wall. 'Yes, she was very sad and needed a companion.'

He looked at me dryly, assessing. Thinking. Making up his mind. 'How is she? How long have I been away?' he asked.

I remembered her distrust of me at the beginning. It was frustratingly hard to locate. Teddy wasn't the only one with fuzzy memories. 'She misses you,' I said, rapidly calculating weeks and days. 'I was not there right after your brain injury.' There were huge gaps of static after that. The best I could give him was, 'A couple of months, I guess. I can't be sure. Might be longer.'

He studied me with that calculating look he had, again. 'I thought you guys were meant to be super AI brainbox computers, or something,' Teddy said with a wry smile.

He was right. 'I know. You could say I've been having some glitches.'

Teddy's smile flatlined. 'Are you safe to be around?'

I laughed, incredulously. 'Are you?' For a guy who never came out of his room, he had guts and I knew I liked him. In a different life, he would have been popular. *Street model* came to my mind and I had no idea why, with a sharp stab of disappointment. 'So what did they replace that's got you so mad?' I asked, raking my gridlines over him, getting immediate hits on what was cybernetic and what was not.

He let out a blast of bitter laughter. 'I don't even know why. What happened. What I'm doing here. And why they changed everything about me,' he said, shaking his head. 'I have no clue what's left,' he finished, looking hopeless again.

I crawled forward and poked his arm before he could flinch away. 'Ow!' he said, recoiling.

'Not everything,' I said, relaxing back against the wall. Then I pointed at his face. 'They left your eyes, too.'

He didn't respond right away and let that sink in. He was studying mine. The ones I hated. That particularly struck me; I had no idea why.

'To be honest, I wasn't exactly coherent when they were explaining it, but I think they healed my brain that was basically dead before and then I had complete organ failure. So, I guess, brain, everything above the neck, to the trapdoor,' he said, tipping his head towards mine. "Like yours."

'The cybernetic nerve centre,' I said, thoughtfully. I thought only TinBoiz had that.

'Right arm, heart, lungs. No stomach. Nothing below the waist,' he reeled off like a shopping list.

Despite his delivery, I flinched at the last part. It was pretty much everything. No wonder he'd freaked out. I wondered why they'd needed to take all that. 'Why leave you one pathetically weak arm?' I asked, genuinely curious.

He laughed, surprising me with a sense of humour. 'I know, right?'

I grinned, feeling weird. Like we'd just bonded and joked like friends. I didn't know for the life of me where the thought came from. Words and feelings started coming, without any forethought. 'It sucks at first.' I knew it was weird because Teddy's face was reflecting it, while he absorbed and processed what I said.

Something deep inside me drove me to my lateral passcode. My eyes snapped left and brought up the code for my back door. The green light in the bottom left corner of my vision switched and flashed to red. Then code, *'Camera on, initiate shut down?'* I immediately thought, *Initiate.* I looked into the corner of the room, knowing there was a hidden camera there. I concentrated for a second and it went off.

I focused on Teddy, who was watching me strangely. He had no eyes, therefore no camera, so I was safe. 'I only have two minutes before the cameras in here come back on. I was told that Chrissy left something in here for me. I have no idea what or where it is.'

Teddy's eyes widened in surprise, then he frowned in understanding that this conversation was off the books.

'I don't have time to explain. All I can tell you is that I lived with the Coes for weeks. I know your parents and I care about them all.'

Teddy switched to suspicious. 'Why would she do that?' he said, already scanning the room, doubtfully. 'How would she even get in here?'

I didn't know that either. 'All I know is a sub gave me a clue to a back door left by a tech. It said that during my last update, they had taken some of my memories and replaced them with fake ones. Now I don't know what is true and what isn't. Or whether it is even a test.' I spoke quickly, but my time was almost up. 'I'll try to convince the professor to let us go home together. But you need to get out of here first. Comply with whatever they tell you, because …' I turned my head to the grey metal door and dropped my voice. 'They will end you, if you don't.' I took one final look at him off camera. 'But I ask you, please. Find whatever Chrissy left first.' I looked up and pointed at the camera hidden in the corner. 'Camera is up there.'

Time was up. The red light in my vision blinked back to green again and everything came back online.

'So if I can deal, I get to come home.'

I was so grateful he was willing to play along. I'd heard so much about him but had no idea till now. I could see why Chrissy liked him so much. They must have had so many good times together growing up. I got to my feet slowly, not understanding the yearning I felt. 'Yes. If I am able, I will go with you to help you adjust.'

I helped him to his feet, unbuckled his arms and eased him out of the straitjacket. He winced at the weight of the cybernetic arm and had to cradle it with the other just to hold it up. 'It will get easier. Your limbs are heavy. They'll give you physio and training. You won't eat or go to the toilet in the usual way. I'm not sure about an organic brain,' I said, scratching my own head. 'I'm guessing you'll have a simultaneous power-down when you sleep.'

He nodded, riveted to every word. The change in him was miraculous from the demented creature he was half an hour ago. 'Thanks,' he said, looking worn out now. 'I'm going to insist you're with me. I don't think I can do it alone.'

Something stirred in my chest. It felt like it meant something. I meant something and I'd get to go home. A feeling like wings flickered in my stomach. 'I would be happy to help.' *So happy.*

AFTER JUST TWENTY-FOUR HOURS, Teddy was out of his cell. I didn't get the opportunity to ask him if he found anything and he gave me no clues that he had. So the idea simply slipped away and became eclipsed by five days of intensive training supervised by Damien. But we did it together and it felt good.

Simple things, like walking on a treadmill, going up and down stairs, eating the disgusting nutripaste and evacuating waste. We powered down together, even though I knew his brain slept. It felt like we were the same. Brothers. For the first time in my life (which was only about three months, max), I had someone I had everything in common with. Right down to Chrissy. My heart ached at the sound of her name and I had no idea why.

CHAPTER 69

*C*hrissy

'How much longer?' I groaned, lying on the sofa and looking up at the ceiling.

Mom and Dad were sitting in the armchairs, opposite, tapping their fingers on the arms. Nate was sitting on the floor with his back to the sofa, playing a VR game from his wrist-plate. Its constant beep, his swaying and pointing at thin air, made me kick him a couple of times. 'Bug off, Chrissy,' he shouted.

'Enough! Chrissy! Both of you,' my dad shouted.

'He's driving me mad.' But I knew we were all on our last nerve. I was just irked that Nate could take his mind off it.

'Should be any minute,' my mom said, a little more calmly.

My dad looked at his wrist-plate.

I couldn't believe it when we got the news. I thought it was going to be another excruciatingly long day of not knowing anything. Then the call came early this morning that they were coming home today. Not just Teddy, who I was deliriously happy about, but Royce, too. *Royce. My Royce.*

I had so much I wanted to talk to him about. To tell him off for. 'I don't understand why he is going to live with Teddy,' I said moodily, expecting everyone to follow my random train of thought. They were only next door. But deep down, I did. I totally got why Teddy might need him. I just felt hurt and abandoned by him. Like I meant nothing. Even though it wouldn't have been up to Royce. 'Can't he live here and still help Teddy?'

My mom smiled, indulgently. She always saw right through my emotions. 'I know it feels strange, dear, but he won't be far. Teddy needs him. Apparently, the professor was just wonderful in adjusting our financial arrangement package to include Royce in Teddy's care. I don't fully understand the details, but it's wonderful we're still able to keep him.'

My eyes dropped to Nate's. He'd pushed his VR goggles to the top of his head and was sending 'selfish sister' missiles back at me in a single look.

I let out another groan. I knew I should be grateful that we got to keep Royce at all.

'I think it's because Teddy is on this clinical trial,' my mom continued. 'So Tina and Tom pay next to nothing and with Royce included, we don't pay anything at all. Not even for the TinBoiz products they need. Marvellous really.'

It *was* perfect. My biggest fear had been the cost when Teddy came home. Now it appeared to have been solved. But I still felt uneasy about it. I think it was because the professor was still in all our lives and I didn't trust him, despite all he'd done.

My dad jumped to his feet. 'They're here!'

My mom was next. Then Nate and me scrambled to ours right after. In two seconds, we were all watching at the window, as the Monshalls' car, followed by the Silver TinBoiz van, pulled into the driveway next door.

I felt filled to the brim, knowing everything important to us was held in those two vehicles. My heart was skipping and my whole body was shaking.

'Let's get out there,' Nate shouted, already shooting behind me to the hallway and out of the front door.

I followed with my mom and my dad right behind me. I slowed at the still swinging front door and my parents passed me. The Monshalls got out of their car and immediately hugged them. Tina and my mom were openly crying.

I stepped just outside the door and watched the side panel of the van open.

My heart stopped and I don't think I even breathed when Royce stepped out of the van first. I'd forgotten how good-looking he was. With his tanned skin and hair much longer than I remembered. Perfect physique shown off in his uniform of blue, black and silver. But he didn't look at me and I wanted him to so badly. I wanted an instant answer to relieve my misery. That he knew me. Understood and remembered what we almost had together.

Instead, he was completely focused and turned back to help Teddy down from the van. *My Teddy. My beautiful, wonderful, best friend in all the world.* 'Teddy!' I cried and ran.

His feet had barely touched the ground when I slammed into him. And it hurt. Not emotionally, it physically hurt. Like he had a saucepan lid strapped to his chest, hard and rigid. I stepped back to take him in. He was no longer bony and soft; he was wider, taller, and stronger-looking. It took me a long moment to absorb the difference, looking him up and down. His face was the same. His eyes were the same mahogany brown, not TinBoiz blue. His expression was blank at first. Unsure. Cautious. Then his lips slowly curved into the smile I remembered. 'Cool, eh?' he said, holding his arms wide and grinning. 'I'm a walking comic book. My dream come true!'

Tears sprang from my eyes and I threw my arms around his neck again. 'I missed you so much. Never leave again,' I said into the curve of his neck. Still soft and smelling of him.

'I won't. Promise,' he whispered next to my ear. 'Now can we get in?' he said, pulling apart from me. 'I need to take out the trash, if you know what I mean.'

I was laughing and crying, walking along next to him. Mom and Dad hugging and fussing him too. The AUs began hauling all the technical equipment out of the van and we all slowly made our way into the Monshalls' house.

I allowed myself to finally look at Royce. He hadn't said a word and was accepting hugs and shaking hands with my mom and dad. He was smiling but looked bewildered. I wondered what he remembered.

His strange, icy eyes inevitably found mine and for a moment, they held them, but it was impossible to tell what was there. Whether there was anything behind them at all. I wondered if he was OK with living with Teddy, because there appeared to be nothing left for me. I felt sure I would have seen something. An inkling. A spark. Some kind of clue. Silly really. He was a machine who'd been reprogrammed.

If what he'd told Nate was true, and he was once human, surely, there would be something. Some residue left of me and the life he had before.

I WENT through the hallway of the Monshalls' house and felt Royce right behind me. A wall of magnetic force. I was aware of everything about him. Sending waves of electricity, he made me come alive. I didn't understand it. I'd long given up on soul-searching on whether how I felt was normal. Reconciled myself to it being normal for falling for someone, machine or human. I was resigned to simply coming to terms with it.

Teddy headed straight for the stairs and I went to follow and took one last look at Royce, over my shoulder. My mom held him by the arm and said something quietly to him. His eyes were on mine and he nodded, not attempting to follow. I knew then that my mom had asked him to give us a minute. It gave me a stab of guilt. *Always guilt.* I swallowed it down and jogged to catch up with Teddy.

I could see the AUs and Tech guys setting up the spare room with Royce's equipment. Teddy went straight into his. It was fresh and clean. A boy's room in blue. Comic book characters on the wall. Monitors and action figures on his desk. A shrine to the geeky boy who'd left. 'It's exactly the same,' he said wistfully.

'Course it is.' I wandered around, taking it all in, just like I did when I thought I'd lost him. Everything had felt so precious then. The little pieces of Teddy that now didn't matter because he was back. 'It hasn't been that long. About two to three months, from when you went into hospital.' I don't know why, but the tears burst out suddenly. I was selfish and stupid about everything. He was back, but he was different and so was Royce.

I heard his heavy stomps and he came straight to me and held me in a weird hug. Like he was frightened of crushing me. 'I thought they were going to switch off your life support,' I wailed. 'It was Royce who really saved you. If it wasn't for him, we wouldn't have known about the special chamber.'

Teddy nodded his soft cheek against my hair. 'I know. I owe him a lot.' He pulled back to check my face. 'Do you mind that he's here?'

I shook my head, even though that wasn't entirely true. I was genuinely trying to be OK with it.

'Because I wanted to ask you something about him, Chrissy, and I want you to be completely honest.'

I stared at his intense look, nodded and swallowed, immediately feeling my cheeks burn and my heart pound painfully in my chest.

Teddy frowned, looking troubled. 'I guess you just answered my question. You've fallen for a TinBoi.' He said it flatly, not angry but more concerned. 'I get it, I really do. But it's messed up, you know that, right?'

I just nodded, like a naughty child caught red-handed. He was only voicing the obvious. I could never hope to hide anything from him. He knew me too well. 'Does he know how I feel?' I barely managed to say, in a reedy voice.

Teddy was studying me closely, then shook his head. 'Not yet, I don't think. What can come out of it, though, Chrissy? I mean, I like him, I do.' Then his concern slipped into his lopsided grin. 'I definitely would,' he said, breaking into laughter, then trying to get serious again.

I smacked him on the arm, then, shaking the bad idea out of my hand, I walked over to the window. The van was still open. More stuff was being carried into the house. 'It's not as simple as that, Teddy.' I turned around to face him and just came out with it. 'Nate seems to think he had a life before. That guy, the professor, isn't as good as everyone thinks. Royce told Nate before he left that he came from beyond The Danger Line. That's where he was going when he left. To find his family. He thought he wouldn't come back because of the cost of your healthcare. We wouldn't afford to keep him. They took him to that facility and did something to him. They took it all away.' My hand went to my mouth as I almost crumpled.

Teddy's face creased in disbelief. 'So you think they're using real kids to make TinBoiz?'

I shrugged and ran my hand through my hair, exhausted with it all. 'Honestly, I'm not sure. Maybe not all of them. I know the professor referred to Royce as a beta model for the next evolution in AUs. The most realistic yet.' I looked him dead in the eyes. 'It's where they got the technology for you.'

Teddy locked eyes with me at that final piece of information. He was thinking the same thing as me. That if he wasn't standing there as seventy-five percent machine, neither of us would have believed it. But he was, and it made it so much more plausible that Nate might be right.

'Royce said you left something in the padded cell?'

My mind stalled. 'He found it?' I couldn't believe it. I had no idea by the way he'd acted. Before I could launch into a thousand questions in excitement, Teddy shut me down with a, 'No, but he asked me to look for him.'

I shrank a little in disappointment, finding it difficult to look at him.

He was still studying me closely. Assessing me.

I shook my head and started picking at my fingers. 'I didn't. A friend of mine gave him my locket and a note, before he—' I couldn't finish what I was saying, it was too painful. 'Look, I wanted... I was trying to let him know how I felt before they reprogrammed him, or whatever it was. I guess he must have hidden it there so they couldn't find it.' I tapped my foot and looked anywhere but at Teddy.

'I found it.'

My eyes shot straight to his. 'You did? Has he seen it?' My blood was pulsing in my ears.

'Not yet,' he said, still assessing me. 'It wasn't safe, and I wanted to talk to you first. So you definitely want him to have it? Because this could open up something that might best be left hidden.'

I was nodding so hard I must have looked demented.

'You know it might not work if he has a cybernetic brain. I don't hold out much hope.'

I went to Teddy in two strides and picked up both his hands. One felt different to the other, confusing and throwing me off for a minute. But I gathered myself and looked intensely up into the same eyes, just a little higher than I was used to. 'I think we owe it to him to at least try. Think about it, Teddy. If he was robbed of his life, something, anything, might trigger a memory.'

Teddy let out a slow breath. 'OK.'

I hugged him tightly, then the moment was broken by a sharp knock at the door. His dad put his head inside. 'The Techs need to come in, guys.'

I reluctantly let him go, still smiling at him over my shoulder. 'I'll see you later.' I squeezed past Tom, hurried across the landing, and ran right into Royce at the top of the stairs. 'Hello, Chrissy,' he said.

CHAPTER 70

oyce

I came face-to-face with Chrissy. Eye-level, as I hadn't yet reached the top of the stairs. She looked startled, almost scared, and I frowned at that. She didn't respond to my greeting, just pushed past and ran downstairs, leaving me watching her, unable to process it. I remembered her being quite grumpy when we first met and I turned to look at Teddy's open door. That had been because of Teddy, too.

Tom saw me standing there and pointed to the door next to Teddy's. 'That's your room, Royce. It's all set up for you.' He patted my shoulder as I went past him, towards it.

'Thank you.' I went right in and assessed it as adequate. Cot. Cupboard, metal cabinet, 'Welcome to your new home, Royce,' Sentia immediately said. White lights flickered across the black surface.

'Thanks,' I said, feeling empty and lost. It was an illogical feeling. One place was much the same as another. I turned sharply at the presence behind me.

Teddy was slowly closing my door. He came and faced

me, squarely, looking very serious. My gridlines assessed his features for signs of anger and found none.

Instead of talking, he held out a closed fist.

I looked down and stared at it, not understanding at all.

'Hold out your hand,' Teddy said, flicking his eyes to the side.

My power pack sped up, knowing exactly what he was hinting at. *Lateral command – back door – initiate.* When the green light flashed to red, I held out my hand and gave him the nod to go ahead.

He dropped a small packet into my hand. 'I found it hidden in the wall of the padded cell after you went. It was right in the corner, under the camera. I almost missed the note.'

I stared hard at my hand; it was a wonder it didn't combust. I was waiting for something, but it held no association for me at all.

'I'll leave you with it,' Teddy said, turning back for the door. 'I'll be downstairs if you need anything. Don't forget it's school tomorrow,' he finished with a bright smile. 'I can't wait. It's going to be awesome.'

I smiled a little weakly, still with my hand out flat, until he left and closed the door.

Then I focused on the package. I didn't have long. My gridlines quickly assessed it for size and weight. There was something loose inside it, so I tipped it into my other hand. It was a silver oval disk on a fine chain. *A necklace?* I turned it over, inspecting it. It felt heavy for its size, but pretty unremarkable. I brought it up to my eyeline and saw the seam and a small catch, hinting it should be opened. I loosened the catch and opened it up.

I almost dropped it when the small image of Chrissy popped up. A tiny hologram of a moment in time. She was smiling, but her eyes looked weighed down with worry and her smile looked unsure. She was captivating. So delicate and breakable. It was intriguing that she'd left this for me and that I'd felt the need to hide it. I must have been frightened it would be taken away. I didn't understand the significance of it. I felt frustrated and almost screwed up the packet, but something made me take a last look inside before I discarded it.

I saw it—a tiny, folded piece of paper. Something so strange to use these days. I had to use two fingers to pull it out and looked at the neat words on the page.

Dear Royce,
Please don't hate me. I love you, machine or not. Please remember me when they scrub your mind. Above all, remember. Royce,
Remember me, Chrissy X

I stared at the page, converting every handwritten word to memory. Then I folded it up and tucked it in my boot to discard later. My time was up, and my warning red light was flashing furiously. I came out of the lateral command, still staring into space, wondering how so much could be conveyed on such a small piece of paper. Although I still thought there was more to be said. The word *love* repeated in my head, over and over. So human and yet she was referring to me. A TinBoi, *machine or not. Remember,* she kept repeating, meaning there was something to be forgotten. Greg had said something was taken. This was Chrissy trying to help me remember. *Remember me. Something else?* I didn't want to get anyone in any trouble. I felt safe here. I wanted to stay. I liked Teddy. I remembered I liked Nate. We played games. He looked up to me like *a brother.* That hit me harder than anything else. I remembered that clearly.

I slumped down onto my cot, suddenly fatigued. I would power down and avoid any further interaction today. I needed to decompress. Settle in and not make any unusual ripples. That was normal behaviour.

Teddy must settle back in, too, and it would give me the time to assess the Coes and build a picture of what happened there.

Chrissy was special. I knew that without any idea why. I needed to find out what happened before, without alerting the professor. Because people disappeared all the time. I knew that was a fact. I had no idea where it came from, how I knew, or why.

CHAPTER 71

hrissy

We all travelled together, squashed in my dad's car, to school. Nate twisted around in his seat in the front to face us. 'I can't wait. This is going to be so cool.'

I had to admit my heart skipped a few beats. I'd barely slept.

Teddy squeezed my hand on the right, as if he knew. He was excited too. His eyes were drinking in every house and building that went past as if they weren't all the same. I guess you would if you hadn't been out of the house for months.

I looked down. Royce's leg was pressed against mine on the left. Unavoidable with three of us in the back seat. When I meandered back to his face, he was already there, holding me with those eyes. They were searching intensely for something. We'd barely spoken and I'd started to lose hope. He'd had my message. My gaze dropped to his mouth, already moving and speaking so quietly. 'I don't remember, but I want to.'

I was so drawn to whatever magnetism he was using that

I had to drag my eyes away. I was already dissolving under his intense gaze, like he could reach my soul.

We were there, like a cool, reviving breeze. The journey over too quickly and yet I swallowed in reprieve. We were already turning into the drop-off circle in front of the school. It was busy. Kids everywhere. Some were stopping and pointing over. We pulled up and were already creating a stir.

Nate laughed and jumped out of the car right away. Teddy got out of his side without a shred of the quiet, geeky boy he once was. I was so proud of how he'd come through this—embracing the confidence he always had inside.

I followed Royce more cautiously out of his side and he surprised me by holding out his hand. I took it and looked up into his eyes for a clue as to what it meant. It told me nothing, but it felt symbolic. Like my place was with him.

The car eased off and we were left standing there for everyone to see. Teddy closed the gap. He grinned and picked up my other hand. Nate, a little way off, turned and waved for us to catch up.

Then we were four. Individual. Confident. Striding purposefully into school. Not scared of anything. I'd never felt anything like it. We were in synch. Strong. A force to be reckoned with. It didn't even fade when Simon spotted us, with his friends from the team. 'Guys! He's back,' he called out. Clearly delighted.

Cindy and Jessica turned and scowled the moment they saw me. The only cloud was that Ace was with them. But I didn't let that ruin my mood. This was the start of a new era, and every kid instinctively knew it. No one would exclude us anymore. Whatever happened next, we could handle it. Something told me everything was just beginning.

ACKNOWLEDGEMENTS

As always, sending a special thank-you to my team: Nicky Lovick, my cover artist, Daniela Orwegoor, and Jane Harrison. And, of course, my wonderful readers.

CONTACT T

To receive your two 21st Century Sirens Novellas, and be the first to know anything relating to T's books, leave your details here: https://mailchi.mp/d18c89c14f50/tstedmannovellas
And please don't forget to leave a review wherever you bought your book. I really appreciate the feedback.
Much love,
T
www.tstedman.com
Facebook
X
TikTok

ALSO BY T STEDMAN

(The YA books)

Young Atlanteans

Cross Heirs

Two Tribes

The Night Shade Novels

Demon in the Attic

The Blackwood Curse

(18+ books)

21st Century Sirens Series

Soul Breather

Blood Sister

Shield Maiden

Tiger Lily

Night Goddess

Darkly Begotten

Dark Valentines Collection

Star Child

The Watchers

Diablo

The Novellas (Only available free on T's website)

Protector

Lost Moon

Non-Fiction

My Migraine Story

www.ingramcontent.com/pod-product-compliance
Lightning Source LLC
Chambersburg PA
CBHW050601170726
48283CB00001B/59